I0773120

MOSAIC

KYSER EDITION

DRAGONFLY
BOOK FOUR

LEIGH T MOORE

TLM PRODUCTIONS LLC

CONTENTS

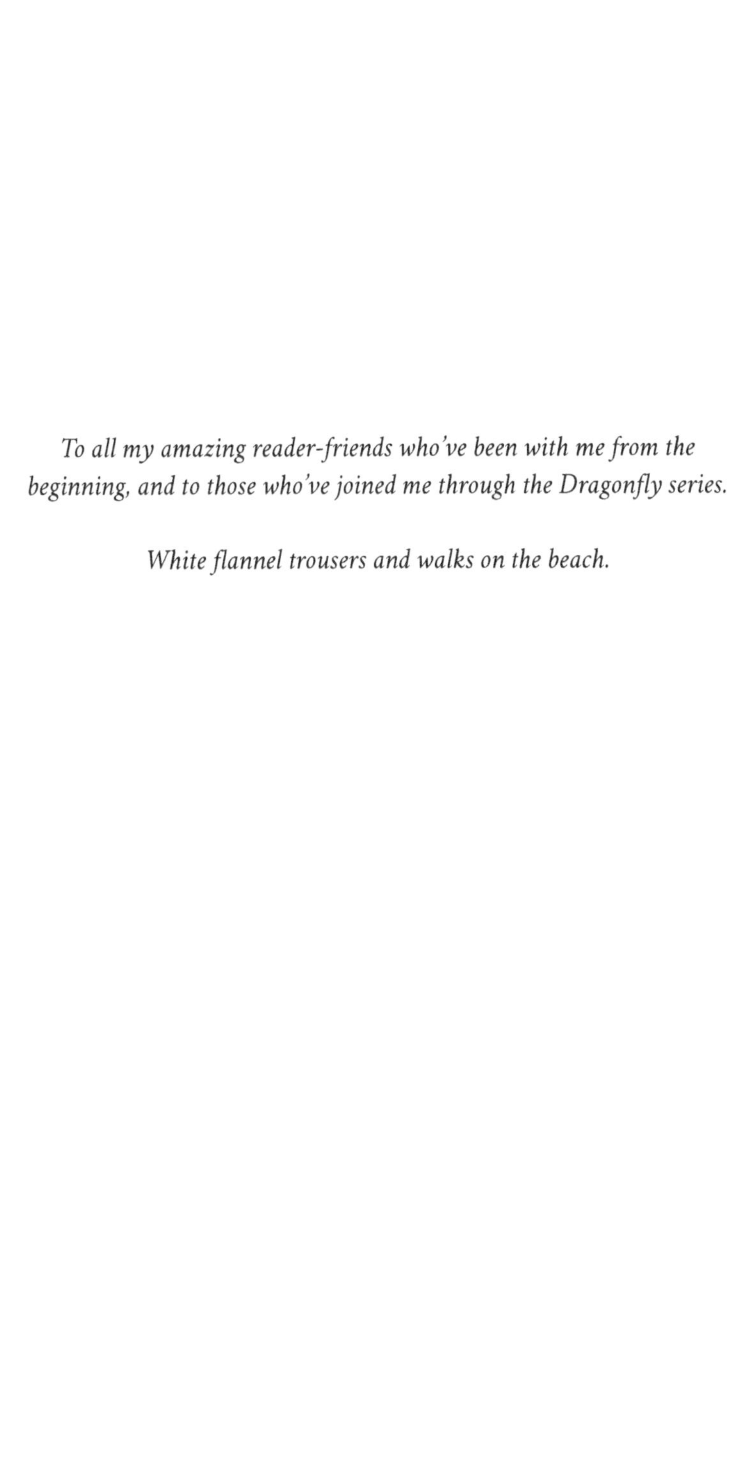

To all my amazing reader-friends who've been with me from the beginning, and to those who've joined me through the Dragonfly series.

White flannel trousers and walks on the beach.

PART I
PRESENT DAY

HIM

The man's feet sank in the soft, white sand of the beach he'd known since childhood. Walking this overcast morning, watching the storm building in the distance, he remembered a time when he'd eagerly anticipated days like this, running to grab a surfboard, hoping for waves high enough to ride.

He'd been in love with life back then, embracing experiences and going for whatever he wanted without caring about the consequences. He'd been pretty lucky, too, with happiness and getting what he wanted, but a lot had changed in the last twenty years.

Days like this were now spent in an office, usually poring over plans. He couldn't even remember the last time he'd picked up a board.

The invitation had arrived months ago, but he'd put off thinking about it until now, the weekend of the event. *Had it really been twenty years?*

The past swirled through his memory as he watched the gray waters, the salty gusts pushing his dark hair back. He was still tall and slim, and most people mistook him for younger than he was. But he'd noticed the small lines around his eyes.

Business. That was the only thing that mattered to him now.

All the colors and distractions of youth were behind him. Marriage, kids, those things had somehow escaped him, and going into this weekend of reunion, he suddenly felt like he had nothing to show for himself.

Which was ridiculous.

He had money and power. Those counted for something—especially around here. He was the son of the most famous real estate developer on the coast, and as it turned out, he'd inherited his father's keen business sense.

He'd been successful at moving into development, and he liked it—unlike his older brother, the golden boy, who now practiced medicine in Nashville.

He could also have any woman he wanted, and occasionally he did. But he also had a past.

The past.

For a second he unclenched the vice grip he held on those memories and allowed himself to see her green eyes the last time they'd spoken. *Hazel eyes.* She'd always corrected him.

They were filled with tears.

He'd said… so many things. He'd been so angry. So hurt and betrayed.

But that didn't excuse the choice he'd made. The words he'd said knowing they'd drive her away for good. He hadn't seen her face again since that night on the beach. She'd told him he wouldn't.

This was the weekend he might.

Lost in these thoughts, he walked back up the shoreline toward his office when he slammed into a small body that seemed to appear out of nowhere.

"Wanker!" The girl hissed, her wild black curls flying around her head in the breeze.

"I'm sorry." He started to laugh at her insult, spoken in a light British accent, when he realized pages were swirling around them and scurried to help her collect them.

"Bloody hell," she continued fussing. "They're ruined!"

"I'm sorry," he repeated. "I didn't see you there."

"You should watch where you're going." She groused as they returned to each other, messy stacks of papers in hand.

He bit back a grin. No one spoke to him this way. *What a funny kid.*

"What is all this?" He looked at the pages filled with words and small sketches.

She answered with a flourish. "My memoirs, of course!"

"Memoirs? How old are you?"

"Sixteen." Momentarily deflated, she quickly recovered. "But Mum says I come from a long line of artists. So I'm writing and illustrating my life now before I don't have time for such nonsense."

"Some people would call it keeping a diary." He studied the pages—a small seagull sketch, a pod of pelicans soaring low over breakers—the kid had talent, he had to admit.

"And some people are not as creative as I am."

"I can believe it." He returned the papers to her, catching her clear blue eyes. "What's your name?"

"Juliet. But you can call me Jules. Everyone does."

He almost noted they shared teenage nicknames, but a strange hesitance stopped him. "That's a very fancy name, Jules. Are your parents big Shakespeare fans?"

She shook her dark curls, and shoved one behind her ear. "Don't think so. I mean, Mum likes to read and all, but I'm named for my dad."

"Your dad?" His brow creased. "You live around here?"

"We flew in from London for a school reunion. Mum, Aunt Gabi, and I are all staying at my grandparents' home in Fairview."

London? Gabi? He paused and studied the girl. "Your dad didn't come?"

"Well, my real dad isn't in the picture, if you know what I'm saying." She slanted a familiar blue eye at him. "*Brandon* stayed across the pond."

"Who's Brandon?" He felt a sting of something. It couldn't be jealousy. He didn't even know who this girl was. For certain...

"My step-dad. Mum finally agreed to marry him a few years ago, but it never took." She exhaled, looking out at the water. "They divorced last year. Poor Brandon. They thought I didn't hear them arguing, but it was hard to ignore."

"Maybe you shouldn't—"

"It's pretty simple, actually." Jules shrugged and started walking. Unable to help himself, he followed her. *Was it possible this girl was...*

Her next words derailed that train of thought. "She's still in love with my dad. She tries to deny it, but Brandon and I know the truth."

Shock and energy surged through him. Was he furious? Was he glad? One thing was certain—he needed to hear this. "How do you know?"

"Oh, it's the little things mostly."

"Like what?"

"Well, she has this painting he did of her in her closet, and once I caught her looking at it."

His brow creased. It wasn't enough. "That doesn't prove much."

"Oh, no?" Jules flashed him a glance. "She was holding out her hand and tracing the brush strokes just so... I know she was thinking of him."

They continued walking against the wind. "Sounds like you read a lot. Romance fan?"

"Well, naturally, but that's not why I'm saying it." She gestured to him as if making her big reveal. "There's also the ring."

He turned his face to the waves so she couldn't see his expression change. "What ring?" He could barely ask the question.

"Well, Dad was brilliant." A smile was in her voice. "He made her this gorgeous dragonfly ring when they were in high school, and she still has it."

His eyes pressed closed. "Does she wear it?"

"No."

"Then how do you—"

"I busted her trying it on one night, and there were tears in her eyes."

He stopped walking and sat down in the sand. The soft white grains were cold and damp from the night before, and the sun hadn't come out to warm and dry it. His slacks would be ruined, but he crossed his arms on top of his bent knees and forced the air in and out of his lungs.

"Hey, are you okay?" Jules asked, dropping beside him.

"Yeah." He struggled to smile. "I like this weather."

"Me, too." She smiled and looked out at the horizon. "Like something's coming, brewing. I hope we move back."

"Is that a possibility?" *Did he want it to be?*

The girl shrugged. "Mum's always saying she misses it here. I can certainly see why."

They were quiet for a moment then he gestured to the growing waves. "When I was your age, I'd be out there surfing."

Jules turned to him. "You live here?"

"Just up the road."

She glanced at his slacks, dress shirt, and tie. "Very formal for a walk to the beach."

"My office is right there. I was on my way to work."

Her brow creased over her blue eyes. His chest tightened at the sight of them, at the knowledge of what it all meant.

"You work in that big condo?"

"In Phoenician I. Penthouse suites."

"What are you? The resort manager or something?"

He exhaled with a laugh. "Something like that."

"Did you go to Fairview High?"

Pushing against the sand, he rose to his feet. "Yep. I'm supposed to be at that reunion, too."

"Hang on." The girl fished a phone out of her pocket. "It's Mum. 'Where are you?'" She read aloud. "She's just waking up, I'm sure."

The memory of how she looked just waking up warmed him, and he glanced at the phone that held her words. A picture was there, but it disappeared before he got a good look.

"I'm at the beach talking to some old tosspot." Jules read her response aloud.

"Thanks." His eyes narrowed, but he smiled.

Her cockiness reminded him of someone from his past, someone he used to be.

"It's okay," she laughed. "I'm just messing with her. Watch this."

They were quiet a split second before her phone buzzed again. Jules burst into familiar-sounding peals of laughter.

"Come home *now*—five exclamation points," she read.

She giggled again, speaking as she typed. "But he asked me to run away with him!"

"You're not being very nice to your mother," he scolded gently.

"She's used to me." The girl poked her chin at him. "She likes to say I act just like my dad."

Frustrated, he pushed his hand into the side of his hair, and Jules caught her breath.

"Hey, cool ink!" She reached for his hand, and he let her take it. "It's a dragonfly?"

"Yeah." He watched as she slid her thumb across the small

tattoo between his thumb and first finger. Her instinctive response, exactly like her mother's, burned in his chest.

So many times he'd considered having that little reminder removed, but he could never bring himself to do it.

The buzzing of her phone interrupted them, and it was followed by the girl's laughter as she read aloud. "911! 911!"

"What does that mean?"

"It means I have to go." She released his hand and turned, but she paused. "It was fun talking to you. Maybe I'll see you at the reunion?"

"Yes, you will," he nodded, making a decision.

"What's your name?"

"Julian."

Their blue eyes met, and a wave of recognition passed between them. Jules's brow creased, but she didn't say what she was thinking. Instead she nodded. "Unusual. I like it."

He watched her walk away and observed that she moved exactly like his mother.

* * *

HER

Pine needles and lemon furniture polish. The woman's nose wrinkled. Had her old house always smelled like summer camp? How was it possible she'd never noticed it before?

Her eyes roamed around the familiar room as she stretched her arms over her head. With Jules in her old bedroom and Gabi in the guest room, her only option was to sleep in her parents' bed, and even though they'd been RV-ing all over the United States for a year, it still felt awkward—comfortable, but somehow like she was breaking an unwritten rule.

At the same time, she couldn't imagine spending the night in her old bed anymore. She imagined lying in it with that window over-shadowing everything. It would've been impossible to sleep without seeing the ghost of him sitting on the tree limb right outside. Or worse, smiling at her through the glass, waiting to be let in.

Her throat tightened at the memories of all the nights they'd spent together in that little bed holding each other close. They were just kids, but somehow they'd found something very real and strong together. Like magnets, it was almost impossible to stay apart.

Her whole body flushed with heat at the memory of their first night as more than friends. She hadn't forgotten a single touch. Every kiss, every sigh, the quiet sense of wonder as they discov-ered how perfectly they fit together was as clear as a bell in her mind's eye.

Sitting up fast, she threw the sheets back, ripping the bottom corner loose from where it was tucked. There was no way in hell she'd go back down that road. Julian LaSalle or Kyser or what-ever he called himself now, would *not* spoil this high school reunion like he'd spoiled her high school memories.

She couldn't even think about those years without a gut-twisting ache pulling at her insides.

Why was she here? Why was she doing this? It was inevitable they'd run into each other. She was doing it for Jules, she reminded herself.

Yes, she fully expected to see him, and it was time he knew the truth, even though she shuddered to think what he would say.

They had a daughter.

She'd kept it from him in the beginning because it was all too much, turning up pregnant an ocean away after the way they'd parted.

As time passed, she'd started to tell him so many times. Every time, she'd only get as far as the first words, *We have a daughter...* Then she'd back down and vow to do it the next year.

Now, almost seventeen years later, with the school reunion

invitation sitting on her desk, she realized it was the only way she'd ever do it. At least in Fairview, she'd have his mother, Gabi, her friends, everyone around to hold her hand.

Still she shivered at the prospect of seeing him again, of giving him the news. A dark flash streaked through the door, and she was plowed back against the pillows.

"I made it!" Jules shrieked, holding her in pretend relief. "Just barely escaped being kidnapped into the sex trade. Thank everything that's holy you called when you did!"

Pinching the slim, ivory arm around her neck, she struggled to get out of her wild daughter's vice-grip. "I'm sending you to your Nana's for the rest of the trip if you don't behave."

Jumping up, her blue eyes twinkling, she bounced on the bed. "Oh, please, yes! Didn't you say she used to dance naked on the beach at night when she was my age?"

"Good lord, Jules, No. And don't you dare tell her I said that!"

Peals of laughter filled the room like water rolling over rocks. "I can't wait to beg her to kidnap me!"

The woman's tight lips curled in a smile as she watched her child. Jules was so much like her dad at that age—confident, in love with life, and able to charm the pants off anybody who crossed her path.

"She'd probably get a kick out of you wanting to do something like that. Your grandmother was very 'new age' at a time when that had pretty much gone out of style."

"From what you've told me, she never gave a rip what was in style."

Lifting her robe off the back of the chair she nodded. "Lexy definitely followed her own drum. But it left her very lonely." She shook the past away as she tied her belt and studied her daughter lying back on the bed, dark curls spread all around her face. "Who was the old tosspot you met on the beach? I probably know him."

That made Jules sit up fast, but while her expression was eager, she hesitated.

"What?" Her mother's brow creased.

"I actually do think you know him."

"Did you tell him I'm your mom? Who was it? Maybe Brad Brennan?"

"I don't think so." Jules chewed her lip, her blue eyes wide. "He was actually quite lovely, with dark hair and blue eyes…"

The girl's hesitation filled the room with a silence that pressed heavy on her mother's shoulders. Was it possible on her daughter's first trip to the beach she met him?

"Which beach did you say you went to? Romar?"

Her daughter nodded slowly, but the moment was interrupted by the other boisterous personality in their group.

"I am *not* cooking today!" Gabi jumped on the bed beside Jules, completely oblivious to the tension. "Make yourself useful, small fry, and get in there and cook me some eggs!"

Jules blinked and then threw her arms around her adopted aunt. "You know I can't cook, but we're at the beach. I want fish for breakfast."

"Fish and chips! Anna, you've birthed a true Brit."

"We can talk more about that later." Anna finished, going to the closet. "Hey, Gab, wasn't the best place for breakfast always Tacky Jack's?"

"If you're wanting seafood it definitely is."

"Give me a second to throw on some clothes."

The canal rolled past in brown ripples just across the break of pines separating the island from the rest of South County. It was a man-made trench dug years ago for some reason Anna couldn't remember.

"It's so lovely here—even with a storm hanging over it all."

Mother and daughter both had their natural curls wrapped in

matching buns at the back of their necks. "Lovely and hot and humid."

Gabi's short, blonde curls blew wild around her head as she scooped a bite of shrimp and cheese grits into her mouth. "The hair is the worst part. Otherwise, it's all good. I miss living near the water."

After years of moving all over the edge of the continent with her Coast Guard father, Gabi had settled, land-locked in Arizona, forced there by her occupation.

She'd followed her dream and landed an amazing job studying astronomical anomalies and running the Lunar and Planetary Laboratory at her alma mater.

Jules shoved a bite of tortilla in her mouth. "Mm... you just like the heat. I don't know how you could ever leave this place."

"I thought you were getting fish for breakfast." Anna took a bite of her wheelhouse pancake, big as the plate and stuffed with pecans.

"How could I resist a menu item referred to as 'Mexican trash'?"

Her mother frowned. "Well, it is called *Tacky* Jack's."

"I think I'd go into a coma if I consumed that much sugar this early." Gabi stole a whipped cream-covered strawberry from her best friend's plate.

"I'm taking my coffee black!" Anna cried, as if that made it better.

Jules quietly stirred a drop of salsa into her sour cream, turning it pink. "So what's our plan for today?"

"Well, your Nana won't be back from New Orleans until tomorrow—"

"I still wish we could drive down and see her show. I can't wait to see her again. One visit was not enough, and I want to see the Big Easy!"

Anna gave her daughter a warm smile. "You two will be thick as thieves by the end of the first day, and I'll take you to New Orleans sometime, show you where I went to school."

Gabi leaned back with a sigh and rested her hands on her stomach. "A NOLA visit would be fun, but I don't know how we could fit it all in. Tonight's ice-breaker reception starts at five. Love how they're calling it that, as if we need to break the ice."

"What about…"

Jules's concerned eyes caught her mother's, and Anna knew this was about their interrupted conversation from earlier.

A familiar tightness pulled at her throat muscles. It was ridiculous to avoid it. Seeing him was part of the reason they'd come back. It was time.

"I think I should see him by myself first," she answered her daughter's unfinished question.

Gabi was instantly at attention. "Are you talking about Julian?"

"Jules thinks she ran into him on the beach today." Anna ran a finger around the edge of her mug thoughtfully. "Can you believe it? What are the chances?"

Chewing her lip, Gabi's eyes narrowed and flickered from mother to daughter. "Do you want me to go with you?"

"What? No!" Anna tried to laugh, but even she could hear how unconvincing it was. "It's just Julian."

"Shit, yeah it is, and I can see you're already freaking out. Don't even try pulling an act with me."

"Gabi." Worried eyes went to Jules. "I'll be fine talking to him alone."

"Oh, good lord, Mum. Like I don't know this is hard for you?" Jules almost laughed. "And from what I saw today, well, a lot was explained."

Taking a huge breath, Anna pulled out her wallet and several bills. "I'm going now. No point prolonging the inevitable."

Standing, Gabi tossed an arm around her god-daughter's

shoulders. "Your mother has always been very impulsive." Then she turned to her friend. "We'll just head back to the house."

"Yes." Jules said, and neither of the women missed the glint in her eyes.

"What are you up to, small fry?" Gabi asked.

"Nothing!" Her fake innocence fooled no one.

"Try again."

"I just stumbled across something curious last night."

"Juliet," Anna said as they walked down the steps away from the tin-roofed restaurant. "Take it from me, try to curb that naturally inquisitive nose you inherited. It will only get you into trouble."

The girl laughed and shook her dark curls. "Whatever, Mum. It seemed to get you exactly where you wanted to go."

"Not every time."

As they parted company, the woman turned her gaze southward, toward the high rises she knew so well. Those imposing structures had played an enormous part in many lives over the past forty years. Now she was headed there again. Penthouse suites.

The first time she visited them, she was only seventeen. Twenty years later, she was just as intimidated. Only the man she'd face today was not Bill Kyser, he was a boy she never dreamed would grow up to be exactly like his dad.

Gabi was right. Seeing him again would be difficult, but it had to be done. Twenty years had at least made her stronger than she'd ever been as a teenager in Fairview, and facing Julian was an event that had been coming for some time.

The time, it seemed was now.

* * *

JULES

Hi, there, I'm Jules, and I am an artist as you well know if you're reading this. Not only am I an artist, I'm the best at what I do, and you'd better damn well thank your lucky stars you'll get a copy of my memoirs eventually.

But back up, that's not why we're here. What we're about to read is something *far* more interesting, and I'm a lucky duck Mum put me in her old bedroom, or I'd never have found it.

See this?

I know, of course you can't see it. Dammit. This should be a video series. Too bad for all of us, technology isn't quite ready for my brilliance, so I'll describe it to you.

On this ancient laptop is the saved password to "Anna's Private Tumblr." Can you believe that?

Right now I'm just going on the record to say Mum was definitely a feather-headed innocent when she was my age. How could *anyone* be so naïve as to label her private tumblr *as a private tumblr*? Doesn't she realize that's like slapping a neon sign on it and begging everyone to read it?

Regardless, I love the heck out of that woman, so don't you dare criticize her, or I'll kick you in the tush. I'm the only one allowed to do that.

Anyway, she left this laptop on her desk, along with a framed photograph of her and some massively hot blond fellow. He's actually *really* good-looking, I'm not going to lie to you. I have no idea who this guy is, but Mum's gazing at him like he's the bloody future King of England. I mean, Wills had better look out if Kate ever meets this bloke the way my mum has her eyes on him.

Back to the now. As my internal clock is all screwed up, and I'm eight hours ahead in my mind, last night I flipped on this old laptop and guess what happened? The whole damn story popped up. It's all here.

I'd only gotten through the first several entries when I finally fell asleep. It starts with the summer before she left for college, and when I stopped she was on her first days at Loyola.

It kind of all skips around a lot because it's basically a diary, and she only wrote in it when she bloody well pleased.

But do you get what I'm looking at now? It's the story of her and my dad! At least some of it—I hope she kept writing through whatever happened.

Today, with this whole day empty, I plan to do some heavy reading and find out. Who's with me?

We might not be headed to New Orleans physically, but that's exactly where this story begins. Here we go.

Switch on...

PART II
ANNA'S PRIVATE TUMBLR

COLLEGE LIFE BEGINS

Heavy, damp air filled with the dark scents of bodies in motion, the luscious aroma of garlic and celery. Musical strains drift past, either live or canned, I can't tell. The heart of the city beats strong and full, and the atmosphere wraps around me like a second skin...

Who am I trying to kid? I'm not a poet. I'm a journalist.

Still I love the idea of keeping a record of this time in my life, and yes, I got the idea from Julian's mom, so don't even bother pointing out the obvious.

The thing is, with Julian in Savannah and me in New Orleans, I've got time to document these years. We're starting college, we're launching our careers, we're completely miserable being so far apart—it's all a huge part of our lives.

So I'm going to keep a record for us to look back on and laugh… or count our blessings. Just don't expect poetry. This will be straight news.

New Orleans is like no place I've ever lived in my life.

I haven't lived in that many places, but I think I can safely say this city has an atmosphere unlike anywhere else. It all has a rhythm I can't explain, like it's beating just outside the walls.

Even the voices of the locals roll along like the river... which is actually higher than our apartment on Oak Street.

It freaks me out a little when the barges go by, stories above us just on the other side of the levee. I try not to think about what that means or allow it to give me horrifying visions of Hurricane Katrina's aftermath.

Since I waited so long to confirm, we lost our apartment on St. Charles Avenue, but it actually worked out for the good. Rachel and I got a great deal on a shotgun duplex just around the corner. It's actually a little closer to Tulane, which is only steps from Loyola, and we're super close to the Camellia Grill and Cooter Browns.

Our next-door neighbor is an ancient lady we rarely see. She doesn't even answer her door if we knock, and I can't decide if it's because she can't hear us or if she's afraid we're burglars.

Loyola is fantastic. I knew college life would be different from high school, but I had no idea it would be so much fun!

I tested out of almost all of my introductory classes, so I'm starting out as a second-semester sophomore. Taking nothing but classes in my major is like finding myself in Wonderland—no more scary science or sleep-inducing geometry. It's all reading novels and writing and theorizing about major issues in Classical and Modern Literature and learning to be a newswoman—all the time. I. Love. It!

I opted not to go for a straight communications major. I'm doing a double in English and media studies. That way I'll have more options when I graduate.

Rachel's taking straight pre-law, and she's lobbying hard for me to join her at the law school at State. I'll cross that bridge when the time comes. For now we're learning the ropes, and the only thing that could possibly make it better would be having Julian here.

HUGE sigh. God, I miss him so much.

When we said goodbye last week, my stomach cramped so bad. We'd been working on stockpiling for the shortage all summer long, but with the day right there, staring us in the face, everything in me was in full-on panic mode at the thought of being separated by so much distance.

No matter how often he'd said the time would fly, I was certain it would feel like forever.

Now I have to confess… he was partially right. Getting set up made the days go by really fast, and now that classes have started, I'm too busy to sit around and miss him. It helps that we text each other constantly—more than when we lived in the same town.

JULIAN

Stretched a new canvas. It's for a figures project,
but the only figure I want to cover it with is yours.

A tingly little smile touched my lips, and I glanced up at the large watercolor he gave me just before prom. It's a painting of me in New Orleans, surrounded by music and purples, greens, and golds, reaching out to him across and above in Savannah, surrounded by the ocean. His hand is stretched back to mine, and our dragonflies hold us together in the center. The sight of it caused a knot in my throat.

ANNA

Your painting is hanging above my bed.

JULIAN

Hope it makes you feel less lonely.

ANNA

I don't think I'll ever feel less lonely until we're
together again.

I lay back, holding the phone close to my chest as if that somehow pulled him closer to me.

JULIAN

Don't look at it as the number of days we're apart. Look at it as the days of adventure we'll have until we're back together.

ANNA

You're the only person I want to have adventures with.

JULIAN

If we're going on an adventure, we're bound to run into a shortage.

That made me giggle.

ANNA

Don't even say the word. It's too cruel.

JULIAN

Love you, Sunshine. I'll make the trip down next weekend.

Thinking of him driving all the way from SCAD to Loyola made me frown.

ANNA

Let's meet back at home. It's a much shorter distance if we both drive to Fairview.

JULIAN

I can't spend the night if we do that.

ANNA

It never stopped you before.

I smiled at the memory of looking out my bedroom window and seeing his face.

JULIAN

I'm getting too old for climbing trees every night.

Then I laughed.

ANNA

You're the same age you were all summer when you did it.

JULIAN

Shortages drive a guy to extreme measures.

With a sigh, I relented.

ANNA

Okay. Come here. I'll see if Rachel will shack up with Brad so we can have the place to ourselves.

JULIAN

Clothing optional.

Laughing again, I ended our chat.

ANNA

Love you, too.

* * *

In the meantime, I go to class, and it is fantastic. The buildings are all ancient and amazing. They have huge windows, cool art-deco style chandeliers, and wood everything. It all smells like the biggest library you've ever been in, which is perfect for me. I'm like Belle in that animated *Beauty and the Beast* movie, spinning around in heaven at the sight of it all.

My literature professor is cool for a fifty-something year-old. He looks just like I expected all my professors to look with messy gray hair, five o'clock shadow, and wool blazer. It's way too hot for wool, but it's just the classic, English-professor look.

We're starting out reading Kafka's *The Metamorphosis*. I read it once before in high school and hated it. But somehow reading it in college makes me feel like I have to dig deeper. Look past the ickiness and find the meaning.

Gregor Samsa awoke one morning from a night of fitful dreams to find he'd been transformed into a monstrous vermin...

Shudders. I remember my high school teacher said he'd been transformed into a dung beetle, which is just nasty. Wikipedia said it was a giant cockroach. I also read it was somehow anti-Semitic, but I don't know enough about that to comment.

I hate the image and the story is almost inexplicable, but I'm trying to be a college woman. I'm far too sophisticated to be disgusted by the main character of the story being a giant cockroach.

Who am I kidding? I hate this book! Bring on the Jane Austen!

* * *

FIRST CHANGE OF PLANS

Have I ever mentioned how much I love Julian? I love his dark, shiny hair that reflects the light like a mirror. I love his smile, his perfect white teeth that are like a line of pearly perfection. (I don't care if I'm repeating myself. I already said I wasn't a poet!)

I love how he always smells like fresh soap and ocean breezes. I love how strong his hands are and how his callouses are just a little scratchy when he smooths them over my skin. I love the way he knows exactly where to touch me...

The boy is pure perfection. And then he pulls off his shirt, and he's just all lines and Vs. Oh, God, I'm shivering just typing this right now.

He got here on Friday, and the moment I saw him, all the days of us being apart hit me so hard, I could barely breathe. Seeing him... I confess, it's possible I was momentarily blinded by the visceral need for him. It was overpowering. A little like going into one of those trances. Temporary insanity.

Luckily, Rachel had already packed her overnight bag and headed to Brad's. I'm not convinced we would've cared if she was still in the house, our reunion was so intense.

Within seconds of him parking his car (Will's old Beemer his dad gave him), I was in his arms. He carried me straight inside with our mouths stuck together and us all wrapped around each other like Asian contortionists. Or spaghetti. Or monkeys.

We sort of flew together then bumped back, knocking over the coffee table on our way to falling on the couch. I'm not sure the front door even made it closed before our clothes started flying. I barely had time to spread my hand over the round tattoo on his torso before he was driving my skirt higher, devouring my mouth, pushing my panties aside.

"I missed you so much," Julian's breath was hot against my skin, and I was pretty sure my body would combust if he paused for even a nanosecond.

"No, I've missed you," I breathed, my fingers threading in his silky hair, inhaling his clean, beachy scent.

My stomach was painfully tight as the magnitude of missing him collided with the intense happiness of holding him again. We stretched and curled, trying to press our lips against every part of each other's skin… and more.

Yeah, typing all this is pretty crazy now, but it was hot. The whole night was pretty much the same. At one point during it all, my eyes grew damp.

I'd let myself think about how our time together was so short —less than two days and he'd be gone again on Sunday afternoon. I tried to smother the feeling, but a sob jerked in my chest. I was wrapped so tightly in his arms, clutched against his chest, that of course he felt it.

"Hey." His voice was low as he smoothed my hair away from my face. His warm lips pressed against my brow, working his way down my temple to my cheek then my jaw before lifting up again and holding my gaze. I was powerless against those Kyser blue eyes.

"I love you." It was a simple statement, but he said it with such conviction, it could've been a mandate. "This separation isn't forever."

My eyes were still burning with unshed tears, but I blinked them back and nodded.

"I know." My voice had the slightest tremble. "I love you, too."

He hovered above me a few minutes more, holding my gaze, as if that simple act would somehow forge a concrete edifice of fact. We loved each other. What we were doing, being in college pursuing our dreams, was so important, but it was also temporary.

In the next breath our mouths were together again, and I'm not sure we would've left the duplex if Rachel and Brad hadn't called and texted repeatedly, insisting we meet up with them for brunch at the Camellia Grill.

It was the next morning, and we were lying beside each other on our backs.

"You've got it right over your bed." Julian's fingers lifted my curls off my shoulder. I turned into him, placing my cheek on his chest listening to his heartbeat. I was drowsy with happiness and love and pure bliss of holding him.

"Hmm?" I wasn't sure what he was talking about at first, and I was reluctant to lift my head and break contact.

"I get it next semester, right?"

The watercolor. The one he'd made of us apart but held together by our dragonflies—I was wearing my ring, and I slid my thumb over the little tattoo on his hand.

"Hmm," I frowned. "If you take it, you'll have to give me something to put in its place."

He chuckled, and I lifted my head to press my lips against his skin. That's when my phone buzzed. Rachel was texting again about meeting for brunch, and I knew Julian wanted to see Brad. The two had become almost inseparable by the end of senior year —just like their dads had been, although Julian didn't know about that. Neither of them did. I was the only one who'd read those diaries.

"Rachel says ten. Can we make it?"

Julian stretched his arms then kissed my head roughly before sitting all the way up. "Sure. I'll just take a quick shower."

"I'm right behind you," I called as I tapped my reply. Glancing up, I caught his grin. "As soon as you're done," I added.

I knew right where it would lead if I got in with him. Not that I minded, but I'd just promised Rachel we'd meet them.

* * *

The heat of August in New Orleans is hard to describe if you've never felt it. It seems like humans shouldn't be able to survive the conditions. It's like trying to breathe hot water or living in a steam room, but I suppose if humans can survive sitting in a steam room, they can survive late summer in the Crescent City.

Rachel had the greatest hair for New Orleans, straight, blonde, always perfect. If it did anything, it picked up a slight wave that made her look all tousled and sexy.

I tried not to hold it against her as I cinched my frizzy spirals into a tight knot at the back of my neck. She was parked beside Brad in a light blue sundress, smiling and drinking coffee. I was ready for a cup as well, only I'd be having the iced variety.

Brad looked up and saw us before she did, and it warmed my chest the way his expression changed at the sight of his friend.

"Whipped," Brad called, sliding his arm around Rachel's shoulders and giving a smug grin. "It's been less than a month, and here you are. When are you transferring?"

Julian answered fast. "You're one to talk."

The guys slapped a handshake as I slid into the booth across from my roommate.

"So, how's Georgia?" Brad's loud voice reminded me a lot of his dad's. "If you ever show up in anything Bulldogs, I'll kick your ass."

"When have I ever worn football shit?" Julian flipped the menu over, scanning it. "Anyway, I'm in Savannah not Athens."

"Right. How are all the gay bars in Savannah? Found one you liked yet?"

Julian exhaled before kissing my ear. "Why do football players always act like football players?" That made me laugh. "What do you want?"

"Iced coffee," I said, smiling up at the server who'd just appeared.

"He'll have a skinny butterscotch Frappuccino latte." Brad winked at the girl, who appeared to be our age.

"Oh," she seemed confused. "We don't have that—"

"Regular coffee." Julian cut in, and Brad just laughed and asked for the same.

Rachel elbowed her boyfriend hard in the ribs. "If you'll quit being a dick for five seconds, I want to know what Julian's working on." She leaned forward against the table. "Everybody's got their eye on you, you know."

Julian didn't answer her right away, and instead fiddled with a sugar packet. "Yeah," was all he said.

I was on instant alert. "Whoa, hang on." Catching his upper arm, I pulled it toward me. "What's this about? Aren't you loving SCAD?"

Lifting his arm around my shoulder, he leaned back and looked at us all one by one. "Don't wig out and start acting like my mom."

"What does that mean?" My voice was hesitant.

I couldn't imagine what he was about to tell us.

"It's not that I don't like SCAD. I just… I dropped a few art classes and replaced them with something different."

We were all too stunned to speak, so Julian continued. "Hell, it's not like I have a terminal illness. All I mean is I'm thinking about broadening my focus."

I wasn't sure how this news made me feel. I knew Julian so well, and he'd always had a plan. I knew he wouldn't just ditch everything without a good backup.

"Broadening your focus?" I turned so I could see him better.

His smile was warm just before he traced his thumb over my cheek. "Yeah. I'm thinking about the future. I love art, but I'm looking at other ways to use it. More practical, real-life stuff."

Rachel wasn't letting him off that easily. "What did you replace them with?"

Brad cut in with a laugh. "Look out. She's going to start pressuring you to go to law school."

I exhaled a shaky laugh, knowing my roommate's passion for her field. "We can talk about it later if you want. Or not?"

The thought of Julian not doing art was a pretty big shock. At the same time, he hadn't said he was quitting. He was so calm about the whole thing.

"It's okay," he continued. "They have a lot of different programs, so I added a few architecture classes to my schedule. I'm also looking into development."

A twinge of worry filled my stomach, and I wondered how much knowing his dad factored into his evolving plans.

As far as I knew, Julian hadn't told anyone about his connection to Bill Kyser. They were still tentatively building a friendship when we left for college. I wasn't sure how often they spoke—I hadn't even thought to ask. All I'd been thinking about was getting on my feet, making it to all my classes, and missing him.

Brad slapped the table with a laugh. "We'll end up partners before it's all over, you wait."

Rachel and I both blinked at her boyfriend. "What's that supposed to mean?" she asked.

His brow creased. "You didn't think I chose Tulane to help me become a career football player, did you?"

Our waitress cut us off, placing coffees in front of Brad, Julian, and me. Then she straightened up, and we all ordered. I asked for Rano's egg-white spinach omelet, while Julian got the pecan waffles. Brad chose the chili omelet and side of bacon, grits, and biscuits, while Rachel ordered the Manhattan, which was sort of like a Reuben-sandwich only made with eggs.

As soon as our server left, we were back to the bombshell.

"What are you not telling me?" Rachel's voice was stern.

"I'm looking at industrial engineering, business, it doesn't matter what I major in, as long as it's related to development."

"I knew that," she pressed.

"And when I graduate, I'm un-silencing Dad's silent partnership in Kyser-Brennan and seeing where that might go with a little concentrated attention."

It was all too much—way too coincidental that Brad would want to pull Julian into the same partnership their fathers had launched decades ago, before either of them were born.

Julian took his arm from behind me and leaned forward. "When the hell did you come up with this idea?" I could see a spark of enthusiasm. "And why didn't you say anything about it to me?"

Brad just laughed. "For all I knew you were headed to New York to be the next Andy Warhol or some art crap like that. Now that I know your head's in the game, we can make real plans."

My brow creased as I watched them. It was surreal, like seeing the journals coming to life in front of me.

"What plans?" I asked.

"Well, the old guys have been letting everything ride for years," Brad started. "Jackie's here pissing his time away partying too hard, but I'm betting if we talk, if he's part of a real team with real direction…"

Brad kept going, but I couldn't help the sick feeling in my throat at the mention of Jack. It was funny. Brad had been trying to get Jack to join him since that first football game last fall in Fairview, when Jack had first transferred to our school.

I glanced at Julian and saw the muscle in his jaw move. "You think he'd be up for something like that?"

"I know Will is." Brad leaned back as the waitress and a busboy unloaded our orders.

I reached for the salt while Julian poured the syrup.

Brad took a big bite of chili and continued. "Have you met their brother Will?"

Focusing on my omelet, I didn't say a word. I'd met Will, and he was the biggest jerk I knew. I hated the thought of Julian working with him.

Julian shook his head no, and I tried to imagine how he was feeling in that moment, knowing this person was also his half-brother.

Someone he'd never met, but only heard about through Lucy.

"I'll introduce you to him, and we can see what we think. He's kind of an arrogant prick, but he's smart. He's also been at it longer, so he's got more connections. And he wants to reboot the business, too."

Julian leaned back again, putting down his fork. "Look, I'm only trying things out, experimenting, seeing what's interesting to me." He studied his huge friend for a beat. "Nothing's set in stone yet."

"Hey, no pressure!" Brad held up his hands, but he was grinning.

I knew he was already working out a plan himself, and I was having a hard time figuring out how I felt about it all.

So much of what Brad described was history repeating itself, and while Julian knew a little bit of the story, he had no idea how much more was left for him to learn.

Brad was willing to put his ideas on pause, and we spent the rest of breakfast talking about senior year and how we'd spent the summer. A few more teasing comments, and finally we were settling the bill, saying goodbye and going our separate ways, with the two of us walking alone back to the duplex.

Julian's arm was across my shoulder, and we were moving slowly. I decided to tease him a little, hoping to get to the heart of how he felt. "Were you going to tell me about this architecture experiment?"

His lips pressed into a line. "No."

His bluntness stunned me, but he only studied the sidewalk in front of us as we kept going.

"I wasn't going to tell anybody." He glanced at me. "Then I wanted to say it out loud. I wanted to hear your reaction. We've always talked about this stuff. Help me decide if it's crazy or not."

"It's not crazy at all. I think it's a really interesting idea." I glanced at his profile and his blue eyes met mine for a moment. Relief was in them. "Did something happen at SCAD?"

His eyes roamed up, around the buildings we were passing. "I don't know." We were quiet for a few more steps before he continued. "Maybe it was the move, everything changing. I just had this idea, and the more I thought about it, the more I liked it."

"Architecture." The image of him following in his father's footsteps made me nervous in a way I couldn't share with him.

"Have you told anybody else?"

By his glance, I could tell he knew who I meant. "I exchanged a few emails with Dad."

"Yeah?" I leaned forward to catch his eye again.

He nodded. "I asked if I could visit his office, maybe try working there some over the break. Just to see if I liked it."

I was pretty confident Mr. Kyser liked the idea. I was certain he loved it. He'd wanted his son by his side for years.

I was also sure his mother knew what was on her son's mind, even if their relationship was still strained. Bill Kyser wouldn't keep anything from Ms. LaSalle, and I wanted so much to know her thoughts. Was she happy? Was she as nervous as I was?

"I probably shouldn't have brought it up." He was back to evasion. "I'm probably just adjusting to the move, having a moment."

"It's a big move for all of us." Still, my future plans hadn't changed.

We were back at my duplex and he stopped, pulling me around to face him. My expression must've given me away, because he cupped my cheeks in his hands, his thumbs lightly touching my skin.

"Why so worried? This doesn't change anything for us."

I swallowed my fear before speaking. "It doesn't?"

His hands moved to my shoulders, pulling me against his chest. I held his narrow waist and tried to banish my doubts.

"I told you, I'm not losing my angel. If I decide to do this, you'll just have to come and work with me."

"What would I do at Kyser-Brennan?" My voice was muffled against his shoulder, and my eyes were closed as I inhaled a deep breath of fresh, ocean air clinging to his t-shirt.

"Be my PR person, of course. Marketing… you name it."

Shaking my head, I managed a little laugh. "Not until I've gotten sick of being a writer."

"Ahh," he growled. "I'll find you things to write about. Just like I'll find time to draw and weld and paint." He caught my cheeks again. "Trust me. This doesn't change anything."

Deep inside, however, a little nagging pain said he was wrong. He was starting a path that could lead him away from us and our dreams. Even if it didn't, I knew for certain Julian working with his dad would change something.

* * *

THE ONE THING

Tonight was the night. I'd been waiting for it, preparing myself, and out of the blue, when I least expected it, there it was.

It did not go how I thought it would. I have no idea how to begin sorting out my feelings. I don't know what to do with what just happened or where to place it in reality.

My head is still spinning, but I won't cry. No way am I shedding another tear over that boy.

I know... I have to back up and fill in the gaps, but trust me. What happened tonight defies all logic. Even more illogical is my stupid eyes that keep trying to fill as I sit here typing this.

Dammit. I am not crying over him anymore.

Deep breaths.

Back it up a little.

Place this in time...

Being a second-semester sophomore is actually way more demanding than I expected. I'm sorry if my entries are sporadic and spread apart. Rest assured, I'll definitely be back to dump crap like what just happened here. God knows, I can't say it out loud or tell anyone else. They wouldn't understand. *I* don't understand.

I've given up on my emotions returning to normal after senior year—as much as I try and force them. All I can hope is that maybe seeing it here, written down in black and white, I'll understand it better.

My last entry was Julian's visit, when he told me about his future goals and how they were shifting. Even though I was worried, we spent our last day together the same way we'd started the weekend, holding each other, catching up on time we'd lost and making up for the days ahead when we'd be separated again, touching and kissing... which led to other things.

We'd said goodbye with me fighting tears and him holding me close, telling me softly in my ear that he loved me, and we'd be together again soon.

Rachel stayed at Brad's, which was fine. They're stockpiling for their own shortage once football season gets into full swing.

Playing for Tulane, Brad won't be quite as slammed as if he were at one of the big state schools. Still, he's going to be on the road, practicing then trying to cram studying around it. At least they grew up in the football life.

Julian suggested we try FaceTiming every evening so we can see each other as well as text. We started the very next night, and I'm convinced he gets better looking every time I see him.

I don't know if it's because we're apart or if he's turning into a man, but whatever it is, he's absolutely yummy. So what's wrong with my stupid head? What happened to me?

It all brings us to tonight…

Rachel and I were doing our usual, Thursday-night meet up at Fat Harry's. We do it every week because between her class schedule, my class schedule, me FaceTiming with Julian, her spending the night at Brad's, it's our only way of keeping in touch.

Fat Harry's is one of the college bars on St. Charles Avenue, east of Loyola. It's a pretty easy walk or even a cheap street-car ride away from our duplex, and it's pretty popular with the Greek kids.

Neither Rachel nor I pledged a sorority. My reason was because of my accelerated schedule and Julian. I didn't want to be distracted by unnecessary social events involving other guys that would slow down my studies and make him uncomfortable.

I wasn't sure what Rachel's reasons were.

So Thursdays are our catch-up dates, and you know how I said Julian's growing up? Well, guess what? We all are.

As I stumbled into Fat Harry's with Rachel last night, I couldn't help thinking how different college life is than how I expected. It helps so much having her with me, and I'm so glad we decided to be roommates.

Even though I miss Julian like crazy, Rachel and I are having a blast learning to be responsible adults together. I even enjoy hanging out with Brad more. School work, football practice, and soon games are keeping him busy, so it doesn't happen very often. Still, it's fun. I'm truly feeling like a College Woman…

Except for The One Thing waiting to happen.

Everywhere I went, I held my breath waiting to run into Jack. Loyola and Tulane were literally built back to back. It was an inevitable meeting, and I wanted to get it over with. I wanted to know how seeing him would affect me, so I could deal with it if I had to.

He knew I was dating Julian. I knew I loved Julian. I just needed to see how I'd handle being confronted with Jack here, alone.

More than anything, I wanted to prove to myself that I was past him, finished being the girl I used to be. The past was in the past, I'd moved on, and my future was waiting for me with someone better.

Last night, my waiting ended.

As I made my way past the tables in Fat Harry's, I spotted him, sitting by himself in a back corner booth. He didn't even look up, but his name was out of my mouth before I could stop it.

"Jack." It was somewhere between a whisper and a squeak.

I was incredibly nervous, and I braced myself to hear his voice. I wondered if it would sound the same, then he looked up and saw me.

His eyes widened almost imperceptibly, and he laid his head back against the wooden panel of the booth.

"Anna." His voice was low and slightly loose, and I noticed a half-empty pitcher on the table in front of him.

He was so amazingly handsome in the dim yellow light, almost unchanged from our last meeting at homecoming—the night I left early and Julian sat with me while I cried. That memory made me cringe.

His eyes seemed to glow from the blue oxford he wore, but all I felt was relief—intense relief. My insides were calm. I wanted to do a little dance when I realized the thing I feared most was *not* happening.

I wasn't melting at the sight of him. I wasn't that fragile little girl anymore, and I knew why. I had someone now who meant more to me than the infatuation that had defined almost a year of my life.

All I felt for Jack was friendship. I only wanted to be friends if that were possible. Julian was his half-brother, after all.

Jack's eyebrows pulled together in a frown. "What are you doing here?"

My voice sounded distinctly calmer. "I didn't expect to see you."

"Well, it looks like you found me." He was still frowning, and even though I was calm, a pain moved through my chest.

We *could* still be friends at least, couldn't we?

"Were you hiding?" I tried to joke. "Wow, it's been what? Almost a year?"

"Six months." His tone was sharp, and it seemed the answer to friendship was *No*.

For whatever reason, that realization made me sad.

"I'd better go. I'm sure we'll see each other around. I'm at Loyola now. Full scholarship. It was the best offer I got, so I took it." The way he was acting, I was hoping he didn't remember how much he'd had to do with my decision to apply.

"You were always very smart. Speaking of smarts, how's Julian?"

"He's in Savannah now."

Was this about Julian? He slid to the side of the booth and stood to face me. I'd forgotten how tall he was as he leaned forward to close the space between us.

"Tell me, was Julian on the pass-fail system as well, or did you grade him on a curve?" His voice was low and sarcastic, and I could smell the alcohol on his breath.

My pulse ticked up a notch.

"I don't understand."

"You were so good at riding the fence. After I left, did you run straight to Julian or did you wait a day or two for appearances?"

"I don't know what you're talking about. You broke up with me."

"Right. No discussion. No argument."

"Do you have a head injury?" My voice rose as my tension built. "You were determined. You said… You told me you needed to end it. Still, I waited for you."

"You waited? Why?" He leaned back and the look in his eyes immediately called up the first night I'd encountered his father.

It could have been the same man standing in front of me now.

"I don't know. I don't even recognize you anymore."

"I'm me," he smiled, holding out his arms, slightly wobbly.

"You're not Jack. Not *my* Jack."

"I was never *your* Jack." The smile left his face, and the cold withdrawal returned.

Nodding, I backed away. "You're right. You told me many times, but I wanted…"

I couldn't finish that sentence. It was all in the past, and I wasn't going back there.

"Wanted what?"

"What's happened to you?" He was being so mean.

For a moment, I thought he would sit back in the booth, but after a pause, he turned back and grabbed my arm roughly, pulling me into his embrace. His kiss was hard and aggressive, and I put my hands on his shoulders to push myself free.

"Stop it! What are you doing?"

"Just trying to remember what I've been missing."

"If you're missing anything, it's your own fault. You could

have called me at any time. I'd have waited forever if you'd only asked me to."

"I didn't know you needed to be asked."

"That's not fair." A tear spilled onto my cheek, and I turned to go.

This was crazy, and why the hell was I crying? He was the one rewriting history, clearly still trying to mess with my head.

I was so angry and hurt, I could barely see where I was going, but I stopped as I opened the door. Looking back through the center window, I saw him slump down into the booth, head back against the wall, eyes closed.

He might be messing with my head, but one thing was certain —something was wrong. Bad wrong. The question facing me was whether to walk away or try and help him. For tonight, I chose to walk away.

I got back to our apartment on St. Charles Avenue and didn't even turn on the lights as I collapsed onto the bed, pulling my knees into my chest.

I didn't know why I was crying. It wasn't like I wanted him back. But dammit, I was worried about him. I loved Jack once, and it hurt to see him so changed.

He was lost and ugly, and regardless of what he said, he was not being my Jack, the guy I knew and fell in love with a year ago.

I grabbed a pillow and held it over my mouth to muffle my crying. The Jack I left back at Fat Harry's could just as well have been his brother Will. The closed cruelty and lack of compassion. He'd been gone less than two years. Less than two years, and already he was an exact replica of Will.

I remembered everything he'd said to me the day we parted. He'd needed to come here, needed to learn the business.

Lucy was the first one to suggest that wasn't happening. Brad was the second. But what did any of it mean? And how dare he try to pretend it was somehow my fault or that I had been the one to end things. My mind reeled at the very suggestion.

My face was wet with tears, and I pulled myself up to go and shower. Standing under the warm spray would help me relax, I hoped…

Now I'm here, typing up the whole thing and looking at it on the screen. I was right. It does help seeing it all in black and white, because most of all, I remember how I felt right away. I am over him.

The second thing I remember is Jack has his own family, a twin sister. I'm not his lifeboat, and I'm certainly not getting on that merry-go-round again.

Brad's here now, and Will is somewhere close. He is not my problem. I'm not worrying about Jack Kyser anymore.

* * *

LONDON CALLING

Media Studies is rapidly taking the place of English in my list of favorite classes. I still love reading stories and breaking them down, even when they're disgusting roach fantasias like *The Metamorphosis*, but finding real-world applications in books like *Responsible Journalism* is far more fascinating to me now.

Maybe it's because I've seen first-hand the effects of writing and reporting events with my feature on Julian's art.

I've also seen the impact of *not* reporting events with his parents and their story. Maybe it's the fact that working at the podcast opened doors for me and gave me more confidence. It got me here. Whatever the case, all I know is I love it!

My ethics professor Dr. Arati has quickly become my favorite instructor. She's about my height, 30s, petite with clipped British tones flavoring her Indian accent, and she's always encouraging me.

Today she asked me to wait after class so we could discuss

something. I watched as my older classmates gathered their things and made their way to the door.

"Anna, I want you to consider applying for Junior Year Abroad next year." Dr. Arati's usually formal voice was tinged with excitement. "I have friends at the BBC World News, and I think an internship there could be a powerful experience for you."

My jaw literally hit the floor. I was so surprised, I almost couldn't speak.

"Oh, Dr. Arati." I couldn't help a laugh. "That would be amazing! The BBC?"

Visions of me in a power suit, straight, professional hair, reading a report on terrorist attacks or international espionage flooded my brain.

My old dream of being Christianna Amanpour blinked through my mind. I couldn't believe it. I couldn't breathe.

"It's only radio, but—"

"But how?" As fast as those visions appeared, the price tag cut through them like an evil buzz-kill. "I don't know if I can afford it."

"It is an expensive trip, and radio isn't as lucrative as something like television." I watched her digging through her file cabinet, lifting out a hanging folder that had glossy pamphlets in it.

She handed one to me that was covered with smiling co-eds holding books and looking very international in front of those lion statues in Trafalgar Square.

One of them was a dark-haired male, and another problem flashed in my brain as she continued speaking. Julian.

"It's very competitive, but I'll write a recommendation for you. You're a strong writer, and with your background in podcasting, you could easily be accepted." She was so encouraging, but the more I looked at the dark-haired model, the further my stomach sank. "We have great relationships with their administration, and our students have always been an asset to the program."

Blinking up at her, I tried to imagine being separated from Julian by a year and an ocean.

"I think..." My voice was quiet. "I think I'm as abroad as I want to be right now."

Her dark eyes creased with her warm smile. "I don't understand. Your resume is very good for someone your age. I think you should capitalize on the momentum you have now. See how far it can take you."

"It's just that going abroad means leaving..." I felt like an idiot. Of course it meant leaving.

"And there is someone holding you here?" A smile touched the corner of her mouth.

I didn't want to answer that.

"It's just... I couldn't have come here without a scholarship, and I don't know if my parents or I have the money."

It was almost the whole truth. Money might not have been as painful a consideration as leaving Julian, but it was definitely a consideration.

She nodded, her glossy dark hair bobbing around her cheeks.

"Of course. You must talk it over with your parents, whoever else, and let me know." She squeezed my forearm. "Like I said, it might not lead to an offer or even to a very lucrative position, but it would be an amazing experience for you. And who knows what doors might open? Just think about it."

Now I nodded rapidly. "I'm sure you're right. Thank you so much, Dr. Arati!"

Her straight, white teeth shone with her smile. I smiled back, but my stomach was a cluster of painful knots as I collected my notebook and bag.

Junior Year Abroad would be the most unbelievable experience, but how in the world could I ever be away from Julian like that? I was already miserable with him just a few hours away.

Heaviness weighed on my shoulders as I pulled open the wooden door. Money was a major factor, but it was the least of my concerns.

I was lost in a cloud of wanting to be a strong College Woman, wanting to seize this opportunity that had just been presented to me, and failing, when I glanced up and nearly dropped all my stuff.

"Anna, hey." Jack caught my computer before it slipped out of my arms. "Whoops—don't drop your notebook."

He smiled, and dammit. I hated that stupid gorgeous smile that always knocked me a little off-balance. He didn't look at all like last night. He looked amazing. His light blond hair was perfectly messy as always, and he wore a gray tee that stretched across his shoulders. His faded jeans hung loose around his hips.

Finding my voice, I asked the obvious question. "What are you doing here?"

"Waiting for you." My brow creased, and he continued. "I wanted to find you, and apologize for last night."

The painful memory of last night only made the ache in my stomach even stronger. I glanced down the empty hall.

"How did you know I had class here?" An impossible idea flickered across my brain. *Had he been following me? Did he know my class schedule?*

"After you left, Rachel was looking for you…"

Dr. Arati stepped out of her classroom then. She paused when she saw Jack and me talking, then she gave me a knowing smile before turning back to lock the door.

I wanted to correct what I feared she was thinking, tell her she couldn't be more wrong. Jack was not the reason I'd hesitated at her offer. Jack would've been the one thing that would have sent me running to London just to get away from him, to stay there until he no longer had the power to trip me up.

He caught my arm and escorted me down the hall, away from class. I resisted inhaling the citrusy scent of his cologne that tried to fill my brain with memories of every time he'd pulled me into his arms. Last night included.

As we walked, he continued. "She told me which classes you had today."

Of course, Rachel had told him. From what I kept hearing, Jack barely knew his own class schedule, much less mine.

Shaking away the crazy, I stepped to the side, out of his grasp. "So you went to all of my classes today?"

"Just this last one." We were outside in the humid air, and we stopped, facing each other. He smiled again. "Want to grab some lunch with me?"

"No."

I answered so fast, he actually laughed. "I don't blame you. I was a jerk last night. I'm sorry."

His hand rose as if he were going to touch me again, and I took another half-step away. He put it in his back pocket, stretching his shirt in a way that told me everything underneath it was just as perfect as always.

I did not care.

"When I first saw you last night, I thought we could be friends." Somehow my voice didn't give away how blindsided my insides felt. "Now I don't think that's a great idea."

His mouth pressed into a line. "Because of Julian?"

"Because of you. You're different now." I thought about it and added. "Or maybe it's like you said last night. You were never the person I thought you were."

His head dropped and for a moment, neither of us spoke. His eyes traveled from the space between us to my hands then up to mine again.

That damn Kyser blue, the same intense color that was so full of love when it met me from Julian's face. It was full of suspicion or annoyance when it came from their father. Now seeing them in Jack's perfect features, they were lost and a little sad.

"I'm not going to apologize for telling you that." His voice was low now, and I heard a touch of weariness. "I honestly don't remember everything I said, and my delivery was… bad. Again, I apologize."

"Save it. There's no reason why we ever have to see each other here." I started to go, but he caught my arm. His strong grip kept me from leaving.

"I don't want it to be like that. I do want us to be friends like you said."

I didn't answer, and he dropped his hand. "That's all I came here to say."

All I gave him was a nod, and he inhaled deeply before turning to go. "See you around," were his last words before he walked away.

I watched him crossing the space crowded with students. His casual way of walking turned a few heads and took me all the way back to that very first day at the beach.

I'd hidden behind my dark sunglasses, fantasizing as he walked down to the crystal blue Gulf. He was as perfect then as he was now.

On that day, I'd dreamed of standing beside him, holding his hand. Now, having been in that coveted spot—and tossed out of it, and pulled back in, and tossed out again—I had no intention of swimming back into that wave pool. Even if I wasn't completely in love with Julian.

Julian. The pamphlet I now clutched with all my other books and computer was like a huge pill stuck in my chest, and I couldn't swallow it away.

With Jack gone and most of the students clearing out for their next classes, I collapsed onto the concrete bench and pulled out my phone. He was probably in class himself, but I called his number anyway.

"Would you believe I was just thinking about you?" His happy voice filled my ear in less than two rings.

Tears clogged my throat, stealing my voice. Somehow hearing

him broke the dam and all my emotions came swirling out in a violent stream.

"Oh, Julian…" Was all I could manage in a pathetic little wail.

He was instantly concerned. "Whoa, what happened? Are you okay?"

Nodding, I realized he couldn't see me, so I sniffed and coughed and tried to get it together.

"Hang on," I whispered and walked quickly to one of the ancient water fountains in the breezeway between the buildings.

The water was hot and tasted like metal, but it helped me to get my voice back.

"You're scaring me a little, Anna."

"I'm sorry." I cleared my throat. "I'm okay. I'm actually good, it's just…"

"You're crying. That usually means you're not good."

"I just needed to hear your voice." Every breath sent a pulse of pain radiating through my chest.

"It's okay, Sunshine." His voice was quiet now. "I miss you bad sometimes, too. But I was just there—"

"It's not that—or not only that. I was just in class, and well… one of my teachers… my favorite teacher said… she told me I should…" I wasn't sure if I wanted to repeat what Dr. Arati had said yet.

"You're really good at building suspense." I could hear his grin, and it made my eyes fill again. I loved him so much. "You should consider writing mysteries."

"She wants me to apply for Junior Year Abroad." That silenced him. "She has a friend at the BBC. In radio."

"BBC," he repeated.

Now we were both hanging on the line, listening to each other's breathing. I knew he was seeing what I had seen in the classroom. Nine months of us being apart. Not separated by state lines, but by passports and oceans and airlines with expensive fares.

After what felt like a mini-eternity, he spoke again. His voice was serious. "It sounds like she's giving you a really great opportunity."

"Oh, Julian." My voice was barely a whisper.

"You've got to do it."

"What?"

"I'm serious, Anna. I'm not going to stop you from doing something that could change your life for the better."

"Even if it meant we'd be apart? I don't want any changes at that price."

He exhaled into the phone and I could hear him walking. "We're apart now."

"But you can actually come and see me." I felt desperate and angry, which didn't make any sense. I knew what he was saying was right. "After last weekend, are you actually saying you want to give that up?"

"I've got to go. I'm in a workshop." He was walking again, and his voice was still determined. "But this isn't something you can blow off. And I won't let you turn down an opportunity like this for me. You'll blame me for it later."

That pierced my forehead. "I would never blame you for anything I chose to do."

"I'm just saying—"

"I can't stand this separation as it is. It's physically painful to me, but maybe you don't feel that way?"

"You know that's not true. I miss you so bad…"

"Then how can you even suggest I apply for this?"

His voice grew quieter, and I could tell he was trying to whisper. "I've got to get back inside, but I'll call you as soon as I'm out, okay?"

With a sigh, I let him go. Then I sat on the concrete bench and looked up and around the quad. The live oak trees with their black trunks and heavy branches hung low in the dense heat. My limbs felt equally heavy and weighted down as all the emotions of the past twenty-four hours pressed in on me.

I knew what Julian was going to say, and deep down in a part of me I didn't want to recognize, I knew he was right. Dr. Arati was giving me an amazing opportunity, and I couldn't just dismiss it without serious consideration.

Everything was changing, just like I said it would. Julian kept insisting we could get through anything, but as the waves kept growing higher, I couldn't help my growing fears for our untested little lifeboat.

* * *

FAT HARRY'S FIASCO

Thursday night again, back at Fat Harry's with Rachel, fake IDs in hand. Only this time, there were no unpleasant Jack sightings. I hadn't even seen him since last Friday when he'd shown up outside my ethics class.

Rachel was pouring her second beer from the pitcher and ranting about a prelaw class she was taking and a judge who'd been caught applying corporal punishment to prisoners, among other things.

"One year later he was running for senator!" she cried. "How's that for going into the legal system?"

"Are you arguing for it or against it?" I laughed, taking a sip of my beer.

My nose wrinkled, and I wished I'd ordered a Malibu and pineapple instead.

"Neither!" Rachel always got louder when she started getting buzzed. "I'm just saying if you have connections and know how to use the law, you can get away with anything. Look at Richard Nixon! OJ Simpson! Michael Jackson!"

"Are you planning on doing criminal defense or prosecution?"

She shook her head and took a big gulp. I watched as she finished and then cried. "Neither. I'm going into corporate litigation."

"That's probably for the best, considering Brad's decided to relaunch his dad's corporation."

She exhaled a deep breath and leaned back. "Can you believe that? It was the first I'd heard of any of it."

My eyebrows flew up. "You and me both! Have they been discussing it when our backs are turned? Brad seemed to have it all worked out!"

"I don't think so. Julian seemed pretty surprised by the whole thing. But who ever knows what those two talk about."

We were laughing when the song changed, and an up-tempo dance song filled the room. It was getting increasingly crowded with frat boys in their button-down oxfords and khaki pants, and that was usually the time we called it a night and caught the streetcar home.

Tonight was different, though. Rachel and I both were happy and excited and a little tipsy. Our eyes met and widened, and we both laughed before jumping up and heading to the dance floor.

"Come on, Anna!" She yelled, twisting her hips and moving her shoulders around.

I noticed a guy checking her out and wondered if I might ought to shoot Brad a text and get him to meet us here. That would probably mean I'd end up home alone, but at least I'd feel a little safer.

"Hang on!" I yelled to her before skipping over to the booth. I grabbed my phone and quickly pulled up Brad's number.

ANNA

Dancing at Fat Harry's. Better come quick!

I was about to put my phone down when it buzzed.

BRAD

Just planning to crash your girls' night. Be right there.

I grinned and tossed the phone into my bag. She'd be happy to see him, and I'd catch a ride to the duplex with them when they left.

My friend's eyes were closed and her long, blonde hair swished down her back as she danced. Rachel really had been one of the prettiest girls at our high school, and some drunk guy had noticed.

He slid up behind her and caught her hips, pulling her against him, but just as fast, she jerked away. Eyes open now, she trotted over to where I was and leaned forward.

"Hate to say it on our girls' night and all..." Her voice was almost too loud in my ear, and I was ready to finish the sentence for her. "I wish Brad was here."

"I just texted him," I laughed, catching her wrists.

We danced together until the end of the song, and she gave me a squeeze before going back to the booth where our drinks waited. The next song was slow and couples-dancey, and I noticed the guy she'd rebuffed making his way to her again. I was about to hop over and intercept when I felt a hand catch my wrist and gently stop me. Turning back, I froze when my eyes collided with Jack's.

In a fast sweep, I was chest to chest with him, a strong arm slipping around my waist. His citrusy scent filled my nose as he leaned forward.

"Dance with me." His low voice was right in my ear, causing an involuntary shiver.

"No," I managed to say, but his other hand held mine, lacing our fingers. My heart was beating too fast, and my throat was tight. "Stop."

"Just one." His breath whispered across my eyelids. "We haven't danced together since that night at Jesse's."

That night at Jesse's, or more specifically, what happened *after* Jesse's, was not the best choice of memories.

My jaw clenched, and I jerked my hand away. "I want you to leave me alone."

I was just about to push him away hard when I heard Rachel's loud voice cut through the music. "Get OFF!"

Jack turned as quickly as I did, and we both saw that same drunk guy from the dance floor reach her hips. Our conflict forgotten, we were across the bar and at her side before the guy could follow-through with grabbing her again.

Jack grabbed his arm and spun the guy so hard, he almost fell. "She said get off, asshole."

"What tha—" He straightened and frowned at Rachel's defender. "What's your problem, barfly?"

In the second it took Jack's fist to rise, I'd caught it in both my arms. "Don't! He's not worth it."

Jack's forearm was clasped against my chest, but I still wasn't sure I could hold him. I could feel his anger. I could see it in his eyes, and it was more than just some drunk jerk harassing Rachel. I didn't have time to sort it out, because Brad walked up and the entire situation changed.

"Hey, babe." Oblivious, Brad caught Rachel around the waist, and she folded into his arms. "Sorry it took me a few. Had to shower after practice."

The drunk idiot took one look at his competition and wisely disappeared into the crowd, but that left me inexplicably clutching Jack's arm in both of mine. It looked like I was hanging on him, and I quickly straightened up and stepped away.

"What did I miss?" Brad frowned at me, and I knew he misunderstood what was happening between me and my former… whatever Jack and I were.

At the same time, I wasn't sure setting the record straight would be wise.

"Uhh…" I tried to think of anything that might make sense. "I was… I—"

"Hey, man." Jack clapped Brad's shoulder. "Where you been hiding out?"

"I'd say the same to you." Brad's expression remained serious, possibly annoyed. "It's almost like you've been avoiding me."

"What?" Jack laughed, but his eyes slanted away. *Had he been avoiding Brad? But why?* "I'm getting a drink. Anybody want one?"

I shook my head, and Rachel turned to her boyfriend. "I'm so glad you're here." Her soft voice triggered an ache in my chest I tried to fight down.

I wished Julian were here so badly.

"Looks like I showed up just in time." Brad was still giving me a look like I'd done something wrong.

Like he needed to watch out for Julian or something. It pissed me off.

Of course, it was a justifiable position after the way I'd acted all last fall. I'd been so caught up in Jack, I'd probably driven everybody crazy, but I needed Brad to know that had changed.

Jack was not dangling me along anymore. I wasn't sure what was going on in Jack's head at the moment, but whatever it was, I wasn't falling for it.

"Yeah, Jack was goofing off, and Anna was very cool about it." Rachel gave me a look that said *Be cool*, so I held my tongue. "He's acting weird. Do you know what's up with him?"

"How was he goofing off?" Brad wasn't ready to let me off so easily.

"Acting like he's so tough. Anna kept him from getting in over his head just now."

Rachel hugged her arms around Brad's neck and made a little laugh. It seemed to ease whatever he suspected I'd done—or thought about doing.

My stomach relaxed, and in that space, I could tell how hard it had been clenched. College had turned into a little more than a series of stressful moments lately, and one repeat offender was part of the reason.

"Yeah," I tried to reinforce Rachel's story. "He's different now. Somehow."

Brad exhaled and rubbed the back of his neck. He almost seemed guilty. "I should be doing more to reach out. Dad would expect me to."

"Do you know what's wrong?" I almost hoped he did.

Brad blew air through his lips. "Shit, I don't know. What do I look like? A psychiatrist?"

Rachel had relaxed her hold and now only had Brad by the hand. "Well, I do know you just got here, but I'm about ready to take off."

I couldn't agree with her more, and I hoped she'd be successful in getting us all out of Fat Harry's. Either that or I'd catch the streetcar alone.

Brad squeezed her hand and looked toward the bar. "Just a sec, okay? Let me see what's up with him."

With that, he was gone, leaving Rachel and me facing each other and hoping Jack knew better than to get Brad all riled up and into a bar fight. I was pretty sure he did, but after the way he'd acted tonight, I didn't know what to expect.

I remembered his story about beating up the teacher who'd hurt Lucy. Brad had helped him then as well, and a nagging twinge inside me said Jack was gunning for trouble.

Rachel collapsed into the booth, and I slid in across from her still worried.

"What was *that* all about?" she sighed.

I decided to try laughing away my worries. "You're too sexy for Fat Harry's."

She jumped forward. "We should play that song!"

Shaking my head, I ran my finger over the table before dropping my head onto my hand. "Too much adrenaline. I'm so tired."

She scanned the dance floor quickly before turning back to me. "That guy was such a jerk. I'm really glad Jack's here, even if he is acting like a crazy drunk."

"He's not a drunk!" Why was I suddenly getting so defensive? I had no idea.

I felt like his father's parrot from when I'd overheard Will saying the same thing to Mr. Kyser last spring.

"Okay!" Rachel's eyebrows rose. "I was just saying what it looked like. Don't get bent."

I exhaled and rubbed my forehead. "I'm sorry. I think all of this is getting to me."

"All of what? We're two weeks behind on catching up. Spill."

"I don't even know where to begin." Part of me didn't want to start because I was afraid I wouldn't be able to stop. The other part wanted to get it all off my chest. "Dr. Arati thinks I should apply for Junior Year Abroad. She has a friend at the BBC radio—"

"Shut up!" Rachel's eyes were huge. "And thanks for telling me. Do I need to find a new roommate?"

"Oh my god!" Shaking my head, I felt even worse. "I'm sorry— I didn't even think of that! I've been so knocked out by the very suggestion."

"But you're excited, right? I mean, that's a huge deal."

"Truthfully? I'm kind of leaning toward saying no."

"What?" Rachel's hand slapped the table. "You can *not* turn down something like that. It's an amazing opportunity!"

"I know, but it's just, well, it'll probably be super expensive…"

"And?"

My stomach clenched at the thought of saying my real reason out loud. I knew what she was going to say. I knew what I would say if the tables were turned.

Rachel wasn't letting me off the hook, though. "*And…?*"

"And there's Julian." I said, squeezing my eyes shut.

She didn't respond, and I dared to sneak a peek at her. Instead of railing on me for letting a boy control my destiny, her lips were pressed into a line, and she nodded.

"It would be hard to be away from Brad for nine months. Especially like that."

Relief hit me so hard, I thought I might cry. "I know, right? It's not like he can just hop over and see me on a moment's notice."

"Well, he can't really do that now."

"But at least we're not an ocean apart!"

We were quiet for a few moments, and I glanced around wondering for a half-second what Brad and Jack might be doing.

Rachel's voice brought me back. "What does Julian think about it?"

That question made me feel like I *would* cry, and my voice cracked when I answered her. "He wants me to go for it."

Our eyes met, and never in our entire relationship had I been more thankful to have her as a friend. Understanding radiated from her to me, and I felt my nose warm.

"I seriously might cry right now," I managed to say through a sniff.

"Don't you dare, or I'll cry, too."

For whatever reason, that made me laugh, and soon we were both laughing. I blinked down, and a tear fell onto my cheek.

Brad walked up then, and he frowned as he quickly looked from one of us to the other. "What'd I miss?"

I sniffed again and shook my head, wiping my cheek fast.

Rachel answered him. "I know you just got here, but we're wiped. Can we go, please?"

"Sure." I heard the smile in his voice and slid to the edge of the booth when I saw Rachel doing the same.

After I stood, she wrapped an arm around my shoulders. "I'm sorry to be losing such a great roommate."

I caught her hand as we walked. "See? That's another strike against the whole thing."

"What whole thing?" Brad held the door as the two of us went through it.

"Not only is Anna queen of the nerds with her amazing scholarship," Rachel started. "She's now been invited to spend her junior year interning at the BBC."

Brad's eyebrows pulled together. "BBC? You mean as in—"

"Right-o, old chap." Rachel did a pretty decent British accent. "In jolly ole England. She'll be across the pond and whatnot."

"I haven't said I'd take it. I haven't even told my parents yet." I shoved my hands into my pockets as Brad pulled Rachel into his side. "For all I know, I might not even get accepted."

"Oh, please," Rachel groaned. "Dr. Arati wouldn't have told you to apply if she didn't think you could get in."

Brad only nodded as we approached his car. "Want me to drive you to the duplex?"

"That'd be great."

Rachel cranked up the radio, and the topic was dropped as we drove the few blocks to our place. Once there, I told everybody goodnight and hopped out. They waited for me to get inside before driving away, and I collapsed on the couch. Grabbing my phone, I quickly tapped a text to Julian.

ANNA

Miss you so much tonight, I almost cried on Rachel.

It only took a second for him to reply.

JULIAN

Don't cry. What are you wearing?

That made me laugh. I glanced down at my outfit and my lip curled.

ANNA

Old jeans, chucks, long-sleeved tee.

JULIAN

I love casual Anna. Makes me want to slide my
hands under that tee and over your stomach.

A little tingle followed the imaginary trail of his touch, followed by the sadness—and that dry ache at the base of my throat.

ANNA

I might cry for real now. Want you here so much.

JULIAN

We'll be together again soon. I love you.

ANNA

What are you doing?

JULIAN

Something to replace the watercolor on your wall
when I have it.

I imagined him painting, and it was almost more than I could bear. How in the world could I go to London when this separation hurt so much?

ANNA

Send me a pic?

JULIAN

It's a surprise. I'll show you next visit.

ANNA

I want to kiss you.

JULIAN

When you close your eyes tonight, feel my lips
on yours. Know I'm doing the same—dreaming
of your little-flower scent…

ANNA

It's called Happy, but it's not working. Still sad.

JULIAN

Soon, Sunshine.

ANNA

I love you.

JULIAN

Sweet dreams of us together.

I kissed my phone and rolled onto my back to stare at the ceiling. Thinking back over the night, I realized Jack didn't return to the table with Brad. I wasn't sure where he went or if I even wanted to know.

Rachel had said exactly what Will did—what his dad denied and Lucy feared. Maybe Jack was in trouble, but for now, that wasn't my concern. At least he didn't get in a fight.

London was pressing on me hard. I knew Rachel was right—I knew Julian was right. I couldn't ignore this opportunity, but I still didn't want to think about it. It was the same painful pressure I felt last spring when my scholarship letter from Loyola arrived. I needed time to process it for myself first and decide how I felt.

The truth was, once again what I wanted and what I loved were in opposite directions of each other, and it was tearing me apart. Why did what was "good" for me always take me away from what I loved most?

My head hurt from thinking about it and from the stress of tonight. More than anything I wished for Julian's arms. If we'd gotten together six months earlier, would any of this even be happening? Would I be facing this "opportunity of a lifetime"?

Sliding doors and playing "what ifs" about roads not taken would only drive me crazy. What I needed was a break, space to think.

I needed to talk to Gabi.

* * *

DESERT REGROUPING

Fall break was just around the corner, and I ended up spending the long weekend in Tucson with Gabi. I really wanted to be with Julian in Savannah, but when I called, he actually encouraged me to go.

"This architecture project is killing me," he complained. "I've really got to focus on it."

"This London thing is killing me." I pushed my hand in my hair, not wanting to think about it. Still it dominated my thoughts. "What if I came and watched you work. I promise, I won't say a word."

"Then I'd look up and see that cute face, and I'd be all 'screw architecture.'" His warm voice made my insides tingle, and I returned the smile I heard there. "I knew I'd have a little learning curve when I switched majors, but man. It's a good thing I'm better at math than you."

"Hey!" My voice rose as I flipped onto my stomach. "I was a Mathlete *and* your algebra tutor!"

"And then you threw it all away to follow your dream of being a journalist."

"Hmm…" It seemed like my dream kept messing up my life. "Maybe I was too hasty in that decision."

"Take it one step at a time, Sunshine. We'll get through this." I could tell he was working and only half-listening.

When I closed my eyes, I could see his face, that expression he got when he was focused on a project. I now knew it made him look exactly like his dad, and I wondered how Ms. LaSalle could bear it all those years, separated from the man she loved. How did she not completely fall apart?

"I miss you so bad it hurts. I want to spend the break with you." It was very possible I was pouting.

"I miss your beautiful green eyes."

"Hazel," I corrected.

"No, it's *Julian*. I've told you this a hundred times. How can I trust you when you never get my name right?"

That made me laugh, and I sat up shaking my head. "So you'll just be doing architecture all break?"

"Pretty much." It sounded like he was lifting something. "When I'm not painting."

"I love that you're still painting."

"I'm painting what I love. It's different."

A huge sigh pushed through my lips. "Well, then I'm going to see Gabi. I've got just enough time to get a cheap ticket, and I've saved up my library money."

"Sexy nerd. I think that's a great idea. Gabi always cheers you up. Just don't forget to come back."

"No worries there. I'm counting down to Thanksgiving break."

"We'll be together every day."

"Goodnight, Julian."

"'Night, Hazel."

I smiled and hit End.

Gabi's fall break didn't exactly coincide with mine. I arrived on Thursday night, and she was in school all day Friday. Still, we had Saturday and half a day Sunday to talk it out.

Being with her was just what I needed to get my head straight and give myself some breathing room. By Saturday, we were on lounge chairs by her apartment complex's pool dissecting my "problem."

"What did Jenni and Frank say about you joining the BBC?"

Gabi leaned back on the chair, pushing her white wayfarers up to hold back her blonde spirals.

"They're beside themselves. Dad wants to borrow against his retirement to pay for it, which just freaks me out even more."

I let out a heavy exhale as I stretched against my chair. Gabi's apartment complex was just off campus near the University of Arizona. My best friend had followed in her father's footsteps, joining the military right out of high school, but unlike her Coast Guard dad, Gabi's focus was on astronomy. She hoped to work in the space program, and I had no doubt she'd be successful.

She turned to study my profile. "So what besides my hottie ex-future-husband who you heartlessly stole is making this decision so hard for you?"

I had to confess, I really loved the way my best friend could cut to the heart of the matter and make me laugh at the same time. "Would *you* want to leave Julian for nine months?"

"Objection! Evasive answer."

"Rachel would say that's not really a real objection, Fake Lawyer Gabi."

"Don't make me get the judge to require you to respond, Hostile Witness Anna."

"Would you repeat the question please?"

"Is Julian the only reason you're hesitating?"

I closed my eyes for a moment and thought about it. Out of all the noise of worry in my brain, being separated from him was the loudest, but he wasn't the only thing scaring me.

"He's not the only reason."

She bent her elbow to prop her head on her hand. "What else is there?"

Sitting up, I pushed my sunglasses on top of my head as well, and bent my knees, hugging them to my chest. "The idea that dad would borrow against his future, and then I might get over there and not be good enough or be too young or too inexperienced for world news… or what if I hated it? The whole thought of that makes me want to throw up."

Thankfully, she didn't launch into arguments dismissing my fears as ridiculous. Instead, like the best friend she's always been, she nodded and leaned back on her chair, restoring her sunglasses over her eyes.

"It's a legitimate concern." She paused for a moment and nodded again. "You're afraid journalism might not be your passion?"

My lips poked out, and I fiddled with my painted toenails. "Bikini so Teeny" was the color I'd chosen. Gabi had opted for "Haute in the Heat." When I didn't answer, she continued.

"Or you're afraid your college professor would urge you to apply even if she thought you couldn't handle it?"

Slowly, my eyes rose to hers, and I knew she was right. I wasn't ready to concede defeat yet, though. "Now it's my turn. You didn't answer *my* question."

"What was it again?"

"Would you want to leave Julian for nine months?"

That made her laugh. "Hells no! That's why I'm not in a field that would send me a million miles away."

"Just to the moon!"

"Or the space station." She took a deep, excited breath. "Can you imagine it? That would be *so amazing*."

I shivered. "No thanks. I'm still trying to get over *Gravity*."

"You need to get over yourself and apply for the internship."

"I know. And if I get it, I'll kill myself."

She rolled onto her side facing me again. "Julian's not going anywhere. He's focused on his thing, and you know how he's always been."

A little smile touched my lips. "Yes—once he's got his mind on something, he holds on until it thunders."

"So you'll miss him like the worst pain on the planet, but you won't lose him over Junior Year Abroad."

Tightening my arms around my thighs, I rested my cheek on my knees. "I'm also afraid of what comes after that. What if I like it? What if they ask me to stay? It's like every step I take is another step away from him."

"Now you're borrowing trouble. How do you know Julian wouldn't want to move to London if he had a choice?"

"Brad's talking about the two of them reviving Kyser-Brennan."

That made her sit all the way up and jerk off her sunglasses. "No shit! Does Brad know about his dad?"

"No!" I shook my head. "It was so crazy. He just launched into this plan with Julian over breakfast. I couldn't breathe. It was like all of the past flying in a circle around us ready to swoop down and repeat itself."

"Did Julian say anything?"

My lips poked out. "I could tell it took him by surprise. He backed away pretty quickly, but still..."

"He's taking architecture classes now."

Nodding, I picked up the sunscreen and sprayed more down my legs. "He says he wants to broaden his focus. He also wants to work with his dad over the break."

"His mom's probably wigging out right now."

Rubbing my hands over my legs, I tried to imagine what Ms. LaSalle must be thinking. I remembered from her diary she was surprised by how much she enjoyed working in development with Mr. Kyser.

"I'm missing a lot being in New Orleans, but when I left, she and Lucy were actually getting close. They've started having regular lunch dates, and Lucy refers to her as 'Dad's girlfriend,' which is just weird because she's as old as our moms."

"Older," Gabi corrected. "Do you think they'll ever tell them? I mean all the kids—that they're related?"

My shoulders rose. "I stopped trying to guess what those guys would do last year. As soon as Julian knew the truth, I hopped off that crazy train."

"Crazy is right." She reached for the sunscreen, and I passed it to her. "Just take it one challenge at a time, Banana Face. You'll get through this."

That made me smile. "Julian still calls me that sometimes."

"He's your home. You won't lose him so easily."

I nodded, warmth filling my stomach. "I can't imagine anything that could come between us. It really is like home."

Her smile was warm now, reassuring. "See? True love lets you follow your dreams. Don't be afraid."

Reaching for her hand, she quickly caught it through the space between us. "Thanks for always being awesome."

"What can I say? I am the fabulous Lady G."

We both laughed then. It was true. No matter what freak-out confusing, mixed-up brain-defying, heartbreaking problem I'd ever run into head-first, Gabi had always been there to help me sort it out. I felt sure London would be no different.

* * *

SAVANNAH SURPRISE

Even though I felt loads better after spending a weekend with Gabi, my entire being ached with need to see Julian. We'd never gone a month apart, and now we were going on six weeks. It was getting hard to concentrate.

My classwork didn't suffer, of course. My professors were encouraging and complimentary as always. I completed the application for JYA, so Dr. Arati was happy.

In American lit we'd started a unit on Tennessee Williams, and reading *A Streetcar Named Desire* only made me long for Julian more. It was hot and sweaty in New Orleans, and the thick air and the heavy subject matter made my desire feel over-whelming.

By Friday, I'd started to feel like I couldn't breathe. I was sitting with my back on a pillow against the headboard when Rachel burst into my room and fell across my bed.

She studied the back of the script I held. "Do you have a test Monday or something?"

"Not really. I mean, we'll probably have a quiz, but I'm ready for it. Why?"

"Brad's got the weekend off. He asked if you might be up for a road trip."

My brow creased. "Back home?" I might be up for a visit to Fairview, and for a moment, I wondered if Julian might as well.

"He was saying how he'd never been to Savannah, and—"

The scream was out of my mouth as fast as I jumped off the bed. "He wants to go to Savannah!?"

Rachel laughed and jumped up with me. "Let's do it!"

I was already moving. "It'll take me less than five minutes to throw my crap in a bag!"

"Good, because Brad's on his way now!"

My body hummed with excitement as I ran to the bathroom, duffel in hand, and started throwing toiletries into it—makeup bag, toothbrush, deodorant, face wash, lens solution, hair prod-ucts, everything! Back across the hall, I jerked my dresser open and threw in a nightshirt (not needed!), panties (needed?), a few shirts, a skirt, and an extra pair of jeans.

Rachel called out that Brad was pulling up outside just as I was running into the living room ready to go.

"This might be a record," Brad laughed as we pushed him back out the door. "I'll have to let Jules know how fast you can be ready for something you really want to do."

"Do what you want, just get us there now!" Three doors slammed and we were on our way.

Brad and Rachel were arguing the value of environmental law over basic, corporate law to his plans for taking over his father's development business while I lay across the back seat trying to decide if I wanted to text Julian we were on our way or not. I kind of wanted to surprise him. At the same time, we hadn't gotten on the road until almost three. It'd be after midnight when we got there.

Pulling up on the back of Rachel's seat, I stuck my head between them. "Thanks for doing this."

Brad's eyes caught mine in the rearview mirror. "Hey, no problem. I really wanted to go, and this might be the only weekend I can do it."

I patted his shoulder. "Still. It's amazingly cool that you're driving me over."

"We had to do something to get that look off your face," Rachel laughed. "I wasn't sure how much more of your moping I could stand."

"I wasn't moping!" Pushing against her seat, I leaned back again.

"Oh my god! You were like a puppy who'd been left home alone too long!"

I crossed my arms hard then I laughed. She was probably right, but I was too excited to care. Now I just had to figure out how to survive another eight hours.

Rachel's soft voice calling was the next thing I heard. "Anna, we're almost here." She was shaking my shoulder gently, and I sat up fast.

"Sorry!" My voice was thick. "I didn't realize I fell asleep."

"I just texted Julian for directions. We're like a block away."

A million butterflies flooded my stomach at her words, and I almost lost my breath. It was after midnight, and we turned off the road next to the park with that famous fountain in the middle, onto a quiet side-street lined with parallel-parked cars.

Brad's voice cut through the tension building in my chest. "This is it." He leaned forward looking through the windshield. "He said he'd be waiting outside. I'll let you out, and then we'll head to the hotel."

I'd already grabbed my duffel when I saw his familiar form lean out from a doorway. Tall, black jeans and chucks. He had a dark-gray hoodie over a white tee, and a stocking cap was pulled over his head.

Still that glossy black hair peeked out from underneath. He hadn't shaved, and the combined effect made his smile seem brighter, his eyes more intensely blue. The car had barely stopped before I was out the door and ran up the short flight of stairs to where he stood.

He exhaled a little laugh, and I only paused a moment to notice how fast I was breathing. Then we were in each other's arms.

At first we only held each other, inhaling deeply. His scent never changed, and I felt his lips press against the top of my head as he breathed into my hair.

We didn't speak. We savored the warmth of our bodies pressed together, shoulder to shoulder, his arms over mine, my arms around his waist. My cheek lay against the warm skin of his neck, and our hearts beat so fast.

The intensity rose until he moved his hands to my face, lifting my chin so he could cover my lips with his. They parted at once, and a little noise ached from my throat.

I didn't remember how I got inside. All I knew was we were there, in front of the couch, stumbling to his room, his hands sliding from my face, cupping my neck, to my shoulders and then to my waist.

Each movement was punctuated by another long kiss. Shirts off, mouths together; shoes kicked away, mouths reunited. Our arms collided as our hands reached desperately for one another whenever we were separated for even a moment.

Energy raced under my skin, and it didn't take long before we were on the bed, first him above me, then me rolling him onto his back.

It was like being without food or possibly even water for days and days, and when it's finally restored, you can't decide if you want to drink it or swim in it. Or both.

We were in heaven. Julian's warm mouth trailed from my cheek to my jaw, making his way down to my neck. I couldn't stop touching, feeling, remembering every part of his body with my hands until at last we...

* * *

Hello, there. Yes, it's me Jules cutting in here.

I know, you're like, "WHAT!?" I'm sure a lot of you romance-junkies are dying to indulge in what comes next right here, and trust me, Mum spared no detail—jeez, give a girl a break. For someone who claims not to be a poet, she practically breaks into song over Dad's... special gifts.

But honestly. Nobody wants to read about their parents getting it on. Yes, I know that's how I got here, but it wasn't on this particular occasion. Even if it was, that doesn't make it any more appealing to me to read.

So we're just going to skip to the afterglow, and you can fill in the blanks using your imagination...

* * *

... Julian's soft lips touched my eyelid, and the scruff of his chin touched the tip of my nose. With every heartbeat, a sparkling pulse moved through my insides.

"Best surprise ever." His voice was warm, and I laughed because it was all I wanted to do.

I was secure in his arms, his face hovering above mine, arms on either side of my shoulders.

"I'm trying to remember when I was ever this happy." My whole body buzzed with satisfaction, joy, contentment.

He leaned down and kissed me again. "I hope every time you're this happy, you're with me."

Reaching up, I traced my finger down his cheek, ran my thumb across his bottom lip. "I never dreamed I'd be with you this way. Then it happened, and it's the most amazing thing. Now I feel like I'm on the edge, like I might lose it all."

"Why would you say that?" He rolled to the side and rested his head on his hand. His other hand moved to my stomach. "I mean, yeah, it's tough being apart. All that works is just, you know, burying myself in schoolwork until we're together again. But nothing's slipping away."

I rolled into him, pressing my cheek against his warm skin. "Everything we're doing is sending us in opposite directions. How will we ever get *us* back together?"

The hand under his head went around my shoulders, pulling me tight against his chest. "We'll get there. I keep telling you this isn't forever."

It was so late, and I'd been running on adrenaline so long, I couldn't help the tears threatening.

"It feels like forever." My voice was a cracked whisper.

He kissed me, and I held him, closer than it should've been possible. We moved together again, but this time it was different. It was bonding somehow, or maybe that was how I wanted it to be. We fell asleep in the early morning hours, wrapped in each other's arms.

Julian was still asleep when I opened my eyes again. Dawn was streaming in too brightly through his windows, and I sat up and looked around his bedroom. I hadn't even noticed the space last night. The only thing I'd cared about then was Julian and touching him, being with him.

This morning all of that was different. It was my first visit to Savannah, and I wanted to see his room.

I carefully slipped out of the bed, pausing to look back at him, asleep on his stomach. His olive skin and dark hair contrasted sharply with the white sheets, and the sunlight threw shadows across the lines in his back. Resting my cheek on my bent knee, I resisted the urge to trace my finger down one of those lines. Instead, I took a breath and swiped his tee off the floor. It was big enough to hang on me like a short dress as I walked around the large area.

On his desk were several different sketches, what looked like elevations. I wasn't sure if they were for the big project he'd been working on or if they were regular class work.

My bare feet softly padded on the floor as I skipped over to a set of canvases leaning against the wall. This was what I wanted to see.

Dropping to sit on my feet, I lifted the first one back. It was a brilliant painting with vibrant, sharply contrasting colors. At the bottom was dark blue, the water of the bay with a bridge stretching across it—black in the sunset. And what a sunset! It was deep orange with clouds in sweeping strokes of neon-yellow and white. For a few seconds, all I could do was gaze at it. Julian was a master of taking my breath away.

Sliding that canvas to the side, I tilted back the next one. It was a colorful chaos of flowers, storefronts, and his metal sculpture of the students lined up reading. I recognized it from the sculpture park in Newhope. Looking around the room, I wondered if he did these from memory or if he had photographs stashed somewhere. Perhaps on his phone...

The last one wasn't finished, but I knew what it was immediately. In broad strokes of green, lighter green, white and dark green-almost black, what appeared to be waves surrounded the form of a girl. A young woman.

Her head was down, one pale, slender arm bent, holding her hair at the base of her neck in a tight bun. It was light brown hair with glints of gold, and spiral tendrils fell along the side of her face, turned just enough away to be unrecognizable. Only I recognized her. She was nude, but the green strokes obscured her private parts.

The woman was me, painted in such an obviously loving manner, my gaze was captivated looking at it. I didn't move as I felt warmth behind me. Julian dropped to sit at my back on the floor, wrapping his arms around my waist and resting his chin on my shoulder.

"You're snooping." I heard the smile in his voice, and I hugged my arm over his. "What do you think?"

"I think being an architect is doing wonders for your art."

He laughed before pressing his lips against the top of my shoulder, right in the crease where my neck came down. It caused a shiver to run down my legs, and I turned my head to find his lips.

One breathless kiss later, my eyes rose to meet his. "These are gorgeous."

Those blue eyes creased in a grateful smile. "I'm not sure I can trust you," he teased. "You love everything I do."

Shaking my head, I rotated so I was facing him. "No. These are truly amazing. Your art is really evolving into something… it's like your mom's style, but it's very different. It's your own."

His eyes traveled down to my lips then over to my jaw and up, around my hair before coming to rest again on mine again.

"I tried to remember you in feelings as well as images."

My hands held his waist as I listened. "What does that mean?"

"I'm not sure." We both laughed then, and he continued. "I mean, I have pictures of us on my phone, and pictures I've taken when you weren't looking…"

"Let me see them!"

"Hang on…" He caught my hands and wrapped them back around his waist. "But I wouldn't look at just one, I tried looking at all of them and letting it mix in my head into this… feeling of you."

Leaning forward, I pressed my heated eyes against the bare skin of his chest.

His voice turned loud. "Do I sound like a pompous asshole?"

"No!" I sat back quickly to catch his gaze, but by doing that, he saw the pools in my eyes. Blinking, a tear hit my cheek.

In a movement, I was pressed close to him again. "I'm sorry. Why are you crying?"

"It's so beautiful." Then I laughed. "Now I'm really not going to London."

He sat back and caught my cheeks again in both hands. "Yes, you are." He kissed me quickly, then stood, pulling me up with him. "Come on. I want to show you Tybee Island. It's amazing."

"Oh, yes!" I remembered the impression it made on his mother, and I was eager to see it. "It's on the migratory path for Monarch butterflies!"

"That was just happening... we might still see a few of them out there."

Holding hands we started back toward the bed, him in his boxers and me in only his long-sleeved tee. That's when I caught the look in his eye, and a little charge sizzled straight to my core.

"I bet it'll all still be there in an hour." His voice was a husky whisper right at my ear, and there was no way I was arguing.

His mouth covered mine, pushing my lips apart, and it was all I could do not to melt on the spot.

Tybee Island was exactly the way his mother had described it—at least this morning. A lighthouse was on one end, and with the tide out, it seemed to be long stretches of dark brown sand.

Once the tide changed, however, Julian said the ocean came racing in, and it was as close as the Gulf off Crystal Shores. Sure enough, several straggler Monarch butterflies were making their way south for the winter. It was amazing. We sat on the sand, and I leaned back in his arms.

"Do you come out here a lot?" I asked, threading our fingers, trying not to think how impossible it was going to be to leave him tomorrow morning.

"Not as much as I'd like." He kissed the side of my neck. "But it's not the same as being home. You're not here."

We were quiet a moment, and I thought about what Gabi had said about home. Sitting here in Julian's arms, I knew home for me would be wherever he was.

I stretched out our hands and imagined us growing old together, lines on our hands, lines on our faces. Gray strands sprinkled in his dark locks.

"What are you thinking about?" He was still holding my back against his chest, the wind pushing our hair back.

"Family."

"The holidays are getting close."

Nodding I shifted around so our laced fingers were in my lap, and I could see his face. "Not to kill the mood…"

"Hmm." I could tell he knew what was coming.

"Have you talked to your mom?" Blinking up to his blue eyes, I saw frustration there, but not directed at me.

"No." His answer was short, and for a moment, I thought that was all I'd get. Then he continued. "I talk to my dad a lot, and I know he fills her in. He's really excited about me working with him over semester break."

Chewing my lip, I went on and said it. "You need to talk to your mom."

He exhaled and deflected. "When are you planning to get home for Thanksgiving?"

"I can take off after my last class Tuesday," I said, slanting my eyes up at him.

"Excellent." He caught my waist and pulled me closer. "I'll be there ASAP on Wednesday, and we'll be together the rest of the week."

"What's the plan for Thanksgiving day?"

"Will your parents mind if I tag along to your house?"

The very suggestion made me laugh. "Of course not. You know they love you."

"And you'll have dinner with me on Friday?"

"Sure! Where do you want to go?" Planning our next visit so close in the future helped me be less panicked about saying goodbye to him tomorrow.

"The Kyser mansion?"

Until he said that. "What?"

"Dad said he'd like to do something special—and you'll get your wish, because I'm sure Mom will be there. I'll have to talk to her."

"If that's the case, then definitely."

He laughed and covered my mouth with his. I was content to go on kissing him for the next twenty-four hours, and besides the two times we met up with Brad and Rachel, that was pretty much all we did… in addition to other things.

* * *

POST-THANKSGIVING KYSER-APOCALYPSE

Okay, so wow. If the world ever *does* end in a dramatic explosion, it's very possible it will look something like what I witnessed Friday night.

I know I have to back up and fill in the blanks again, and I will, don't worry. I'm just getting a chance to sit down and think about how it all went down for myself.

After my weekend in heaven with Julian (*shivers*), we headed back to finish the short weeks leading up to the Thanksgiving holiday. It was pretty much the end of classes, as we'd have dead week and finals when we got back.

Then we were done. *Done.*

It's hard to believe my first semester of college is behind me! So much has happened, and so much is uncertain.

I filled out the application for JYA before my trip to Savannah, but the selection process would continue into the spring. We wouldn't know who was selected until at least March. For distraction (and because I had no other choice), I threw myself into my studies.

We were reading *A Streetcar Named Desire* in American lit, and I had to write an essay on what Tennessee Williams' depiction of Blanche and Stanley's lives said about desire. I'd already gone into what I thought the whole play said about my desire… Still, I loved the assignment. Exploring literary themes and concepts was one of my favorite things. It was a fun paper to write.

In my communications classes, we started a video project that would continue across both semesters. We had to have the planning half finished by Christmas break, and it would culminate in a fifteen-minute news story, complete with tags, interviews, and location shots due at the end of spring semester. It was a group project, so two of my classmates and I chose the history of Algiers Point.

We were including John McDonogh, one of the world's largest landowners until he died in the mid-1800s. He owned most of Algiers. From him, we'd move to the oil boom and bust and the impact it had on development, along with the aftermath of Hurricane Katrina.

The only thing more fascinating to me than the fictional characters in my English classes were the nonfictional ones I met and interviewed on the streets. Their stories were sometimes even better than fiction.

Julian's right. Gabi's right. They're all right, and it breaks my heart. Journalism *is* my passion, and it keeps pulling me further away from the person I love.

Julian says I can't get hung up on that right now. He says we'll get through this, and I'm doing everything I can to trust him and see the amazing in all of it.

Rachel's prelaw classes wrapped up around the same time as mine, and we were both packed and making the two-hour drive home by Tuesday afternoon.

"Brad's sticking around Tulane?" I leaned back against the seat to let the unusually cool, crisp air filter in through the window. It sent my light-brown spirals jumping around my neck.

For the briefest of seconds, my thoughts drifted to Jack. I hadn't seen him since that night in Fat Harry's, and I wondered if he'd stay in the city or be at the Friday dinner Julian mentioned.

Shaking my head, I figured it would be just Julian and me, possibly Julian's mother, and Mr. Kyser.

"He had a project due tomorrow for one of his engineering classes, but he'll be home for Thursday." Rachel's straight blonde hair blew around her neck as well.

"Still excited about him relaunching his dad's business?"

Her eyebrows shot up. "Definitely! It makes total sense. The name-recognition alone is worth millions. I mean, Mr. Bryant never said why they all shut down and let it go, but it's a total waste of potential."

I nodded and returned to looking out the window. I knew exactly why they shut down and let it go. Mr. Kyser and Ms. LaSalle had an affair; they had Julian and kept his paternity a secret from everybody until Meg Kyser found out—the same night she caught Bill and Lexy embracing and kissing in Lexy's office at the Kyser-Brennan Christmas party.

The same night she died in a car crash.

Will, Jack, and Lucy weren't the only ones to lose a parent that night. Julian lost his dad when Bill and Lexy parted ways for more than fifteen years. Kyser-Brennan was set adrift, shuffled aside in the aftermath.

But I couldn't tell anybody that story. Instead, I studied the expanse of blue-brown water racing past us beneath the bridge.

We were more than half-way across Lake Ponchartrain, the giant brackish lake separating New Orleans from the rest of eastern Louisiana, on our way to Interstate 10. From there, it was a straight shot east all the way to South County.

"It *is* the most logical decision," I said, shifting my mental focus. "They're all heirs to this amazing thing their dads accomplished."

"Well, he and Jack are at least."

My bottom lip pulled between my teeth. "Right."

"Speaking of the guys, when's Julian headed back to town?" She slanted her eyes at me with a grin, and for some silly reason I blushed.

"He said Wednesday, but you know how long that drive is."

"Oh, man, no lie." She shook her blonde mane. "Still, I'm glad we did it. It was so cute reuniting you two. I swear, I almost cried."

"Thanks," I snorted, rolling my eyes. "Glad I'm a soap opera now."

"More like a free romance. First you're all mopey, dragging around campus like you lost everything to the hurricane. Then Brad and I swoop in like superheroes to produce the sweetest reunion scene this side of a Nicholas Sparks movie!"

"Jeez, Rachel." Catching my hair in my hand, I propped my elbow on the doorframe. "I do not feel patronized right now at all."

She laughed. "Are you kidding? After that display of passion, we couldn't get to the hotel quick enough. Old, practically married couples like us live for that shit."

"Don't be gross." I snorted and cut my eyes at her.

She started laughing, and so did I. We almost couldn't stop for a minute.

"I think we've been in school too long," I finally said, when I could breathe again.

"Definitely." She took a deep breath and drummed her fingers on the wheel. "I'm planning to spend part of every single day walking on the beach."

"God, I miss it so much." Propping my feet on the dash, the breeze fluttered my loose skirt around my knees.

"Hey, I don't know if I've said it a thousand times yet, but I really love being roomies." She gave me a quick, warm smile. "I'll be sorry to see you go."

I looked down and smiled before glancing up. "Don't rent out my room too fast—I don't have anything yet."

"Oh, please. If there's anything you've always been good at, it's school."

"I *think* that's a compliment?"

"Of course it is! And your personal life's coming around."

"Maybe one day I'll be as perfect as you and Brad."

"Hmm… I'll give you another twenty years."

I shook my head, and the rest of the ride was spent singing too loudly along with the radio or brainstorming Christmas get-togethers with friends we hadn't seen since July.

We agreed Thanksgiving was simply too quick to try for anything meaningful. Rachel, being the lifelong party-planner promised to make something happen.

Before long, we were entering the lowlands of Fairview and taking the turn toward my parents' home.

A quick goodnight, a promise to get together before time to head back to New Orleans, and I was dashing inside. Mom and Dad were waiting, ready to hug me too long and too hard and hear everything about college life, as if I hadn't been calling them regularly every week since I left.

Dad ran over to Scoops to grab hamburgers for dinner, and after we'd all eaten and Mom asked her five thousand questions, I climbed the familiar old stairs up to my equally familiar old bedroom.

Dropping my suitcase and bag on the floor, I sat on the bed and looked around. The walls were still painted a pale shade of pink, and my bedroom furniture somehow seemed smaller than it had when I left. My twin bed rattled when I sat on it. Mr. Bear was still in the corner, and I exhaled a smile, remembering how I'd used him to comfort me those miserable nights when Julian and I had broken up.

My eyes traveled next to the dark window. The one leading out to that wonderful, old tree that so many nights had held the boy of my dreams sitting out there, smiling and waiting for me to let him in.

I stood with a sigh and walked over to it. For a moment, I leaned my head against the glass and looked down the dark street to where his car would be parked.

Tonight it was just an empty space.

With a sigh, I straightened up and went to my bathroom to wash my face. I couldn't help thinking how nothing seemed to change here.

Back in my room, cleaned, scrubbed and ready for bed, I pushed the covers aside and slid beneath my old sheets, cuddling my pillow to my cheek. I was in my usual little sleep-shirt, and I wished so hard Julian was driving in tonight instead of tomorrow.

I dug out my phone and shot him a quick text.

ANNA

Made it home. In my bed. Staring at the window.

Dropping my head on my arm, I waited, thinking of the last time we'd been here together. It was the night before I'd left for New Orleans, and I'd barely slept for holding onto him all night, trying not to cry. My phone buzzed.

JULIAN

Where's that bear? I've got my eye on that guy.

That made me giggle.

ANNA

He's in the corner, but he's giving me a look.

JULIAN

His ass is grass if I catch him in bed with you
again.

ANNA

Speaking of, your tree seems very lonely tonight.
It misses your ass.

JULIAN

One semester in the Crescent City, and already
swearing like a river rat.

ANNA

I was talking about that little donkey you used to
ride around.

JULIAN

I've traded that guy in for a real car.

I shook my head and laughed through the pain.

ANNA

How much longer?

JULIAN

Not much. Get some sleep and try to dream
about me.

ANNA

I always do that.

JULIAN

Love you, Banana Face.

ANNA

Back to the nicknames. I'm definitely home now.

JULIAN

See you soon.

I rolled onto my back and stared at the ceiling. Then I hopped up and walked over to the window, raising it just a little bit. The noise of frogs singing in the cool night drifted in, and I dropped onto my knees to look out at the dark, starry sky.

November here was always a mixture of cool and the occasional, odd 80-degree week, but tonight was perfect. I was home, and I could feel my muscles starting to relax. Only one thing was missing.

I pushed off the windowsill and walked back to my bed. Mr. Bear got a passing glance before I climbed in, curling into the warmth of my soft blankets. I was asleep before I knew what happened.

I know this, because I woke with a start to arms sliding around my waist, and a warm body curling in behind me. Flipping over fast, I pressed my mouth against Julian's to muffle my squeal. His lips curled in a smile over mine, and he rolled me onto my back for a better kiss. My entire body vibrated with happiness.

"What are you doing here?" I managed a whisper that was almost a shriek.

"I was on the road when you texted." He kissed my nose and warmth bubbled in my chest, right at my heart.

"Texting and driving is bad bad bad, Julian!" I kissed his cheek.

"Then stop texting me when I'm driving." He kissed my ear, and I couldn't help a laugh.

"I never seem to know what you're doing these days." His mouth moved along the line of my jaw and then down to my neck as bliss surged through my insides. My arms were around him, and I squeezed. "Ugh! I'm so happy to see you! How did you get away so soon?"

"Finished earlier than I thought. I was already packed, so I just hopped in the car and drove." Propping on his elbows, he smoothed his hands on either side of my face. "I'm happy to see you, too."

I reached up to place my palms on his warm cheeks, and for just a moment, we looked into each other's eyes. *Home.* The word sounded like music in my head. Everything was right now.

He broke the spell by leaning forward and kissing me quickly. "Gotta run. It's almost dawn."

"Julian! You just got here!"

Laughing, he pulled me against his chest and gave me a long squeeze. "And I couldn't pass through Fairview without stopping to see you, but your dad'll kick my ass if he catches us."

My lip poked out. "But we haven't even… you know."

A little spark hit his eye. "We haven't what?"

His sly grin was too sexy, and I was smiling too big. "We haven't said a proper hello."

Both of his hands caught my cheeks, and he kissed me so hard, it stole my breath. My eyes were still closed when he rested his forehead against mine. "You are seriously irresistible."

"You're seriously a tease."

"You're right." He reached back and pulled off the tee he was wearing, causing my jaw to drop. "Screw it. I'm not leaving you. We'll deal with it if your parents catch us."

He leaned in and pressed his mouth against my neck, working his way lower as his hands rose under my nightshirt. My heart rate rose right along with them.

"You're wearing my favorite PJs." His voice was hot against my skin.

"It's just a shirt…"

Breathless, I couldn't help checking the window, where sure enough, orange light was warming the darkness. My hands slid down his bare back, and he covered my mouth again with his. It was so good, for a moment, I was lost in sensation.

But he was right. "Mm—you've got to go now."

"What!" Pushing me back on the bed, he moved down to my waist. "Who's being the tease now?"

"Ooh, heck!" I groaned as he pushed my shirt up and kissed a line to my navel. "Julian…" His lips moved lower, and I wanted to die. "That feels so good, and you're right. It's morning. You've got to get out of here!"

"I'll be fast." He kissed my lower stomach, then he laughed, a swirl of warm breath against my ultra-sensitive skin. "I'm only nineteen—give me five minutes."

"Julian," I laughed, and he slanted a grin up at me.

"Not cool?"

"Are you going to start being one of those boyfriends?"

One last kiss, and he sat up. "No."

He stood and scooped his shirt off the floor, jerking it over his head as he went. I was up, pulling my shirt down as I followed him to the window.

"I'm staying out on Hammond Island with Dad this week." Catching my waist he pulled me to him for one last hug before he went through the window. I caught his chin and kissed him again. "I'm about to crash, but I'll call you this afternoon."

"Are you okay to drive? You won't fall asleep?"

"Yeah, just no texting."

"I'm sure if you wanted to go down and crash on the couch, Mom and Dad wouldn't mind…"

"And then I'd have to be up in an hour." He was out the window, pulling my hand to his lips for one more kiss. "I'll be okay to get to Dad's."

"Can't wait to see you again. And get that proper hello."

I watched as he went down the tree, and when he got to the bottom he looked up with a smile. "See you in a few."

I leaned my head against my hand and reached down to him. He held his hand back before taking off in a jog to his waiting car. I stayed in that spot until I couldn't see him anymore, then I stood with a sigh and went back to my bed.

Confident I'd never get back to sleep after that, I lay on my back and closed my eyes, replaying all of the sensations of his surprise visit over in my mind. Next thing I knew it was broad daylight, and I was waking up.

Thanksgiving with my parents meant heading to Navarre to spend the afternoon with Nana. Julian tagged along, and while it still bothered me that he wasn't spending the day with his mom, I was so happy to have him with us. Mom was equally thrilled.

"Julian, I want to hear all about your latest project." She smiled as she blobbed a spoonful of dressing onto his plate. "Especially the part about when we can display it at the Performing Arts Association."

He laughed, but I jumped in. "Oh, Mom, you should see the paintings he's done. They're absolutely gorgeous."

"Do you have any pictures we could see?" Nana was equally excited about Julian's art, and though she'd never say it, I was pretty sure she preferred him to the boy with the boat. "I've always loved local art in this area. It's so unique and vibrant."

"I think you love anything that has the ocean as its subject," I teased, hugging my grandmother's waist.

"It's true." She kissed my head. "I'm a bona fide beach bum."

"Make that two of us." Dad was cutting the turkey as we all stood around waiting for our slices. "Anna, how are you taking it? You're the only one not near the coast now."

I got my slices of turkey and headed to my seat at the table. "You know, it's almost like I am near the water. I've got the river so close to our duplex, and there's Lake Ponchartrain. I can go there and watch the sailboats."

Julian followed me over to the table and sat, grabbing a roll for each of us from the basket in the center. "We should get the surfboards out."

He gave me a wink, and I smiled, remembering all those days last year when he taught me to surf. It was really hot. Me in my bikini, him with his arms around me all day. We were seriously not together then, or I'd never have learned anything.

Mom cut through my steamy memories, grabbing a roll as she sat in front of us. "Come on now, Julian, tell me what you're working on. What do you think of your art professors? Is there anything they can teach you?"

"Here she goes again!" I stuffed a piece of roll into my mouth. "You should've heard her cross-examining me last night."

Julian laughed. "I'm sure there's lots they could teach me, but…"

"But?" Mom leaned forward to catch his eye.

"Anna hasn't told you?" He sat back and put down his fork. "I'm taking a break from art classes."

Mom's shocked expression mirrored exactly how I'm sure Brad, Rachel, and I looked when he told us.

"You… wait." She shook her head. "If you're taking a break from art… are you still enrolled at SCAD?"

"Oh, yes, I'm definitely still enrolled." He seemed more comfortable talking about it now than he had in September. It was probably having a semester behind him, and from what I'd gathered, a pretty successful one. "The first week of classes, I looked at all the different options, and well, I just decided to expand my realm of possibilities."

He gave me a wink, and I let out the breath I didn't realize I was holding.

Mom's eyes moved from him to me and then back. "What does that mean?"

"He's taking architecture classes now, Mom. Julian's thinking about working with…" *Crap!* I'd almost said *working with his dad*, which my parents still didn't know about. "With Mr. Kyser. Remember how encouraging he always was to Julian?"

I didn't think it was possible for Mom's eyebrows to go any higher, but they did. "You're working with Bill Kyser? In development?"

Julian shifted in his chair. "I just asked if he might be willing to let me intern in his office over the break. We haven't really committed to anything, but I think he's open to the idea."

"Julian, that's amazing!" Mom's shock morphed into excited pride. "Working with Bill Kyser, why... that could open doors that I can't even imagine!"

Dad clapped Julian's shoulder before he sat. "What does it feel like to live a charmed life?"

Julian looked down. "Exhausting. And really stressful."

"The flip-side of being given amazing opportunities is getting to live up to them, yes?" Mom's voice was warm.

"Anna-Banana's getting a little taste of that as well, isn't she?" Dad was cutting his turkey.

I just rolled my eyes. "Here we go again!"

Nana was with us at last, giving me an encouraging look. "It's time to go around and say what we're all thankful for."

We covered the usual bases, being with family, being healthy, having good food and good friends. Then Mom launched into a discussion of funding for art education in schools, and Nan followed up with the issues of conservation and working with turtle habitats. It was each of their favorite "causes," and I'd been routinely recruited to help with both through the years.

My favorite had been the spring break I'd spent with Nana in Navarre helping with "Share the Beach" when I was only a sophomore.

Baby turtles hatched from their eggs in the early morning light, all alone. They were left to race to the ocean to survive. The only problem was all the seagulls, pelicans, and other birds hanging out, waiting to gobble them up as soon as their tiny dark brown bodies appeared on the sugar-white sands from South County through the panhandle of Florida.

"Share the Beach" volunteers all lined the small ditch we'd dug from the nest to the Gulf. All they had to do was scamper to survival, and all we had to do was not touch them or interfere any more than we'd already done.

"Hey," Julian's voice was low and soft by my ear, pulling me back from the memory. "You ready to go?"

I blinked up at his crystal blue eyes—almost the same color as those waters we all loved—then I glanced around the table. Nana, Mom, and Dad were splitting a bottle of wine, and they seemed to be pretty embroiled in some new political discussion.

"Julian and I are going to walk down by the surf," I interjected.

They all took a breath and looked up at us.

Dad was the first one to speak. "I think that's a great idea! We should all go."

He rose and dropped his napkin on the table. I bit the side of my mouth and glanced at Julian.

He only shrugged. "It's a family walk, then!"

I caught his hand knowing very well that was not what he had in mind. Outside in the cool air on the crisp white sand and gorgeous turquoise waters, it was hard to think that anything could go wrong here. Mom, Dad, and Nana walked ahead still talking about whatever new problem needed to be solved.

Julian and I hung back, keeping close enough to the shore that our feet were wet and he decided to cuff the bottom of his jeans. The wind pushed his dark hair around his face, but it sent mine flying in all directions.

"I feel like all we do is talk about me and my change of plans these days. Tell me about Loyola. What's happening with your cool project?"

Our fingers were laced, and with my other hand, I held my curls. "We've only done the planning part. Next semester is when we'll set up our interviews, do some 'man on the street' stuff, and really get out there."

He smiled. "Algiers sounds like a neat place to research."

"Just like every other place in the city."

"And you hang out with Rachel and Brad all the time? No new friends?"

Pressing my lips together, I looked up at the faint white clouds drifting past. "Not really. I mean, I have friends in class, but I'm just so slammed. Whenever I do go out, it's usually with those guys."

"Yeah, it's the same at SCAD, although a group of art students usually goes out along The Strand every weekend. Sometimes I tag along with them."

"What's The Strand?"

"Bars, karaoke, standard college stuff."

I stepped closer, hugging his waist. "Sounds fun."

"It'd be more fun if you were with me." His hand was on my shoulder.

Slowing down, I pulled him to sit beside me. For a few moments, we only watched the waves rolling in. Seashells were everywhere, but most of them were broken. Still, Julian found a white one that was intact and it even had a little hole at the base.

"I can make a necklace with this." He held it out to me, and I took it. "I just need some dental floss."

Wrinkling my nose, I laughed. "Waxed or unwaxed?"

"Waxed of course."

He took it back, then glanced up at me once more. "You never see anybody else you know on campus?"

I knew who he was talking about, but I decided to play dumb for a little bit. I scooted around so I was facing him with my legs crossed.

"Summer's supposed to be at Tulane, but thankfully I didn't see her this entire fall. It's weird—as close as the two colleges are, it's really easy to avoid people."

"Well, now you've jinxed it. You're going to see her everywhere come spring."

"Noo!" I cried, putting my hands over my face. "What have I done?!"

"So that's it?" His arm was still propped on his knee, and I reached forward to lace our fingers.

"I did run into Jack one night at Fat Harry's." I took a deep breath, remembering how strange that night had been. "Rachel and I were having so much fun, and some drunk guy kept hitting on her, grabbing her waist and stuff. I thought Jack was going to get in a fight with him, but Brad showed up and the guy took off."

"Smart asshole." Julian's jaw tightened, and he dropped his knee. "I don't really like hearing that, you know."

"But nothing happened! I mean, we talked a little, but as soon as the drunk guy left, Jack did too."

"That's not what I meant. Sounds like you and Rachel were in a dangerous situation. I'm glad Jack was there."

My head ducked. "Oh—oh my god. I thought you meant… no, I mean, you don't have to worry about that either. Fat Harry's is fine, and it's not far from where we live. It was really a random thing."

Julian reached for my hand and pulled it into his. "I trust you."

I lifted our laced fingers and kissed the back of his hand. "Good. Now, I bet we'd better catch up with those guys!"

Pulling him up, we took off jogging toward the parents.

Later that night, after everyone had gone to sleep and Julian was snug in my bed, I felt safe enough to bring up our dinner plans for the next day. We were lying on our sides facing each other, our "proper hello" said, he was tracing a curl down my cheek with his finger.

"So it's just going to be us and your dad?" I asked. "Will your mom be there?"

"Don't know." His long finger traveled across my cheek to my bottom lip. "Dad just asked if I'd please save Friday dinner to have at his house."

"Wait, are you sure it's okay if I'm there? He wasn't planning some father-son bonding time or something was he?"

"I asked before I invited you." His finger slid down my cupid's bow, and I caught it between my teeth. "Ow! Didn't you get enough Thanksgiving dinner?"

"You're much better than turkey." I laughed, and he leaned in to kiss me.

His lips parted mine and our tongues curled together. Heat flared low in my stomach, but before we traveled too far down that path again, I pulled back.

"Hang on."

"Anna," he groaned. "I've been hanging on all day. Talk after."

He reached for me again, covering my mouth, but I pulled back.

"I'm just really worried about your mom. I mean, it's a holiday. This separation must be breaking her heart."

With a heavy exhale he dropped his forehead onto my shoulder then rolled onto his back. "I don't know. I send her an email every now and then."

I moved closer and rested my cheek on his chest, reaching out to thread our fingers again. "I have a feeling you email your dad more."

"He tells her everything I say. It's not like she doesn't know what I'm doing."

Lifting my head, I propped it on my hand. "Would you do something for me?" His lips pressed together, and I knew he knew what I was about to say. "If she's not at dinner tomorrow, please go see her while you're in town."

For a few moments he didn't answer me, and it was my turn to trace my finger down the center of his lips.

His blue eyes cut to mine, and I saw that spark, and I knew what it meant. "Will you let me in your pants again if I say yes?"

My hand covered his mouth. "You're impossible."

He took that as the open invitation it was. Flipping me on my back, he caught my wrist and held it above my head before covering my mouth with his. I didn't care so much about his answer anymore. Still, I felt pretty confident he'd do what I'd asked.

Since Julian lived with his dad now, I drove myself out to the enormous mansion on Hammond Island for dinner. He'd offered to pick me up, but four trips back and forth seemed crazy-ridiculous. Not to mention Nana and her environmentalists would not approve of all that wasted fuel and pollution.

The only thing I couldn't figure out was how Mr. Kyser was managing Julian's presence with his other children. During school, at least, Jack and Will were in New Orleans, but as far as I knew, Lucy still kept her room at the mansion.

When I turned Mom's old Civic, which was pretty much *my* old Civic now, into the drive, I saw Mr. Kyser's silver Audi and Julian's Beemer, but no other cars.

I stepped out into the warm night and took a second to admire the gorgeous neon pink, orange, and yellow glow of the sunset over the Gulf.

Hammond Island was perfectly situated less than a mile from the waterfront, but secured by a break of land and several lakes and inlets.

Julian was waiting, and before I'd even touched the bell, he pulled the door open and swept me into his arms. "You're beautiful."

My insides lit at his words, but I'd only worn a plain yellow sundress and tan ballet flats. A leopard-print cardigan was tossed over my arm because I wasn't sure how cool it might get, and my hair was in a loose braid over my shoulder.

"I'm not sure beautiful is accurate, but thanks. You look great!"

Julian was in his usual black jeans, but tonight he'd put on a chambray oxford. It made him look slightly more formal. He kissed my nose and my lips quickly before continuing.

"You'll be happy to know I've already fulfilled my promise from last night."

My brow lined in confusion. "What promise?"

"I talked to my mom. She's here." He kissed me again and then leaned into my ear. His warm breath was a delicious whisper against my neck. "Does this mean I can get in your pants again?"

"Julian!" I laughed, pinching his arm. Truth was, he could have whatever he wanted, and he knew it. "Be serious. It seems like your dad's trying to do something special here."

"I want to do something special here."

His friskiness was working. My whole body was buzzing from his touches and kisses, but I really wanted to see what was going to happen.

"Come on."

We clasped hands and walked through the familiar hallway that opened up to the large kitchen. I remembered the very first night I'd come here on a study date with Lucy. It was the first time I'd had a real conversation with Jack.

Lucy had gone out to the store, and he and I were the only ones in the house. We'd talked about our English lit assignment. It was *Song of Solomon* by Toni Morrison…

"You ready to face these guys?" Julian's voice blinked me out of the past.

"We're not *facing* them. We know them. It's your parents."

He took my hand and pulled it into the crook of his arm. "I wish it was your parents."

"It's true. My parents are a lot less intimidating." I whispered, not sure why.

"It's no wonder you're so sure of yourself. You never had this shit to deal with."

"I wouldn't hold myself up as a role model."

We passed through the big, open living room past natural-wood doors that opened onto a formal dining room I'd never seen.

That wasn't saying anything. I'd only been in four rooms total in this house.

Ms. LaSalle stood at the far end, holding a glass of red wine. Her long, dark hair hung straight down her back, and she was dressed in a sleeveless, navy shift dress. Mr. Kyser stepped away from her when we entered and strode toward us.

"Welcome," he said with a bit too much enthusiasm.

I wasn't sure, but it seemed like Julian's dad might actually be nervous. I almost couldn't believe it.

Julian met him. "Anna's been here before, Dad."

"Of course. When was that?" His father took a sip of his beverage, and I wasn't sure why he was acting this way.

He knew the last time I'd been here.

"At the birthday party." Julian didn't seem interested in pursuing it. "And once before… and after."

His mother's smooth voice cut through the confusion. "You look very well."

It wasn't clear who should answer, so I did. "So do you."

She did. She was beautiful as always.

Mr. Kyser spoke again in his weird, almost jovial-host mood. "Well, we can't get started just yet. We're waiting on a few more guests."

"Oh, yeah? Who?" Julian took the scotch his father held out.

I wanted to protest, but I didn't. We were at their house, and I was pretty certain nobody would be driving tonight. Julian and I would work out our sleeping arrangements later—in private.

"Your siblings are joining us tonight." Now I understood why he was acting so strangely, and I decided it was nerves. "I wanted you to come a little early so you wouldn't feel ambushed. Your mother and I have decided to clear the air."

The soft sound of a throat clearing in the background led me to believe it might not have gone exactly that way. Mr. Kyser had wanted his family "reunited" for years, but Ms. LaSalle had always fought him on it.

I wasn't sure whose side I was on in whether the truth was the best approach now. I'd only ever wanted Julian to know his dad and how much Mr. Kyser loved him.

"Wait." Julian's voice sounded like he might agree with his mom for once. "What exactly is happening tonight?"

Mr. Kyser walked over to him and slapped his shoulder. "Your brothers and sister…and her fiancé, I suppose… are coming for dinner, and tonight I want to get it all out. Lay our cards on the table, so to speak."

"Hang on." Julian stepped away, toward me but not really in a way that implied he needed my support. "I'm the one who knows these guys. Maybe this is something we should ease into—"

"Ease, my ass. We're going to pull this Band-Aid off in one fast swipe and be done with it."

Julian was about to argue when the door opened, and a high, musical voice filled the space. It was Lucy, beautiful as always in a bouncy, tiered pink dress. A.J. was right behind her.

"Hello, Dad!" She paused and kissed him on the cheek. "Lexy!" I watched as she went to Julian's mother and gave her a warm hug. "If Will's a jerk, which I'm sure he'll be, just know I'm on your side. I think it's wonderful that we're telling everyone you're dating Dad."

I almost couldn't breathe because of Lucy's misinterpretation of events. She clearly thought this was about introducing her dad's new girlfriend to the family. A.J. only smiled and held Lucy's waist, supportive as always.

Ms. LaSalle glanced at Mr. Kyser, and he did something I couldn't remember ever seeing him do as long as I'd known his family—he stepped forward and hugged his daughter.

"Thank you, Lucy." His voice was low and close to her ear, but audible.

When he released her and stepped back, her eyes glistened in her surprised face. She cleared her voice and smiled, and I decided no matter what happened tonight, it was worth it to see that moment pass between them.

"A.J." Mr. Kyser reached for her fiancé's hand. "Lucy said you got into med school in Birmingham. Congratulations."

"Thank you, sir."

"Oh, Dad?" Lucy took her escort's arm. "A.J. wants to go by Robert now."

Her father's eyebrows rose. "Is that so?"

"Yes," she continued. "No more initials."

Robert only laughed at what I guess was an inside joke. "If I'm going to be a doctor, I should probably lose the redneck nicknames."

We all made noises of support, and Lucy stepped over and gave me a huge hug followed by Julian.

"It's so good to see you guys! I want to hear all about college, art school, New Orleans… Anna, you are going to flip when you see the bridesmaid's dresses I've picked out. Spring break can't get here soon enough!"

"I love the name Robert," I said, squeezing her back. "It's very elegant."

She shook her light blonde head. "I confess. It's taking a little getting used to, but I'm glad he made the decision before all the invitations were printed."

We didn't have time for any more words because the door opened again, and Will marched in followed by Jack. My chest squeezed at the sight of them. They were both dressed in khaki pants, but Will had on a thin, black V-neck sweater, whereas Jack was wearing a green polo. As usual, his older brother's expression was impatient and irritated.

He went straight to his father and shook hands. "Hello, Dad. I suppose we'll find out soon enough what this is about."

"Will." Mr. Kyser shook his eldest son's hand. "Thanks for driving over."

"I don't get all the cloak and dagger, but I'm here. And I managed to find him."

Jack had walked to the other end of the room, where he was filling one of his father's crystal tumblers with two fingers of scotch. Lucy gave me a worried look before walking over to her twin's side. I watched her say something to him quietly, and he gave her a bored smile and a brief hug.

"I noticed my old car out front." Will stood waiting, his eyes narrowed suspiciously at Ms. LaSalle. They'd just grazed Julian before he saw me. I got the usual sneer. "What's this about?"

"Let's have dinner," Mr. Kyser said. "I hired a caterer. They'll begin service once we've taken our seats."

Lucy was still smiling as she gave her father a little wink, thinking she knew what was coming. I was sure I'd never be able to eat a thing because my stomach was so tight. Even Julian seemed apprehensive as I held his hand.

Will had already taken his seat, and he stared the three of us visitors down from where he waited to his father's right. Finally, Jack wandered over and sat, but he still either hadn't seen me or had decided to pretend I wasn't in the room.

Once we were all sitting, a male and a female dressed in black slacks and white shirts entered the room carrying platters of salads and ice water for everyone. I sat back and waited as they placed a portion on everyone's plates and then exited again.

I stared at the dark greens in front of me wondering how much longer this agony would last. Lucy had taken the spot beside Ms. LaSalle, who sat at her father's left. Robert was on her other side, and Julian was beside him, leaving me at the very end of the line. I was practically across from Jack.

Mr. Kyser spoke first as he stabbed a bite of salad. "I trust you boys had an easy drive up from New Orleans?"

Will didn't touch a thing. "It was fine."

Jack didn't even answer.

Everyone was on edge. Lucy was the only one who seemed

giddy with excitement as she happily stabbed a bite of salad and ate it.

"Will, I'm not sure if you know Ms. LaSalle, but she was a very important artist in this area back in the day. Her son Julian seems to be following in her footsteps."

Will's eyes flicked from Ms. LaSalle to Julian as he picked up his fork. "To what do we owe the pleasure of such esteemed dinner guests?"

The way he said *pleasure* indicated he meant the exact opposite, and I remembered that night last fall when he'd subjected me to his overt disgust with my presence at the mansion. I'd driven over to check on Jack after an ill-fated visit to New Orleans. It had been the beginning of the end for me.

The black-and-white-clad male and female re-entered the room and served us all plates of crispy golden-fried chicken, buttery red-skinned new potatoes, and steamed asparagus. It smelled delicious, but I still hadn't been able to start my salad.

Jack finally glanced up, and mine was the first face he saw. His brow creased, and his normally bright blue eyes were stunned and bleary. I knew then he'd only just realized I was in the room. He was drunk.

My heart hurt a little, but his gaze moved from me to Julian then back to me again. After that, he picked up the crystal tumbler and drained it.

"I'd hoped we could enjoy our dinner before we got to the heart of the matter." Mr. Kyser placed his fork beside his plate. He reached to his left and covered Ms. LaSalle's hand with his. She focused her attention on the physical connection between the two of them. "Alexandra, or Lexy, is an old friend of mine from before you were born."

Will only stared at her, expressionless, while Lucy almost started clapping.

"I met her a few months ago," she said, reaching out to

squeeze Julian's mother's forearm. "Jack and I were in school with Julian last year, so we have a little connection."

"I believe I recall the name." Will wasn't letting up. "But I still don't understand the purpose of this get-together, or I should say why I had to drive up from New Orleans on a moment's notice for it."

His father took a deep breath and slid his place setting a little further from him. "Lexy and I were very close when we were younger. She was on the original Kyser-Brennan development team."

Ms. LaSalle's glance flickered up from their clasped hands to Will's blue eyes, and she gave him the smallest smile. He did not return it, and I wanted to kick his shin under the table.

Julian didn't look up from his plate. He seemed to be bracing himself.

"So this is about the business?" Will asked, and his father continued.

"Not necessarily. Lexy and I reunited several months ago, last spring, and I wanted all of you to know... we're very much in love."

At that, Will placed his fork down and straightened in his chair, putting his hands in his lap. Jack finally tore his attention away from the booze and focused it on Julian.

"You said *reunited*." Will was catching up fast, I could tell. His blue eyes traveled from his father's paramour to the boy sitting beside his sister's fiancé. I watched as he scrutinized Julian's face. "That means you have a history together."

"A long time ago." Mr. Kyser pushed his chair back and stood, slowly rounding the table behind Ms. LaSalle's chair, passing Lucy's, then Robert's, and stopping behind Julian. My throat grew tighter the closer he came. "You're all old enough now, and I'd like you to know the truth."

Lucy turned in her seat, her brow creased as she looked up at her father. My heart was beating so hard, and I couldn't even imagine how Julian must be feeling.

His mother, by contrast, seemed to have gone completely still. She watched Mr. Kyser like she was resigned to whatever might happen.

Mr. Kyser placed his hand on Julian's shoulder. "I'd like you to meet your brother. Julian LaSalle. Kyser."

For a half a second, the entire room went deadly still. Then several things seemed to happen at once. Lucy's jaw dropped and she exhaled a whispered *"Brother?"*

Jack sat back in his chair abruptly and blinked at the new identity on a familiar face. Will was another matter.

He threw his cloth napkin beside his plate. "Are you saying—" His voice had risen in volume, but his father cut him off.

"I'm saying a long time ago, Lexy and I had a son together. Julian is that son, and I hope you'll welcome him as part of our family." Mr. Kyser's hand was still on Julian's shoulder, and I reached under the table to lace my fingers with his.

At that moment, Julian looked up first at Jack, then he glanced at Will before looking at Lucy, who was still staring wide-eyed and open-mouthed.

"A son?" Will was still speaking too loud. "Who's the same age as Jack and Lucy?" What you're saying is this *bastard*—"

"I will not hear your brother referred to by that term." Mr. Kyser's voice matched Will's in volume.

"You won't hear it?" Will roughly shoved his chair back and stood. "You're damn well going to hear it. You cheated on Mom with this—"

"William!" Mr. Kyser's jaw was clenched. "Take care how you address the woman I love."

"The woman you *love*? The woman you LOVE?" Will's upper lip curled. "What was our mother? The female who bore your children and kept your house clean?"

"That's a conversation for another night. Tonight is about reunions. Welcoming a new family member."

Lucy's astonishment had slowly dissolved into something different. She was still holding Ms. LaSalle's arm, but now she reached out for Julian's hand. It caught his attention, and he looked up at her.

He took her hand, and she gave him a warm smile. I wanted to kiss her sweet face.

Will was undeterred, however, sweeping his arm toward Jack. "As if things weren't bad enough, I've got this loser, who won't do anything but drink all day and squander what little potential he might've had. Now you're telling me I've got some bastard brother and his social-climbing mother coming in to wreck things even further. Great move, Dad. One of your best."

Mr. Kyser started to speak, but Lucy cut him off. In a flash, her hand left Julian's and grabbed a plump, red tomato wedge off her salad plate.

"SHUT UP, Will!" She cried, hurling the tomato with surprising force at her brother.

The deep red fruit stuck to the front of his black sweater, and he flashed at her with pure shock on his face. "What the HELL?"

As if encouraged, she grabbed a round, buttery new potato and threw it too. "I said SHUT UP!"

Will flinched away. "Have you lost your mind?"

She grabbed another potato and threw it, and each item hit his black sweater and slid down, leaving a trail of shiny grease. "I've lost my tolerance for YOU!"

"Dammit, Lucy! If you throw one more piece of food at me..."

She did just that, grabbing two handfuls of potatoes, asparagus, and even a chicken breast, pelting her brother with them. The rest of us only sat, open-mouthed, watching.

"Shut your stupid mouth, you... you BULLY!" She yelled. "I'm sick of you pushing everyone around!"

"For God's sake... Lucy!" Will was completely derailed, taking the cloth napkin again and dabbing it against his shirt. "This is Tahitian silk!"

Lucy jumped out of her chair, grabbed her water glass, and started in his direction.

"Need to wash it off?" She reared back, but Jack was out of his chair, catching her around the waist. I wouldn't have thought he could move that fast in his condition.

"Take it easy, spitfire." He laughed a little too much, holding her back and taking the water glass.

"Let me go!" She twisted in his arms, but her father stepped in at last.

"Stop this behavior *at once!*" His voice was stern, and his children did stop. But Lucy's lips were so tight, I knew she was barely holding control. "I will not have you acting like this."

I could barely breathe. Julian's eyes were a mixture of shock and pride for his sister.

"I need to wash my hands." Lucy pushed roughly out of Jack's hold and stormed out of the dining room with Robert right behind her.

Jack dropped back into his chair, and Will stood for a moment, dabbing his sweater with his cloth napkin. "I'm going to change." His voice was a low growl, but at least his tirade had ended. "This isn't over."

When he left the room, it felt too quiet and still all of a sudden. I was still trying to breathe. Ms. LaSalle's face was pale, and her eyes went to Mr. Kyser's.

He gave her a weak smile and walked to where she sat. "In all of my imaginings of how this would play out, I never saw *that* coming."

Julian's mom stood slowly. "I need some air."

She left the room, and Mr. Kyser followed her out, leaving Jack, Julian, and me sitting at the table. I finally remembered how to breathe, but Julian continued studying the plate in front of him.

"I can't believe he just did it like that." Julian's voice was quiet, and I reached for his arm.

"I'm so sorry," I whispered.

"So." Jack's voice was only a little off. "How about that, Brother?"

Julian's eyes flickered across the table. "I guess it explains a few things."

Jack pushed himself out of the chair. "I need a drink. You?"

Julian nodded. "Sure. Thanks."

"Anna?" Jack looked back over his shoulder, but I shook my head no. "That seems familiar."

Tumblers refilled, Jack handed one to his brother and sat in Robert's abandoned chair. Then he exhaled a laugh. "Dad sure knows how to break up a dinner party." He clinked Julian's glass and took a long sip. "That takes the edge off."

I wanted to say something, but I had absolutely no idea where to begin. Julian took a short sip and placed the glass by his plate. He seemed as disoriented as I felt, but just then Lucy swirled back into the room.

"Where did everybody go?" Her voice was quieter now, calmer. Robert entered after her and pulled the doors closed.

Jack leaned back in the chair and looked in her direction. "Nice work, sis. Of all the ways Will's had his fat mouth shut in the past, that might've been my favorite."

Speaking of the devil, their older brother stalked in and looked around, pausing only to give his sister a withering glare. "Where's Dad?"

"No idea," she said off-handedly. Her expression turned serious as she approached her twin. "I don't like seeing you this way. What's happening in New Orleans?"

"I've turned into a total ass, haven't I, Anna?" Jack stood and went back over to his chair, pausing behind Julian for a beat. "Sorry I kissed your girl, bro. I wasn't thinking straight that night."

My eyes flew wide. After all we'd witnessed here, those words were literally the worst that could've been said. Julian didn't look at me, but he straightened in his chair.

Pulling my bottom lip between my teeth, I intended to see what Lucy's response to her brother's words might be, but instead my eyes caught on Will.

His eyes narrowed slightly, but in a blink it was gone. "I'm not spending the night here. Jack, are you riding back with me tonight?"

Instead of sitting, Jack kept moving to where his brother stood. "I don't know how else I'm getting home. You drove."

Will's eyes cut one last time toward Julian and me. "Let's go."

They walked out and Lucy's shoulders dropped. "I don't like this at all. As much as I hate siding with him, Will's right. Jack's got a problem."

My mouth was completely dry, and I could feel the irritation in Julian. He'd had a pretty rough night as well, and Jack's words poured a can of gasoline on the whole thing.

Lucy turned to me. "Did Jack say he saw you at school?"

My voice was quiet. "I ran into him once." Julian shot me a glare. "Or twice, I guess."

His sister exhaled deeply. "I wish there was some way I could get down there, but I know he'd never let me help him. Just like he'd never admit to having a problem."

Julian stood and went over to her. "I want to thank you for what you did. That was pretty brave of you standing up to that guy."

She shook her blonde waves. "*That guy* now known as your brother?"

"I guess you're right." Julian glanced down. "Not sure he's too thrilled about it."

"Will's an ass. He's had that coming for years." Catching his hand again, she gave it a squeeze. "I guess I should feel angry or something, but I don't."

Julian nodded. "Thanks for that. It's all been pretty weird for me, but… I like knowing who I am."

"I'm glad we never got serious! Talk about gross!" She stuck her tongue out, making big eyes. Then she laughed. "But I love my ring. It's so much more special to me now."

"Thanks, sis."

They smiled, and Lucy pulled him in for a quick hug. Then she caught Robert's hand. "I need some dinner! My first course is all over Asshat Older Brother's sweater."

Robert laughed. "You could eat his serving."

"And die of whatever poison lives in his mouth? No thank you!" She pulled her fiancé's arm. "Let's go to the Shrimp Basket. I've earned a honeydew daiquiri."

Robert smiled, watching her with so much love. "Okay. See you guys later."

Lucy paused before departing. "Text me before you head back. I want us to get coffee or something."

I nodded, and they were gone. Julian and I were alone in the room, but he didn't come to me. It hurt so badly.

After all the drama, after I knew he had to be feeling winded and wounded, now Jack's words had put a wedge between us, and I couldn't even comfort him.

His voice was impatient when he spoke. "You didn't think I needed to know he kissed you?"

"Julian, I swear—"

"Just stop."

My voice was too desperate, and I knew it worked against me. I took a moment to collect myself then I tried again in a calmer tone.

"It was one of my first catch-up nights with Rachel. All the way back in October." I studied the Oriental rug at his feet, not daring to look in his eyes. "He said a bunch of stuff that was completely stupid, and I argued with him. Then he kissed me, and I pushed him away and left. That's all it was. I'm sorry I didn't tell you, but it was so random and pointless, I didn't see the need to upset you over it."

"It would've been better if I'd heard it from you first."

"I'd practically forgotten it." That wasn't entirely true, but I wanted it to be true.

Julian didn't respond, and for several moments we faced each other in silence. Finally, he closed the space between us and wrapped me in his arms.

I was sure I'd have dropped from the combination of relief and fatigue if he hadn't been holding me up.

"I believe you." His voice was soft at my ear. "Let's forget it."

My eyes were hot, and I hugged him tightly around the waist. "I'm sorry. I should've told you the whole story and not let you be ambushed twice in one night."

"I still can't believe he did it that way."

For a few moments, we only held each other, breathing together, coming down. I thought about what he'd said and how different things were from the spring. Our relationship had grown, and we did trust each other. Even if I was still working on stupid, emotional flare-ups.

"Thank you," I said, leaning back. "For trusting me, for not being angry."

With one hand, he smoothed my hair away from my face. "I can't resist that cute little newsy nose. Or those green eyes."

I laughed, the relief making me slightly giddy. "Hazel."

"You always call me that." Leaning forward, he kissed my cheek. "It's Julian. Juu-lien."

That made me laugh more. He grinned and pulled me toward the door. "I never know what to expect with these guys."

"Lucy was fantastic."

"Yes. She definitely was. If I was never in love with her before, I am now."

"She's been through so much, and she's been alone so long. A... I mean *Robert* has really been good for her."

Julian nodded. "Even though it's an 'insta-family' type of deal, I already feel sort of protective of her. It's weird… but I like it. And I like him. I like having a family."

I thought of what I'd read in Mr. Kyser's journal about how his own mother had left him and his father behind. I remembered the nights he'd documented lying awake at night, alone, with his father passed out drunk. He'd described taking one of the horses from their ranch and riding it down to Soldier Creek, vowing not to grow up to be like his dad. For a while it was exactly what he'd done, but now he had a family, too, and Ms. LaSalle was helping him heal.

"I think your dad always wanted the same thing himself."

"We're fumbling our way toward happiness."

Lucy was bright and beautiful as always sitting in the coffee shop, waiting for me Saturday afternoon. It reminded me of the day we'd met last spring. Right before she'd insisted I take her to see her father's girlfriend, a.k.a., Julian's mom.

A tiny crease was between her perfect brows, but it instantly disappeared when she saw me.

"Anna!" She hopped up and hugged me before I slid into the booth opposite her. "Can you believe last night? I couldn't sleep for thinking about it. My mind's still a little blown."

"It was pretty bomb-shellish the way your dad did it."

A small laugh bubbled out before she sipped her coffee. "Who knew Dad could be so dramatic?"

"Are you still… I mean, do you still feel the way you did last night?"

"It helps that I knew her a little while first." She blinked at the table a minute, thinking. "I know I should be mad about it, but it was all so long ago."

She paused, but I didn't know what to say. Instead, I sipped the large cappuccino I'd ordered.

"I don't remember my mom. I love her..." Her lip caught in her teeth. "I should be loyal to her memory, but I can't seem to find it in me to punish them. They've punished themselves better than I ever could."

It was such a difficult situation, and I had no basis to relate to any of it or offer any help. So I tried a different approach.

"It was really cool how you stood up for Julian."

Slim fingers scrubbed her forehead. "I suppose Will was right. I lost it for a minute, throwing my food." Then she blinked up at me. "I don't want any more fighting. I want a family. It's something I've never had. Dad's happy... I just want us all to be happy for once."

"Well, you've got a knack for derailing arguments, I'll give you that."

She smiled and for a moment we sipped our coffee. "You like New Orleans?"

"Maybe." I shrugged. "I haven't really had a chance to check it out."

"Oh, you have to! You can't be there and not experience the city." She gave me a teasing look. "Get out of the classroom and hit the streets."

"You're right. I will."

"Promise me you'll do it when you get back."

I laughed, but she didn't. Her lip was back between her teeth, and I knew there was more to this meeting.

"I'm so worried about Jack. I know he's not Julian's favorite person, but you have to be worried, too." It came out so fast, I couldn't argue.

I'd have been lying if I'd even tried.

"He has been different." I took a sip, trying not to commit.

"Why?" She leaned forward against the table, desperation filling her blue eyes.

"I-I don't know."

"Somebody has to help him. Will obviously isn't going to do anything but sneer as he goes down the drain."

I remembered the few times I'd been around him and my personal vow not to get involved. "Sometimes you have to let people realize for themselves they need help."

She began shaking her head before she'd even finished her coffee. "Jack's been there too many times for me. I cannot let that happen."

Everything inside me resisted this conversation. Yet, I said, "What did you have in mind?"

"I have no idea." She shrugged and leaned back again. "I know it's too much to ask, but if there were any way you could just... keep an eye on him for me? Let me know if things get too bad—"

"I've got an incredible amount of work going on this semester..." I couldn't get involved. Julian wouldn't like it.

"Anna, please." She reached across the table and caught my hand, and it was difficult to tell her no, especially in view of how she'd stood up to Will.

My eyes met hers, and I caved. "I'll do what I can... but, Lucy, you have to understand—"

"Oh, thank God!" She slid down and out of her seat then rounded the table to hug me. "Just think. One day we'll really be sisters."

I gave her a tight smile. Making that dream a reality was top priority for me, and I wouldn't let Jack derail it because his life had gotten off track. I'd have to figure out a way to help Lucy and stay away from her brother at the same time.

It wasn't going to be easy.

* * *

DEAD WEEK

Only two short weeks were left before the end of first semester. It had gone by so fast, and I'd spent most of it either studying too hard or pining for Julian.

But somehow, knowing so little time was left, it was like a weight lifted off me. I thought of what Lucy said, and I wanted to see more of the city. I wanted to forget about all the stress and anxiety, and get out and explore.

My finals were all either written reports or progress reports for projects we'd complete next semester. It was the last Saturday of Dead Week, so I grabbed the digital camera I'd checked out of the journalism library and took off before the sun was fully risen.

I headed out toward St. Charles Avenue and the street car lines. For a couple dollars, I could ride all the way, round-trip, to the French Quarter, and I wanted to get some early-morning shots of Algiers before it got too crowded. I'd grab my coffee at Café du Monde before the tourists flooded the place.

Black, wrought-iron benches lined the top of the levee, where tourists could sit and watch the riverboats go by or the barges. Or the crazy locals. As the day wore on, more and more people would venture out and the whole atmosphere would change, but right now, it was quiet, anticipatory.

December was cool, but not cold. I wore jeans and a light sweater, and all of the businesses were decked out for Christmas. Wreaths hung on the lamp posts, and every shop window either had an alligator in a Santa hat, or Santa in a pirogue, or some other type of "Christmas on the Bayou" scene.

The holiday mood was catching, or maybe it was just residual spending almost a week with Julian, knowing I'd see him again in less than ten days, knowing I'd done very well my first semester of college in spite of it all—whatever it was, any dark feelings I had were far behind. I was light and happy.

With my back to the Mississippi River, I had a full view of

Jackson Square, with St. Louis Cathedral towering over it all. The sun was rising, and the partly cloudy sky was a mixture of yellow, blue, and orange. A stand of tall banana trees clustered in the center along the iron fence, creating a nice layered effect with the statue of Andrew Jackson on horseback front and center.

The small video recorder I had with me was top of the line, and I was sure the footage would be gorgeous. Still, nothing compared to seeing it live. Hearing the noise of the river traffic, seeing the street vendors shuffling out, laughing and calling to each other in their unique accents.

They'd spend the day sketching, telling fortunes, twisting balloons into animal shapes, or selling works of art, hung on the wrought-iron fence that lined the flagstone sidewalk along Decatur Street.

The voodoo practitioners were my favorite, with their chicken feet and assorted *gris-gris*. Horse-drawn carriages brought the smell of livestock to the scene, but it was mixed up with the scent of sugary beignets, coffee, seafood, and humans.

With Mardi Gras just around the corner, the occasional brass quartet or trio would come down and play for tips, filling the air with the distinctive, jovial sound of "Joe Avery's Blues." Depending on the group, they'd mix in a little "When The Saints Go Marching In," and it would turn into a regular New Orleans street party.

If I kept walking toward Bourbon Street, I'd get shots of the children who clustered around cardboard boxes, tap-dancing for tips. If the crowd got big enough, they'd do fast-tapping tricks, choreography, and even the occasional back flip. More and more they were being replaced by bucket drummers, and I was sad to see the talented children go.

I loved filming them, and of course, I filled their coffers with my lunch money. At least I could grab a Lucky Dog for a dollar, and my ride home was already paid.

Walking around the Quarter by myself with my camera was

instantly one of my favorite experiences of living in this ancient city. A huge part of why I loved communications was the documentary component of the genre.

I considered heading up to Elysian Fields, since I'd finished *A Streetcar Named Desire*, but I probably needed Brad with me for that adventure. Even though the city was mysterious, or perhaps *because* it was, certain parts were best explored in groups.

We had a little time before the break, so after *Streetcar*, our professor had made us read and analyze "The Love Song of J. Alfred Prufrock." It was a T. S. Eliot poem I had always enjoyed, and I'd read it many times, over and over, trying to catch everything.

I loved the fog rubbing its back like cats against the window-panes, the arms downed with light-brown hair, and the almost stand-up-comedian humor of this funny little man, obsessed with going bald, writing a love song.

> Let us go then, you and I,
> When the evening is spread out against the sky
> Like a patient etherized on a table.

It made me laugh how he killed every beatific image with an ugly reality.

There were parts I didn't totally get, but I still loved the rhythm and the rhyme, like the

> Women who come and go,
> Talking of Michelangelo.

That's how my birthday tiptoed in, on little cat feet. Okay, that's not Eliot; that's Sandburg, but that's how it felt.

My birthday is in that twilight period between Thanksgiving and Christmas, when nobody is paying attention, when I can sneak it past everyone. Except for my parents, only a few people never miss it.

I came home that afternoon, my head full of Bourbon Street and tap-dancing kids and Eliot, and when I opened the door, I froze. Everything in the room with the capacity to hold something was filled with yellow chrysanthemums, bright daisies, and red roses.

Whipping out my phone, I saw the missed calls from Gabi and my parents, but I quickly typed a text to Julian.

ANNA

How did you do this?

My hand clasped over my mouth, and I was floored.

JULIAN

What's this? I have no idea what you mean.

ANNA

You filled my room with flowers!

JULIAN

Don't know what you're talking about. It must be
one of your other boyfriends.

ANNA

You know exactly what I'm talking about. You're
my only BF. Why did you do this?

JULIAN

Because I want you to smile today, Sunshine. I
love you.

I remembered last year, the note in my locker from him with the single yellow flower. So much had changed in one year. For starters, he could afford to buy me a lot more than one flower, and while I missed the old days, I was happy he was right about this year so far. The distance sucked, but our love was stronger than distance.

ANNA

I love you, too. So much.

Yes, fall semester had started out badly. I'd had shocks and unexpected encounters, and I'd spent most of the first half heartbroken and wishing I was anywhere but here. Well, not *anywhere*. One place in particular. Still, regardless of how it began, nothing could steal this moment from me.

The end was better than the beginning, and I was happy I'd come to the Crescent City and learned to love it and to be independent.

I'd stopped fighting my choices, and I was starting to appreciate the path I was on and what the future might bring. And Julian and I had found a way to hold on to our love in spite of it all.

I was certain things could only get better.

* * *

Hi, ho! Jules cutting in again!

I have to go on record right here—my dad was pretty cool. Mom's not so bad herself, but I know her, and her love of books, her funny, nerdy self. It works. She's cute and guys dig it. Brandon sure did. Dad clearly did.

So are you with me here? I'm not seeing how they could possibly break up. How in the world did they have all this, have me, and separate for so long? This silly blog had better tell me. If it cuts off, I'm going to be pissed.

But first I need a sandwich. Grab yourself one... meet you back here for the rest.

* * *

SPRING SEMESTER

You *really* didn't think I was going to spend Christmas break writing in my blog, did you?

Good, because it went by way too fast, between visiting family, getting together with friends who were also in town for the break, and cramming in as much time with Julian as I could, I was off the writing game.

Julian's break was consumed with working for his dad, and I could tell, even though he wouldn't commit to anything, he loved it. He'd even visited his mother a few times during the break, and I was thrilled and relieved.

Lucy was a big part of that—she insisted the five of them spend Christmas morning together.

Jack was only in Fairview briefly, and I hadn't even seen him. My promise to Lucy lurked in the background of my mind, but I'd only committed to do what I could. I had no intention of going out of my way or doing anything to make Julian uncomfortable.

Mr. Kyser was happier than I'd ever known possible, and the more time Julian spent with him, the more excited he got about a future at Kyser-Brennan. We'd gone out with Rachel and Brad a few times, and Brad took it as a sign from heaven that Julian was Mr. Kyser's son. It was like God himself ordained his plans, and all he could talk about was how great it would be when they were working together, rebooting their fathers' vision, taking over the business world and becoming billionaires in the process. I didn't point out that both of them were already pretty well set as far as money went.

Julian did note the biggest obstacle to Brad's dream: Will hadn't even come home for the holiday, and as far as I knew, the eldest Kyser sibling wasn't on speaking terms with their father.

Brad dismissed it with a wave, and they were back to plotting the future. Unfortunately, *my* future came much too quickly, and we were saying goodbye before I was ready.

I'd rounded a small corner on life in south Louisiana before the break, but three weeks of sleeping in Julian's arms, being together as often as we wanted, and catching up on our shortages made me feel like I'd gone all the way back to August.

Heading back to college and being separated again felt like the cruelest torture I could imagine. I struggled with wanting to quit and stay with him (or transfer to Savannah), but there was no way anybody… including me if I thought about it long enough… would let that happen.

"We'll FaceTime more," Julian said before we parted, giving me a wink. "Virtual nookie."

My chest was tight with desperation. "How can I do something like that with Rachel in the house? She'll hear everything."

"When she's with Brad, silly." He tweaked my nose before kissing it again. We were probably in the running for the World Record on the number of times you could kiss someone before saying goodbye. "Hang in there for just a few weeks. Mardi Gras is early this year, and we'll all be back together for that long weekend."

"February feels very far away."

"I know." He exhaled and wrapped his arms around my shoulders, pulling me tight against his chest.

I only held him, breathing in his clean, beachy scent, listening to his heartbeat against my ear, and trying not to ugly cry.

When we'd finally parted, I drove all the way to New Orleans with a boulder in my stomach and intermittent tears on my cheeks. I'd left my heart and all my insides behind me. Even worse, they were being driven almost 700 miles in the opposite direction.

Back at school, Dr. Arati was very encouraging about my prospects for landing JYA. I intentionally hadn't thought about it over the break, figuring I'd cross that bridge if it appeared. Now here I was, and if last semester were any indication, it would be May before I knew it.

Even more bad news? Summer Daigle was now in my photo-journalism course, of all things. She'd been in another section the previous semester, and apparently some scheduling conflict had landed her slap in my class.

We eyed each other warily when she entered the first day, and I'd done everything to avoid her. The only good thing was we weren't in the same group, but New Orleans wasn't the biggest city in the U.S., and most of the photo-worthy sites were in the same location. I knew it was only a matter of time before I'd have to speak to her.

"Can you believe it?" I wailed that night, watching Julian laugh through my laptop screen. "I jinxed it just like you said!"

"But come on. You said you'd managed to deal with her last year. Weren't you almost friends?"

I hadn't told him about Summer's strange plot our last semester of high school, how she'd been spying on me for Will, trying to figure out my connection with their father. She'd said it was because I'd tried to steal Jack from her. As if. Ugh!

"For like five minutes." My voice was seething. "Then she went back to being the most annoying person on the planet."

Julian looked up and smiled, and even though he was miles away and only on a computer, his blue eyes made me forget everything bad. "You'll do fine, Sunshine."

I reached out to run my finger down his cheek on the screen. "I miss you so much. I think I hate FaceTime. It's awful to see you like this and not be able to touch you."

His lips twisted, and he rested his head on his hand. "You're right. It's hard with you sitting over there in that little nightshirt. And I love the bun."

I hadn't expected his call tonight, and he'd caught me getting ready for bed. Still, there was no way I was too vain to take his call on a moment's notice. "We should start planning these calls so I can at least look cute."

"Are you kidding me? I love how you look. It's how you look when you first wake up in the morning."

"Right before you leave me."

Apple computer needed some special award because I actually saw his eyes sparkle. "We should come clean. Tell your parents everything and let the chips fall where they may."

"The chips wouldn't fall, my dad would hit the ceiling. We're still in the south, you know."

"I know." His voice had taken on the warm tone I loved. "You just let some jackass like me try and mess with our daughter. I'll meet him at the window with a shotgun."

The idea was lovely, both of us with a daughter, and him with a shotgun. I started to laugh. "You're not so bad."

"I'm not so good either. What panties are you wearing? Pull up that shirt."

Electricity surged through my limbs, and I couldn't help laughing more. "You're so crazy. Rachel's here."

"At least give me the PG-13 version."

My eyes searched the edges of the box holding his face. "You're alone?"

"Totally."

Chewing my lip, I lifted my shirt quickly. Five seconds later, I fell back on the bed laughing.

"Nice. My girls."

Heat flared low in my stomach, making me laugh harder. "Julian!"

"Night, Hazel."

I was lying on my side now, looking at the screen. "I thought you were Hazel."

"I'm whatever you want me to be, baby."

"I want you to be here."

"See you soon."

* * *

UNEXPECTED ENCOUNTER

Saturday mornings in Jackson Square with my camera had become my weekly ritual, and I loved it.

Friday nights I'd stay in, FaceTime for a while with Julian, then read a book or watch a movie until I got tired. Then Saturday mornings, I was up with the dawn, running down to catch the streetcar and head out to watch the city slowly come to life.

It helped me forget the pain of separation and made me feel like I was part of something here.

So what if I was miles away from the one I loved? I was plugging into the city. I was even making friends.

Pierre, who ran the counter at Café du Monde had gotten to where he had my café au lait ready to go at 8 a.m., and he'd be waiting for me to reappear an hour later for beignets.

"Why you're not with a fella, cher?" He was an attractive man, brown skin, and light brown eyes. "I'm thinking those college boys aren't very smart."

I just giggled, and I was sure my cheeks were pink. "I told you. I have a boyfriend in Savannah."

My embarrassed response only encouraged him. "Savannah's far, far away, sweet petite. I can make you forget all about that careless guy."

Rolling my eyes, I took a sip of the milky dark coffee with chicory. "Nothing will make me forget Julian."

Pierre's eyebrows rose, and he smiled with approval. "Then it's true love, cher. The best kind."

Nodding, I sipped the bitter drink. "It is."

"It is what?" That voice made me jump out of my skin.

"Summer!" I spun around, almost spilling my coffee. "What the hell?"

"Hi, Anna. I saw you here, and I figured it was time you stopped ignoring me."

A spark of anger burned in my stomach. "I'm not ignoring you, I'm avoiding you. There's a difference."

"You know," She nodded at Pierre, who held up a paper coffee cup, "What happened last year was really dumb, and I'm totally over Jack now."

My eyes narrowed. "You spied on me and basically lied to my face. It was a lot more than dumb."

She took the cup from Pierre and passed him her cash. "I'm sorry, okay? Love makes you do stupid things. You of all people should know that."

It seemed we were back to Summer speaking her mind.

"I was only off track for a few months," I reply. "Julian has changed all of that."

"So you see? No reason for us not to be friends."

"I can think of a few."

I started toward the door, and she was right with me. "But why? Let bygones be bygones. Let stupid high school behavior stay in high school."

We were back out in the sunshine, and the foot traffic was already picking up. I squinted into the light a second before a click brought me back to my companion.

"Did you take my picture?" I frowned as she looked at the back of her camera.

"I'll send it to you." She turned the device toward me, and I saw my face bathed in sunlight. "You should think about broadcast news. The camera has always loved you."

"It's kind of rude to take someone's picture without permission." As if rudeness ever stopped her from doing anything.

She shrugged. "Send it to Julian. I know he'll like it."

I was ready to jog up to my favorite spot on the levee and then down into Jackson Square.

"Look, we're in this class together, so I know we'll be in the same place a lot. I'd appreciate it if you'd give me some space. And don't take my picture without my permission."

She held her hands and the camera up. "Sorry! I was just trying to make amends."

Suppressing the urge to growl at her, I took a deep breath. "Apology accepted. I'm willing to try and let it go. I just need space right now."

"You got it."

We stepped out onto the flagstone, and after about five steps, Summer was still right beside me. I stopped walking abruptly and so did she.

"You're going this way?" Her voice was meek.

"Yes," I snapped back.

A pivot on her heel sent her west toward the square. "I'll head over this way then."

"Thank you."

Turning back toward the river, I headed up the hill toward the wrought-iron bench where I had the best view of Algiers Point. It seemed my Saturday morning ritual was in danger of derailment by a very unwelcome intruder.

We'd see how this played out.

* * *

MARDI GRAS MADNESS

Mardi Gras season in New Orleans always started twelve days after Christmas, after Epiphany, so the building sense of excitement ran from January until Fat Tuesday, whether it was early February or late March.

Lucky for me, this year it was early February, which meant I'd see Julian again very soon. We celebrated Mardi Gras along the coast as well, since the tradition actually began in the U.S. in Sterling.

Still, nothing compared to the big business of New Orleans carnival.

My Saturdays in the Quarter were becoming more and more crowded and festive by the week. I hated to miss the big day in the city, but we had events of our own in Fairview and Dolphin Shores.

The "secret" Kyser-Brennan krewe had a huge masquerade ball planned, and Rachel insisted we go to Bourbon Street to find masks for it. We spent a day sipping hand grenades and laughing at the T-shirts in the trashy shops lining the street as we explored different options.

With the help of much back-and-forth photo-texting with Julian, I got a gorgeous black mask with silver glitter fanning across the nose and out from the eyes. For Julian, I bought a velvet eye-cover that had tiny silver studs sprinkled over it. He'd look more like Zorro than a reveler.

Secretly, I hated masked balls. The thought of all those creepy eyes peering out from behind masks sent a nervous shiver through my stomach. It helped that I'd bought the masks we'd be wearing—at least I'd be able to keep up with Julian in the sea of "strangers."

So even though we'd only been back at school a few weeks, once again Rachel and I were headed back to the coast for a weekend of festivities.

Starting mid-November, college had taken a backseat to social activities, but I wasn't complaining. I couldn't wait to see Julian again.

"I bought a floor-length baby blue satin dress online," Rachel said as she studied the road. "It should match the mask I got, but I'm afraid I'll look like Cinderella."

Rachel's mask was silver with white accents and feathers. "I love your mask. I think you'll look gorgeous even if you are a Disney princess."

She laughed. "So what are you wearing?"

"Probably that black dress I bought for prom." My actual prom dress had been a short, Tiffany-blue chiffon that I adored, but I had a back-up just in case.

"Black?" Rachel's brow creased. "You know Mardi Gras is supposed to be colorful and festive."

"Yes, but the store was doing a two-for-one sale, so Mom picked it up. We can't really afford three formals every year."

"Sorry. I bet you'll look gorgeous in it. I can't wait for the ball."

I didn't say I could.

SCAD wasn't technically out for the holiday, so Julian was only in town for the weekend. Still, it was a whole weekend together. After Rachel dropped me off, and I did the required catch-up with the parents, I hopped in the Civic and headed straight to Hammond Island.

It was strange to be so welcome in the giant mansion on Peninsula Avenue. I pulled into the circle drive and saw Mr. Kyser's Audi, Julian's Beemer, and a new Lexus I didn't recognize. Somehow I'd managed to forget all of the Kyser children would be at the ball. That meant Jack… and Will.

I'd just closed my car door when Julian appeared, trotting down to greet me with a kiss. "I'm thinking about playing hooky on Monday. Staying one more night."

The wind pushed his shiny dark hair around his face, and I couldn't help returning his grin. Julian's happiness was contagious. "I love that idea!"

He leaned in close and kissed my nose on the way to whispering in my ear. "Will's inside. Want to go?"

I was about to say yes when the sound of a car horn almost made me jump two feet in the air. A voice called out, and I looked over my shoulder to see Lucy in her bright, yellow Cabrio pulling in behind me. The top was down and she was waving.

"Or not." Julian dropped his arm to my waist and smiled back at his sister.

"Anna!" She hopped out of the car, bouncing over to us. "I'm so glad you're here. I need a second opinion on my dress."

Pressing my lips together, I looked up at Julian, who only shrugged. Lucy caught my arm and pulled me away. "You two can snuggle on the dance floor. She's coming with me."

I followed her inside, through the short entry hall and into the enormous kitchen. Julian was right behind us. The only person in the room was the one person I hadn't wanted to see, but despite how our last encounter had gone, Lucy didn't even pause.

"Hello, Will." Her tone was light, but not exactly happy.

Her oldest brother blinked up to us. When he saw Lucy holding my arm and Julian right behind me, he actually sneered. Then he shook his head and left the room.

Lucy kept going toward the staircase. "Ignore him. We are going to have a blast tomorrow night. Just you wait."

She had a dozen ball gowns in assorted colors and styles. The one she'd bought for this year was strapless silver with green and purple tulle wrapped tightly over the body, going down into almost a mermaid style.

"What do you think?" She turned in front of the mirror looking over one shoulder at her reflection. "Too Ariel?"

Julian had stayed downstairs, and I had flopped onto her bed to watch the fashion show. "Your hair's not red. Are you planning to sing?"

"No!" She started to laugh.

"Then I don't think anyone will get *Little Mermaid* when they look at you. It's gorgeous."

She gave me a huge smile. "Thanks. I really loved it too, but you know. Sometimes I can be off."

"I have never seen you 'be off' when it comes to fashion."

She caught her silky hair up in a make-shift up-do. "What are you wearing?"

"Black, floor-length. It was one of my prom-dress possibilities from last year."

Her nose wrinkled. I was clearly new to the whole Mardi Gras social scene. "You need to wear something colorful. Here, borrow something of mine."

A stubborn knot of inferiority formed in my throat. Mardi Gras balls were not world-changing events. "Won't people recognize it?"

"Of course not. A few drinks and everybody forgets everything." She went deep in her closet and came out with a flowing, bright green chiffon dress. It had clusters of fabric roses in the same material over one shoulder, but it was otherwise strapless.

"Here." She held it against me. "Go try it on. Your eyes will absolutely glow in this."

I stepped around the screen and quickly slipped the dress on. Hopping out, I went over to let her zip me up, then I turned in front of her three-way mirror.

My breath caught. "Oh my gosh."

Lucy bounced, clapping her hands and squealing. "I'm giving it to you! This dress has never looked that good on me."

For just this one moment, I decided it was possible she could be right. I'd never worn anything so fine, and it did make my eyes glow green.

"Have your hair done up, and you will look *amazing*."

"How can I get it out without Julian seeing it?"

She ran up behind me and squeezed the top of my arms, putting her chin on my shoulder. "He is going to flip when he sees you tomorrow night. I hope you make it to the ball."

We did make it to the ball. Mom was ecstatic at the dress, Tamara was more than happy to work me into her schedule so she could hear all about college life, but all of it was a torturous blur as I waited for the day to hurry up and end. Suddenly I wasn't feeling so skittish about the masquerade, I only wanted to see Julian—or more accurately, him to see me.

I borrowed a pair of Mom's heels and some red lipstick. She smoothed my hair and helped me get my mask in place, then she hiccupped a breath.

"Oh, Anna!" Another sniff, and I looked over my shoulder.

"You okay?"

Shaking her head, she snatched a tissue to dab her eyes. "You're just so grown-up and beautiful."

"Mom…"

We didn't have time to talk because Julian was downstairs with Dad. I gave her a quick peck and scampered to the door. "Come on! I can't wait for Julian to see me."

My date was dressed in the standard Mardi Gras tux, which is black tails and white accessories, and as predicted, his jaw dropped when I appeared at the top of the stairs. I'd have enjoyed it more if I weren't so afraid I'd catch my heel on the hem and tumble the rest of the way down.

"Wow." Julian's low murmur sparked an excited flutter in my stomach, and with a trembling hand, I held the rail until I finally made it to the bottom.

Dad was equally shocked, and now I was starting to feel awkward and self-conscious. "Guys! I know I'm wearing a mask, but it's just me. Anna."

Part of me hoped Dad would add *Banana* for the first time in… never. But I was ready for anything to cut the tension.

Julian was the first to snap out of it. He pulled the cloth mask I'd bought for him out of his pocket and held it over his eyes. "Okay, hot stuff. Take a good look at this. I'm your date. Right here."

Blue eyes twinkled at me from behind black velvet, and I laughed. "I'm not forgetting you."

He dropped it and caught my hand. "Back by…"

Dad shrugged. "You guys have been setting your own curfew for almost a year now. Just be safe."

Stepping forward to kiss Dad's cheek, I took Julian's hand and followed him out to the waiting Beemer. Before I got in, he pulled me close against his chest. Our noses were a whisper apart, but he didn't kiss me. Everything in me was humming, but he only looked into my eyes.

"You're gorgeous tonight." His lips lightly touched my cheek. "I don't want to smear your lipstick or I'd kiss you good."

"I hate red lipstick now."

He chuckled and kissed my other cheek. "I don't. You look hot, Hazel."

I gave him a quick hug, and we were on our way.

The civic center was decked out with purple, green, and gold feathers, balloons, wreaths, and streamers. A live band was playing in the background, and everyone was masked and either milling around, chatting and having refreshments, or dancing. I wanted to dance, but first I wanted to find Rachel and Lucy.

Rachel would be looking for me in that black dress, but Julian's sister knew what I was wearing. Other than the two of them and my date, I'd have a hard time figuring out who anyone was.

"I'll grab us some drinks. Don't wander off." Julian kissed my cheek, right next to my ear and took off for the bar.

I stood for a few moments twisting my hands and wondering why I hadn't gone with him, until a female dressed in a long, flowing purple dress approached me from the side.

"Anna?" Her mask was gold with matching purple and green detailing. "I thought that was you. It's me, Summer."

I recognized the voice, and did my best not to frown. "Hi, Summer. Yeah, I recognized your voice."

Brown eyes flashed up and down my outfit. "You look really good. I wasn't expecting you to go all out for this."

"Umm… thanks?" Summer had not lost her ability to be completely inscrutable. "You look good too. Who's your date?"

She shrugged. "I came with my cousin. We're all old neighbors, so you know. They let us in."

"Your cousin?" Conflicted emotions pushed back and forth in my chest. "You mean Casey? Casey Simpson?"

"The one and only! Or I don't know. I guess there could be other girls named Casey Simpson in the world." That airhead tone was back in her voice, but I stopped myself.

There was no reason to be angry with her. So what if Casey Simpson, Jack's ex-girlfriend, the girl he'd broken my heart over, was here. I was with Julian now.

"That's great. I hope you guys have fun." I willed myself to mean it.

Summer's cousin hadn't knowingly done anything to me, and anyway, if she were here, maybe she would recognize the change in her ex-boyfriend. Maybe she could help him and get me off the hook with Lucy.

"Hey, I see you've found a friend." Julian was back, handing me a clear plastic cup of wine.

"Hey, handsome." Summer stepped forward and hugged him, and my eyebrows shot up at her boldness. "How's art school?"

"Summer? I'm good. Thanks." He appeared as surprised as I felt. "How's… your college?"

"Didn't Anna tell you?" She shook her head. "We're in the same photojournalism class this semester."

"Yeah, I heard." His eyes flickered to mine then back. "How's it going?"

"It's fun. I'm enjoying seeing her again."

The band started a slow song, and Julian caught my waist. "Well, good seeing you. We're going to dance."

He pulled me out onto the floor, and I couldn't have been happier. "What's gotten into her?"

"I don't know!" I couldn't help it. I started to laugh. Then I laughed more, dropping my head onto his shoulder. "You should've seen your face."

"She's never even spoken to me, much less grabbed me around the neck like that."

I straightened up then and leaned close so our lips barely brushed. "Don't get used to it, Mister."

He caught my chin and lightly kissed me back. "Don't worry. I'm ready to take you home now."

Warmth tingled in my stomach. "We're supposed to stay at least a few hours."

"Longest hours of my life."

We finished our dance, and went back to the crowd, where I soon spotted Lucy in her mermaid dress. She went on about how perfect her selection was for me, and soon Rachel joined us. She was gorgeous and only slightly reminiscent of Cinderella.

"I guess balls bring out the princess in all of us." She teased, and we danced to the live music and chatted while the guys hung around the sidelines, drinking and talking.

The night continued pretty much like any other dance I'd ever attended. I only caught sight of what I thought was Jack once. It was nearly impossible to know for sure, since all the guys wore the exact same tuxedo in various sizes. Still, at one point, I was certain the male I thought was Jack danced with a tall, slim model-type girl in a long, gray gown. It was strapless and flowing and perfectly elegant, and with a bitter twinge, I acknowledged that Casey, with all her status and social confidence, really was more Jack's type than I'd ever been.

When he'd come to find me that day after his birthday party, after I'd watched him kiss her and then slip his hand down the front of her dress, he'd said she knew their kind of life and what to expect from his family. I was so stupid, all I knew was to be miserable because I'd lost him. I had no idea how twisted events were going to get starting then.

Lost in memory, I didn't notice a tall, slim man approach me from behind. He lightly touched my waist, and I jumped. He smiled, and his blue eyes seemed strangely familiar. I wished I hadn't had that last glass of wine, because my head was too fuzzy. He motioned toward the dance floor, and I scanned the crowd for Julian. He wasn't anywhere to be seen, and I wavered, trying to find a reason to say no.

Whatever fear I would've normally felt didn't register through the haze, and I set the Dr. Pepper I'd switched to on a nearby table. It was just a friendly dance, after all.

"I… I need to find my date." My eyes blinked too fast, and the guy put his hand on my waist, touching my lips lightly with his finger.

"Shh," he whispered.

My chest tightened. It wasn't attraction, but it wasn't alarm either. It was mysterious.

It was just like a masque—strange and unexpected. Whoever this person was, he was confident and handsome. We were at the Kyser-Brennan Mardi Gras ball, so I knew that meant he had money and connections.

As we danced, his eyes never left mine. The image of a snake hypnotizing one of its prey floated through my inebriated brain, but I shook it away.

Halfway through the dance, he finally spoke in a low voice. "Enjoying yourself?" Dread clenched my stomach, and my entire body stiffened in alarm. *I was dancing with Will!* "You're very beautiful in my sister's dress."

"Let me go." My heart hammered in my chest, but he held me firmly in his embrace.

"You seem to like dancing with all the Kyser men." A wicked smile curved the sides of his mouth.

"I'll scream," I threatened, my voice cracking.

I'd never been this close to him before. Everything about him was overwhelming, from the strength of his grip to the firmness of his body against mine.

"You'll do nothing of the sort. You'll close your mouth and listen to me."

Intimidation held me in place. He was so different from Jack and Julian, and yet at the same time, they were all strangely similar. Will was handsome, of course, when he wasn't scowling at me. The problem was, he was always scowling at me. And while his brothers had only gotten a small portion of their father's coldness, Will seemed to have gotten both his share and their leftovers.

My voice was shaky. "What do you have to say?"

We moved a few more steps before he spoke. "This family has weathered many storms, and it's survived them all."

The words weren't threatening, but his tone was. "I don't understand. That's a good thing, right?"

"It is for us." His ice-blue eyes held mine. "*You* don't get comfortable."

Dread crept up my shoulders as he continued to speak. "You can trade in one brother for the next, dress up in my sister's clothes and pretend to be one of us, but you're *not* one of us."

"What—"

"Let me spell it out for you." He leaned in close so his lips were right beside my ear as he hissed. "You will *never* be a part of this family."

At those words, I did push against him. I struggled hard, but his grip only grew tighter around my waist. I jerked my hand fast out of his, and pushed against his shoulder, but he grabbed my wrist and twisted it behind my back. Ice blue eyes bored a hole into mine, and the scream was at the base of my throat when a warm firm grip caught the tops of my shoulders.

"Here you are, Anna." My knees almost gave out with relief at Brad's loud voice. "Julian's looking for you."

Will released me and straightened.

"Brad." He nodded to my savior, then to me. "Thanks for the dance, Anna."

I watched him stalk away as I clung to the front of Brad's coat, trying not to cry.

My friend's big arm went around my shoulder. "You okay?"

I held onto him for a moment longer, then I swallowed the knot in my throat and managed to blink away the tears. "Thanks. I wasn't really in the mood for dancing."

"It kind of looked like he was upsetting you."

If Brad only knew. My insides were shredded from the pain of Will's words, and small shivers kept moving through my limbs. Still, I didn't want to repeat what Julian's brother had said. I wanted his threats to vanish along with him.

"He's kind of overwhelming, I guess." Straightening my back, I smoothed my hand down the front of Lucy's dress. "I appreciate you getting me out of that."

"No problem." He put my hand in the crook of his arm and escorted me back to our friendly group.

His lips pressed into a smile before he handed me off to Julian and returned to Rachel. I didn't leave my date's side for the rest of the night.

Later, curled in his old bed at the little house on Crystal Shores Boulevard, I held Julian's arm tight around my waist. I hadn't told him what had happened with his brother, and when he'd asked me if I'd enjoyed the ball, I just said yes.

But Will's words kept replaying in my mind. They wouldn't let me sleep, and every time I closed my eyes, I saw his piercing blue ones.

It was stupid. How could he say something like that to me? How could I even consider believing him? I *didn't* believe him.

He was an evil, bitter person, and he had no power over Julian and me. Still, he touched on the inferiority that had defined my senior year. He poured a mountain of fertilizer on the seeds of fear planted when Julian started working with his dad.

Twisting around in the bed, I put my cheek against Julian's bare chest, snuggling deeper into his embrace. His lips lightly touched my head before he returned to sleep, but I blinked against his skin. I took a deep breath, and fresh ocean breezes flooded my senses. I loved being with him here in this little cottage by the shore, and once we'd done all that we needed to do, we'd come back here and live.

Then we'd be married and have babies.

Julian was mine, and I was his. The little dragonfly was on my finger, and the tattoo was on his hand. He'd taken the painting of us held together by these symbols to Savannah with him at Christmas, and in its place was the beautiful portrait he'd made of me surrounded by the ocean we loved.

Only now the waves covering me were his family and a hatred we couldn't control. As much as I fought against them, I knew they still threatened to pull us under.

Still, Julian was different. He wasn't the same as his brothers, and I had to believe that meant our future would be different. But with my uncertain plans hanging over us, I couldn't completely shake the tiny possibility his brother might be right.

* * *

MARCH LIONS

Will's words hung like a dark cloud over my head as I returned to New Orleans, and they continued troubling me through the rest of February. It was silly, I told myself. What could he do to hurt Julian and me? But no matter how hard I tried to dismiss him, his cruel threat lingered like a cut that wouldn't heal.

The only thing that took my mind off it (besides Julian) was working on the Algiers project for my photojournalism course.

Saturday morning, I headed out as usual toward the Quarter, but today I had only planned to be there for less than an hour. I was supposed to be meeting the rest of my group members at the ferry to cross over and get some interviews on the street.

Winter was mild this year, but the morning air was chilly. I was wearing a Northface jacket one of my Indiana relatives had sent me for Christmas. It was never cold enough for it here, but I tried to work it into my wardrobe.

After hopping off the streetcar and picking up my coffee from Pierre, I headed up the levee to my usual spot. Summer was not around this morning, thankfully, and I figured it was too cold for her to be following me out, annoying me.

Dampness made the air feel colder than it was, and I stood for a second looking out at the brown waters. Currents zigzagged across the center, and I thought of all the boat traffic that passed through here on a daily basis.

Instead of taking my usual seat, I decided to stroll down the levee as I sipped my warm beverage. I'd only taken a few steps when I saw a man hunched on one of the benches.

He wasn't exactly hunched, more slumped over with the collar of his coat turned up around his ears. He appeared to be passed out, and I was about to hurry past when he made a noise. Stopping was not in the plan, but I couldn't help a glance. When I did I almost dropped my camera.

"Jack?" All hesitation gone, I hurried to him and pushed him back, straighter on the bench. "Jack, what are you doing out here? Were you sleeping?"

He groaned again, and a bitter stench of alcohol hit me right in the face. It turned my stomach.

"Jack!" I shook him, but he didn't respond. His chin dropped to his chest. "You have to wake up!"

His head wagged side to side for a moment, and then he straightened clumsily. "Anna?"

He frowned, but he didn't focus on me. He couldn't seem to

focus on anything. His face was pale, and his thin body shook in my hands. I let him go and he slumped over again.

Chewing my lip, I looked up and down the path I'd taken. Nobody was around to help me. I couldn't leave him here, but who could I call? Rachel and Brad were in Baton Rouge for the weekend, and Will was not an option, even if I had his number.

The only thing I knew to do was call 911. I caught Jack's cheeks and tried to get him to look at me again.

"Jack?" My voice was loud. "I'm sorry, but I've got to call EMS."

He didn't respond, and Lucy's words were ringing in my ears. I'd promised her I'd help him.

So with shaking fingers, I took out my phone.

Almost a year had passed since the last time I'd been in a hospital waiting nervously to hear if a friend would be okay, but it all came back as vividly as if it had been yesterday.

I'd called Lucy, but it would be another hour before she arrived. The doctors wouldn't tell me anything, since I wasn't next of kin. But they were at least being friendly.

For a moment, I considered lying and saying he was my husband, but that had major backfire potential. So I sat in the waiting room and bided my time, praying.

Lucy texted from a rest stop to say she was halfway here, and I let her know I hadn't heard anything. I put my phone back in my pocket and paced the hall. I was about to give up, when a blonde nurse walked up to me.

"Miss Sanders?" She looked down at the clipboard she carried.

I jumped up and went to her. "It's Anna!"

Her smile was warm. "Hi, Anna. I'm Celeste, your friend's nurse. I understand you brought him in?"

"Yes," I nodded rapidly as I spoke. "I found him out on the levee. I-I don't know how he got there or how long—"

"It appeared he'd been in the elements all night. He was in an advanced state of hypothermia, and his blood-alcohol content was point four."

"I'm sorry," I shook my head. "I don't know what that means."

"It means he was going into shock and potential alcohol poisoning." Her warmth had morphed into more of a stern admonishment. "Your friend has a serious problem."

My lip pulled between my teeth. "I knew he'd been drinking a lot. He's not really my friend. He's my ex-boyfriend. Sort of." The details of Jack's and my bizarre connection weren't pertinent to what was going on here. "What happens now? Is there anything we can do?"

Her sternness faded as I explained our connection. "He's actually awake now and asking for you."

I blinked several times as I took in what she'd just said. "So… he's okay now?"

"Far from it, Miss Sanders." She glanced at the clipboard she carried. "I have several recommendations at this point I'll discuss when his family arrives, but you can see him now."

"Thank you." I was breathless, and I wasn't exactly sure why I was thanking Nurse Celeste, but I took off in the direction of Jack's room.

Stopping just before I entered, I took a deep breath and collected myself, but nothing could've prepared me for what I saw when I pushed through the door.

Lying in a hospital bed, he was thin and vulnerable with wires attached to his arms and machines monitoring his vitals. His eyes were closed, but he must've heard me enter. They blinked open, tired and defeated, and he struggled to sit up.

"Anna, hey." Even his voice was changed.

I went quickly to his bedside and took his hand.

It was all so horrible, the only thing I could think was to try and be light. "Hey, yourself. Don't you have a bed to sleep in?"

He managed a weak smile. "I didn't feel like going home."

Or you forgot where home was, I thought.

Still going for light. "You're a good-looking guy. You couldn't find somewhere warm to sleep besides a park bench?"

His expression grew still, and I felt him withdraw. It killed all the easygoing feelings I was trying for.

"Oh, Jack." I leaned forward, squeezing his hand. "Tell me what's wrong."

His thumb moved back and forth over my hand. "Nothing's wrong. It's just… I didn't feel like going home. That's all."

"But why? Is it because of Will? Did he say something to you?" As angry as I was at his brother, I was just waiting for an excuse to confront him, to prove he was no better than me.

But Jack didn't answer that question. Instead his tone shifted. "Remember when we were in school?" His voice was so resigned it hurt my heart. "Those early days before I came to New Orleans?"

"Yeah?" I nodded, studying his face.

"You used to look at me like…"

I squeezed his hand, worry tightening my stomach. "Like what?"

He exhaled a bitter laugh and didn't meet my eyes. "Like I was so special."

My brows pulled together. It was true. I did.

"You are special. Whatever you saw was only your reflection in my eyes."

Leaning his head back on the pillow, he laughed a little more. "I'm not special. I'm a jerk."

Somehow I always managed to get myself into these situations where my qualifications were no match for what the person needed.

So I just spoke the facts. "Well, you did kind of yank my chain one too many times, but that didn't make you less special. That just made me sort of…"

A jerk.

He slid down in the bed again and looked at me. Deep in his eyes was that same old expression that used to slay me—sexy and slightly mischievous. In that moment, I knew he was still in there. He wasn't beyond saving. The question was, could I handle being the one to save him or did I need to pass the baton to someone else?

"I'm sorry," he said. "I was a stupid kid, and I didn't know how to handle… this."

"It looks to me like you still don't know how to handle whatever *this* is."

His eyes flashed to mine with a look I'd never seen before. It was like respect, and it caused an unexpected tingle in my midsection. "Don't try to save me, Anna. I'm not worth it."

"Are you seriously saying that to me? Say something like that again, and I'll kick you in the nards."

Silence filled the room, and I was afraid I'd gone too far. Until he laughed—so loud it rang off the walls.

My head dropped forward. I laughed, too, and in that moment, I confess, I was proud of myself. I took a deep inhale and straightened. I could help him, but if I did, I'd have to be as strong as him. I couldn't be old Anna anymore.

I *wasn't* old Anna anymore.

"Anna Sanders," he breathed. "I could kiss you right now."

I leaned away, still smiling. "You better not try it."

Where this sudden surge of empowerment came from, I had no idea, but I liked it. We laughed again until he put a hand over his face and exhaled a groan.

"I think dating my little brother has been good for you."

"Dating Julian has definitely been good for me, but back to you. Tell me what *this* is all about."

A few seconds ticked past. The vulnerability, that strange weakness was back, but it seemed he was making a decision to let me in. I had no idea if I was prepared for what he might say or to give the right answer, but I said a silent prayer I wouldn't let him down.

I never got the chance, because the door flew open, and a streak of blonde shot into the room.

"Jack!" Lucy flew to his bedside and hugged him. "Oh, honey. Everything's going to be fine. Don't worry about a thing." She leaned back and smoothed his messy bangs off his forehead, and I remembered when I used to do that. "We'll have you out of here and home before the close of business today."

"Lucy." Jack caught her hands in his. "It's okay. I'm not in jail."

He might not have noticed, but I saw her tremble. I also recognized something I never saw in Lucy—fear. She'd been afraid this was coming for months, and now it was here.

At the same time, I remembered being in a similar situation with her, Jack flying to her side. I'd been shut out of the hospital on that particular occasion as well, but her rock bottom had looked a lot like his.

It was probably best to let them work it out privately.

"I'll go ahead and take off now." I backed to the door, but Jack sat up.

"Hang on." His earnest tone startled me.

It seemed to startle Lucy as well. She shot me a pleading glance, so I stopped.

"Um…" I wasn't sure what he wanted. His sister was here now. "I kind of need to get back. I was supposed to meet some classmates to work on a project today."

"Right." He was faltering about something, but I couldn't tell what. "We'll talk soon, okay?"

"Oh." *Talk about being put on the spot!* Seeing Jack again did not feel like the best idea. "I… uh… sure. I mean, okay. If you need to."

He seemed to relax, and Lucy was still holding his hand. She lifted it and pressed her lips against it briefly. "Be right back, okay?"

Then she headed in my direction and pulled me out the door.

"Oh my God, thank you so much, Anna." Throwing her arms around my neck, I could feel her shaking. "I can't even think what might've happened if you hadn't—"

"It's okay! Thank God I go out there every Saturday."

She straightened up and pushed her tears away. "It's like a miracle. You're our angel or something."

My smile was more of a squint. Julian had called me *his* angel, but I refused to look at myself as some sort of Kyser-family supernatural being.

"I think it was more a lucky coincidence. New Orleans isn't really that big if you think about where everybody tends to go."

"Well, I don't care what you say, you saved him, and I'm forever grateful."

I didn't want to point out that he wasn't out of the woods yet, so I gave her a quick hug. "Okay. I've got to go now."

She hugged me back. "I'll call you soon about the wedding plans."

"Sounds great."

I left her and her brother to take care of themselves.

It had always been that way with them, and it would go on being that way. It wasn't my business.

* * *

THE REASON

Julian's voice was always optimistic when we talked. He was working hard and learning his dad's business fast. It reminded me of the journals I'd read so long ago.

"You've really found your passion." I lay on my bed looking at him on my computer screen. His head was rested on his hand, and his dark hair hung in his eyes.

"I found my passion a few years ago." His blue eyes twinkled, and I reached out to touch his face on the screen. "But if I have to work, architecture is cool."

Rolling onto my side, I rested my head on my hand. It was almost like we were in the same bed together. I just couldn't bury my nose in his chest and take a deep breath of his Julian-scent.

"How about you?" he asked. "What's the latest on London?"

"Ugh. Still haven't heard. But Dr. Arati said it could be May before we know anything."

"Doesn't give us much time, does it?"

Pressing my lips together, I shook my head.

"Anything else going on? Your Algiers project all you hoped and more?"

"It's had some unexpected moments." I thought about finding Jack almost dead on the levee. It had been almost two weeks, and I hadn't heard from or seen him. I had heard from his sister, though. "Lucy's in full wedding-planning mode. Have you been keeping up?"

"Not really. She sent me an email telling me what to wear and where to be, but you know guys aren't as important at weddings."

"What? Julian! Guys are the most important part. You can't get married without a groom."

"But I'm not the groom."

I sighed as my eyes traveled around his perfect face. *Maybe one day soon*, I thought. "I'm just happy we'll be seeing each other again."

"I know." He smiled. "I was worried when our spring breaks were at different times. Big sis saves the day."

My nose wrinkled. "It's so weird to hear you call her that."

He shrugged. "I'm getting used to it. She texts me pretty regularly. She's getting really close with Mom."

"I love that, and I'm sure your mom does, too. It's like she has her best friend back somehow."

Julian's brow lined. "What do you mean by that?"

"Oh!" My eyebrows flew up. "I mean…"

"Anna." His eyes narrowed. "What do you know?"

"Just that… well…" I heard myself gulp. *How was it possible I was still keeping secrets from him?* "I found a photograph when I worked at the paper office of your mom and dad and… their mom at Scoops. They were all old high school friends."

He didn't say anything for a minute. He rolled onto his stomach and looked at his hands.

"Julian?"

He didn't look up, but I could hear his low voice. "And my parents… me…" He shook his head. "No wonder Will hates me."

His tone sent an ache through my chest, and I wanted to be with him so badly. "What they did is *not* your fault, and Will hates everybody. He even hates Jack and Lucy."

We didn't say anything for a few moments, and I decided to hold off on telling him what happened with Jack. He was already dealing with enough.

Instead, I tried to comfort him. "I wish I was there with you."

"Me too." That sunny optimism I loved was dampened. "I'm going to go now. Just feeling a little tired."

"Okay. Remember I love you."

He nodded. "Ditto."

The screen went dark, and I lay back on my bed.

What his parents had done was something he'd have to work through in his own way. I knew that, but I also knew so much more of the story than he did. I couldn't help wondering if it might help him to know everything the way I did.

Shaking my head, I sat up, planning to head to the kitchen when my phone buzzed. I picked it up to see a text from Jack.

JACK

Any chance you might check your peephole?

Frowning, I walked quickly to the door and looked out. There leaning against one of the narrow columns lining our front porch was Jack. He appeared very much back to normal and handsome as ever. I glanced down at the short, black mini-dress I was wearing, I shrugged and flipped the two locks open.

"What are you doing here?" I whispered, stepping out into the cool evening. Even though we never saw our aged neighbor, we still tried to be courteous.

Jack exhaled a little laugh. "It's nice to see you, too."

"Sorry. I mean, yes, how are you doing?"

"Much better, thanks." He pushed off the column and stepped toward me. "Have you had dinner yet?"

"No…" It was eight, but I'd been doing video editing since I got in, and then Julian called. "I was just going to grab a sandwich."

"Walk with me over to Ninja."

"Oh… I don't think so." Shaking my head, I looked down. "I mean, thanks, but no."

"Anna. It's the best sushi in New Orleans, and I owe you dinner."

"You don't owe me anything." That wasn't exactly true. I still felt like he owed me multiple apologies, but I was willing to let that slide. "And I don't think going to dinner with you is a good idea."

I couldn't help remembering how our last dinner date ended, in his Jeep parked out by the shore, making out until he pushed me away when I'd told him I was a virgin.

Most humiliating night of my life.

"It's a great idea," he insisted. "It'll give us that chance to talk. Come on. I insist."

He held out his elbow for me to take his arm, but I didn't. "I'll just walk beside you, thanks."

"So you'll go?"

"I am hungry."

I thought about the struggle Julian was having with his new family arrangement, and I thought about how I'd found Jack. I thought about my promise to Lucy, and I did want to know what it was he couldn't handle.

"I'll let you buy me dinner, but that's all. No drinks. Nothing else."

"Not a problem." He turned and we headed out into the street. We walked for a few moments in silence, until he broke it with a confession. "Not having drinks is actually my preference."

I glanced over at him. "Oh really?"

"Yeah. I've been talking to a counselor since that night, and I've agreed to cut back on the alcohol for the duration."

"Are you doing AA?"

"No, just seeing if I can grab the reins myself, get it back together."

I nodded. "I think that's good. You can do it."

He smiled, and we were quiet again.

It was more of a long stroll up Oak Street to the restaurant, but the weather was pleasant, and I liked walking the historic streets. We arrived at Ninja, and he held the door for me.

"Thanks," I said. "Parts of New Orleans have such cool neighborhoods. I love being here."

"You say that like you expect to leave soon."

"Oh, I guess you don't know. I've applied for Junior Year Abroad. One of my professors thinks I should do an internship with BBC radio."

The hostess led us to a booth, and we took seats across from each other.

"That's really cool." His eyebrows rose, and he seemed genuinely impressed. "You were always into your stories, but I gotta say, you're not meant for radio."

It was a compliment I'd heard before, but not from him. I didn't want compliments like that from him. Pushing my hands under my thighs, I leaned back on the vinyl-cushioned bench and didn't respond. A waiter appeared with sheets of paper, but Jack held up a hand.

"Mind if I order for us both?"

I raised my eyebrows and shrugged. "You know more about this place than I do."

"I'll have a Coke, and she'll have a…?"

"Diet Coke's fine."

The waiter nodded, and Jack continued. "And One Spicy California Roll and a Sushi Combination."

The man left quickly, and Jack returned to me. "It really is the best sushi."

"I'm sure," I nodded. "I've also heard Tru Burger's really good. I need to get out more around here."

"I can help you with that." He smiled and my stomach felt uncomfortable.

"I don't think—"

"Table that." He smiled and leaned back as a busboy put our drinks in front of us along with small plates and little dipping bowls.

I took a sip and studied the guy across from me. Dressed in a maroon long-sleeved shirt and jeans, he seemed completely changed from the person I'd taken to the hospital two weeks ago. Still, I knew better than to think whatever demons he'd been fighting could be shaken off that easily.

"You look different," I said. "Much better."

"Thanks. Apparently it helps my recovery that I used to run away from my problems." He poked his straw in his drink and didn't meet my eyes. His voice grew quieter. "Or sail away from them."

Chewing my lip, I studied his face. "I know your boat's still in Crystal Shores, but you can run."

He nodded. "And I'm bringing the boat over next time I go home."

I started to say "good idea," but the waiter reappeared with a large platter of sushi selections, including slices of deep red tuna or white-pink shrimp lying atop sticky white rice, avocado-filled

California roll, seaweed-wrapped rice with yellow or orange centers.

Jack snapped his chop sticks apart, but I unrolled the silverware at my place. "This looks delicious."

We both added portions of the pasty-green Wasabi to our small bowls followed by a healthy dose of soy sauce and mixed the two until it was smooth. Then he clipped a tuna roll and dipped it. I started with the California roll. The fresh avocado was one of my favorites.

"Thanks for dinner." I went for a shrimp roll after I'd finished the first piece. "This really is delicious."

"Thank you for helping me."

I took a bite of fresh shrimp and shook my head. "All I did was what anybody would've done."

He shook his head to argue as he popped one of the seaweed-wrapped pieces into his mouth, but it derailed whatever he was about to say. "Mm—try the maki. It's really good."

I couldn't help a laugh as I followed suit. A salty-fresh ocean was in my mouth. "Oh my gosh. I love it."

He smiled, and that old spark was back. I loved seeing him approaching normal, but I couldn't help feeling a creeping guilt about having dinner with him.

I told myself this wasn't a date—I insisted it was not. I was only letting him thank me for helping him, which was completely unnecessary.

I would tell Julian about this next time we talked. He'd understand. After I told him about what had led to Jack's feeling the need to thank me. *Ugh!* It was all getting tangled again.

"Why do you look like you got some bad fish?" Jack's blue eyes glowed as bright as they always had.

"What are we doing right now? I mean, what do you want from me? Why are we here?"

He sat back in the booth and his brow relaxed with his grin. "I gotta tell you. I really love College Anna. You're so… direct."

"You said you wanted to talk. Let's talk."

He nodded and looked down. "I'm trying to figure out what I want to say."

Then a voice I didn't want to hear interrupted us. "Wow! Anna and Jack. What's this all about? Rekindling?"

Summer stopped at the table, and I felt my eyes widen twice their normal size. Everything she'd said to me at the paper office that day, about how she was supposed to be with Jack and how I'd stolen him blared in my brain like an emergency warning siren.

There was no way she was cool with this, and of course she had a camera.

"Lean in and say cheese!" She snapped before I could protest.

"Hey, Summer." Jack's voice was friendly as he slid out and stood to give her a hug. I saw her melt a little. "Haven't seen you since Mardi Gras. Doing okay?"

"Oh, yeah." She sounded like a gushing teenager. "Just, you know, going to classes."

Jack sat back in the booth, and she managed to tear her moony gaze away from him to me. I saw her expression change even if Jack didn't, and my stomach sank like a lead balloon. This could *not* be good.

"What a funny coincidence we're all having dinner here." She smiled at me, but it didn't go to her eyes. *Shit.*

"Yeah..." I didn't know how to finish that sentence. I was sure Jack didn't want me talking about what had happened on the levee with everyone. Yet, what other reason could I give for us having dinner together? "We all had the same idea, I guess."

Maybe I could plant the idea that Jack and I just happened to bump into each other here?

"Oh, are you two *not* on a date?" Her voice was trying to sound innocent and failing.

"No!" I said quickly, cutting Jack off.

"That's okay. You guys lean in, and I'll get one more for the reunion."

"I'd rather not—" The words were still coming out of my mouth when she'd already snapped and was walking away.

"Enjoy your sushi. It's the best in New Orleans!"

She was gone, but I was completely winded. Two photos—*two!* I needed to get home and call Julian and tell him everything immediately.

"You look like you just robbed a bank." Jack was watching me, but I wasn't interested anymore in hearing his problems.

I wanted to get home before *I* had a problem. "I'm not really hungry anymore. I think I'll just go."

I started to slide out of the booth, but Jack was right with me. "Hang on! I'll walk you back. You don't need to be on the street by yourself at this hour."

"I can get an Uber." I was pushing my arms into the jacket I'd worn, but he was digging in his pocket, pulling out his wallet and counting out cash.

"I said I'd take you home. Just wait."

I didn't wait. I started for the door, leaving him to worry about the bill. I was out in the cool night in less than ten seconds. Checking my watch, it was only nine-thirty. Julian was an hour ahead of me on Eastern Time, but it still wasn't too late to call him and explain.

Jack was at my side again, but I ignored him. I kept looking up and down, then I started walking toward the street corner.

"You're heading in the wrong direction to get to your duplex." He touched my arm, but I pulled it away. "Anna. Let me walk you back."

I wouldn't look at him. I was furious, but I couldn't decide if it was at him or me. He'd only showed up and asked me to dinner. I was the one who'd said yes.

He tried again. "I'm not sure why Summer upset you so much,

but I wish you'd let me walk you home. I'd really hoped we could talk tonight."

That brought me around slightly. Turning to him, my shoulders dropped. "She tends to have a knack for showing up at the worst times."

"I wouldn't know. She's the little cousin of… of a friend of mine."

I didn't bother pointing out that *friend* was Casey Simpson. Who cared? "We have a history."

"I take it not a good one."

I wasn't going into it with him. "Let's get going."

We didn't talk much on the way back. My heels clicked on the sidewalks, and Jack seemed preoccupied. My thoughts were all focused on what I'd say to Julian when I called him in a few minutes, and as steps turned into blocks, it wasn't long before we were at my door.

"Thanks for dinner." I stretched out my hand to shake before I dashed inside. It still wasn't too late to call.

"Would you hang on for just a minute?"

"Jack, I—"

He stepped closer, and I stepped back. But the front door was at my back, and I couldn't go any further. He was so close to me, warm and familiar, and completely not what I wanted.

"That day… at the hospital, you asked me what this was."

I'd still wanted to know at the start of tonight—until the flash of Summer's camera put a spotlight on what I was doing.

"It's probably not my business." I wouldn't look up and meet his eyes. "It really never was."

He leaned a little closer and his voice dropped. "I'm sorry about that night at Fat Harry's, when I was drunk and came on too strong."

"Apology accepted." I was blinking fast. "You were dealing with things I didn't understand. Water under the bridge."

"These last few weeks I've thought a lot about who I used to be. Past mistakes and all. I'm sorry, Anna. I'm so sorry for how I treated you last year, how I hurt you. I was such an ass, and I took from you over and over because I needed you. I needed the way you used to look at me. It kept me going."

The desperation I felt caught on his words. It was exactly what I'd wanted him to say, all the apologies he owed me.

Cautiously, I blinked up to meet his eyes, so blue and open. "Why are you saying this now?"

He looked up and exhaled, but he was so close, his breath whispered across my cheek. "I've been thinking about everything, and through it all, one thing stands out so strong in my memory."

I studied his square jaw. His blonde hair, dark at the roots but light and shaggy around his collar. I remembered him so well.

Timidly urging him on, my voice was a hoarse whisper. "What?"

He looked down at me, and I felt paralyzed by his gaze. "You."

"Me?"

My brain was barking orders for me to go inside now, but I needed to hear this. I *had* to hear this.

His eyes traveled around my face in a longing way, and the vindication was so sweet. "You've given me a reason to try, and I'd give anything if you saw me through those old eyes again—like I was something worth having."

I swallowed the lump in my throat. "But… you are worth having."

We were standing close, and when he looked down, his expression was so serious. So determined.

"I miss this so much." He leaned forward and before I could even think, his mouth covered mine.

Lips parted, and our tongues met. My knees buckled, but his arm went around my waist holding me up.

He pressed me against the wall, catching my cheek with one hand. A little noise came from my throat as he kissed me deeper, and for a moment I was lost in the whirlwind of what was happening.

I knew what he wanted. I could feel it, but somehow, through it all, I managed to fight. I found my feet, and I grasped desperately at the strength I'd been so proud of.

My hands fumbled to his shoulders as I pushed him away. Our lips parted with a smack, and I covered my face.

"Oh my god." I cried in a whisper. "Oh my god!"

Tears splashed between my fingers onto my cheeks, and I was drowning in the tsunami of guilt over what I'd just let happen.

"Anna…" His voice was husky, and he was back, leaning in for more.

I ducked and spun out of his embrace. "You have to go. *Now!*"

I took a shuddering breath and wiped the tears away. *Oh, God. What had I done?*

"Are you crying?" The desire that was in his voice was now replaced with confusion. "What's wrong? Why are you crying?"

I didn't have time to explain what he should already know. "Goodnight, Jack."

Stepping through the door, I slammed it shut, turning the lock before I slid down to sitting. I put my forehead on my knees and sobbed.

Rachel had spent the night with Brad, so I wasn't sure how long I sat on the floor in front of the door crying. Jack had knocked a little while, begging me to open up and talk to him, but he finally went away. I leaned to my side and cried, staring at the crack under my door where the light was still on, where my laptop still sat on the bed, where I'd just talked to my love before I went out and betrayed him.

I couldn't move from all the emotions weighing me down. Of all the things I'd feared would come between us, me kissing Jack had never been one of them.

I hadn't been able to imagine any scenario that would lead to such an occurrence. How had I let this happen?

My phone buzzed in my pocket, and somehow I managed to lift it.

JULIAN

Sorry about tonight. I guess I'm still processing everything.

Closing my eyes, I could see his dark head. His blue eyes and sweet lips, the only lips I ever wanted pressed against mine. My stomach cramped harder.

ANNA

No worries. It's a lot to process. I can wait. I love you.

JULIAN

I love you. Night, Sunshine.

Fresh tears flooded my eyes, and I decided to wait. I'd tell him in person what happened, so he could see my face. So he could know no matter how badly I'd screwed up, I was so, so sorry.

I loved him so much, and I'd do whatever it took to prove it to him.

* * *

APRIL STORMS

Julian and I continued to FaceTime like always, and while the heaviness of what I'd done pressed down on me, I was able to put it away in my mind, waiting until we were together again to come clean.

I'd actually been able to forget about it. Spring break was getting closer, and apart from school, his family, me, our friends, were all preoccupied with the preparations and the buildup to Lucy's wedding.

It was only a week out, and while seeing him again, knowing what I had to say, filled me with dread, I was ready to get it out in the open. I was prepared for him to be angry. I was ready for him to shout or pull away or even say he needed a few days to process.

I wasn't ready for him to call.

I hit connect, and his face popped up on my screen. His expression was serious, but it had been for the last few weeks—ever since we'd talked about his mother and her relationship with his dad.

"One more week." I stretched out on the bed, finding it impossible to hide my smile. "This is the longest we've ever been apart. I expect you to be glued to my side the entire weekend."

He didn't respond, and I propped my head up to gaze at his sweet face. His blue eyes set off dramatically by his dark hair and tanned skin. So gorgeous.

"I'm changing my plans."

"Okay! You know I love all your ideas." Lucy was already dropping hints about how she wanted mine and Julian's wedding to be, and I loved every suggestion and theme she floated past me. "Are you ditching the tux? Let me guess. The wardrobe choice is now sexy rock-n-roll."

I remembered the night of his presentation at the National Athletic Center. I'd tried to go formal, and he'd shown up at my house one hundred percent Sex Pistols.

"Maybe. I never tell Renee how to dress."

"What?" A spear of ice drove down the center of my torso. I sat up confused, searching his face that was miles away, yet still right in front of me on the screen.

Was he joking? And if he was, did he realize how hurtful it was?

I tried to laugh. "I don't understand."

"Renee's in town. She's one of the bridesmaids. I thought she might like to be my date to the wedding."

Painful flares kept radiating through my stomach. "But… what about me?"

"What about you?"

My eyes were wide as they flew around his face. His expression was closed, giving nothing away. He had withdrawn, and his tone was informational, unemotional.

I managed to speak, even though my throat was closing. "I'm your date."

"I'm sure you'll be too busy keeping Jack company to notice."

"Keeping Jack…" The words died in my dry throat. He knew. "I'm not keeping Jack company. I'm keeping you company."

"That's not what I heard."

"What have you heard? What—"

"Save it, Anna." He flashed then. "I'm up here working my ass off, dealing with all this shit, and I'm believing the one thing I can count on is us. You."

"And you're absolutely right! You can count on me!"

"Until he shows up."

"No! It's not like that!" My voice rose. "Julian. You're wrong. I love you."

"Goodnight, Anna." The screen went black.

"NO!" I shrieked, gripping my laptop. I lifted it, but Rachel was somehow in the room, and she caught my hands.

"Whoa, don't throw it! You need this."

She took the computer out of my hands and placed it safely on my desk, but I slid to the floor as tears poured from my eyes. I kept going until I was lying on my side, knees clutched in my chest.

"Tell me what happened." She kneeled beside me, rubbing my back, but I was temporarily paralyzed.

My insides throbbed with the pain of his words. He'd found out. Somehow he'd found out before I'd had a chance to explain in person, and now he'd never listen. He thought I was hiding that first night. Two times was too many, and now he was pulling away.

Desperation pulled at my scalp so hard, my temples throbbed. The pressure of my headache made me want to vomit, but I crawled to my feet.

"I've got to go to Savannah." My voice was broken. "Tonight."

Rachel's brow pierced. "You're not going anywhere. Tell me what happened!"

"There's no time." Shaking my head, I started moving around the room grabbing clothes. "I have to talk to Julian. I have to make him understand."

"Anna!" She took the clothes out of my bag as quickly as I put them in. "All of Lucy's wedding events start in four days. You've got to go to class."

"I don't care about class. I don't care about anything…"

"Right now you don't." She caught my hand. "Listen to me. Okay, you had a fight. It sounds like a bad one, but you'll make up. Trust me, you will. You can't let school suffer in the meantime."

I blinked up, staring into her face as my insides slowly disintegrated. "I can't."

Tears were coming again, but she pulled me into a hug. "Yes, you can. Just be strong a little bit, and we'll all be together again by the end of the week."

* * *

LUCY'S WEDDING

Somehow I managed to get through the last few days of class, but I was the walking dead. Everything was a blur of noise and bodies, and I didn't care about any of it. My stomach was a lead weight, and each passing second ticked the vise of desperation tighter across my chest. Every breath was a silent prayer for Julian to please understand, please listen, please forgive me.

He wouldn't return my texts or pick up when I called. It was killing me.

At night I wore my ring and slept under my portrait, the placeholder one. I hoped that hundreds of miles away, he was looking at the one we shared. I hoped he saw the dragonflies, our hands bound together, and knew the truth—nothing could ever come between us.

Finally it was time to drive home. Rachel kept talking as we crossed the miles from New Orleans to Fairview, but I wasn't listening. I was counting down the hours until I'd see him again.

Since we weren't communicating, I didn't know when he'd be in town, but I planned to drive to Peninsula Avenue as soon as I got home and bang on the door until he saw me. I didn't expect his car not to be there.

He didn't come home.

At all of the pre-wedding events, Lucy was radiant and glowing, so happy. Every time she'd ask me about Julian, I would only smile and shrug, trying to make up some excuse that might sound plausible.

She had way too much on her plate this weekend because every time, she'd frown and let it go. Any other time, she'd have dragged me to a coffee-shop pow-wow.

So we had our wedding-party event, then we had rehearsal dinner. The bridesmaids, which included Summer and Renee, planned a bachelorette, but I made an excuse. I couldn't take any more questions from Lucy about where Julian was, and even worse, there was no way I was hanging out with Renee Barron all night if he really had asked her to be his date.

I spent the night home, alone. I wanted to call Gabi and get some friendly reassurance, but I was actually afraid she'd tell me it was my fault. I should've told him right away about Jack taking me to dinner and the kiss.

He was still dealing with the fallout of his dad's revelation, with realizing what his parents' affair had meant for his new siblings, how his creation had shredded their young lives. I didn't want to add to his stress, and I really wanted to be face to face, in person, when we talked, when I confessed and then begged for forgiveness.

It was all my stupid pride. Jack had finally said all the things I'd always wanted him to say. He'd finally validated all those times I'd taken him back, and I was such a stupid little girl, for a moment I'd lost track of what was most important—Julian.

Nothing else mattered.

Now he wasn't here, he wouldn't talk to me, and I had no way of knowing if he was even coming. Why was he staying away? He said he'd be at the wedding. He had to give me a chance to explain.

Lucy's wedding day was gorgeous. Spring break is hard to predict in South County—it can either be cold and rainy or sunny and breezy. This day was the latter. Flawless.

The ceremony was to take place on the large flagstone balcony that led off the downstairs living room. It was an open space that looked out over Bayou Saint John toward Evangeline. Since I was one of the bridesmaids, I'd arrived early to get ready and help Lucy with whatever she needed.

My hair was blown out straight, and the bubble-skirts on the coral bridesmaids dresses we all wore were thigh high. Each of us had the choice of strapless, one-shoulder strap, or two narrow straps. I went with the latter. Rachel had opted for the one-shoulder strap, but of course Renee went strapless. One swift pull and her top would be down, her stupid perfect boobs would pop out. I couldn't even let my mind go there.

Julian apparently had arrived during the night. I couldn't breathe when I pulled into the circular driveway and saw his car.

I'd have run into the house to tear the place apart until I found him if Summer hadn't intercepted me.

"Excited for the big day?" She was back to clueless voice. "Lucy's dress is so gorgeous. By the way, we missed you last night. Did you beg off so you could spend it with Julian?"

My mouth dropped open. I was about to say no, but I knew she'd ask why. I didn't want Julian's and my problem to be the focus of the day. Lucy and Robert were that.

Instead I shook my head. "No." I gently rubbed the front of my neck. "My throat's been so sore. I might have a virus, and I don't want to get Lucy sick on her wedding day."

"That would be the ultimate party pooper! Can you imagine? Sick on your honeymoon?"

Nodding, I touched my throat again as if it hurt. I wasn't lying. The sight of Julian's car had my neck muscles so tight, I was afraid I'd burst into tears at any moment. At least it was normal to cry at weddings.

We went inside, and all the girls were holding mimosas. Lucy hustled up to me in that gorgeous dress. It was off-white strapless and form-fitted all the way to the floor with a soft-white tulle overlay accented with tiny clusters of seed pearls. Her hair hung down her back in soft waves, and a slim silver headband accented with crystals would hold her veil. She was stunning. "Where have you been? I was sure we'd have morning coffee together since my little brother finally showed up!"

I could feel Renee's eyes burning into my back, so I continued the lie. "Sore throat," I whispered, touching the front of my neck.

"Oh no! How awful!" She started to hug me, but I pulled back waving as if to preserve her health. "Do you even want a mimosa?"

"Better not." I continued whispering.

"Darn." She air-kissed me and headed back to her seat in front of the mirror.

The other girls were at varying stages of readiness. I'd arrived dressed, so I didn't need to do anything. Instead, I went to where Rachel was finishing up her makeup and slipped between an armoire and her mirror, partially hidden.

"Love your hair like that." She gave me a quick glance and finished applying her mascara. "You're claiming sickness?"

She and I were the only ones who knew the real truth. Well, and possibly Renee if she was truly Julian's date. At this point, she hadn't made a move toward me. She was helping Lucy fasten the pins that would hold the delicate veil at the top of her head.

"I don't know where he is." My voice was low, as I tried to avoid notice. "He must've driven in last night, but he's either with the guys or in his room."

Rachel packed her makeup bag and glanced around. "Let's slip out. See what we can find."

Nodding, I followed her out the side door. Drinks were going around, and the other girls didn't seem to notice us leave.

The small room we were in was just off the balcony. When the wedding march began, Lucy would emerge from the glass French doors right into the aisle between the chairs. We were all expected to assemble at the front when the first piece of music began.

"There's Brad." Rachel took my arm and led me through the guests to where he stood with Jack.

I noticed Jack's eyebrows rise in my peripheral vision, but I didn't make eye contact.

"Hey, babe." Brad kissed his girlfriend when we approached. "You look hot. Hey, Anna."

I nodded, hoping he'd say something about Julian. He didn't. Any more of this pressure, and I was sure I'd lose it. More of the bridesmaids were spilling out onto the balcony area, and wedding guests were taking their seats.

Lucy had included Ms. LaSalle in her wedding arrangements, seating her where the mothers were traditionally placed. Mr. Kyser stood down front talking to her, and I could tell by his expression he was in heaven. Lucy's embrace of Julian's mother had gone a long way toward healing her relationship with her dad.

During the last few days, the sight of him smiling at his daughter and lavishing praise on her made me so happy, but it wasn't the sight I longed to see.

Once again, I turned and scanned the room, sweeping past the guests, past the columns of flowers, to the back and down front again. I was just checking the other side when a pair of blue eyes stopped my heart.

He was there, gorgeous in a tux, and standing with his back to a column that held more roses. He didn't acknowledge me. I wasn't sure if he even saw me, but just then my question about Renee was answered. She crossed the room quickly to where he stood and threw her arms around his neck. His hands held her waist, and my stomach cramped so hard, I had to find the nearest exit.

Tears were coming fast as I ran through into the enormous living room, taking the first door I saw. It was another room I'd never been in before. Elegantly decorated in sky blue and white with lace curtains.

Several pristine wood and silk chairs were arranged in half the space. Several end tables with Tiffany lamps on them were dotted throughout, and in the back corner near the window was a large piano. As far as I knew, no one in the family played, and I wondered why this room was designed like a private concert space.

I walked to the back and sat on the piano bench, propping my elbows on the closed keyboard. Tears spilled over from my eyes, but I tried to catch them with my fingertips. It was too early to be crying for the wedding, and my carefully applied makeup would be ruined. I had to get control of myself or everyone would know what had happened.

We'd broken up, and now Julian was inside with Renee. The

sight of her hanging on his arm like the green-eyed spider she'd always been magnified the pain beating in my chest.

"You look very beautiful today." Jack had followed me. He crossed the room at a leisurely pace and sat on the bench beside me with his back against the keyboard.

It didn't make any sense for me to push him away now, but I really didn't want to discuss it with anybody. So I tried to joke.

"I'd return the compliment, but you look great every day."

"Already crying for Lucy? I think A.J.'s going to work out after all."

"Robert." I corrected then shook my head. "I'm not crying for them. He's perfect for Lucy."

"So why the tears? My little brother getting you down again?"

I looked away and Jack handed me a small cloth. I glanced back and took it from him. "You had a hankie?"

"There was one on that little table." He pointed across the room.

"What is this place?"

"I guess our conservatory? Music room, maybe? From what I've been told, Mom was into all that kind of stuff when they were building."

"She had very refined tastes."

"Hm." Jack looked down. Then he grinned. "So if he's going to keep running back to Renee, you should start running back to me."

The words burned in my chest. "Is he with Renee?"

"Hell, I don't know. But she's always ready to play catch."

"I hate her."

He laughed out loud then. I winced at the noise, but I was glad he was laughing. It meant he was getting better. "Still holding out for him?"

I nodded.

"In that case, we could just what? Practice? Keep those pretty lips warm?"

My eyes narrowed. "You know me better than that."

"I'm just saying. If he's going to break up with you for kissing me, we should make it count."

"How did you know—"

"What else could he possibly be angry at you for?" He leaned in closer to my mouth, but I stood up and went to the window.

"Not everyone cries after I kiss them, you know."

I never did before Julian...

I looked back at his perfectly handsome face. "Lucy got a beautiful day for her wedding."

He stood and crossed the room to where I stood. I turned and looked out the window across the water, and he slid my hair back, kissing the base of my neck at the top of my shoulder. A charge moved down my back.

"Please stop." My voice was a whisper.

He smiled. "Just testing the waters."

"I'm not interested."

"Julian's an idiot."

My insides flashed. "You're one to talk. You broke up with me over a kiss."

He exhaled and looked out the window. "You had a problem picking sides, but it was more than that."

"No, it was just a kiss."

"Several kisses and you getting all steamed up about Renee and then spending the night in the hospital with him. Jesus, Anna. I didn't have to get hit over the head."

"I was committed to us."

"And you were in love with him. I didn't have time for that. Not that year."

I looked down. "I'm sorry."

It was strange to be talking about those days with all that had happened. He'd told me a lot since that day in the hospital, but I still didn't know what demons he'd been battling in New

Orleans. I know all of that year was wrapped up in whatever it was.

"Well, don't beat yourself up about it now." He pulled me into his arms. "I told you, I'm willing to give it another shot—"

I pushed back. "I'm still in love with him."

"He's an idiot."

"Stop saying that."

"It's the truth."

"I can always count on you to defend me." Julian's loud voice made me gasp.

I turned my back to the window, my heart thudding. *This was not what it looked like...* Julian wasn't smiling, and Jack slid his hands into his pockets, heading for the door.

"So, Jules," he said in passing, "where'd Renee get to?"

"I don't care." Julian hadn't taken his eyes from mine, and I was having difficulty breathing.

Jack chuckled. "In that case, I'll see if I can't find her."

He left the room, but all I could see was Julian.

Even without a smile, he was so handsome. I'd missed him so much. I would've done anything he said at that moment. Instead, he just walked to the window and stood beside me looking out.

"I'm sorry," he said. "I was listening."

I nodded, expecting as much.

"I never thought I'd agree with my brother."

"About what?" My voice was soft, cautious.

He glanced at me. "Renee really is always waiting around for me."

That wasn't what I expected. "Julian!" I started to turn away, but he caught my waist and pulled me into his arms.

"And you are so beautiful in that dress."

He leaned down to kiss me lightly on the lips, but I couldn't resist. I caught his cheeks and pulled him closer, opening my mouth. Longing pulsed through my chest so hard as he lifted his chin and kissed my forehead.

"Would you be my date to the wedding?" He breathed against my eyes.

They closed as my body vibrated with relief. "I-I thought you were asking Renee."

His voice was thick. "I couldn't do that. You're my angel."

"Oh, Julian." Two more tears hit my cheeks. "I'm so sorry I didn't tell you about Jack. I swear, I was just waiting for the right time to—"

"Hang on," he whispered, touching my lips.

I went silent, and that's when I noticed music playing outside. The first wedding song.

"I think we'd better get out there." His arms relaxed around me, and I hated to walk away before I'd told him everything.

Our eyes held each other's a moment, and all the time we'd been apart felt enormous between us. I hated that only one night was left before the break ended, but at least he wasn't angry… or at least he was holding me now.

He quickly slid his hands to my cheeks and kissed me once more. It was soft and gentle, and just when I thought he'd stop, he kissed me again. Was this forgiveness? Was he saying he understood?

Trying to speak made me realize I was panting. "You're not angry anymore?"

"I love you, Anna."

I blinked, and fresh tears dropped onto my cheeks. He touched them away with his thumbs.

"Don't cry. It's too early."

I turned my head and blotted my face with the handkerchief Jack had given me. "I need to explain what happened. I was going to explain as soon as we were together again—"

"We've got to get to the wedding. We'll talk after."

"I've missed you so much. I thought I'd die these last few days."

"I've missed you, too."

The look in his eyes was warm, but I could tell we still had a conversation ahead of us. He took my hand and slipped it through his arm, leading us back to join the guests. I was at his side, but I could feel it between us. We had more to say.

* * *

POST-WEDDING PROMISE

The wedding ceremony was intimate and touching and beautiful. Surrounded by roses and lilies, Lucy and Robert promised to guard each other's hearts both from outsiders and from their own carelessness.

They'd written their own vows, and as they said them, I remembered the days before they were together and how far Lucy had fallen. It had only taken one person to give her hope, to help her find her way back to standing, and from there she'd grown stronger and stronger—enough to embrace her father's mistakes and forgive them; enough to embrace her mother's best friend as a source of happiness for her family.

Lucy was the one to start the healing here, and it seemed she'd be the one to see it through to the end.

My eyes traveled down the line of groomsmen, past Robert's brother, skipping over Will, until I got to Jack. I studied his face, and the change was remarkable since that bad night when I'd found him. Something had given him hope, and while he wanted to say it was me, I chose to believe it was the counseling.

Perhaps they'd found the key to whatever it was he hadn't felt strong enough to face. Whatever he still hadn't told me about.

From there, my eyes moved to Julian, and of course, he was looking at me. Automatically, a little smile touched my lips, and the warmth of love filled my chest.

The minister had just gotten to the part of marriage and what it meant. Joining two lives, two becoming one, for better or worse...

He smiled back, and as we looked at each other, I dreamed of the day when we'd stand this way, making these promises to each other. We'd had a rough patch, sure, but it wasn't going to derail us. We were meant to be together, and it was just a matter of getting through the separation until we'd found a way to merge our future.

These thoughts were in my head when the minister instructed the groom to kiss his bride. A brief, passionate smooch later, and he introduced Mr. and Mrs. Robert Curtis. We all clapped, the guys pulled out confetti poppers, and the party was on.

The reception was held at the house, and while we'd been focusing on the ceremony, a team of caterers from Cobalt, an upscale restaurant on East End Beach, had set up the house for lunch. Only a small group had been invited to the wedding, but they'd thrown the doors open for the reception, and guests were already filing in. My parents were in the last row on the balcony seats, and Julian took my hand, leading me to them as soon as Lucy and Robert had left the area.

"I'm so glad to see you two holding hands again." Mom reached up and hugged Julian. "She's done nothing but lie on the couch all week."

"Mom!" I cried. "I went to Tamara's to get my hair straightened."

"And I saw her get up to eat a whole pint of ice cream," Dad added.

Julian glanced at me, and I gave him a sheepish grin before he pulled me close to his side. "This year's been harder than we planned."

Dad patted him on the shoulder. "You're doing great."

The photographer stuck her head in the door and called for the wedding party, so we said a quick goodbye.

For the next several minutes, we were pushed and pulled,

arranged and posed, until everyone was satisfied enough documenting had been done. At last we were free.

"Let's get a drink." Julian pulled me inside to where trays of champagne flutes were circulating along with clear platters of all sorts of hors d'oeuvres and finger foods. In the kitchen were chafing dishes of shrimp and grits, sausage and shrimp étouffée, and bland pasta for the finicky eaters.

I didn't care about any of it. I wanted to get alone with my guy as soon as possible, clear the air, be sure he understood and I was forgiven, and spend the rest of the afternoon and night making up for shortages. I was just about to suggest it when his parents approached, holding hands.

"Anna." Ms. LaSalle leaned forward and kissed my cheek. Her long brown hair was over one shoulder, and she wore a flattering beige sheath dress. "I wasn't sure I'd get to see you this trip."

"It's been pretty hectic, but that's weddings," I said, and she smiled.

Mr. Kyser released her hand and touched his son's shoulder. "I've had some contact with that project we're working on in the Caribbean. I wonder if I might discuss it with you."

"Oh…" Julian's eyes darted to mine, but I nodded, hoping it would be a fast discussion. "Okay."

The men left, and Ms. LaSalle put her hand through the crook of my arm. Her face was close to my ear as she spoke. "I've never had a chance to thank you."

You could've knocked me over with a feather. "Thank me?" I stepped around to face her. "Are you saying…?"

"This time I've had with Lucy has been… better than I hoped it would be. I didn't believe you when you said she'd understand, but she did."

"Jack won't be difficult. But Will—"

"He'll be more of an issue. It's understandable. He was old enough to know what he lost."

We'd moved to a private area of the house, and it struck me

that Mr. Kyser's need to talk to Julian might've actually been a cover for his mother's desire to speak to me.

"I don't know if I'll ever understand Will." I took a small sip of the champagne Julian had handed me. "Or like him."

His mother's smile softened her face. "I've been given so much more than I ever had a right to dream possible, I can only believe it will get better."

"I hope it does."

"I like you with Julian very much. The two of you remind me so much of…" She took a deep breath. Then she shook her head. "But it was wrong. We weren't supposed to have that."

I stepped to her. "Your past has been paid for—so many times and for years and years. They need you now. Lucy needs you."

Her eyes glistened when she looked at me again. "She should've been here."

My eyes flooded at her words, and I dropped my chin. I couldn't speak, but she continued.

"Lucy looked so much like Meg today, and I remember their wedding day so well."

I sniffed, and she touched my shoulder. "I'm sorry."

Wiping my eyes roughly, I shook my head. "No, I'm sorry. It's been an emotional day."

"I hope you'll understand that I know." She looked at me pleading. "I'm not letting myself off the hook. She should have been here."

Chewing my lip, I studied my hands clasped in front of me, searching for the right words.

"It's true." I took a deep breath. What I was about to say could go either way. "But she made that choice. She drove the car drunk, and she… she didn't think about how it could mean she'd miss this day."

My whole body was tense. I wasn't trying to disparage Lucy's mom, but I had to find a way to keep the healing that had started in this house moving forward.

Ms. LaSalle had to find a way through her guilt.

She looked down and sniffed. "She wouldn't have done it if I hadn't broken her heart. If I hadn't stolen her dreams."

"She was a grown woman. She made her choices." Blinking quickly, I dared to peek up at her, hoping she wouldn't withdraw again.

She didn't. She only nodded and touched her fingers to her eyes. "I'm sure on some level you're right. But I'll never be able to let her go."

"She was your best friend." Images of Gabi and me filled my mind, and I couldn't even think of going through what Julian's mother had with her best friend. I couldn't even imagine how it might be possible. "It's right for you to carry her memory. But I think… I think it's also right for you to live the life you have."

We were quiet for several long moments. She walked slowly to one of the windows and looked out at the water. "Thank you. Again."

Searching my mind for anything to say, all I came back with was the obvious. "You're welcome."

She looked over her shoulder and gave me a sad smile. "You'd better find Julian. You don't have much time together."

Quietly, I nodded and left her, and sure enough, my date was not with his father when I emerged from the small room. He was hanging around with my parents, smiling and eating boiled Gulf shrimp.

They were chatting as always in the easy way they did, and I couldn't help agreeing with him. My home life was worlds different from his.

"Worked out the details in the Caribbean?" I teased, taking a piece of shrimp.

"Anna!" Mom held an arm out to me. "Come take your lovely boyfriend away and catch up."

"Mom?" I blinked at her, wondering how many champagnes she'd drunk.

I was pretty certain her idea of "catching up" meant hugs and kisses… at least I hoped it did. Otherwise, it was just too weird.

"We'll be taking off soon." Dad leaned forward and pecked my cheek. "If you have too much fun, just spend the night. I won't fuss."

"Thanks, Dad."

They walked away, and I was left facing my boyfriend. He'd lost the tie and cummerbund, and he stood in front of me, top button undone, hair shaggy around his eyes, looking absolutely scrumptious.

"I think we should follow my mom's orders."

He smiled, but it wasn't the usual full-on beam I typically got. We still needed to talk, and I knew it. I took the hand he held out to me and followed him through the enormous living area to the kitchen through the small hallway and mudroom out to the circular drive.

Stopping at his car, he held both my hands. "How would you feel if we ditched this place and went surfing?"

The sky was clear blue and while it was breezy, it wasn't frigid. The water most likely was, but I liked the thought of getting away to our beach with him.

"I'd love it."

"Grab a suit and meet me at Mom's old place!"

Catching his chin, I stepped forward and kissed him briefly. "Be there in less than twenty."

The surf was rough for a day without storms, and as I anticipated, the water was frigid. It didn't stop Julian from charging into the pounding white breakers—of course, he was wearing a long-sleeved rash guard and board shorts.

I wore my black one-piece, but I stayed in my green hoodie and lounge pants, wrapped in my towel on the shore.

Even with the cool breeze, sitting on the white sand, watching the crystal-blue waters rush in and out soothed me. Somehow, it always put every problem into perspective, as if the enormity of the ocean made my worries feel small.

We were quiet when I arrived at the cottage on Crystal Shores Boulevard. Julian was ready to go, waiting with his board in the garage, but I decided then to sit it out today.

So we walked the few short blocks to the Gulf, and I stopped as he kept going. I didn't know what he wanted to say to me or when he'd say it. Watching him ride in on the curling waters and then paddle back out, I was sure our current misunderstanding would be sorted.

The sun was slowly dropping in the west, turning into a deep, red-orange display of heat when he finally came in for good. His towel was beside me, and he dropped the board on the other side of where I sat. He lay on his stomach with his elbows bent looking out, noticeably less tense.

"Nothing replaces the way this feels." I said, following his gaze out to the dark blue water at the horizon.

"I miss it. When I'm in Savannah, I can take a break and run down to the water, but it's not like this."

"You don't have your board."

He didn't answer, and I took a chance to reach out and hold his hand. He didn't pull away, so I laced our fingers. "I wish we had another day."

Dropping his chin, he turned our hands so mine was on top, then he traced a line down the back of it. "I wasn't sure I was coming home at all."

Pain twisted in my chest, and I tightened my grip on him. "I'm so sorry I didn't tell you. The time never seemed right, and then I decided to wait until we were together again—"

"And then it would've been some other reason." He pulled his hand away and sat up, but I couldn't let him get angry again, not after the way we'd been earlier. "It's the second time it's happened, Anna. I thought we'd agreed—no secrets."

"Isn't there anything I can say that will make you forgive me?" My voice broke, and I could feel the tears heating my eyes. "Just tell me what you need to hear, and I'll say it. I love you, Julian."

His blue eyes cut to mine, and for a half-second I saw him soften, but the anger wasn't far gone.

"I just want you to be honest with me. How do you think I feel when people ask me if we've broken up—if you're back with Jack? Shit, Anna, of all the people you could go to dinner with."

"Who asked you that?"

"It doesn't matter. What matters is that you didn't tell me."

"It matters to me." I had a good idea who'd be keeping up with him, asking if we'd broken up, and her name was Renee Barron.

Nothing had changed since high school. She was still making plays for him just like always.

We sat for a few moments longer in silence until he pushed up and held his hand to me. "Come on. We don't have a lot of time left."

Squinting up at him, I slowly put my hand in his and allowed him to pull me to my feet. The board was under his arm, and we walked back, hand in hand, until we were at the garage again. I waited while he stowed the board and then we went inside the dark, quiet house.

"So tell me now. Why were you with him? Why did you kiss him?"

"It wasn't like that! He was talking and… he kissed me." I had to back up. It wouldn't make sense if he didn't know about Jack's hospital visit or me finding him on the park bench. It was a long story, and I hated wasting our precious time on it. Still, I'd do anything at this point.

"Remember how I told you he'd been drinking a lot, something was wrong, but I didn't know what it was? I still don't, and that night—"

"He just showed up at your house and kissed you? Was he drunk then?"

"No…"

"Then what happened?"

"I've told you about my Saturday morning ritual? How I like to go down to the Quarter?"

Julian nodded, and I rubbed my forehead. I hesitated a moment, wondering if Jack wouldn't want me to tell his newfound half-brother the extent of his problems. It didn't matter. He'd lost that right when he'd stolen that kiss.

"About a month ago, I found him there on a bench. He was incoherent, almost freezing, and completely drunk."

That got Julian's attention. His brow lined. "What are you saying?"

"He almost died. I called EMS and Lucy, and I took him to the hospital. They got his vitals under control, and Lucy finally showed up. That's where I left him."

"Why didn't you tell me this?" Julian shook his head and paced the room. "It's things like that you need to tell me about."

"I didn't know if it was fair to tell anyone. I didn't know if he might want to keep that problem in the family."

"I am his family, Anna."

My lips twisted into a frown. "That's very new, and I guess I just… I didn't want to talk about it. But I'm telling you now!"

"After I've spent a month thinking the worst."

I took a deep breath and sank onto the couch. "It's only been a week."

He walked over and sank on the couch beside me. "Longest week of my life."

My eyes rose to his, and at last I could see the pain in them. He was opening to me again, and relief hit me so hard, I dove forward into his arms.

"Oh, Julian. Last week, he just showed up wanting to buy me sushi. He said it was to thank me, and he wanted to tell me why it had happened. Only, he never did. Then when he walked me home, he… he said a lot of things. He apologized for how he'd been in high school, and then he just... kissed me." Saying it out loud flooded my body with shame, but I had to keep going. "I pushed him away. I locked the door. I actually cried."

Holding him around the torso, I could feel the slight relaxation of his body. "I heard that part before the wedding. I'm sure that was a nice buzz-kill. Why did you?"

For a while I only held him, breathing deep of the fresh scent of the ocean always surrounding him. "I'm not sure. I was stunned, and his apology... well, it was something I'd needed to hear for a long time. But more than that, it wasn't *you* kissing me."

His arms were around me, and for the first time in days, the knot of fear in my chest released. I was able to hold him; he was here with me.

Lifting my chin, I found his lips, the ones I *did* want to kiss. No tears, only rising heat that neither of us were able to deny any longer. We quickly found a way to fulfill the shortage, to lose the swimsuits and come together until I was holding him, my arms wrapped around his neck, my legs straddling his sides as he sat on the couch.

We were both breathing heavily, and I held him, my cheek against his. "Please say this means you forgive me." My voice was thick from nearly crying and desperation and making up.

I felt his cheek move just before his warm lips pressed against my bare shoulder. "I do. I already had after I overheard your conversation earlier. It's just hard to be away and not see you for so long, and then to hear that."

Relief, happiness, all of it surged through me. I leaned back to catch his face in my hands and lifted it so I could kiss each of his eyes, his nose, his lips. "It's the worst thing in the world, but I promise. I will never do that to you again. I won't put myself in a position to be alone with him. I won't make you worry or doubt me or even feel that way ever again."

He took a deep breath and then smiled a little. "You don't have to say that."

"I know, but I am saying it. I love you too much."

Moving me to the side, he jerked his shorts loosely up his hips before going to the kitchen. "I'm starving." He peered into the refrigerator then shook his head. "Mom must never stay here anymore. We'll have to order in or go somewhere."

I pulled the hoodie over my shoulders and zipped it up. "Order in. That way we don't have to leave." Walking over to him, I slid my fingers over the skin of his waist, causing him to rest his forehead against mine.

"I like the way you think."

Thirty minutes later, pizza and beer were spread all over the table. We'd ordered sausage, cheese, and Hawaiian. I didn't care for pineapple on pizza, but Julian loved it.

We sat on the floor in the living room around the coffee table with the television on low as we caught up on the last few weeks.

"The last time we talked, you were kind of upset about your parents." I managed around a bite of cheesy-tomatoey-goodness. "Is that any better?"

He shrugged, picking off a bright yellow cube of fruit and popping it into his mouth. "You've seen how these guys are. They don't talk. It's all work, all the time. Dad's cool and Lucy's great. But I don't ever hear from Jack, and well, I'm not sure I want to hear from Will."

My nose wrinkled. "He's just a big bully. Lucy was right when she said that."

"I'll have to figure him out, though. I want to get more involved with what's going on here."

"You deserve to be a part of it." Placing my slice down on the plate, I thought about what it meant if he got more involved with his dad. "So you're going to pursue Brad's plan?"

His lips poked out a moment before he answered. "I haven't officially committed to anything, but he's making really great points. It's our heritage, and with his business and engineering degree and my business and architecture work, why not get the old ball rolling again? Will's still adjusting to the idea of me, but Brad says he's been trying to jumpstart operations for years."

"And your dad pulled you aside today to talk about the Caribbean. It sounds like you're fitting right in."

He crawled over to where I sat and rested his arm on the table. "Why does that make you sad?" Reaching out, he touched my cheek, which I leaned into him.

"It doesn't make me sad. It just means you'll be here. This will be your permanent residence."

"That's okay, though, right? We love it here."

I only nodded. I couldn't agree more about how much I loved it here. I also couldn't forget about JYA and what might happen with my career path. What kind of choice I might have to make between the man I loved and my dreams for my future.

He studied my troubled expression before changing his statement to a question. "We do love it here, don't we?"

"Of course. It's home." I blinked up at him.

His earnest expression, his blue eyes, shiny dark hair, and full lips made me want to forget these hard questions. We only had a few hours left, and I only wanted to spend them in his arms.

I stretched up and covered his mouth with mine, the sweet-tart flavor of pineapple touching my tongue with his, and that's exactly what we did.

* * *

LABYRINTH

After spring break, the days leading up to summer hung over everything like a giant countdown clock.

I tried to focus on my Algiers project and not think about it, but since I'd done much of the B-roll, the background shots and setting, the other two members of my group were handling man-on-the-street interviews and voiceovers. I wrote the narrations they read, but once that was done, my part was over.

So I developed a new habit. I started walking through Audubon Park every day. It was steps from campus and similar to Central Park in New York—an enormous rectangle of green in the middle of a bustling city. But unlike Central Park, Audubon was absolutely magical. I discovered it by accident when I was researching sites in Algiers, because it was purchased by the city in the 1800s.

It had the typical, ruined statues and quatrefoil-shaped fountains, but what made it feel enchanted were the rows of enormous, ancient live-oak trees. Some were as wide as six adult men, and in some places, their huge roots—bigger than branches—wrapped over the ground like prehistoric tentacles.

The actual branches stretched out for several feet until they drooped down, almost touching the earth. It all formed a dark-green canopy, and on foggy morning walks, I felt certain the spirits of the past walked alongside me.

One tree was actually called the Tree of Life, and it was incredible, with those same branches and an enormous, undulating trunk.

The park also had a zoo, a carousel, and a vast, green lake that stretched through the center with arching bridges. After the hurricane, an enormous mosaic of small, square bricks was constructed in a circular pattern to form a labyrinth. It was a meditation path that visitors were supposed to follow without question, with only trust, until they found healing. So far, I'd only looked at it, wondering if it actually worked.

Each week, I spent a few days there, trying to find peace with the future, with the decisions that were coming.

It was where I ran into Jack again on a rare, cool April evening.

I was by the pond, sitting on a root of the Tree of Life,

studying the six branches and wondering how it had gotten its name.

"It's creepy." His voice startled me at first. "But I guess it's beautiful, too."

I stood and dusted my hands, thinking of my promise to Julian and looking for a way to excuse myself politely. "I think it's more the base, how all the roots seem to be spilling toward us like a bark waterfall."

Trying not to be obvious, I backed away. When I'd promised never to be alone with Jack again, I hadn't counted on accidentally bumping into him.

He laughed quietly. "I hadn't thought of it that way, but that's exactly what it's like. A bark waterfall spilling toward us from hundreds of years ago."

I frowned up at him. "You're feeling poetic tonight?"

"I guess." He was dressed in the usual, khaki pants and a chambray oxford untucked. His light blonde hair was messy over his forehead, and I remembered always sliding those bangs to the side.

By contrast, I was dressed in black yoga pants and a tank, with my old green hoodie and sketchers. Occasionally, I joined the joggers along the path, but I was not a jogger—I walked.

"Well, I should get exercising. It was funny running into you here." Then I decided to tease a little as I left. "Almost like you were following me."

"I was." His quiet answer momentarily snared me.

"You were?"

"Sort of. I've started running again."

My brow creased. "That's good, but I don't see the connection."

"I'm getting back to the things that helped me." He put his hands in his front pockets and started walking slowly. Cautiously, I followed him. "I was out here a few weeks ago and I saw you, then I saw you again last week."

"It's like therapy, I guess. When we were back in Fairview, sitting by the shore used to help me clear my head. I just found this place, and at certain times of the day, it feels magical."

"Magical." He'd almost said it with me. "I agree."

I looked around at the dying light and the lamps flickering on and thought how this was one of those times. We were at the Labyrinth, and he went to the large round mosaic. I watched as he slowly followed the pattern, hands still in his pockets.

"So you didn't really follow me," I said, remembering I needed to leave now. "You just guessed that I'd be here."

"No, I followed you."

Again, that stopped me. "Why?"

He turned to face me. "I needed a guinea pig, and you're the perfect person for the job."

I stood at the edge of the huge round monument, and I thought of mice in mazes. "If you're trying to say something, you're going to have to stop talking in riddles, because I've got to go."

With slow, measured steps he followed his own path to where I stood, stopping directly in front of me. "I'm leaving the family business. I'm not working with Dad anymore. I might not even stay in New Orleans."

My mouth had dropped open as he spoke, so I closed it. His brow was creased, but as it all came out, I could see the invisible weight lifting.

"What will you do?"

"I'm going to study medicine." He waited for me to say anything, but I didn't. "That doesn't shock you?"

"Is it supposed to?"

"I expected you to say something about it being random or out of left field or too radical of a shift." Shaking his head, he pivoted and slowly started the path of the stones again. "I'm prepared for everyone to say that."

"But…" My mind traveled across the miles and the years to a journal I'd read, his mother's.

He didn't know what it said, and he didn't know how much I knew about his family. I couldn't open that can of worms, so I tried to approach it a different way.

"Why would they think it was random? I mean, sure, your dad's into development and business, but you have other relatives. Are any of them… doctors?"

He shrugged. "We never see other relatives. Neither of my parents had siblings, Dad's dad never comes around. I think he was a rancher."

"Horses." I nodded, watching his feet pause on the meditative stones.

"How did you know that?"

"Oh!" My bottom lip caught between my teeth. *Think fast.* "You remember that story I did about your dad for the bicentennial series? I found it when I was doing my research."

"I'd forgotten about that." He took another step, and I had a brain flash.

"There was more… I'm surprised you don't know this, but your maternal grandfather was a surgeon. He was kind of a big wig at the hospital in Fairview."

Jack spun on his heels and faced me. Then he walked to me quickly and caught me by the shoulders. "What did you just say?"

His expression was such a mixture of excitement and relief, my own stomach fluttered. "He was! He even had a wing in the hospital named after him. I can't believe you don't know this."

He pulled me fast into a big hug then just as fast, he released me and walked out to the center of the labyrinth.

Once he got there, he turned and headed back, pacing. "Dad never said a word about him. I got the idea they didn't get along."

"But you lived with your grandmother. She didn't have any pictures of him or talk to you about him?"

Blue eyes, relieved and full of hope met mine. His expression was so changed, it was like nothing I'd ever seen as long as I'd known him. He was inspired.

"Nobody told us anything!"

They were the forgotten ones. When Meg Weaver died, her little body wrapped around the light pole in a tangle of metal and car parts, she didn't just take the loving mother out of their house, she took their history.

Bill Kyser had completely closed himself off from them, and only now did I realize the extent of the damage.

I walked out into the swirling paths to where he stood and caught his hands. "It's not random or out of left field. It's perfectly normal for you to be interested in medicine. It's in your genes."

For once, it seemed I'd managed to say the exact right thing at the right time. I saw the change in him in the pale, evening light. He was released, and all the questions were answered, puzzle pieces clicked into place.

"Why didn't I think to make you my guinea pig before?" He smiled that gorgeous smile that had stopped everything almost two years ago when he'd walked into my English class.

"I think you did. At least, not in a way that was healthy." Memories of everything he'd said that night after our sushi dinner trickled through my mind.

"We'll have to put an end to that." His tone was authoritative. "If I'm going to be a doctor, only healthy choices are allowed."

I laughed. "You're going to be a wonderful doctor. I can see patients lining up for miles to see you. Majority females, of course, and most perfectly healthy."

"Miss Sanders, are you implying my patients would be dishonest?"

"Once the word gets out you're a doctor, yes. I have a feeling there will be many healthy ladies feeling the need for medical treatment."

He laughed with me, and I looked down. Night had settled in

completely, and I needed to go. "I'm heading home. Thanks for telling me, for trusting me with this."

"Thanks for telling me what you knew. I don't feel like a freak now."

"You're not a freak."

He walked with me along the wide path that ran through the park, back in the direction of my duplex. His hands were still in his pockets; my arms were crossed over my stomach. I'd planned to walk home alone, but I couldn't think of a way to ditch him. Not after that confession.

"I was so afraid to tell him," Jack mused. "He's always made such a big deal about how I would finish school and come back to work with him."

"Maybe your dad wanted you to feel like you had a place?"

"It didn't feel that way. It felt like an order. That was what I was going to do. Work with him, work with Will, sit in that box and stare at building plans all day. I was completely trapped, and I didn't see any way out of it."

We were on Oak Street, passing neighborhood businesses and restaurants or bars with music filling the background.

"Most people would look at you and think you had everything you ever wanted."

"Trapped in that house?"

"You're not trapped." We'd finally reached my place. "And I predict you'll be happily surprised by your dad's response to your change of plans."

His brow relaxed and he stepped forward to pull me into a grateful hug. My body was tense, but I patted him back, taking a deep breath of his soapy-citrus smell. He was the former boy of my dreams, now making the transition into a man.

"Thank you." He whispered into my hair.

I stepped back, putting several feet between us. "You're welcome." Then I smiled. "Goodnight."

* * *

OPPORTUNITY OF A LIFETIME

My head was a whirlwind of different thoughts as I stripped out of my workout clothes and hopped into the shower.

Jack wanted to be a doctor. He was just like Dr. Weaver.

Ms. LaSalle had said it to Mr. Kyser last year as we waited through the night after Julian's accident. She predicted it then, and Mr. Kyser dismissed her correlation out of hand.

Back then, if anyone had suggested Jack might do anything but follow in his oldest brother's footsteps, in his father's footsteps, into the family business, Mr. Kyser would have squashed that notion.

Julian had changed all of that.

Julian's sudden, unexpected fascination with his father's work had given Mr. Kyser the heir he wanted and had taken Jack off a career path that had never made him happy.

It all made sense—every bit of it. Why he'd acted so strangely toward me, why he'd slowly spiraled into self-destructive behavior year after year he spent in college pursuing a life that would make him miserable.

The creation of Julian might have hurt his siblings in the beginning, but now, it was helping them. He was making life better, for Jack at least.

I wanted to grab my laptop and tell Julian all of these things, but the minute I stepped out of my room dressed, Rachel cut me off. She was working on a mock debate for one of her prelaw classes, and she begged me to be her test jury—just for an hour or two. I glanced at the clock. It would still be early enough to tell Julian everything tonight, after I helped her, so I agreed.

As she paced the floor back and forth in our living room, spelling out the facts of her case, I realized the facts of my own case. My epiphany was courtesy the three journals Mr. Kyser had entrusted me with two Christmases ago. I'd promised him then I wouldn't tell anyone what they contained, and if I started connecting all the dots now, I'd have to break that promise.

"Anna!" Rachel stopped pacing and was now facing me with both hands on her hips. "You're not listening. I need your help!"

"Sorry," I said, shaking my head. I'd sort out how much I *didn't* care anymore about the ridiculous promises Julian's parents had used to control me later. "Please continue. I'm all ears."

"And curls." She giggled and then cleared her throat. Her voice turned immediately back to professional, firm. "As I was saying…"

Rachel continued working out the kinks in her debate, while I made a dinner of turkey sandwich and Funyuns. I'd just flopped down on the couch again when my phone buzzed with a text from Julian.

JULIAN

Where are you?

I smiled, instantly seeing his sweet face.

ANNA

On the couch. Listening to Rachel pontificating.

JULIAN

Pontificating. College Anna uses v big words.

ANNA

College Anna is v smart, haven't you heard?

JULIAN

That's the rumor.

"Anna! Stop texting with Julian." Rachel's hands were back on her hips.

ANNA

College Rachel is also v bossy. Thinks I know about legal issues.

JULIAN

Should be illegal.

ANNA

What are the legalities of being forced to listen against my will?

JULIAN

What are the legalities of keeping secrets?

That made my forehead crease. I knew he wasn't still angry about the kiss… what could he be talking about?

ANNA

Statute of Limitations might apply.

JULIAN

Not in this case. The crime has just been committed.

Maybe he was talking about something else? His parents?

ANNA

Counsel needs more information to make an educated decision.

"Seriously, Anna."

ANNA

Have to go. College Rachel v demanda. Love you!

JULIAN

To be continued.

I couldn't help a little frown at his strange line of texting and lack of love or kisses at signoff, but Rachel insisted. I temporarily forgot about Julian's mood and the time as I attempted to give her feedback.

Rachel and I worked until after midnight, and my short texting session with Julian had distracted me from my need to call him. I would do it immediately after class, even though I was completely groggy. Still, my physical exhaustion didn't stop Summer.

"Hey, Anna. You look tired. Hot Thursday-night party?" She sat in the chair next to mine, fiddling with her camera.

For half a second I almost ignored her altogether, but I didn't. "Rachel had a debate today. I helped her prep." *As if it's any of your business*, I added in my head.

She clearly missed my tone. "Have you ever looked at the houses around campus?"

My brow creased at her random question. "A little. Why?"

"There's this enormous mansion on St. Charles near Audubon Park. One of them looks like Charlotte's house in *The Princess and the Frog*, don't you think?"

"The white one?" I really wasn't interested in chatting about Disney princess films. "I hadn't thought of it, but they could've used it as the model."

"I was walking around sight-seeing, and then I went into the park. Talk about photo ops! Have you been there? I need to go back with my camera."

Glad for once she was giving me the heads up. "I've walked through it a few times. You should check out the Tree of Life, and the Labyrinth they built after Hurricane Katrina."

"I will!" She was so excited, but I was sad that my magical little refuge was no longer private.

Oh, well, I sighed internally, it's not like it ever really was.

Dr. Arati entered the room and called me to her desk. I wandered up, my mind distracted by Summer tromping through all my formerly sacred spaces with her stupid camera.

"I'm very pleased with your work on the Algiers project. Your location shots show a real eye for framing. If your writing wasn't so strong, I'd suggest switching focus."

Her praise was always so specific, I was almost embarrassed. "Thank you. I guess it's because of my boyfriend."

"Ah, yes. The one who met you in the hall." She nodded. I was about to correct her, but she continued speaking. "I'm afraid you have some bad news for him. Unless he's an English major. They do have a Shakespeare program abroad…"

It took me a second to realize what she was saying. Then my breath disappeared in a whoosh. "Did I get—"

"Accepted for JYA? As a matter of fact, you did. My friend Liam is eager to welcome his new intern at the *BBC World News*."

My mouth dropped open, and I experienced the strangest twist of emotions. I wanted to jump up and down and scream, and at the same time, I wanted to drop to my knees, crawl under the desk, and cry.

"Well, don't stand there gaping," my professor laughed. "Say something!"

My chest was so tight. "I can't breathe…"

Her black eyes danced. "Are you hyperventilating? Shall I send one of the boys to fetch a bag?"

"Dr. Arati… I-I don't know what to say!"

"Say you're headed to London! Say you're on your way to joining one of the top teams in the news radio circuit."

Summer ran up behind me then and started talking way too loud. "Anna! Oh my god, Anna! You got it! You're going to London!"

My knees were weak, and I needed to sit down. More than that, I needed to get out of here and go back to the duplex and sit in my room for a bit. I didn't like being shocked with enormous, life-changing opportunities in front of everyone. It was like last year when I got the scholarship to come to this school.

I needed a minute. I needed to catch my breath and think about what my professor was saying. I was happy, of course I was happy, but I also felt like as soon as I got comfortable, got my feet under me, something new and huge swept in like a tsunami and changed everything.

I needed to swim to the side, get out of this rip tide of emotions, calm down and think about everything.

"Would it be okay if I just go home? I-I just need to think—"

"Of course." Dr. Arati's lips pressed into a proud smile. "Take a break and consider this wonderful news. We can talk about it when you're ready."

"Thank you." I nodded, going to the door. "I'm sorry."

"Don't apologize. It's an exciting thing, and I'm sure a little overwhelming. Take your time."

I nodded and headed out the door, down the quiet hall, and out into the hot, sticky air. It was uncomfortable, and the sun was too bright. I hurried home and went straight to my bedroom, closing the door and dropping my book bag onto the floor. Then I went around the bed to the other side facing the wall and sat all the way at the head, leaning against the wainscoting, knees bent, pressing my face against my hands.

Deep breaths, in and out...

I'd done it.

I'd gotten another huge opportunity that would drag me across the ocean as far as I could possibly get from Julian.

My chest squeezed and my throat ached, but I didn't cry. I only sat, every muscle tense, trying to think of what a great opportunity this was. An opportunity of a lifetime.

I tried to remember what Julian kept saying, the separation was only for a little while. We would do our thing, lay the groundwork on our futures, and then we'd start our life together. Only, why did the groundwork keep taking us farther apart?

Still, our love was solid, and that wasn't changing. We were growing up, but it didn't mean growing apart. Right?

I wanted to go to Savannah, but I couldn't drive like this. I wanted his arms around me, but like always, he was so far away.

So I sat in the growing darkness. I didn't want to move, speak, or even leave this quiet room.

So I didn't.

* * *

COMING UNDONE

I realized I'd fallen asleep when my buzzing phone woke me. Lifting a heavy arm to grab it off my nightstand, I saw five missed texts from Julian. They all asked where I was, and the final one said,

JULIAN

Can you FaceTime?

I quickly pushed myself up and texted back.

ANNA

Yes!

My laptop was in my bookbag, so I pulled it out and quickly booted it up. It was buzzing as soon as the screen lit up. I clicked on the icon, and there he was, eighteen inches across, blue eyes blinking at me. Tears finally sprang to my eyes.

"Where have you been? I've been texting all afternoon." His expression was concerned, and I swallowed the thickness in my throat.

"Sorry. I fell asleep when I got in. Rachel kept me up pretty late last night."

His lips twitched, and his eyes seemed to travel around my face. "Is that all?"

"Yeah, I didn't even hear my phone, that's all. I'm sorry."

"What are you doing this weekend?"

I took a quick look at his background. The last time he'd asked me that, he'd shown up at my door, and the longing for a repeat of that scenario hit me so hard, my stomach hurt. But he was in his room in Savannah, and I let out a sigh.

"I don't know. Missing you, hanging out." I looked down at my hands and thought about what I'd just learned.

I knew what he'd say if I told him—he'd be excited and tell me to go for it. He'd be my best cheerleader, sending me as far away as I could possibly get. I wasn't sure I could handle that from him right now.

The silence caused me to look up at the screen, I hadn't realized neither of us was speaking. His serious expression caught me off-guard.

"Is something wrong?" I sat up a little straighter.

"I never expected to feel this distance between us."

My stomach sank. "Do you feel distance? I-I don't. I mean, I feel that you're away from me, and like right now I want to see you so much. But I wouldn't say that was distance between us. At least not figurative distance. It's only physical—"

Yes, I was rambling.

"I feel *figurative* distance."

"Julian…" My voice cracked. I'd just gotten into JYA, and already it was falling apart. "What's wrong? Please tell me."

"I don't know what's going on with you." He exhaled, looking down. "You don't tell me things like you used to. You make promises, and you don't keep them."

My phone buzzed in my lap, but my eyes were glued to his on the screen. "I tell you everything. I promise—"

"Now it's like you're not even listening to me."

My phone buzzed in my lap again. I still didn't look at it. "What do you want to know? I'll tell you anything!"

My phone buzzed again.

"What do you need to tell me?"

"Julian!" Again my phone buzzed. "Dammit! Somebody keeps texting me."

I picked it up, and the face was covered in messages from Rachel.

RACHEL

Anna, where are you?

RACHEL

Need ur help!

RACHEL

Anna pls answer.

RACHEL

911! 911!

"Oh my gosh, hang on!" I held the phone in front of the camera so he could see. "It's Rachel, something's wrong."

I quickly texted her back, and her reply was instantaneous.

RACHEL

Please come to Brad's! He's hurt. I need help!

"Julian, I've got to call you back. I don't know what this is about." I started to rise, and while he was partly understanding, he was also still angry. "I'll call you as soon as I help Rachel. Is that okay?"

He exhaled and nodded. "Sure. Of course. I hope it's nothing serious."

"I love you?" My eyes were wide as I studied his on the screen. "Are you asking me?"

"No. I mean... I don't know. You still love me, don't you?"

His eyes rolled and he shook his head. "How can you even ask that?"

My heart was thudding in my chest, but I couldn't make Rachel wait any longer. "Please just hang on. I'll be right back." I stood, but then I paused. "And it's not a question. I love you."

He only nodded, but I took off, grabbing my bag off the counter before heading out to my car.

Brad's apartment was close to ours, but not close enough to walk. By the time I'd found street parking, it was closing in on fifteen minutes since Rachel had called, and she was panicked.

"Anna, oh my God. What took so long?" She grabbed my hand and dragged me up the steps.

"I was talking to Julian… something's wrong, and then I couldn't find a place to park." She kept going through the house, headed to the bathroom. "What are you doing? What happened?"

"He fell." She stopped in front of the door. "He was in the shower, and he fell. He lost consciousness for a second, but he's awake now. I just can't get him to the car and to the ER by myself. He's not walking too good."

"Rachel! Holy—why didn't you call the real 911?" She opened the door, and I followed behind her then stopped short. Brad only had a towel around his waist. "Is he naked?"

"Focus, Anna! I need you to help me!" She bent down to put one of his arms around her neck.

"Glad to help, but it's going to be crazy-awkward if that towel comes off. We need to belt it or something."

"We don't have time!" She was still trying to get him up, coaxing quietly near his ear. "Can you stand now? Anna and I can get you to the car if you can help us."

"Hang on!" I took off toward his bedroom and threw his closet open, flipping quickly through pants, shirts, until I found a hanger of leather belts. Skipping those, I grabbed a canvass one. "Here! I ran back—we can just tie this around him on top of the towel."

Brad had managed to stand, but one hand was on the sink. I leaned forward, then stopped. "This feels a little too close for me."

"Oh, good grief." She grabbed the belt out of my hands and slipped it around his waist, cinching it quickly. "Good thing you're not going into medicine. Grab his other arm."

Lifting Brad's arm across my shoulder, we all turned sideways to go out the narrow door. "Why didn't you call one of his football buddies?" I grunted. "Those guys could throw him over one shoulder and carry him out."

"I don't know their numbers!" We were going down the front

steps, slowly approaching my car. Brad was actually helping quite a bit. "Of course, you have the smallest car ever made."

"Not true! Minis are smaller."

Finally Brad spoke, but his speech was slurry. "I'm okay." He stopped, taking a long pause. "Sorry. What did you say?"

"This isn't good." I opened the door, and we struggled to get him into the passenger's side. Once he was secure, we both jumped in, and I took the wheel headed to the ER. "What happened?"

Rachel was leaning in the middle, gently stroking his forehead. "I don't know! He was showering before we went out, and I heard a thud. Then I didn't hear anything, so I went in, and he was down."

"You should've called 911 that second!"

"I tried to get him to wake up, and he did come around. But then he kept fading, and I just... called you."

"Well, we're here now." I pulled into the circular drive and shoved the car into park. We both jumped out and ran around to his side. I left Rachel at the car and ran through the automatic sliding doors. "Help! I need help, there's been an accident!"

Two men in scrubs jumped up and followed me out. A female in scrubs grabbed a wheelchair and was right behind them.

"What happened?" The first man pulled out a pen light and shined it in Brad's eyes. "Head injury?"

"He slipped in the shower!" Rachel was right there. "He hasn't vomited or anything, but he was knocked out for a little bit."

"You're his girlfriend?" The other man leaned down and took Brad's arm.

"Yes, and this is a good friend of ours."

"Any family in town?"

"No, we're all from Alabama. He's a student at Tulane. He's on the football team."

The female's lips pressed together, and she seemed to shake her head.

"What?" I jumped in. "Why did you shake your head?"

"Those kids get hit so much," she said. "He could've had a preexisting injury that was aggravated."

Rachel answered this time. "He had a concussion last year… He was in a car accident."

"Come on." The men had him in the chair, and they were all headed inside. "Can you help fill out the paperwork? I'm not sure he's able. We need to contact his family as soon as possible."

Rachel's hands were shaking, and I could tell she wasn't handling this well.

"I can help!" I stepped forward, catching her hand and holding it. "What can I do?"

Rachel blinked at me then turned to the nurse. "Uhh, yeah. What can we do?"

The nurse only passed us both a glance. "Who knows the most about his medical history?"

"Rachel." I backed up. "Give me your phone, and I'll call his dad."

She passed me her cell and followed the nurse to the small room to the side. I wasn't thrilled about calling Mr. Brennan to tell him Brad was back in the hospital. I remembered him after the car wreck with Julian last year, but we had to let him know.

After that I had to text Julian. All the excitement had only slightly distracted me from what he was saying before, how he seemed angry. We needed to get back to that conversation.

As anticipated, Mr. Brennan was in his car before we'd even finished speaking. He said something about a friend with a plane and that he could be here in an hour. I gave him all the hospital information and ended the call. Then I dug out my phone and texted Julian as I walked to where I'd left my car in the circular drive. I needed to move it to a parking place.

ANNA

Brad fell in the shower and might have a
concussion. At the hospital.

I hit send and chewed my lip, thinking as I guided my Civic into a nearby space. I really wanted to see his face—I really wanted to go home and talk in private, but Rachel was so shaken up. I couldn't leave her here alone.

JULIAN

Is he OK?

ANNA

Think so. Probably MRI. His dad's on the way.

JULIAN

Watch out, he'll take over the whole show.

ANNA

Hope so. I'm hanging with Rachel, she's real upset.

JULIAN

OK.

ANNA

We still need to talk.

JULIAN

I'm ready to listen.

ANNA

I love you. I want to see you.

JULIAN

Only a few weeks til summer.

ANNA

Hurts so much. I want to be with you now.

JULIAN

Soon.

My arm dropped, and I looked through my windshield at the dark night, the empty parking lot. Why wouldn't he say he loved me? What had I done? Leaning forward, I rested the side of my head against the wheel. How could I bear things like this next year in London? I couldn't bear it now. I had to turn down JYA. It wasn't worth it to me. Nothing was worth losing Julian.

Back in the hospital, I waited with Rachel until Mr. Brennan finally arrived. He really did make it in less than an hour, thanks to a friend with a small plane, and he *did* take over the whole show, much to both Rachel's and my relief.

When it was getting close to midnight, and I could hardly keep my eyes open, I decided to call it.

"What's with you and making me pull these all-nighters?" I said through a yawn.

Rachel smiled a little, which was a huge relief to me. "I'm sorry. I really appreciate you coming and helping me."

"Still don't know why you didn't call 911 right away."

"I guess I panicked. Yours was the first number I saw on my phone."

I leaned my head against her shoulder. "I've got to quit calling you so much."

"Oh!" She jumped, and I lifted my head. "Speaking of calls, I need you to call Jack and tell him what happened. Tell him we can't make it tomorrow."

"Why me?" I frowned. "And what's tomorrow?"

"Or today, I guess," she sighed. "I've been trying to call him, but all I get is voicemail. He invited us all to go out on his boat tomorrow. On the lake. But obviously we can't go now."

Grunting a little sigh, I shook my head. "You still haven't said why I have to call him. I wasn't even invited."

"Actually, you were." Her top lip curled, and she looked sheepish. "I didn't tell you because I didn't think you'd want to go, because of Julian and all."

"I don't!" My mind instantly raced to how Julian would feel if I even mentioned Jack and his sailboat.

"See? I was right. I was going to make some excuse for you

and not even tell you about it, but now I can't even go. Somebody has to show up. It's too cruel to just leave him hanging."

"First, I don't think not telling me was the best approach." Even as I said it, I acknowledged my hypocrisy. "And second, just leave him a voicemail. Done."

"Anna, please? I looked out for you. It's just a quick call." Then she squinted. "Or a quick trip to the marina?"

"I'm not going to the marina!"

"If he's not checking his phone, he'll just be out there waiting, and Brad'll feel like shit. Jack's been doing so much better lately. Please? It's not really that big a deal."

Shaking my head, I pushed to my feet. "I'll take care of it." My voice was a low grumble. "But you owe me now."

"Thanks so much. I do owe you. Or maybe this is makeup for the Savannah surprise?" She narrowed her eyes, and I rolled mine.

"Blackmail."

"Technically, it's not blackmail, it's payback."

"Yeah, you're going to make a great lawyer."

"I'll text you the directions."

* * *

SLIP AWAY

Lake Pontchartrain was pretty most days, shining dark blue under cloudless skies, but then it would get muddy brown, depending on the weather and the tides.

Water from the Mississippi River fed into it, diluting the saline content, and like most things in this city, it was a total contradiction and completely fascinating.

It was the body of water that had flooded New Orleans in 2005, destroying so many lives, yet a lone dolphin had taken up residence in it following that hurricane.

The fishing industry was coming back, and now the lake was bringing revenue into the battered metropolis it almost destroyed.

South Shore Harbor Marina was easy to get to, and I spotted the familiar Jeep as soon as I pulled into the parking lot. With a deep inhale, I got out and headed toward the pier. It was early, and only a few sailors were stirring around. *Slip Away* was tied not too far down the line.

I'd worn khaki cargo capris, and I'd remembered to wear my Keds because of the light-colored soles. I'd also grabbed a red windbreaker out of Rachel's closet, not that I planned to stay.

I was just walking up when Jack appeared, dressed in long khaki shorts and a long-sleeved navy tee. He moved quickly around the stern, checking the sails and clearly getting ready to take her out, and for a moment, I only watched him, lean and tanned and sporty.

It took me all the way back to that first day in Navarre, when he'd sailed down to meet me at Nana's. I'd stood on the shore, wondering if there could be anything more perfect than this golden boy sailing over to find me. He was like a prince.

I quickly found out there were loads of things more special than being Jack Kyser's princess—being Julian LaSalle's angel, for one.

My lips pressed into a frown, but I shook it off. All of that was ancient history, and I needed to complete this errand and get out of here fast. And immediately call Julian and tell him and get to the bottom of whatever was troubling him.

He said I wasn't telling him things. Well, the list of what I needed to tell him for the last two days should make him feel very included.

Jack looked up and saw me, and his face relaxed into a handsome smile. "Anna! Hey!" Ducking under the bow, he hopped over to the side and grabbed the railing before stepping onto the pier. "You're here early! I wasn't expecting everybody for at least another hour."

The breeze pushed his shaggy blond hair around his head, and it helped remembering how he'd apologized for being such a jerk to me all that fall.

"About that." I looked down as the wind shoved my curls straight into my face. "Brad had an accident last night. They can't come today."

His face lined with concern. "An accident? What happened?"

"He's okay, but he hit his head, and they want to keep him for observation. It's because of the wreck last year."

Jack was still frowning, but he nodded. "Makes sense, I guess. Brain injury is really serious."

"Yeah, and his dad's here. So you know."

"Oh, then he's fine." Jack laughed. "If anybody can take care of Brad, it's Papa Bear Brennan."

"Right, so that's all. I just came down to tell you what happened." I started to back away, but his head snapped up.

"Wait! You're not leaving?"

"I… yeah." Nodding, I pushed my flying hair behind my ears. "I've got work to do, and I was just—"

"No way, you have to come out for a little bit. I've got her all ready."

"I'm sorry, but no. Can't do it."

"What?" He actually seemed confused for a second. Then his expression changed. He winked one eye at me. "You're not worried about my little brother are you?"

I hesitated, wondering if being honest was a good idea. I decided to go for it. "I kind of am. You and me going sailing alone would not make Julian happy."

"Tell you what." He straightened and crossed his arms. "It won't be you and me going sailing alone."

My brows pulled together and I looked around the marina. Nobody was hanging with us. "It won't?"

"It'll be you getting your final sailing lesson. Didn't I owe you one more?"

"No." My eyes squeezed shut as I shook my head. "I mean, I don't know. It's not like I paid you for them or anything."

He caught my hand and gently tugged me toward the boat. "I always keep my word. I need to evaluate your skills since our last lesson. That was what? A year ago?"

I remembered my last "lesson" vividly. "More like eighteen months. At least."

"See? We're way behind on keeping you qualified."

The boat rocked as he stepped across and down. Then he turned and held out a hand to me. "Come on, Skipper. I need to see that clove hitch."

"Jack, I'm really not—"

"Don't make me report you to the port authority."

My nose wrinkled. "What does that mean?"

"You're losing points already. And where's your life preserver?"

"You never made me wear one."

"Don't try blaming the teacher." His hand was still waiting for mine, and in that moment, I made the decision.

"I'm sorry, but I said no." Calm filled me as I said the words. "Thanks for asking. You know I always enjoyed sailing with you. Have a fun day."

I turned to walk up the pier, and he called out to me. "Okay, no worries. But just hang on a second. I want to show you something."

Pausing, I glanced back over my shoulder. "What is it?"

"Just wait there." He hopped over to the ladder leading into the boat's insides, and despite my initial hesitation, it warmed me to see him so happy and light.

It reminded me of how he used to be.

"Hurry up, okay?" I yelled, slowly walking back.

A few minutes longer, and he reemerged from below, pushing the door all the way open.

"Come across and look," he held out his hand.

My lip caught between my teeth, and I froze in one spot. "Jack…"

He looked back and laughed at my response. "I'm not going to kidnap you. We won't leave the dock. I just don't feel like jumping over again."

My shoulders dropped with an exhale, and I held the line as I carefully extended a leg and stepped into the gently bobbing vessel. "This had better not take long," I groused, and he caught my hand, steadying my transition.

I found my footing and looked up, and he was digging under the small cabinet. All at once, low music filled the air.

"Wow, you got a radio. That's a nice touch. I like it."

He straightened up and smiled. "She's a regular party barge now."

"Not hardly." I smiled and for a few moments we listened to the sounds of classic rock filling the air around us.

"Okay, then." I started to go, but he jumped.

"That's not all." He went to the hold again and disappeared down below, before coming back up the steps holding a small frame. "Check this out. Lucy gave it to me. Can you believe how young we look?"

He held it close as he finished climbing, then he wheeled it around, and my breath caught. It was the same picture Lucy had given me at Christmas two years ago. My hands fumbled to hold it, and for a moment, I only stared at him and me, gazing into each other's eyes.

"I have this…" My voice was quiet.

He walked up behind me, looking at it over my shoulder. I was keenly aware of his body too close to mine.

"Who are those kids?" he joked. "They look so happy together."

"Seems like they were. For a month or two anyway." It was time for me to go, and I made my voice very casual, very end-the-conversation. "Well, I'll see you around."

I turned and pushed the frame into his chest, but before I could move away, his arms encircled me, pulling me close.

"I was so stupid, Anna," he groaned, leaning forward into my hair. "I made such a stupid mistake throwing that away."

My heart pounded, and I struggled to get out of his embrace. "We already talked about this."

He lifted his head, blue eyes searing into mine. "Don't you want that again?"

I pushed him back. "I'm sorry, No." I shook my head, blinking down to my feet. "I mean, I'm *not* sorry and *No*. I already have it. I have everything I need, and it's not you."

"It's Julian."

"Yes. It's Julian, and I think it was always Julian." My eyes flashed to his, and a spark of anger singed that silly girl inside me Jack Kyser always managed to fluster. "I'm sorry you want something that's gone, but the past is past. I want good things for you, and I wish you good luck, but I'm leaving now."

He nodded and walked back to the captain's chair. I started for the side to get off the boat and back to my car before anything else unexpected happened.

"Anna, wait." He moved quickly to where I was balanced, trying to get my footing and braced my arm so I could step across to the pier. "I'm sorry."

I wouldn't look at him. "Apology accepted," is all I said.

Still, he held my arm.

Then he exhaled a little laugh, letting me go. "I'm not really sorry." My eyes flashed to his, and that little spark of anger grew bigger. "Don't give me that look. You felt it. We've always been pretty hot together, and if I hadn't tried, I'd have regretted it."

My voice was sharp. "I love Julian."

He nodded, and looked down. "I know."

As far as I was concerned, this conversation was over, but his voice stopped me right as I took my first step to go. "I also wanted to tell you it's my last semester at Tulane. I'm leaving next year."

"What? Where are you going?"

"Since I've decided to go into pre-med, I talked to Dad about transferring to Vandy."

I thought for a moment. "Where Casey is?"

Jack's brow lined. "No. I mean, she started there, but she transferred to Belmont freshman year. It's better for music majors." Shaking his head, he continued. "Anyway, Dad's pretty happy about it. He always had his heart set on me going to the Ivy League."

That memory was as fresh as everything that had happened today. "You're right."

"Vandy's not technically the Ivy League, but it's the Ivy League of the South."

It all made sense then—why he kept fumbling around for me to stay, why he'd tried one last time. I wasn't angry anymore, I was glad. This chapter was over, and I'd even gotten closure. It was more than I ever expected to get.

"I think that's fantastic." I reached out and caught his hand. "I'm so glad your dad's supporting you in this."

"He was actually surprised I didn't know about my grandfather." Jack shook his head and looked out at the water. "Sometimes I wonder what he thinks he did with us all those years. If he has his own version of events."

Chewing my lip, I remembered how much his father used to drink, and I wondered the same thing.

"Try not to look at it that way. Things are getting so much better with him, don't you think?"

He shrugged. "I don't want to sound cold, but it's hard for me to care."

Pressing my lips together I nodded. "I understand that."

I also hoped that once he was happy, once everything was how it should be with him, his feelings might change.

"Can I have a hug?"

He frowned. "Are you serious?"

"I want to thank you."

"For what?"

"What you said out there, what you said here, for trusting me, for giving me better memories of us together."

I reached out, awkwardly across the space between the pier and the boat, and he gave me a brief, friendly hug. I quickly straightened and smiled.

"It's all turning out like it was supposed to, and you're going to be happy. Trust me."

He smiled then. "Take care of yourself, Anna."

* * *

GO TO LONDON

When I got back home, I went straight to the shower. Rachel was back when I got out, and she was collecting her things and packing an overnight bag.

"Hey!" I wrapped the towel around my wet hair. "What's the news? How's Brad?"

She stopped and gave me a relieved smile. "He's going to be fine. They released him, but he needs someone there just to make sure nothing happens, that he doesn't lose consciousness or anything."

"Oh, Rachel! I'm so glad!" I hopped over and pulled her into a hug.

She hugged me back tightly. "I'm sorry I asked you to help with the Jack thing. I know that's an awkward situation for you."

Waving my hand, I smiled. "It turned out to be a good thing, so no worries."

Her brow lined. "I want to hear more about this, but I don't want to leave Brad home alone too long."

"Where's his dad?"

"His buddy was still in town with the plane, and he managed to catch a ride back before he left."

Nodding, I realized Mr. Brennan would've been without a car otherwise. "Lucky break."

"It was." She pulled the strap over her shoulder. "Otherwise, Brad's mom would've had to come get him. Well, let me take off, but we have a night at Fat Harry's in our future."

All the events of the last two days filled my head, and I grinned. "Yes, we do."

I ate a quick breakfast, and around mid-morning, I sat down and called Julian. I tried FaceTiming first, but it only rang and rang with him never answering.

It was silly of me to think he'd be sitting at home waiting for me to call, so I grabbed my phone to send him a text.

ANNA

I'm here, ready to talk. No more interruptions.

Sitting with my back against my bed, I waited. And waited.

I looked up at my ceiling, resting my head against the mattress. I lowered my legs and opened the photo-sharing app on my phone, scrolling through everybody's party pix, double-tapping the ones I liked.

Still no answer.

ANNA

You there?

I tried to imagine where he might be. It was Saturday. He could be in the park, down by the shore, painting or... something. In a lab? Without his phone?

The pain in my throat grew tighter, and all I could think about were his last words. He felt like I wasn't talking, like we were growing apart. The night before he'd texted something about a secret, and now he wasn't talking.

The whole idea of it, of him being so angry again made my insides start wigging out. It felt like my heart and lungs and stomach were flailing and kicking like a little kid throwing a tantrum.

I know that's weird, but Julian was a part of me, and for him to try and pull away felt like he was pulling everything out of me with him. I had to try again.

ANNA

> Sorry it's later than I realized. Brad was just released. Rachel's over with him.

What else could I text? He wanted me to talk… I hadn't wanted to text this, but maybe it was a start?

ANNA

> She asked me to run an errand this morning. Jack has his boat, and they were going out. He wasn't answering his phone, so she asked me to go and tell him about the accident.

I took a deep breath and waited. What happened next I'd planned to explain over FaceTime, where I could see his face and he could see mine. Where he could see my love for him in my eyes and not read these disembodied letters.

ANNA

> I know I promised never to be alone with him again, but I figured you'd understand because of what happened with Brad. I hope I was right. It was nothing, really.

Chewing my lip, I waited again. Minutes ticked by, and still no response.

I stared at the little blue bubbles containing all my words, and

I wanted to scream, *Answer me!!!*

I hated these 700 miles between us so intensely, I wanted to slam my phone against the wall. I wasn't sure I'd survive this silent treatment from him. What did he think I was hiding?

I slumped down onto my side, lying on the floor. Closing my eyes, I remembered something else he didn't know.

ANNA

Found out Friday… I'm accepted into JYA. Still having second thoughts. Even if we don't get to see each other as much now, at least we still can.

The continued silence of my phone made me feel like I was going quietly insane.

I felt like my room was a small prison, and I'd been forced into solitary confinement.

Only, I wasn't sure what crime I had committed, since the judge wouldn't speak to me.

After a few more minutes of silence, I pushed off the floor and went to the kitchen. At least prisoners were allowed to eat. I boiled water on the stove and made myself a cup of dehydrated black bean soup.

While I waited for it to thicken, I toasted a slice of bread and grabbed a Coke out of the fridge. The entire time, I watched my phone like it was a firecracker ready to explode.

Only it never did. It was one of those duds where the wick either went out or got disconnected.

With a deep sigh, I carried my late lunch back to the living room and sat on the couch. I didn't want to watch television. I didn't want to read or go out. I didn't want to do anything but hear from Julian.

Lunch finished, I lay on my side staring at the silent device. An hour had passed, and I knew he had seen my messages. There was no way he hadn't. He wasn't answering me, and I didn't know why. I decided to try one last time.

ANNA

Please talk to me.

Seconds passed and my phone buzzed. A little squeal leaped from my throat, and I flipped it over fast.

Three short words ripped out my heart.

JULIAN

Go to London.

My brow lined as pain radiated all the way to my bones.

Sliding onto my side again, I lay on the couch like a trauma victim. I couldn't even cry. I didn't know what to say.

My eyes closed, and I saw myself screaming "No!" as he turned and walked away.

* * *

GOODBYE, NEW ORLEANS

My brain carried on the last few weeks of school as if it was completely disconnected from my broken heart. Maybe it had always been disconnected, because it sure seemed to lead me wrong most of the time when love was involved.

Brad continued to improve, but Rachel still stayed with him most of the time. In an effort to distract myself from the intense pain radiating from my hollow chest every minute of every day, I threw myself into final projects, film editing, reading, and writing. Until finally it was all done.

I handed in my last assignment, ready to say goodbye for the summer.

Dr. Arati was my last class to meet, and she pulled me back to the one unresolved issue on my plate.

"We never had that chat about JYA." Her posture was calm, experienced. "I need to send them your final decision this week."

Julian's last text echoed in my memory like some horrible death sentence. He still wasn't talking to me, and I still hadn't been able to get any answers. What had happened? How could he push me away so completely?

"My parents are really excited about it." It was the only response I could give her.

It was the truth. I hadn't told anyone about me and Julian, but my parents knew I'd gotten the internship, and they were already working out the financial arrangements.

"But you're not so excited?" She gave me a warm smile, her black eyes full of empathy.

"I'm not sure how I feel. I'm honored, of course, and I'm sure it would be an unforgettable experience." My eyes dropped to her shoes.

"But?" She gently prodded.

For a few moments, I was silent.

He had told me to go. It was the only thing he'd said to me in almost three weeks. My parents were beside themselves buying me all sorts of devices and gadgets. Apparently the wall outlets are completely different in Europe.

In truth, nothing was stopping me from going except my destroyed heart.

"Anna, I know this can be a hard decision at your age. It can feel monumental—especially if you have someone special you'd be leaving behind."

Lifting my chin, I made a decision then. "I'm sorry it took me so long to decide, but I'm going."

My professor seemed taken aback, but she quickly recovered. "That's wonderful. I'll send Liam your answer today, right now, and we can start getting your paperwork sent over."

Relief wasn't what I felt. Resignation was closer to the emotion moving through my body. In the center of my chest was that hole where my heart had been. It continued to radiate misery through my stomach, but somehow, I felt like I wasn't going to die if I just kept moving.

"Thank you so much, Dr. Arati." I hugged my books and took a step toward the door. "I'm really so grateful for this opportunity."

She smiled and gave me a hug. "Let me know if you have any questions or problems. I'm here as your adviser."

Finally, I was back at home. All of my furniture and clothes had to be packed because Rachel was getting a new roommate, but it wasn't an enormous amount of stuff. I'd only taken up half of a half of a duplex, which was as small as it sounded, and I'd never been much of a hoarder.

The most important thing I brought back with me was the painting hanging above my bed—me holding my hair back, surrounded by all shades of green waves. I took it off the wall and held it a few moments, studying the careful brush strokes, lightly touching the curling greens around my torso and head. Julian had painted it from memory, he said he'd painted it from feelings, and the thought of him creating it, capturing me on canvas stroke by stroke was the only thing that kept me going. He loved me then; he still loved me now. I was certain of it, and no matter how angry he was, I could make him see that.

Mom was giddy and emotional that I was "back in the nest" for a few weeks before I left for London mid-July. Dad just laughed at her and teased me about being a bird. Both wanted to know when Julian would be home from Savannah. I wanted to know as well, but since we'd stopped communicating, I had no clue.

The prospect of hanging around the house alone not knowing where he was or what he was doing was unbearable. Lucy and Robert hadn't moved to Birmingham yet, so I shot her a text.

ANNA

Back from college! Any chance we can meet up?

I was anxious to see her again before we all went in different directions, and even though she wasn't staying at her dad's anymore, she'd most likely know what was going on with her brother. She replied quickly.

LUCY

Of course! Let's do The Hangout tonight, dinner?

ANNA

Meet you there at 8.

The Hangout was more of a tourist-trap, but most of the local kids went there anyway. It was a huge restaurant right on the Gulf, with outdoor seating and live music. The bands played in a giant courtyard area that included games and vendors selling glow sticks and ray guns. On the other side of the space was a sandy playground with rides for kids.

Lucy and I sat at the outdoor bar, listening to the band and catching up. The sun was just starting to set, but under the lights of the outdoor patio, we didn't notice the growing dusk.

It was hot and sticky, but we were both dressed for the weather. She was in a filmy, dark blue handkerchief-print maxi dress. I'd picked up a knee-length, spaghetti-strap green dress at one of the beach shops. It had little white shells scattered like polka dots all over it, and it reminded me of her ring. I touched the dragonfly still on my finger.

"Look at you! So fresh and pretty." Lucy hurried up and clutched me in a hug. Her long hair was swept over one shoulder.

"Just like you!" I squeezed her back. "Married life seems to be agreeing with you."

"I love it very much." She smiled, taking her seat. The waiter came and took our drink orders, but she only got a Diet Coke. I just asked for water. "It's like I have a thing now."

"What do you mean?"

She laughed. "Everybody's got a thing they love. This is what I've got. Robert and my family. I'm hoping…"

My mouth dropped. "Are you pregnant?"

"Oh, God no. We've got to get through medical school, but I can't wait." The waiter returned with our drinks, and once he'd gone, she leaned forward on the table. "Tell me all about London! I'm so excited for you, I can't stand it."

A line pierced my brow. "How did you know I got in?"

"Rachel, of course! She emailed me asking if I knew anybody looking for a roommate next semester."

"Oh, yeah." My lips twisted into a frown. "One of the bad parts is losing a great roommate."

"But not as bad as being so far from Julian?" She took a sip of her drink.

Shrugging, I looked out toward the Gulf, wondering where he even was right now. I stabbed my straw up and down in my water.

"Hang on." Lucy's hand fell, hitting the table and making me jump. "What is that supposed to mean? Are you and Julian fighting?"

My eyes rose to her bright blue ones. "Honestly? I don't know. He's been pulling away since spring break, and for the last month, he hasn't returned any of my texts."

She hopped off her stool and quickly ran around to hug me. "Anna! You must be going crazy—is there anything I can do?"

Her unexpected display of affection made my breath hiccup. My eyes heated, and I was afraid I might cry.

"I don't think so. I just want answers. I want to know what happened, whatever it is he's not telling me, or whatever he thinks I'm not telling him."

She leaned back, studying my face, her eyes full of concern. "You don't have any idea what it could be?"

"No… I mean… he said something about a secret. I didn't know what he meant, but he said he felt distance between us. We didn't see each other much during spring break, and when we went back, it was like that space just got bigger."

"He barely made it in for the wedding."

My mind traveled back to the reason. "He was angry with me. I hadn't told him… some things."

Was that all it was? Jack? But it didn't make any sense, we'd worked that out. I told him about the sailing trip. Yes, I'd promised not to be alone with him again, but he had to understand it was for Rachel. And I'd told him right away.

From the corner of my eye, I noticed Lucy jump. She suddenly sat very straight and reached across the table for my hand. "Brace yourself. He just walked in."

Pain squeezed my chest, and for a second, I forgot how to breathe.

My eyes followed hers looking behind me, moving to the right. "Does he see us?"

She nodded in the direction of the small bar behind us, and I turned, stealing a glance over my shoulder. What I saw made me jump out of the chair.

He was there, facing the bartender, wearing jeans and a gray tee, but what had me ready to run was the brunette in the strapless dress hanging on his arm.

"He's here with Renee?" My whisper was almost a hiss.

"What can I do?" Lucy's voice was equally low, and I felt her reach for my arm.

Just then, he turned around and our eyes met. In my peripheral vision, I could tell Renee was smiling, but I couldn't tear my gaze from his.

I was sure my heartbreak was pouring from my eyes, but I

couldn't read anything in his. His expression was completely neutral.

My feet moved on their own, as if my body were drawn to him. I didn't make a conscious decision, I simply couldn't stop myself going straight to where he stood, until we were facing each other.

He took a half step away from her, and Renee's smile melted into a frown.

I was the first to speak. "What are you doing here?"

He didn't answer, but Renee did. "Hi, Anna. Just get in town for the break?"

I didn't even acknowledge her. "Why won't you talk to me?"

At that, his brow lowered, and he seemed almost angry.

Instead of answering, though, he caught my arm and pulled me away from the bar. "I'm not doing this here."

He released me and kept walking through the patio space to where the small playground was located. I followed him, not sure if that was what he meant, but unable to let him go without an explanation.

He kept walking through the gate, across the parking lot, and over the boardwalk. I followed him out to the sand, away from the crowd, until at last he stopped and turned to face me.

His expression was still that neutral almost-irritation, like he would patiently listen to whatever I had to say, but his decision was already made. I'd seen him treat his mother this same way, and it panicked me.

"Julian, you have to talk to me. What happened back there?"

Finally, I got a response. His eyebrows pulled together, and I saw real anger. "*I* have to talk to you? I'm not the one still keeping secrets."

Shaking my head, I pushed my hair back from my cheeks. "I don't know what you're talking about! I don't have any secrets from you."

"Then we have nothing to say here." He made a move like he

would head back to the bar, but I lunged forward catching his arm.

"Why won't you tell me why you're so angry? Why are you here with Renee?"

Our bodies were so close, the pain was excruciating. "I told you once before. She's completely honest."

"I'm completely honest!"

"Are you?"

"Oh my God!" I threw up my hands and paced in a circle. "This isn't us! We don't play games. We've never played games."

He crossed his arms, and I couldn't believe the coldness in his blue eyes. "I seem to remember you playing lots of games."

He looked so much like his father, my panic only intensified.n"Never with you. I love you."

The tiniest spark of something flickered in his eye, but it was gone just as fast. "High school relationships rarely survive college."

"Don't you say that," I snapped, that old pain back in my chest. "We were more than just a high school relationship, and you know it."

With a deep breath, he uncrossed his arms and pushed his hands into his back pockets. The gray tee stretched across his chest, and I wanted nothing more but to bury my face in it, inhaling his scent of soap and the ocean. I needed him so badly.

"I don't know." His tone was still distant, aloof. "Maybe Renee was right. Maybe this was all just some little high school obsession of mine, wanting something I could never have. Until I did."

My burning eyes met his, and he completely pulled away. I didn't know what I could say to bring him back to me. I couldn't speak, but he didn't stop.

"Only I never really had you, did I?"

"You had me. You know how much you had me." My voice was weak and trembling, my whole body felt numb. Closing my eyes, I thought about how deep our love had been last year, the things he'd said to me. "What about tenth grade? What about math class, and how I couldn't look at you?"

Stepping forward, I caught his hand. "What about this?" I held it so that my dragonfly ring lined up with the little dragonfly tattoo on his hand.

He stood and looked at it for several long moments, not speaking.

When he did speak, he broke my heart all over again. "Kid stuff."

Instead of tears, though, I felt anger. I was furious at him now.

"It is NOT kid stuff!" I pushed him back with both hands, but he caught my forearms and held them. I saw my anger reflected in his eyes, and I jerked them away, confused. "Why are you so angry?" My voice was a broken whisper.

He turned away, but before he left, he repeated what he'd told me earlier. "Go to London, Anna. Do JYA."

The desperation was back in my voice. "I am going to London —I already told them yes. But it doesn't change anything. We won't lose each other."

"We're already lost."

He walked away from me then, and a weak little cry slipped from my aching throat. I couldn't stop him. He was determined to walk away, and I knew him too well. I had to let him go right now.

Somehow, I managed to hold myself together. This was not the end. I wasn't sure why he was doing this, why he was telling himself we were nothing more than a high school thing, but I would not let him give up on us.

I'd seen him angry before. I'd seen him angry with his mother, and I knew I had to wait. He wouldn't let me in right now, but I hoped with everything inside me—with everything I believed in—that like his mother, he could see a time when he'd forgive me.

It was all I had, but I held onto it so hard. I had to believe it if I was ever going to get through the coming months. I just wished with everything in me he would tell me what had happened.

Either way, standing on the beach, with the waves crashing behind me, I made a vow. When I got back from London... when we were back here, we'd be together again.

* * *

BBC NEWSWOMAN

London was amazing. I was technically enrolled at University College, and I lived in the Ian Baker student housing near Ramsey Hall, which was less than a half-mile from the main BBC offices.

It took me less than ten minutes to walk to work past enormous brick apartments and glass-fronted businesses. Trees were planted in the stone sidewalks, and it reminded me vaguely of being in New Orleans, only without the music. And the heat.

Broadcasting was the fastest job I'd ever had. We started early in the morning, and the days were eaten up with chasing stories and doing research. Stories would start at the break of dawn or sometimes late the night before, and if we didn't have them ready by show time, it was too late. Yesterday's news. Over.

Personally, I had to catch up fast on world events and major European players, who were pretty much foreign to me. When I wasn't reading the wire, I was monitoring other news outlets or honing my broadcast writing craft.

Part of my job as an intern was reading through the press releases and finding newsworthy events. It was the same thing I'd done at the podcast studio, so I was at least experienced in that task.

What I hadn't done before was write copy to be read on-air. I had to take into account the narrative element of the process. I had to write sentences that could be read quickly and smoothly at a glance.

An unexpected benefit was that time also passed incredibly fast. It was easy to get lost in the work, and I truly loved it. Liam Stockton was my boss, but I primarily checked in with his assistant Brandon Elliot.

Brandon was a recent graduate, and as such, he was a great mentor for me. All my questions were fresh on his mind, because they were questions he'd had starting out as well.

So I lost myself in research and chasing the days' stories, pushing my shredded insides to the deep background.

My birthday came and went with calls and care packages from my parents and Gabi, but it was the first time in two years I didn't receive a single yellow chrysanthemum or a note telling me to smile today.

I killed that pain with a healthy shot of *Is the Euro Losing ground in the West?* followed by a chaser of *What in the World is Russia Up To?*

Christmas holiday came and went, but I only visited home for a week. Even that was too long, considering Julian wasn't there.

I'd stopped trying to text him long ago, focusing instead on getting through this year, building my resume and finding my way back to him next summer.

That was the plan at least.

By spring, I felt like a regular part of the news staff. I wasn't on the payroll, but that was the only thing keeping me from reading on-air. I did pretty much everything else in the office.

One of my last three Sundays before my internship ended, I was holed up at my computer, reading about Christine Lagarde, president of the European Central Bank, who BBC had declared the "most powerful woman," when Brandon interrupted me.

"Anna!" he barked.

I'd grown to love the British way of saying my name. It was like *Ah*-nah.

"What are you doing here on a Sunday?" He stopped at the desk. "You've got to take a break or you'll burn out. In all these months of busting your arse, have you even toured London?"

I blinked up at his brown eyes. He was dressed in navy slacks and a white tee with a dark brown cardigan over it. His wavy brown hair was parted on the side, and curled down around his ears.

"I, uh… No, I haven't." I looked back at the screen where a photograph of the stern-faced, white-haired female looked back at me. "I need to watch these. I know nothing about Christine Lagarde."

"She's from Normandy," he said, leaning over and flicking off the video.

"Hey!" I tried to reach for it, but he caught my hand.

"She takes Sundays off, and you must, too." My eyes narrowed, but he smiled and continued. "You can't spend a year in this country and not at least see Westminster."

I slouched back in my chair. "You want to give me a tour of London?"

A dimpled smile broke across his face, and for the first time I recognized Brandon was very cute. Not that my missing heart even cared.

"Yes," he laughed, pulling me up. "Hyde Park, Buckingham Palace, and if you're very good, I'll show you Geoffrey Chaucer's gravesite."

"Isn't it in Westminster?"

"So you do know something about the city." He winked at me then. I allowed him to pull me up and lead the way. "As much as you love British Lit, it would be a shame for you to end the year in a newsroom. Especially an old dodgy one like this."

"I like our newsroom!" I cried as he pulled my hand into the crook of his arm.

"Good, because I've heard our newsroom fancies you, as well."

I stopped walking, frozen on the spot. "What?"

He leaned toward my ear. "You didn't hear it from me, but there's talk of offering you a permanent position."

Words escaped me, and when he turned back, he laughed again. "Your eyes are quite round, Miss Sanders. Yes, that's the rumor. But you Americans work yourselves to death. Today, we're going to have some fun."

"Brandon, are you joking? Are they seriously going to make me an offer?" I was clutching his arm now, trying to slow my swirling thoughts.

"I think so. Liam has been very impressed with your work ethic, and Arati did nothing but sing your praises to him."

"But I haven't graduated. I don't have a degree…"

"Minor points in this business." He patted my hand. "Remember, it wasn't so long ago that experience was the biggest qualifier. Most of these old codgers worked their way up from the mailroom."

I stopped walking and pulled my hand out of his arm. "Then I really should stay and finish my research. I'm so behind on who everyone is and how they got started."

Brandon exhaled and paced to where I stood. With exaggerated affect, he took my hand and pulled it back into the crook of his arm.

"Tomorrow and tomorrow and tomorrow. All of this will be waiting for you when we return."

I considered for a moment fighting him, but the expression on his face changed my mind. "You're really into this?"

"It will be *fun*. Have you ever heard of that word? It's important for team-building if we're to be potential coworkers."

Shaking my head, I relaxed and followed him. "I never said I'd take the job."

"That's just what I expected you to say. Come on."

Brandon and I spent the day running all over London. We

started in Hyde Park because it was springtime, and he insisted the flowers there were better than anywhere else in the world. I had to laugh, but when we stepped off the double-decker bus at Speaker's Corner, my breath literally caught.

A sea of tulips spread out in front of us, in all shades of red, purple, yellow, white, and pink. We wandered to the Diana Memorial Fountain, and I noticed Albert Hall so we ran over to check it out. From there I saw Kensington Palace, but Brandon pulled me aside and said we could see these things from the Eye, the giant Ferris Wheel towering over the city. He wanted to go to the Abbey.

Westminster was even more gorgeous in real life than on television. The size of it was enough to steal your breath, and looking up at the gothic arches and enormous chapels made me feel very small in the face of history.

We paid our admission, and for the first part, I was simply wandering around looking at it all with my mouth open, until Brandon leaned over and whispered in my ear.

"Hogwarts."

My brow lined and I looked up at him. "They modeled Hogwarts after this part. That's why it looks familiar."

"All of it looks familiar," I whispered back. "It's on television every time something major happens."

"Why are you whispering?"

"Because it feels very grand and sacred." Then I pinched his arm. "Shut up."

He showed me the Tomb of the Unknown Soldier, Chaucer's grave, Poet's Corner, and the bright green lawn outside the cloisters.

We viewed ancient tombs of kings and queens that had statues with crowns and scepters on top of them. There were colorful tombs for some, and all were ornately decorated with plaques and long descriptions.

We spent almost an hour before we left, headed to Trafalgar

Square, where the four enormous, bronze lions surrounded the statue of Lord Nelson. From there we went through the magnificent Admiralty Arch, a series of three arches opening onto The Mall, a wide, red-bricked lane that went all the way to Buckingham Palace.

It was breathtaking with the golden statue and the royal guard. We were too late for the changing of the guard, which Brandon played off as basically a marching band performance, but even I knew better.

There was plenty more to see by the time we called it a day, but he promised to take me up in The Eye and let me get a good view of the rest.

We finished at The Mayflower, a pub overlooking the Thames River, where he insisted I have the Scurvy, a bitter home brew. He also ordered a ploughman's special, which was basically a meat and cheese plate with boiled eggs and a pickle, and the requisite fish and chips.

"Now you've seen our fair city. Or at least the high points." He winked, taking a sip of the amber drink. "What do you think?"

"I love it. Of course, I love it. It's an English major's dream come true." I tasted my own ale, and my nose wrinkled. "Except for the warm beer."

"Don't be so clichéd, Sanders. It grows on you."

I looked down at the plate, and picked up a piece of the hard cheese. It was tangy with a hint of saltiness.

"Thanks for doing this. I really did need to get out today."

He smiled. "You're welcome, although no thanks is necessary. I'm as much a fan of this city as the next tourist. Next time, we'll catch a play in Covent Garden."

"Next time?" I took a crisp bite of one of the pickles, the tangy sweet flavor filling my mouth.

"Sure, we can make it a regular date if you'd like." He leaned back, evaluating the effect of that suggestion.

My bottom lip pulled between my teeth, and I looked down at the plates. "I'm sorry, Brandon. I didn't mean to mislead you…"

"You have a fellow back home." He leaned forward on the table and lifted his ale, taking another sip. "I should've figured as much the way you work."

My hands were clasped in my lap, and I hated that this might be the end of the fun times we'd shared. "Putting my head down and working has been the best way to drown out the missing."

"Well, he's a lucky fellow. I'm not ashamed to say it." He smiled and broke off a piece of bread. "I suppose that's also why you're not taking the job?"

"Don't… put that out there." Contradictory emotions warred in my chest.

I wasn't completely onboard with accepting a position here, at the same time, I didn't want to lose my offer.

He leaned back then and arched an eyebrow. "Really. So you might be interested? Doesn't bode well for Boyfriend."

"Julian," I interrupted. "His name's Julian, and I'd want to talk to him about it. If it happened."

"Oh, it's going to happen." He gave me a little nod. "Count on it. And I'll be watching to see how it plays out with this Julian chap."

So will I, I thought, but I didn't say that out loud. Instead I sipped my warm beer and finished my dinner.

JYA had turned out exactly as I'd hoped and feared it would, with the possible exception of the friendly guy sharing dinner with me.

Now I had to see how the story actually ended.

* * *

Hey all, Jules here breaking in again.

I'm basically saying this because I know Brandon so well… I'm a little in love with him right now.

Dad's being a git not telling Mum why he's angry, and she's being a flipping featherhead not remembering to tell him about the Labyrinth and Audubon Park and all these accidental run-ins with sodding Jack.

Still, it doesn't make sense. None of this is adding up for me. How does Dad know about it all? I can only guess that he does—why else would he be so mad?

So I'm suuuper frustrated. I don't know if you are. I guess the only solution is to keep reading.

Cheerio, chaps, I guess we're heading back in now.

* * *

REWRITING HISTORY

Being home in Fairview felt both familiar and like culture shock after nine months in London.

For starters, it took me a week to recover from the time difference, but most significantly, London was a big city, like New York City-big. Fairview was a small town, miniscule by comparison. I had to make the mental adjustment back to the slower pace, the change in amenities, driving instead of walking everywhere.

When I'd left for London, I'd been accustomed to New Orleans, which wasn't quite as big but still a city. Back at home, everything felt strange to me.

As Brandon forewarned, Liam had called me into his office before I left and asked if I'd consider coming back to work full time with them. I didn't say no, and he agreed to give me a few weeks to consider their offer.

It was a great starting gig that even included me being in short videos for the website. I'd earn a good wage that would allow me to live in town… but I'd be worlds away from my family and from Julian. So in addition to all the other adjustments, that was hanging over my head.

"You've picked up a little accent." Mom watched me with a grin as I made my breakfast. "I like how you say your *-er* words now."

"Oh no." I put my hand on my forehead. "Do I sound like a royal jerk?"

She laughed and hugged my shoulders. "I think it's cute! Don't worry, I'm sure it'll fade after a few weeks."

I hopped up on the bar, sipping a mug of coffee. "Just so long as I don't sound like one of those sodding gits with their dodgy fake accents."

"What?" She laughed, leaning on the bar beside me.

"I'm just teasing. I just don't want to sound like a showoff."

"You don't, but that was a pretty good imitation!" I smiled, and she hesitated a moment. "I confess I'm a little surprised. I thought you'd be headed over to Phoenician I as soon as you got in town."

My brow pulled together. "Whatever for?"

I couldn't imagine my mom thinking I'd visit Bill Kyser, no matter what had gone on before I left.

That's when she stood up straight, arms crossed. "Because that's where Julian is now. Only you didn't know he was working there, did you?"

"Oh." I relaxed my forehead and tried to play it off. "Right. I just wanted to freshen up a bit first."

"When did it happen?"

"When did what happen?"

"Did you two break up or what?" Her eyes went to my hand where the little dragonfly ring still sat.

I lowered my mug and jumped down from the bar. "No... We just sort of put this year on hold or something. Because of how much work I had to do. And there was the time difference, and you know. International rates are so high and all."

"No way." Mom shook her head. "You honestly think I'm buying that after how you two were?"

My stomach tightened. I wasn't ready to explore whatever was going on between Julian and me with my mom at this very moment, but at least I knew where he was.

"It was something we decided last summer. You had to notice we weren't together as much."

"I noticed you leaving the house all the time. I assumed you were meeting up with him or surfing or whatever you two do."

"Surfing." That was as far as we needed to go on that topic.

Her voice grew quiet. "How does your job offer change things?"

The tone in her voice was like a stick jabbing all of the feelings I'd been pushing down for the past year. All of that pain, my shredded insides, came rushing to the front of my mind. A year of ignoring them and burying myself in work had done nothing to dampen the intensity of how badly his words had hurt me.

It didn't matter. I wasn't giving up on us, and whatever he was thinking, I wasn't letting him give up either.

"I don't know how it changes things. I guess I'll have to see him and talk to him about it."

She pulled me into a hug, smoothing her hand down the back of my hair. "I love you sweetie. Just remember, no matter what happens, the right thing will happen. Does that make sense?"

New Age philosophy wasn't exactly my favorite thing at the moment. I knew what *should* happen. Julian and I had to figure out what went wrong and fix it, so I shrugged.

"Thanks, Mom. I'll keep that in mind."

I stared at my phone for five whole minutes before working up the nerve to text him. Then I composed ten different messages before finally settling on the one I liked.

ANNA

Just got in. Hope to see you soon?

But before I actually hit send, I stared at the words. What if he still didn't reply? Could I handle that again?

Thinking of Brandon somehow made me feel bolder, even if I wasn't interested in him. Something in me turned his interest into validation. No matter how Julian was acting, I had somebody out there who thought I was worth having.

It made my stomach hurt. He wasn't the one I wanted. Nobody was.

I picked up my phone again and was about to hit send when it rang. I jumped and nearly dropped it. Rachel.

"Rachel—Hey!" I was so relieved for the momentary reprieve, I probably sounded too excited to hear her voice. "How was your year? How was the new roommate?"

"Horrible." Rachel's voice was completely flat.

My jangly nerves made me burst out laughing. "Oh, come on, she couldn't have been that bad!"

"She was a filthy slob, and I almost kicked her out before the end of the year. I swear, some people have no home etiquette." She exhaled in my ear. "You're coming back next year, right?"

I hesitated. So much depended on what happened when I finally saw him again.

"I-I'm not sure."

"Anna! Why? What will you do?"

"I've kind of been offered a job over there." Chewing my lip, I waited for her response.

Her voice was resigned. "Well, of course you have. You're going to take it, I'm sure."

"I'm not sure yet."

That perked her up. "When will you know? Seriously. I'm at the point where I'm about to give up, shock the family, and just move in with Brad."

"You're practically doing that anyway."

"Oh, man. You really have been in London too long. When are we going out? I want to hear all about it."

"It's Thursday. Want to meet up at the Hangout?"

"Wink is supposed to be playing at Tacky Jack's. Want to go there instead?"

Sounded like things were changing here as well. "Sure! You know the cool stuff to do in town."

"See you at eight."

Even though the place was called Tacky Jack's, I decided to wear one of the dresses I'd bought in London. It was thigh-length fuchsia knit with a racer-back top, and I loved how the flippy skirt made me feel like dancing.

I chose a pair of tan stack heels, and I styled my hair in a low, side ponytail. It had grown longer than I'd ever worn it before, and the curls spilled in a chestnut waterfall of spirals down my front. I smoothed on red lipstick and a little mascara then I added silver hoops and a cuff bracelet before grabbing my bag and heading out.

Dad called from the couch before I went through the door. "Well, look at my Anna Banana!"

"Dad," I groaned, stopping at the bar. Then I started to laugh and stepped over to where he lay on the couch watching some show. "I love you." I kissed his nose and straightened up. "I'm meeting Rachel at Tacky Jack's. I won't be too late."

"Tacky Jack's won't know what hit 'em when you get there."

Shaking my head, I went through the door to my car, and in less than ten minutes, I was pulling into the gravel parking lot. Stepping out, I realized I had changed as well from the last time I went out in Dolphin Shores, but it was okay.

Time meant change, and I could deal with some of it.

Walking inside, I was surprised by the size of the crowd. I'd never heard of the band Wink, but clearly they were local celebrities. It took me several minutes and two passes through the room before I found Rachel hanging at the bar with Brad.

"Anna!" She squealed, jumping up and running to give me a hug. "Look at you! You're so sophisticated. Very London."

That made me laugh. "No, it's just me. I did get a few cute dresses across the pond."

"I can't wait to see them, and I love your hair. Julian's going to drop when he sees you."

All of my insides seized at her words. "Julian?" My hands went shaky. I hadn't expected having our reunion without a little preparation.

"Brad called him. He'll be up here in a little bit." She had a sneaky glint in her eye, and I knew exactly what was going on.

"Rachel. What are you guys up to?"

"Just be cool, girlfriend, you are smokin' hot tonight." The music cranked up, and I couldn't hear a thing.

Brad cut in at that point with his loud voice, giving me a rough hug. "Anna! You haven't forgotten your old home town have you?"

"No way," I shouted back. "One trip to the beach was all it took. I love it here."

"Glad you're home, girl." He looked up behind me, and the change in his expression made my chest squeeze.

I knew what was about to happen.

"Jules!" he shouted. "Over here!"

For a second, I was afraid to turn around. Then I heard his voice, and my arms instinctively crossed over my stomach.

"Hey, man. I just came over from work." They clapped hands, and I stole a glance over my shoulder.

Blue eyes seared into mine, and for a second, I forgot how to breathe.

His voice grew softer. "Anna?"

Swallowing the lump in my throat, I faced him, managing to smile. "Hi, Julian."

His eyes quickly scanned my outfit before returning to my face. "You look... really good."

"Thank you." I took him in as well—dark slacks and a white oxford unbuttoned at the top, a blazer slung over his arm.

He looked so much like his dad, all business. The only thing that was still him was the longish, inky brown hair. But even that was cut in a more adult fashion and styled back, behind his ears.

"You look different... *good*, too."

"Your hair's longer." His eyes moved over me in a way that was both hesitant and hungry.

It made me feel self-conscious, and at the same time, I wanted him to take me away from here so badly. All I could think of were our reunions in New Orleans, our bodies wrapped together like Asian contortionists. Or spaghetti. Or monkeys.

"I let it grow." I was so distracted, I tried to think of anything to say. "There was some talk about me doing more broadcast."

"Of course. The camera loves you." His words were oddly familiar, but I couldn't place why.

It didn't matter. The heat between us was so palpable, I was certain anyone within two feet of us could feel it. Brad just laughed and left us to find Rachel.

"I'll buy you a drink." He motioned to the bar. "What would you like?"

I realized he was twenty-one now. "Just a Malibu pineapple."

I didn't really want to drink anything, but I needed something to calm my racing heart. I needed something to do with my trembling hands. It was the first time we'd spoken in almost a year.

He turned back with my bev, and I noticed he was having something clear that looked like vodka with a little wedge of lime. He leaned forward, and that fresh, ocean scent flooded my senses.

My eyes almost closed, but he shouted. "Want to go outside where it's quieter?"

"Sure," I said in my best, casual tone.

Outside, on the back patio, the volume of the band was much

lower. A light breeze was blowing as always, and I walked over to look out across the canal.

"Did you like being in London?" The way he asked almost felt like we were meeting each other for the first time.

But we knew each other so well. How much had changed in a year?

"I guess. I mostly worked." Looking down, I remembered burying myself in work, trying to forget how badly I missed him. "But the few times I explored the city, it was really amazing. So much history."

He nodded, and I took the lead. "I heard you're working full-time now. At the Phoenician?"

He blinked up to me. "Who told you that?"

"My mom. She wondered why it wasn't my first stop when I got home."

His brow lined. "She didn't know we—"

"I didn't tell her." I looked down again. "I didn't tell anybody."

He didn't speak, and I decided it was now or never. I couldn't be here with him like this and not try.

"Julian, what happened to us?" My voice was a cracked whisper. "How could you push me away, give up on everything we had?"

His expression changed, and I saw the old anger brewing there. "That's the best case of rewriting history I've ever heard."

"How? What is this history you think I'm rewriting?"

"Just let it go, Anna." He bent his elbow and rested it on the patio column, putting his hand over his eyes. "It's water under the bridge."

Stepping forward, I caught his arm. "It doesn't have to be. I don't want it to be."

He lowered his elbow and faced me, looking straight into my eyes. "I was pretty young when I imagined our future. I thought it would be easy, all we needed was love."

Taking another step closer, I held his gaze, my own eyes

heating from the mist pooling there. "You don't believe that anymore? I still do."

We were so close, mere inches and our lips would be together. That same, familiar pull was between us, my heart reaching for his.

The longing I'd suppressed burned in my chest as his blue eyes flickered to my mouth. I was sure he'd kiss me. Instead, a group of kids burst out onto the patio, killing our mood.

They were laughing and singing too loud, and all at once, I didn't want to be here anymore. I didn't want to be anywhere but my room, my bed, far, far under the covers.

"Thank you for the drink," I said, glancing at the full cup I hadn't touched. My voice was thick with unshed tears. "Please tell Rachel I had to go."

Without giving him a chance to speak, I took off for my car, not stopping until I was back at the house. It was dark and quiet when I got there. I'd only been gone a little more than an hour, but I supposed my parents turned in earlier now. They were getting older.

I climbed the stairs to my room, took off my flirty dress and shoes and threw them in a pile in the corner. I jerked on my old sleep shirt and stepped across the hall to wash my face. I wasn't sobbing, I wasn't even really crying, but every so often a stray tear would leak onto my cheek.

The house was dark and quiet when I went back into my bedroom and shut the door. I was about to turn on the lamp when I heard a noise at my window. My heart jumped when I saw him. He must have followed me when I left.

Quickly, I turned the lock on my door before crossing the room to throw open the window and let him in.

We didn't speak. We didn't have to. His lips covered mine, and a little noise of happiness ached from my throat. He kissed me fast, claiming my mouth. I held his cheeks, doing my best to keep up as my chest grew tighter with every heartbeat.

We broke apart, his forehead rested on my cheek and we held each other, panting.

"I couldn't let you go tonight." His voice was a hoarse whisper. "I couldn't… I don't care about the rest."

Holding his neck, I kissed his lips again and again, savoring the familiar sweet, minty taste of him, loving him kissing me back. "There's nothing but us. None of that other stuff matters."

He led me to the small bedside, and I stopped, unbuttoning the rest of the buttons on his white shirt until his tan chest was exposed. Smoothing my hands over the body I knew so well, I pressed a kiss against his skin. He reached down and pulled the sleep shirt over my head so nothing was between us.

We held each other a moment longer before he lifted my chin and kissed me deeply. Like so many nights before, we maneuvered our way into the tiny twin bed, tangling limbs until we were complete.

Being with Julian was so easy, so beautiful. Everything in me relaxed with him, with us together. Every kiss, every touch was like we were intended to know exactly what the other needed.

But it was more basic than that, more instinctive or spiritual. Nothing we could've done could've stopped this reunion. Like a piece of music waiting to be written or the fragments of glass waiting to be put together in a beautiful mosaic.

All our broken pieces came together in a gorgeous work of art.

We both groaned quietly. My body trembled with the intense feelings he always aroused, and it wasn't long before we both found the satisfaction we'd been craving.

When it was quiet again, we held each other. We didn't speak. He kissed me again before shifting to the side and pulling me against his chest.

Nothing had changed, and I was sure nothing would ever change. This was where I belonged. His strong arms were around me, and waves of happiness moved through me with every heartbeat.

Lacing our fingers, I pulled his hand to my lips, kissing the little dragonfly he'd inked there. My ring was just above it—I'd never taken it off. I believed the watercolor he'd made. These little symbols were a part of the love that held us together. They'd been his dream first, and then he'd shared it with me. Now it was mine, and nothing could make me give up on it.

When I opened my eyes the next morning he was gone, but for the first time in a year, I was calm. That horrid, gaping hole that was left when my heart had been ripped out was finally filled. It was a space that belonged only to him.

Rolling onto my side, I reached out for the pillow where he'd slept, pulling it to my face and inhaling deeply. I loved his fresh, ocean scent. All I could think about was seeing him today. I wanted to spend every minute with him. I grabbed my phone and sent a text.

ANNA

Miss you already. What time did you leave?

Lying back to stretch my arms over my head, I smiled, remembering his touches, his kisses, the sounds he made when our bodies moved together. Warmth stirred in my middle, and my phone buzzed.

JULIAN

Set my phone alarm like always. Old habits die hard.

My nose wrinkled.

ANNA

Smart habits. We're still not able to tell all.

I waited, but nothing more came through. It was okay—if he was working with his dad, I'd have to learn his new schedule.

I kissed the face of my phone and decided I'd surprise him at his office, maybe bring him a picnic lunch. It seemed like the perfect day for one.

All my worries were behind me.

* * *

COMPLETE BACKFIRE

The Kyser-Brennan offices were exactly like they'd always been, not that I expected them to change. It had only been three years since I'd come here as an aspiring journalism student, hoping to get an exclusive interview from the area's richest, most influential businessman.

It was the start of a journey that would change my life.

The elevator opened at the penthouse suites, and I stepped out into the familiar wood-paneled lobby. A small sitting area was arranged with magazines and tables. The only new addition was the perky, blonde receptionist behind the desk.

She looked about my age.

I hadn't told Julian I was coming. I'd only packed a basket, thinking we could go down to the beach just outside the building to share it. Being together last night was so gorgeous, I was sure he'd be as eager as me to slip off alone again.

The girl behind the desk looked up expectantly.

"Hi, Anna Sanders here to see Julian… um—" I wasn't sure if he went by LaSalle anymore or if he'd switched to Kyser.

"I'm sorry?" The young woman arched her brow as if she were suddenly impatient, as if helping visitors wasn't her job.

"I'm here to see Julian LaSalle or Kyser?"

"Hmm…" She looked down at the calendar on her desk then back up at me. "I'm sorry, but Mr. Kyser has a meeting in ten minutes. If he's not expecting you, I'm afraid you'll have to wait."

"It's okay," I said with a sweet smile. "We're old friends. I'll just say hello if he has a prior commitment."

"I'll let him know you're here." Then she used her pen to point past me. "If you'll just sit over there and wait."

I definitely did *not* like the new help. Still, I thanked her and walked over to the small sitting area. I'd been in this spot before waiting on his dad. It reminded me of my ride in the elevator with Will, and my nose curled. Not pleasant memories.

Pulling out my phone, I shot him a text.

ANNA

You're more guarded than the Queen of England.

My phone buzzed right away.

JULIAN

Are you in the office?

ANNA

Yes.

At once, a door behind the receptionist's desk opened, and I looked up to see what could've been a younger, slightly darker version of Bill Kyser.

He wore gray slacks, a white dress shirt, and even a tie, although it was loose and his top button was open. He was gorgeous.

"Anna?" He smiled, and I had to swallow the butterflies that had swarmed in my stomach and lodged in my throat.

That had just spent the night with me?

"Hey," I managed to answer as I walked to where he stood waiting. "I thought you might be hungry."

He reached out for my arm, escorting me into a large, bright office. It had the same huge windows as Mr. Kyser's, but broad tables covered in architectural drawings took up the majority of the space. In the back corner was a model of one of the Phoenician complexes.

"This is really nice." I walked to a window and looked out at the crystal blue waves stretching out to the horizon.

"They put me in Mom's old office." He came and stood beside me. "It's better for looking at plans and drawing. Better light."

I looked up at him. "You're so official now. Do you like it?"

He exhaled a laugh and looked away, rubbing his eyebrow with his thumb. "I do." Those blue eyes cut to me, and I felt a little wobbly inside. "I know, it's kind of weird, but I really do like it."

"I don't think it's weird at all." I didn't tell him his mother had loved it too. Maybe one day she would tell him, if she hadn't already. "Are these some of your projects?"

"Yeah, you can take a look." I set the basket on the floor and walked over to one of the tables. It was all lines and angles. "Most of this is done on the computer now, but I guess I'm a little old school. I visualize better if I start on a canvas. You can see the three-dimensional version on my computer, though. It even shows the building finished."

He left me to go to his desk, but I stayed by the drawing table. I didn't understand any of it, but my eyes were caught by a scrap of paper peeking out from one of the plans. It was another of his sheets of doodles, his old brainstorming device. Small, in one of the corners was a girl's profile he'd sketched. It had crazy-curly hair, and my lips pressed into a smile. It was me, and a hopeful tingle stirred in my stomach.

"Want to see?" He looked up from his large computer, and I walked to where he was leaning over the keyboard, moving the mouse. "It's something we're going to propose for down in Jamaica or the Bahamas, similar to a Sandals-type resort. He clicked on various screens. "It's modeled after an old property in Costa Rica Dad visited a while back."

The computer animation showed the rollout of a tiki-style resort complex, with infinity pools, a golf course, and a spa. Paths and waterfalls running down the natural landscape surrounded it all. I remembered the descriptions of Tengo Sol in his mother's journal.

"It's gorgeous." It was all amazing and very impressive.

He was so different standing in front of me. He was a businessman now, but at the same time, the loose tie and dark hair pushed behind his ears, the little doodles that helped him think, the sketch of my profile—all of it said he was still the boy I'd fallen in love with.

We were quiet for a few moments. I was unsure what to say, but he glanced across the room. "Did you bring a picnic basket?"

"Oh! Yeah." I walked over and picked it up, carrying it back to his desk. I lifted one side of the lid. "It's just sandwiches. I threw in some Funyuns and two Cokes. Nothing major."

"Funyuns?" He shot me a pure Julian lady-killer smile. "You know I can't resist a Funyun."

I started to laugh. "They give you bad breath. I'm not sure why I packed them."

"If I make you eat some, too, you'll never know."

We were being so formal. All I wanted to do was pull him to me and kiss him like last night, but a brief rap on his door broke the moment.

What happened next stomped on it.

"Come in?" Julian called, and Will sauntered into the room.

"You ready to talk tikis?" He was studying a packet in his hand, but when he looked up and saw me, he lowered it. "I didn't see you had a visitor. It's… Anna?"

Was he actually going to pretend he didn't know me?

"Yes," Julian straightened. "You remember Anna. She's just back from London. She did a year abroad with the BBC."

His lip curled in disgust. *So* not surprising. "And she came *back?*"

"This is where I live, after all." I answered, not appreciating the third person.

After nine months of covering world news in a foreign country, it was going to take more than Will Kyser to throw me.

"Lucky you." His dismissive tone was so irritating, I blurted my news without thinking.

"Although they *did* offer me a full-time position if I stayed." I slid my hand over the handle of the picnic basket as if my announcement was no big deal. "I'd start as a junior reporter in the world news HQ. I've got a few weeks to decide."

The first thing I noticed was Julian's posture change. He straightened away from his desk, slipping his hands into his back pockets.

The second thing I noticed was a real smile creeping across Will's face. It made me slightly nauseated.

"Well, that *is* good news," Will replied. "I'm sure you're going to tell them yes. How could you not?"

Somehow it felt like my brag had completely backfired. "I'd have to live in London, and I'm not sure if I want to move there permanently."

"But you *are* interested in being a journalist. Isn't that why you were always here talking to my father?"

God, I hated Will. "Yes. It's what I've always wanted to do."

"Then naturally, working at the BBC would be your dream job. It's like getting an offer from the *New York Times*, if that lousy rag were still worth reading."

I couldn't decide which of his comments angered me more. "Whatever I decide, it's really none of your business."

Grasping the handle of the picnic basket, I lifted it off Julian's desk and moved quickly toward the door. Julian was right behind me.

"Hey, wait a second." His voice was quiet, and he glanced back at Will before pulling me out into the reception area and closing the door. "I do have a meeting scheduled with him right now. I'm sorry about the picnic."

"It's okay. I should've checked with you first." Everything in me felt flustered and mixed up.

Stupid Will. He'd said all the things I knew were true in his typical evil fashion. As if my golden opportunity were the best thing to ever happen to him!

"Hey." He caught my hand, and gave me a little grin. "What's going on under all those curls?"

It was a question he'd asked me so many times. In the past I'd taken it for granted, but now I thought I might cry. "Your older brother is the worst."

He laughed, and no Armani suit, fancy office, none of it could change the fact that at that moment, he was still my Julian. "Don't I know it. Still, he has a few good points—"

"He does not."

"When it comes to business. You didn't let me finish."

"He's an evil jerk, and I hate him."

Julian laughed more, and I started to leave again. But he caught my waist. "Can I take you to dinner? Make it up to you?"

My irritation melted away. "I'd love that."

He released me and turned to the door. "I'll pick you up at your parents house. Seven?"

I nodded, and he disappeared into his office. I stood for a moment staring at the closed door. All my emotions were a conflicted mess in my chest. I wished he would've kissed me just then. In the past, it seemed he was always stealing kisses.

Taking a deep breath, I turned slowly into an annoyed glare coming from the little blonde behind the desk. A light bulb went on over my head, and I realized she had a crush on him. Of course she did! Who wouldn't?

"Thanks again," I said, giving her a sweet smile, then I headed for the elevator.

* * *

MOMENT OF WEAKNESS

Mom was thrilled when I told her Julian was picking me up for dinner. I wished I'd asked for more information before I stormed out of his office in a twist. Standing in front of my closet, I had no idea whether to go formal or casual…

A year ago, I'd have grabbed jeans and a tank or a light summer dress. Now he had an office. He wore expensive suits, and I assumed he was paid very well. It was strange not to know how to dress for a date with Julian.

ANNA

I'm standing in front of my closet clueless.

JULIAN

Are you searching for treasure?

ANNA

I'm searching for clothes. Where are we going?

JULIAN

Cosmo's? Or if you like, Cobalt catered Lucy's wedding. You pick.

Chewing my lip, I thought about the two upscale restaurants on East End Beach. I'd never been to either.

ANNA

Cosmo's sounds good.

JULIAN

You didn't like the food at Lucy's wedding?

I snorted a laugh.

ANNA

You saw me eating it.

You're right. We need our own place. Cosmo's it
is. On my way.

For a moment, I stared at my phone face reading the words "our own place" over and over. That sounded very promising. Then I realized if he were on his way, he'd be here in less than twenty minutes.

Snatching a red dress off one of my hangers, I dashed across the hall to finish my hair and makeup.

I was just stepping into my tan wedge heels when I heard voices downstairs.

"It has been too long since we've seen you." My mom's voice was animated as always talking to Julian. "When was the last time? Lucy's wedding?"

"I think it was." Julian's voice was noticeably less flirty than it used to be.

I kind of hated that, but with a sigh, I realized it meant we were growing up.

My eyes were made up in smoky browns, so I smoothed beige lipstick over my lips and did a little turn in front of the mirror. The red knit dress I wore was narrow at the waist and then flared out to my knees. The top scooped in from my shoulders, showing them off and making them look slightly broader. It was a very flattering silhouette.

My hair was smoothed, and with a strand of costume pearls around my neck, I felt very sophisticated. Picking up my phone, I headed down to meet my date.

His back was to the stairs as I descended, but I noticed he was in tan slacks and a navy short-sleeved polo. It was casual, but still went with what I was wearing. My mom, did a small gasp.

"Oh, look at you two!" Her voice caused Julian to turn, and the change in his eyes when he saw me made my stomach tingle.

He might not make comments anymore, but I could see he still thought them.

With a grin, I leaned forward and kissed his cheek. "You look very handsome."

His gaze made my legs weak.

"I can't get over how grown up you both are," Mom continued, her hands clasped. "It seems like just the other day you were going to one of those fall dances. How many of those did y'all go to together?"

I managed to break away and hug her. "Two. We went to two fall dances together and prom."

"Well, you were very formal for prom, that's true."

"We won't be too late, will we?" I glanced at Julian, and he seemed to come back from wherever his mind had gone.

"I don't know. We can do whatever you want."

Mom jumped right in. "Stay out as long as you need. You guys are adults now."

My eyebrows rose, but Julian caught my hand as we left the house. The silver BMW was sitting in my driveway, and I thought about Will and his nastiness. I wondered how Julian had made it through the hostility. Now it seemed they were actual business partners, and the whole "bastard half-brother" outburst was forgotten.

"You look really beautiful." Julian's voice cut through my thoughts. "Your mom's right. A lot has changed since high school."

I put my hand over his, and my thoughts drifted to sleeping in his arms last night. "A lot has stayed the same, too."

"I hope you like this place. It's the first time I've been able to afford to take you to a fancy restaurant."

Looking up at his profile, I couldn't help being impressed by the man he was becoming. He eased into the Kyser lifestyle so seamlessly.

"I never cared about those things with you."

"I did." His voice was quiet, and it seemed his mood shifted. "For you."

Cosmo's Restaurant was on the canal, and it was closer to the Kyser mansion than to my house. While it was more high-end, it still had a relaxed feel.

The hostess showed us to our table, and Julian ordered a bottle of wine. I studied the menu, trying to decide if I wanted Asian or American cuisine.

"If you miss New Orleans, they have a Muffaletta pasta. They also have a sushi menu." He held the menu in such a way that I couldn't see his face. It felt strange that he mentioned New Orleans and sushi, since it was the source of our first big disagreement, but I let it go. I hadn't eaten much sushi when I lived here, after all.

"I'm really curious about the banana-leaf wrapped fish."

He closed the menu and placed it on the table with a grin. "Get it, then, Banana-Face."

I couldn't stop a snort. "What are you getting?"

"Tournadoes."

That caught my eye, and I read the description of grilled tenderloin stuffed with feta and served with polenta and asparagus. "That sounds delicious."

"I'll let you try it."

The waiter came and took our order and menus leaving us facing each other, and for a moment, I wasn't sure what to say. We were out of context here, and my visit to his office, the encounter with Will had stirred up all my former insecurities.

"Your office is really nice." I took a sip of wine, feeling like that was a dumb thing to say.

He didn't respond at first, touching the base of his wine glass as if he were thinking. "It took a month for me to feel comfortable in it. My creativity was seriously stumped."

"So you left SCAD then?"

"Yeah." His blue eyes flickered up to mine. "It was the right time, and I was ready to get started."

Nodding, I fiddled with the cloth napkin in my lap. "I think that's okay. If it was what you really wanted, why wait? And you said you really like it."

He nodded, but I could tell he had withdrawn. I couldn't be certain of his normal demeanor now, but something had changed from before. It was as if something were on his mind, and he almost seemed a little sad.

"So everybody knows now?" I asked, and he frowned up at me. "That you're Mr. Kyser's son?"

"Oh, yeah."

"I really missed a lot last year."

"It wasn't that big of a deal. I mean, he didn't do an announcement party or anything. It just sort of trickled out." His eyes were back on his flatware. I watched him straighten his knife. "Most people already knew or at least suspected anyway."

I didn't really want to bring up a bad subject, but I was very curious. "How did you manage to get Will to be so nice to you? He acted like you were a regular business partner today in your office."

"I guess it's like I said, he's not such a bad guy. And he has a lot of contacts in the business world." He took a sip of his wine, but I couldn't let that pass.

"I can't agree with that first part. Has he really changed so much since last Thanksgiving?"

Julian shrugged. "I don't know. He's never said anything more to me about that, and Brad's right. He's been at it longer than us. He's a good member of the team."

It troubled me to hear him defending his evil older brother, but I decided not to press it.

"I'd rather talk about you." His eyes flickered up, and he smiled.

He was still holding something back, and I chewed the inside of my lip before conceding. "Okay. What do you want to know?"

I didn't like the question. It was so reminiscent of our old argument, and after last night, I didn't want us to go backwards.

Julian didn't seem to notice. "You said today they offered you a job? In London?"

"They did." I exhaled and took a sip of my wine.

He waited a few moments, but I didn't say more.

"Do you want to take it?"

We were at dinner together, we'd slept together. It had felt like we were making progress back to how we used to be, and now we were right back to the things that were trying to pull us apart.

Still, I had to answer truthfully. I'd always done my best to be honest with him. "I don't know. It's a neat opportunity…"

"*Neat*?" He glanced up at me, and my sadness intensified.

"Okay, it's an *amazing* opportunity." I sighed, looking down at my plate. "It's just not here."

The waiter appeared at that point and placed two small salads in front of each of us. He held the pepper grinder, but I shook my head. Julian asked for a few cranks. We were alone again, but I'd lost my appetite.

I picked up my small fork and turned the dark green and purple leaves over, stirring the tomato in the light vinaigrette. Julian took a bite of his, but he didn't look up at me.

We were both sitting here, in front of the enormous mountain of a problem I'd always known was coming.

"You don't like your salad?" His eyes found mine.

"I'm sorry." Shaking my head, I put the fork down. "I'm just not hungry. I don't want to spoil our fancy dinner, but—"

"No, no—we can get it to go. Hang on." He motioned to the waiter, who appeared immediately at our table. "Yes, Mr. Kyser?"

"We'd like to get our entrees to go, would that be possible?"

"Certainly, sir. They're still being prepared."

Julian glanced at me, then he took out his wallet and handed the man a card. "I'll come back and pick them up."

The waiter left, and Julian stood. "Let's take a walk."

I thought he meant we'd cross the road and walk along the canal, but he escorted me to his car and we drove back the short distance to the Gulf. He parked at the Hidden Pass lot and we left our shoes by the pier, heading down to the ocean.

It was a perfect night, warm but not too humid. The breeze whipped my hair around my head, but I had a band from my purse to tie it back in a ponytail.

All of the events that had led us to this moment were crashing in my head like the waves on the shore. I thought about him being here, working with his dad, and how I didn't even know about it. I thought about JYA, and how he'd practically ordered me to go to London, knowing it could lead to this.

Up until now, I'd had hope. For nine months, I'd held on so desperately to something I'd thought we both wanted until I got back here and found everything had changed.

I stopped walking and turned to face him. "Why did you send me away?"

My voice was sharper than I'd intended, but I needed to know.

"What?" His brow creased, and he actually seemed not to know what I meant.

But I was tired of waiting for answers. "Last year. You pulled away from me. You cut me off and shut down without an explanation, and then you sent me away. I want to know why."

He put his hands in his pockets and continued walking. "Don't spoil it, Anna. Just let it go."

"No!" I jerked his arm, making him stop and face me. "I want to know what happened."

"Why?" Now his voice was raised. "So you can lie to me again? So you can make promises you won't keep and then tell me how it was nothing?"

"How what was nothing? What are you talking about?"

"All those times you were with Jack. Having dinner with him, going to the park with him, kissing him on his boat. I don't want to hear any more lies about how it didn't mean anything to you."

My breath had disappeared. I felt like someone had jumped out from behind a rock and thrown a bucket of cold water directly in my face. I needed a moment to recover.

"I-I don't know what you're talking about. I told you everything—"

"Dammit, Anna, that's exactly what I'm talking about." He looked off and shook his head. "Don't deny what I saw with my own eyes."

I was so confused. "What you saw—but how? I don't know what you mean!"

My mind was ripping through memories like I might tear through clothes in a drawer, searching for anything that would make sense out of what he was saying.

We'd discussed the sushi night and that stupid kiss. I'd explained to him about the run-in at Fat Harry's. I'd texted him about going to the yacht for Rachel. When did I lie to him?

"Julian, please." My voice broke, and I felt the tears threatening. "I told you everything, I promise. There was nothing going on with him."

"I can't listen to this." He started to walk, but I held his arm.

"What about last night? Why did you come to me if you felt this way?"

He stood facing the water, not looking at me for several moments. Then he pressed his lips firmly together. "I don't know why I came over last night."

My stomach sank, and I wasn't sure I could hear this. The waves crashed on the shore, and he looked at them as if he were making a decision.

"I've been seeing Renee again." His words froze my heart. My eyes snapped to his, but only cold blue greeted them. "We've been together pretty regularly now, and I guess I had a weak moment. It was wrong of me."

I thought I might collapse. I didn't even realize I was crying until I blinked and the tears hit my cheeks.

"You should take the job in London," he continued, his voice sounding far away. "It's an amazing opportunity, and you can't turn that down. Good luck to you, Anna."

He patted my arm.

He actually reached out and *patted my arm.*

Something in me snapped. I raised my fists and hit his chest as hard as I could.

"LIAR!" I screamed, pounding my clenched hands against him. "Stupid, lying, *LIAR!*" My insides were broken, but I continued hitting him through my sobs. "I believed in you. I believed in US! I spent a whole year believing if I could just get back here, we could fix it. We could have what we had before. The greatest thing in BOTH our lives."

He didn't look at me, but he didn't back away from me either. He only stood there and let me hit him as if he didn't feel a thing.

I couldn't take his cold indifference anymore. I reached back and slapped him hard. His lips tightened, but still he didn't look at me.

"I'm taking you home now," is all he said.

"I'm not going *anywhere* with you! Not anywhere in that stupid car... that car..." For a moment I thought my head would explode. "You have no idea all the things I've done for you!"

That brought him around, but his voice was harsh. "You mean all the secrets you've kept? All the lies you've told? I'm sure I don't."

My voice was hoarse from crying and yelling, my cheeks were wet with tears. I couldn't think of another thing to say.

Only one thing was on my mind at this point—getting home and calling Liam. I was going to London. Damn right I was going to London, and I was never coming back here.

"I'll call a cab. You'll never see me again."

I walked away from him standing on that lost beach, my insides shattered and blasted to a million pieces. I knew I'd never be able to put them back together again.

* * *

That's it. She didn't write any more. I suppose she left this flash drive behind with all the rest of it when she moved to London.

I have to be honest, chaps, I feel a little winded right now, and I have so many questions.

She said she'd never come back here, yet here we are. We're at this bloody reunion, and all I can think is I want answers.

And if she doesn't demand them, I will.

~Jules

PART III
PRESENT DAY: HER

The woman lifted her face to the high-rise condominium building. It had been seventeen years since she'd stood in this parking lot looking up at the beige stucco behemoth.

Back then she'd been so young, so unsure of herself and her place in the world. She'd doubted everything—her ability to find success, to find love. Her ability to stand beside his family.

Then she'd done what he told her to do all those years before, after the fateful birthday party, when she'd sat on the beach and cried in his arms. Before their worlds started to twist and change.

She'd gone after the things she wanted. She'd worked hard, and she'd achieved award-winning success. She had her own money now and the ability to live wherever she chose.

None of it would have happened if she'd stayed here.

Somewhere along the way, she'd heard a speaker talking about success. He'd said where you see great success, you also see great sacrifice.

The flip side was if one *wanted* great success, one had to be prepared to *make* great sacrifice.

Looking up all those feet toward that penthouse office suite, she was ready to concede she'd made the biggest sacrifice of her life.

Today she was back, ready to face him. Ready to tell him the truth about the last secret she ever kept, knowing he already knew.

The muscles across her chest tightened, making it difficult to breathe, and instead of going straight up, she kept walking across the boardwalk and out to the soft, white sand. She walked all the way to the turquoise waters of the Gulf.

Before anything was said, she needed to see those waves again. The beach was getting crowded, but not as crowded as it would be in another month, when summer vacation kicked into full swing.

For now she had a bit of peace to think about what had happened.

It all started on a public beach.

Well, truthfully, it started in tenth grade algebra class.

She laughed remembering what a studious little coward she'd been back then. School was the only thing she was ever really good at. In relationships, she usually made an *F*. Possibly *F-*.

Until him.

Until she opened her eyes and saw what was right in front of her.

She'd tutored him in math, and he'd held onto her until she managed to score an *A* in relationships.

Then he walked away.

Dropping to sit on the dry sand, she allowed the sadness to trickle back in. That night was burned into her brain, and she'd replayed the scene over and over so many times. His cold indifference, her screaming and hitting him. The slap she could still hear across an ocean.

She hugged her knees to her chest. Funny how her eyes still misted whenever she thought of that night.

She also remembered the first day. The day she'd sat on this beach longing to be somebody else.

She'd done it. Now she was somebody else, although inside she was still that same girl. The girl who walked down to the shoreline and wished for anything to make her life more interesting.

So many wishes she'd made, that was the one that came true.

The constant breakers were a familiar soundtrack. Their rushing in and pounding then rushing back out put everything into perspective. It always had. No matter what happened here on these shores, those waves would keep going, over and over until the end of time.

Now it was time.

The tightness in her chest had relaxed, and she knew she couldn't put it off any longer. Standing, she dusted off her skirt and walked slowly back across the dry sand, back across the boardwalk, to where she'd left her shoes. Slipping her feet into the wedge heels, she went all the way to the elevator.

The shiny metal doors opened to the familiar, penthouse waiting room, but it had changed through the years. The furnishings were newer, and the magazines on the table were different. A different receptionist sat at the desk, a brunette with a pixie-cut. She smiled when the woman approached.

"May I help you?"

"I'm here to see Julian Kyser. Anna Sanders." Her voice was so formal.

Internally, she laughed, realizing she'd expected to sound as young and small as she'd always felt in this building. That too had changed.

"Oh, I'm so sorry, Ms. Sanders!" The girl seemed genuinely distressed. "He just left for the day, would you like to leave a message or a card?"

"Ah, no. That's okay. Thank you."

"Would you like to see someone else? I believe Mr. William Kyser is in his office."

Anna laughed aloud then. "That's okay. I think I'll skip that one today."

The girl gave her a confused smile, but nodded. "Okay, then. Sorry!"

"Thanks."

She turned and went to the elevator, trying to decide what to do next.

* * *

Gabi was on the couch watching television when she arrived back at her parents' home. The minute she walked through the door, however, her best friend jumped up to greet her.

"How'd it go? I've been dying. Tell me everything."

Anna dropped her bag on the counter and walked into the living room to flop on the couch, too.

Gabi was right on the edge. "Well?"

Inhaling a deep breath, she let it out. "I didn't see him."

"*What!*" Her best friend hit her with a pillow. "I oughta—how could you build it up like that and then say you never saw him? What happened?"

"I didn't build it up! You shanghaied me at the door."

"Pfft!" Gabi waved her hand. "Stop using British slang. I don't even know what that means."

Anna's lips curled. "Actually, I think that's Frank Sanders slang. I'm not even sure what it means."

"Wasn't that an old Madonna movie?" Her friend picked up the remote.

"You have the most random memories. How should I know?"

"I was alone a lot as a kid." Gabi hopped up and went into the kitchen, opening the refrigerator. "You were gone a long time. What did you do instead?"

"Hand me one of those." Anna rested her head on her hand as her friend brought her a soft drink. "I walked out to the beach. It's so beautiful, and I hadn't seen it yet."

Gabi popped the top on her beverage and sat in the old, worn armchair near the couch. "So what's the plan now?"

"Not sure really. I'm not going to his house."

"You could. It's partly Jules's house, too, you know. At least her grandparents live there."

Anna scratched her neck. "True. But I'd rather not talk to him there. I was hoping for a more *neutral* location. Before tonight."

"You think he's going to lose it?"

"I don't think so. I mean, I wouldn't expect that. Still, I don't want their first introduction to be at the reunion. Reunions are awkward enough without turning all… Jerry Springer."

"Juliette LaSalle, this is your father!" Her friend mocked a television announcer's voice, and Anna threw the pillow back at her hard. "Ugh! Gut wound!"

Her friend fell back, sending the old chair's footrest shooting forward.

"But hang on." Gabi sat up. "From what you've said, it won't be their first meeting."

"I can't believe that actually happened." Anna shook her head. "I wonder if Jules only thought it was him, you know how imaginative she is. Speaking of, where is she?"

"Haven't heard a peep since lunch. I think she went up to your old room to sleep off the jet lag."

"Gabi! You can't just ignore a teenager all day. And that's the worst thing she could do for jet lag. She needs to stay awake!"

"Sorry! I don't have such offspring of my own. Go do your motherly duty and check on her, but hurry. It's almost time to break some ice."

Climbing the short flight to the second floor, she stopped at her room, the only one now upstairs. Her parents had added a master suite on the first floor and relocated in her absence. She couldn't help thinking how useful that would've been in the old days when they'd done everything possible to keep their voices quiet.

"Jules, you in here?" She tapped softly on the door before opening it. "Jules! What's wrong?"

She dashed over to the twin bed, where her daughter lay face-down clearly sobbing. Sitting beside her, she gently rubbed the dark-brown curls.

"What's the matter, honey? Why are you crying?"

Several sniffles, and her normally free-spirited Jules sat up and buried her head in Anna's lap.

"Oh, Mum. I don't want to go to the reunion anymore. I don't want to see him. I don't care if I never see him again!"

Surprise momentarily stole Anna's voice, then she caught her daughter's face and lifted her chin. "What happened? Have you heard from him?"

"No!" Jules wailed. "I haven't seen him or heard from him, and I hope I never do."

Her mother's brow creased. "I don't understand. I thought you said you already liked your dad."

"I was wrong. I hate him!"

Anna sat and listened to her daughter's sobs, trying to figure out what could have possibly changed since breakfast. Then she had an idea. Jules did have half his genes, after all.

"Baby," Anna stroked her shiny dark locks. "Is it because he was never there for you? Is it because you think he didn't care?"

No answer; only more sobs.

"I'm so sorry about that, sweetheart, but you can't blame him. It was my fault. He never knew about you. I'm sure if he had—"

"How can you be sure of anything with him?" Jules sat up quick, her face splotched and wet from crying. "I want to go home! Back to England, back to Brandon! He loves us. He wanted to make a home for us!"

A sick feeling twisted in Anna's gut at her daughter's words, and she dropped her chin. "I'm sorry, Jules, but you know we can't do that. I don't love Brandon. I've only ever loved your dad."

"Then you're an *idiot!*" Her daughter fell back on her pillow again.

Anna stood quickly, her voice sharp. "Juliet Alexandra LaSalle!" But before she said anything more, she thought of all that had gone before, and it sapped her spirit. Her shoulders dropped. "You're probably right. You don't have to go tonight if you don't want to."

She was halfway to the door when wild arms flew around her middle in a tight hug. "Oh, Mum! I'm so sorry, I didn't mean it!"

Wrapping her arms over her daughter's, she soothed her. Lifting her miserable face, Anna wiped the fresh tears away with her thumbs. "Won't you tell me what happened? Why are you carrying on like this?"

Gabi's voice rang out from below. "Anna! Have you seen the clock? We've got to get out of here. The reception's about to start."

Exhaling a curse, she loosened her daughter's death-grip around her waist. "Look at me." The teen blinked at her. "Don't leave the house while we're gone. I won't stay the whole time. We can finish talking when I get back." Jules nodded, and Anna kissed her nose. "Now wash your face."

Running back down the stairs to her parents' room, Anna threw open the closet and hastily scraped the dresses she'd brought out of the way. "Gabi! This is casual right?"

"I hope so!"

"Not reassuring," she muttered under her breath and pulled out a faded denim halter dress that tied behind her neck.

It was backless, so she couldn't wear a bra. But she'd never been very well-endowed. Besides, it showed off her trim physique and hit mid-thigh. She stepped into strappy leather heels and dashed into the bathroom.

Sitting on the beach had fluffed out her hair, but thanks to the keratin treatment she'd gotten at the salon in London, her formerly wild locks were gentle waves now. Not too bad, and worth every penny, she thought.

Dusting powder on her nose, followed by a smear of red lipstick on her mouth, she ran to the door, and the two of them dashed out to her mother's old Accord.

"Can you believe it?" Anna joked. "I finally graduated to an Accord!"

"What did you drive when we were in school?"

"I don't think I drove anything when you were here, but I had Mom's old Civic after you left." She turned the car onto the main highway navigating the five turns it would take to get them to the high school gymnasium where the ice breaker reception was to be held. "Do you know who all's coming?"

"Nope, but we're about to find out."

The two friends stepped out of the car and adjusted their clothes. Gabi was a little thicker than when they were in high school, but she still looked healthy and ready for fun.

"You look every bit the BBC broadcasting star you are," her friend teased. "I've gotten used to it, but you're going to turn some heads tonight."

"Stop." She pinched Gabi's arm, eliciting a loud *Ouch!* "You're making me nervous, and it's just the old gang."

Inside, the gym was decorated in their senior prom theme, "A Night to Remember."

Gabi returned her pinch, causing Anna to squeal, then pulled her ear down. "Think that's prophetic?"

"You're doing it again," Anna hissed, pinching her a second time.

"We're both going to have bruises tomorrow if we keep this up."

Rachel and Brad were the first to spot them. "ANNA!" Rachel's voice seemed to echo through the aluminum building decorated with twinkle lights, fake columns, and arbors draped in white tulle.

Her senior-year bestie and former college roommate caught her in a laughing hug that spun her around. Then she threw an arm over Gabi's shoulders. "I'm so glad to see you guys! How have you been?"

"Great!" Gabi answered, looking around the room. "Was this the prom theme I missed?"

"Oh, please," Rachel's eyes rolled. "Don't beat that dead horse any more. I've heard for years how much that theme sucked."

"No way! I was going to say the exact opposite! I would've killed for a night to remember when I was in high school."

Rachel and Anna both laughed, and a huge man with two equally huge middle-school aged boys walked up. "Anna, Gabi, meet my guys, Brendan and Chad."

"I'm not one of your guys?" Brad leaned over and pulled Anna into a hug. "Hey, girl. You look great. Seen my boy yet? Need me to call him?"

Anna felt her face get hot, but Rachel cut in. "Julian's not coming tonight. You can relax."

It wasn't clear if Brad relaxed, but Anna sure did. She actually felt her entire body let go in those two sentences, and now she wanted Jules with her.

"Hi, Brendan, Chad." Winking at Rachel she teased. "I see you finally got away from the B-names."

"She just insisted on bucking the system," Brad complained loudly.

"Please. I was so sick of that reign of B-terror. How corny can you get? Bryant, Brad, Brendan…"

The boys stood around with their hands in their pockets, and Anna grinned. Brad caught her by the arm. "Let me buy you a drink!"

"What? I thought the whole party was catered…"

"He just loves saying that," Rachel called after them.

Brad handed her a clear cup of wine, and Anna's eyes landed on a huge guy she remembered very well. On his arm was a very elegant woman, clearly his wife, whose white smile was friendly and confident.

Jerking Brad's arm down, she whispered in his ear. "Is that Montage?"

Brad's head snapped up, and he shouted. "Hey, Mo! You made it!"

The big guy held up a hand before returning Scotty's shake. Anna continued whispering. "Did he go pro after leaving State?"

"Hell no," Brad laughed, his voice too loud. "Mo's an econ professor at Northwestern in Chicago now. He's one of our go-to guys when we have a question about business valuation or investment issues."

"You're kidding me!" She couldn't help but laugh.

The next pair of shrieks were so familiar, she jumped around to see.

"Yes, we made it! Of course we did!" Lucy and Robert were shaking hands and hugging old friends. "We actually drove straight from Birmingham to this gymnasium, so I expect Meggie's going to be screaming her head off in about five minutes."

Anna rushed over to her, and they both squealed and hugged. "You look *amazing*!" Lucy cried, waking the sleeping infant in her arms. "My goodness, you are literally a supermodel! Look at your hair!"

The little body twisted in her mother's arms, and Anna scooped her up. "Give me this baby!" Anna hugged the infant against her chest. "Who is this?"

Lucy smiled rubbing her little back. "This is Meggie, our newest. We sent all the boys to Dad's place on Hammond Island."

"*All* the boys?" Anna's brow wrinkled.

"All three of them!" Her friend started to laugh, and Anna couldn't help laughing, too.

"I can't even imagine your dad with three grandsons. How is he? Grumpy? Sweet? Does he give them candy or scotch?"

"Scotch, of course," Lucy cried. "Don't you know that's how all the men in my family are raised? Now where is my gorgeous niece I've only heard about?"

"Jules wasn't feeling well tonight. I'm not sure why… maybe it's that time of the month?" Meggie started to fuss, and Lucy pulled her out of her friend's arms.

"Lord knows, I'm not looking forward to all *that*. Boys are much easier when it comes to puberty."

"Oh, I'm sure." Anna pressed her lips together in disbelief.

"Hold that thought, I have to nurse her. Jack's just parking the car—be sure and say hello."

She had just finished her sentence and gone when her twin stepped into the crowded hall. Brad was right with him, handing him a drink and walking him around the room introducing old friends.

He looked so good, relaxed and happy. Anna's heart filled with joy, and when he saw her, his face broke into a smile.

Leaving Brad's side, he crossed the room to where she stood. "Anna."

Their embrace was brief.

"Doctor Kyser, I presume," she teased.

"You look amazing. Have you been in London all this time?"

"I have, and you're still in Tennessee?"

"Nashville. You know Casey and I got married?"

"I didn't! Congratulations!" She stepped forward and hugged him a little tighter this time. "I'm so happy for you."

"I finally convinced her she couldn't live without me."

"Oh, please."

He laughed, and nodded. "Honestly, I think she realized being my wife would make it easier for her to keep chasing that music career. Our schedules are both wild, but we make it work."

Memories of Jack's paternal grandmother filled her mind.

She'd abandoned her husband and a very young Bill to pursue a singing career in Branson. It was funny how Jack had such similar tastes to both of his grandfathers.

"Is she still singing?"

"Yes, and I told her she could keep on singing as long as she wanted. That sealed the deal."

"It sounds like you found the magic formula."

"You have cheekbones now." He winked, and Anna flushed.

She immediately blinked back up to face him. "Working in broadcasting tends to do that. Bye-bye, baby fat."

"I can't say I don't miss those round cheeks, but you look great."

Lucy returned, with Meggie on her chest, patting her little back. "I see you two found each other. Is Jack downplaying his role as adoring husband again?"

He stepped forward and took his niece out of her mother's hands. "You're not holding her right. I told you, that's going to make her colicky."

He put the baby higher, over his shoulder and patted her little back as he walked away.

Anna and Lucy exchanged a glance and burst out laughing. "Does he do that all the time?"

"Oh, he's impossible now that he's got that M.D. behind his name. You should hear the discussions he and Rob have. I just go to the boys' room and play Roblox. Now, when do I get to meet Julian's gorgeous girl? I can't believe you kept her a secret for so long. Lexy showed me her pictures, and she's the most amazing combination of you two."

"She really is. Let's do lunch tomorrow?"

"Yes! I can't wait to meet her."

Anna felt a light grip on her arm, and turned to meet a face she knew all too well.

"Summer." Her smile fell a notch. "Hello."

"Anna, would you mind if I spoke to you for just a minute. In private?" Her old nemesis-turned-friend-turned *whatever she was* appeared contrite for the first time in… never.

"Sure." Saying it, Anna could tell how much she'd changed.

Not once had she felt insecure or unsure what to do. Fifteen years of taking care of herself and Jules had taught her a lot.

Outside in the dim courtyard filled with picnic tables, she couldn't help remembering that fall night they'd all met out here.

Jack had swept her away to a dreamy make-out session on a moonlit beach, and she'd left Julian behind, alone.

Silly girl.

"I've had this on my mind so long, and so many times I wanted to write to you and apologize." Summer was pacing, wringing her hands. "I need to apologize. What I'm saying is, I want you to know how very sorry I am for what I did."

Anna was baffled. "What in the world are you talking about? Whatever do you need to apologize for?"

Not a thing stood out in her mind… except that one incident senior year, but that had been so long ago. Surely, she wasn't still hung up on it?

"What I did for Will. I never should have helped him, but I was still so bitter and jealous. Jack was still in love with you, and I just couldn't take it. When he came to me… I wanted to hurt you."

Anna's brow creased. "Are you talking about the spying? At the podcast studio? Seriously, forget it. I practically had until you brought it up again. I forgive you, okay?"

Summer's round eyes blinked up to Anna's hazel ones. "No… I meant at Loyola."

The patio was very quiet for a few moments.

It was early spring, so the frogs were singing, but otherwise, the two women looked at each other in utter silence.

"What do you mean… at Loyola?" Anna's breath hitched as certain shattered pieces slowly found their way back together.

"When Jack would meet you, the night he took you to dinner,

when you walked through the park. That day on his boat. Will would text me when Jack left the house. He'd tell me where to go, and I'd show up with my camera."

A picnic table was close by, and Anna put her hand on the top, easing herself to sitting. "You were spying on me in college? And taking pictures?"

Summer dropped her head, and Anna saw two tears fall. "I'm so sorry. I thought I was keeping you away from Jack. I never dreamed—"

"You were breaking up Julian and me." Her limbs felt weak as she said the words.

It all made sense now.

Yes, she'd told him what happened—when she'd finally worked up the courage or when she was finally with him again, but by that point he'd known about it for days if not weeks.

He'd known since the moment it happened. He'd seen it *with his own eyes...*

Remembering his words caused Anna's eyes to close briefly.

"So Will was sending Julian the photos as texts?" *Did Julian know Will sent them? Could that have been why he defended him?*

Summer shook her head. "I don't know. All I know is I sent Will the pictures. That's all I did, and I'm so ashamed." She rubbed her forehead. "He said it should've been me with Jack. He said I was part of the group, and I was more fit to take Casey's place than you ever were. I was such an idiot, I believed him. I thought Jack would see it, too... Until he moved to Nashville. Of course, he married her. He never cared about me."

Summer's voice trailed off, and Anna stared at the brick-lined patio, processing. It all made sense now. Will's Mardi Gras threat rang clear as a bell in her memory, and she should've known it wasn't an empty promise.

Distance alone would never have pulled Julian and her apart. Something more sinister was at work back then. The question was did it change anything?

"Can you ever forgive me?" Summer was waiting, her hands still clasped, but she was the least of Anna's concerns.

"I-I guess. I mean, I don't know. I really just… don't know. But I appreciate your honesty. Thank you for telling me."

The woman nodded and turned to go back inside the gym, but Anna stopped her.

"You were wrong," she said. "Jack was never in love with me. I was just a friend to him at a time when he really needed a friend. People tend to confuse the two emotions."

I know I did, Anna thought. It was possible he did, too.

Summer left, and Anna was alone in the courtyard. Rachel was quick to find her, looking back after their classmate as she walked out into the night.

"Are you okay? Why are you out here by yourself?"

Blinking up, Anna wasn't sure how to answer. She felt strangely numb.

"Is Julian bringing Renee with him to any of these things?"

Rachel breathed a laugh. "Why in the world would he do that? She's not in our class."

"I thought since they were dating when I left… They might still be together."

Her friend's brow lined. "What are you talking about? Julian never dated Renee after we graduated."

Anna looked up at her confused. "After college?"

"Renee started nursing school at the University of Sterling the year you left for London. Then she met some guy and they moved to Birmingham before the semester ended. I haven't heard from her since."

Anna's mouth dropped open, but no words came out. She closed it, and tried to think. "That can't be right."

"Oh, it's right. Trust me. I know." She studied her friend's bewildered expression. "Why are you asking me this?"

"When I came back… before I left for London again… Julian

said they were together. He said he… Why would he say that if it wasn't true?"

"Hang on." Rachel sat at the table across from her. "When you came back from London the first time. *After* JYA? Julian told you he was with Renee?"

"Yes! Why would he say that if it weren't true?" Her voice was rising in volume with her desperation.

She had to know the answer to this question.

"Did he tell you that night we met at the bar?"

"No." She remembered that night. She'd left, and he'd come after her. It had been… incredible. She was sure they would be together again after that night.

Only they weren't.

"When did he tell you then?" Rachel watched as her friend struggled with the memories. "Did he know about your job offer?"

The next day in the office, her brag to Will…

"He'd just found out." *And he'd begun acting strangely.*

"Is it possible," Rachel cleared her throat, and her voice grew serious. "Maybe he did it because he knew you'd take the job?"

Anna was on her feet in an instant, pacing the courtyard. Her stomach cramped like it hadn't in years.

"I have to go. Where is he now? Do you know where he is, Rachel?"

She jumped up, brow lined. "No. I mean, I don't know, but Brad could find out, I'm sure."

"I need Brad to find out. I need him to find out right now, and I need you to text me as soon as you know." She dashed into the gym with Rachel right behind her.

Anna's heart beat so fast. She wasn't sure what she was about to do, but fate had dropped a load of bombshells in her lap this evening, and she knew from covering world news, when that happened it was time to move.

Stopping before she got too far, Anna caught her friend's arm. "Rachel. Please don't tell Brad I wanted to know."

"Got it." Her old roommate dashed off in the direction of her husband.

Gabi was easily found, sitting with her drama club friends and laughing about the Fabulous Lady G, her high school persona in her short-lived music video career.

"It only failed because I can't sing!" Gabi cried. "They found out I was lip syncing the whole time, and that was the end."

Anna caught her eye, and quickly waved her over. "I've got to go. Do you want to stay a little longer and catch a ride? Or do you want me to take you home now?"

Concern registered on Gabi's face. "Is Jules okay?"

"Oh, crap!" Anna clutched her forehead. "I told Jules I wouldn't be too late."

"What's going on?"

"I just found out something… I have to talk to Julian now."

"I'll find a ride. You go." Gabi turned her friend's body toward the door and gave her a shove. "Don't worry about Jules. I've got it covered."

"Thanks, Gab."

PART IV
PRESENT DAY: HIM

He'd spent the entire day in his office, staring out the window, contemplating the past. His desk phone had rung, but he hadn't answered it. His smartphone buzzed, but he didn't pick it up.

He had a daughter.

She was an artist and a writer, and she walked exactly like his mother.

Why didn't he know this?

Even as he asked the question, he knew the answer. The night she left had been beaten into his memory with every strike of her fist against his chest. It burned across his cheek with the slap she'd given him.

He'd stood there and let her hit him, knowing everything he'd planted in her mind was a lie. His lie.

He'd lied to her and broken her heart. *Of course*, she didn't tell him she was pregnant. But why hadn't *somebody* told him?

That question tormented him, but not as much as the idea that they were both here, short miles away, close enough for him to touch.

They were staying in that house. The memory of how many times he'd climbed that damn tree twisted a pain in his chest.

After so many years of telling himself it was his choice, that he was satisfied being alone, the idea that he could have a family with her was killing him. It was the most acute torture he'd ever known.

Would she come here and tell him? Or would she make him find out in front of everyone at a high school reunion event? He never remembered Anna as being that dramatic. She wouldn't do that to their daughter.

Although he was discovering he was one of the few who didn't already know. It was like history repeating itself.

These small towns and their foolish secrets. How could they keep something like this from a person?

Another hour passed, and still she didn't come.

He stood and walked to the small table by his bookcase. On it was a crystal decanter and two heavy crystal tumblers. Even though it was early afternoon, he took the stopper out and poured a finger of scotch. Then he thought of his father.

Grabbing his suit coat off the back of his chair, he left the drink on his desk and walked out the door. "Mandie, I have to be gone for the rest of the day. Please take messages and send anything urgent to Will."

"Yes, sir." The pleasant young receptionist he'd hired was a nice change from the elitist blondes his older brother always installed at that desk.

Mandie was a friendly girl, who happened to be one of the most helpful members on staff, and Will's antics were starting to annoy him.

Before getting into his Audi, he pulled out his smartphone and sent a text to Lucy.

JULIAN

Can't make it tonight. Will see you tomorrow at
PIV. Please apologize to Rachel for me.

He'd see his sister and her mob of children tonight, and it always lifted his mood. For years, he'd played backup dad to them. Not that Rob did a bad job. It just kept him from feeling so alone.

Had Lucy always known about his daughter? He didn't want to think about it.

Pulling into the circular drive, he went into the huge mansion that was now his parents' joint residence, when his mother wasn't staying in the old home out on Port Hogan Road.

Why she held onto that place was beyond him, but he'd given up trying to figure out that woman. At Anna's and his father's request, he'd put the past behind him and drawn closer to her again. Or as close as authenticity allowed.

She was in New Orleans at one of her art showings this weekend, but his dad had stayed behind. Julian found Bill Kyser sitting out on the flagstone patio of his huge estate, looking toward the east.

"Dad?" He walked up and touched the man's shoulder.

"Julian." His dad eased himself out of the chair and hugged his son with a little less strength.

The warmth that glowed in his father's blue eyes every time they were together had gone a long way to heal the anger Julian had felt growing up.

"How are you feeling?" He sat across, facing his dad.

"Tired, like shit as usual, but that's part of getting old, isn't it? There's even a song written for it. The Rolling Stones wrote it."

Julian laughed. "Sixty is not old, Dad."

"Boring topic." Before returning to his chair, his father walked over to the small table holding a decanter of scotch. He pulled the stopper and poured two fingers in each crystal tumbler, bringing one to his son. "What's on your mind?"

Julian took the drink and turned it in his hand, thinking. His father knew about his child, he had no doubt. He also had no doubt his mother had forbidden him to say anything to Julian, and the entire family knew Bill Kyser did not cross Lexy.

He leaned back and put his ankle over his knee, thinking how to broach the subject. "I had an unexpected morning."

"Contractor giving you hassle? I'll take care of it if you want me to. I know all these rednecks. I gave half of them their start in one way or another." Then he glanced up at his son. "But you've never needed my help that way. You're a great businessman on your own."

Julian's brow relaxed with a smile. "Thanks, Dad." He sat forward then, putting his forearms on his knees. "It's not a contractor. It's a daughter. Apparently, I have one."

His dad was still for a moment then he took a pull off his drink. At that moment, all the uncertainties became clear.

Julian was the last to know.

Bill cleared his throat and sat straighter in his chair. "That wasn't a question."

His son stood and placed the untouched scotch on the small table. Walking to the edge of the patio, he stared at the eastern view. It faced Florida and other points along the south Alabama coast.

The more he thought about the entire situation, the more he felt an internal shift. His goals were changing, what he wanted. He didn't want to be angry with anyone anymore. He didn't care about holding onto the past. He wanted his future.

Turning back to his father, he had a new question on his mind. "You and Mom were apart for what? Seventeen years?"

His father's brow lined. "One could argue we were never together. But I guess you could say that. We didn't talk much for about that long."

Julian nodded. "When you *did* come back together, how did you make it work after being apart for so long? After so much had happened? I'm sure you both had changed a lot."

Bill considered this. It wasn't the question he'd anticipated his favorite son asking, but it was one he was ready to answer.

"Your mother and I spent a long time punishing ourselves for a mistake we made as kids. Our love broke a lot of lives, and we both sort-of… shut down that part of who we were." He took another sip of scotch, while his son waited. "When we came back together, that part, well, it was like it came right back to life. Like no time had passed. Granted, we'd raised families during our separation, and she was clearly a better parent to you than I was to any of my children—"

"That's not right, Dad. You tried so many times—"

"Thanks for saying that, son, but I do know what I'm talking about better than you do."

Julian turned and walked to the railing again.

His father chuckled. "I spent so many sleepless nights killing myself over the notion that Lexy might marry someone else. I was sure I'd throttle any man you called Dad who wasn't me. I was so screwed up. I believed I'd earned the right to be your father after all I'd sacrificed." His voice dropped lower. "I was such a self-centered jerk."

Julian went back to his father and sat in the chair facing him. Then he leaned forward and caught his hand. "I think we're all pretty self-centered at some point in our lives. The important thing is that we see it and change. Yes?"

"We were all pretty broken by what I did. But love came in and filled the cracks, and I think we're stronger now." His father softened. "You have always been the best thing that came out of that tragedy."

His son smiled and looked down.

"So." Bill slapped the top of his thigh. "What do you want, Julian? Tell me what you want."

A few moments passed as the youngest Kyser turned the question over in his mind. Then he looked up at his father. "I want her."

His father nodded, but Julian wasn't finished. "I want what's mine. I want my daughter, my family." He exhaled and leaned back. "But more than any of that, I want her."

Bill gripped his hand, pulling him close. Their blue eyes met, steel against steel. "Then go get her."

Julian stood, but before he left, he added. "I love you, Dad."

Bill smiled. "I love you, son. I've always been proud of you."

PART V
REUNION

Anna didn't know where she was going, driving away from the reunion with only a promise of a text. All she knew was the worlds were crashing in on her now. All the broken pieces were finding their way back together, and it was all making sense in a way it never had before.

Rachel's words stood out strongest in her mind—why he'd lied to her. *Maybe he did it because he knew you'd take the job.*

"Julian…" Her voice was a frustrated plea in the silent car as she drove down the beach road, trying to decide what to do. "Where are you?"

She'd never find him this way. Common sense wasn't what pulled the two of them together. It had never made sense that he would understand her like he did, or that he would wait for her the way he did.

Slowing the car down, she made a U-turn and headed back in the direction of their beach shelter. The place she'd sat and realized he was standing beside her all along. Where she'd realized she would follow him anywhere because she trusted him. Where she'd taken his hand and let him teach her to surf.

Parking the car, she ran out to the Romar Beach Pavilion. It was dark, and the sky was black with clouds obstructing the moon. No one was there.

The storm was growing, and most visitors and locals were safe in their homes. She ran toward the sound of the waves crashing. If the sun were out, he'd be riding those waves. At least, he would have been back then.

Slowing down at the water, she remembered another night they were here together. They were so desperate for each other, but he'd refused to do more until he knew who his father was. She'd spun around and screamed at the high rises. He'd jumped into the ocean to cool off...

Looking up, she let out a laugh, remembering how they'd been in those days. She'd finally figured out what she wanted, and she wanted it right then. Immediately. No more waiting.

He'd gone from trying everything to get into her pants to suddenly pushing her away. God, the frustrations of high school.

Her eyes climbed that old building and the lights were on in the top floor. Her breath stilled as she studied the lit penthouse office suite. *Was it possible—?*

She didn't worry about trying to figure it out. She ran back, all the way to the garage elevator, pushing the button repeatedly until the door opened.

Riding up in the shiny silver box, she tried to sort all the feelings racing through her brain. She tried to tame her scattering emotions. She had no idea if he'd even be up there, if she could even get in.

They didn't leave the offices open at night. It was most likely the cleaning service.

The doors opened on the familiar reception area, and she stepped out into the waiting room. Sure enough, a friendly group of cleaners were in the space, vacuuming carpets and dusting tables, emptying trash cans.

She dropped her head as the crew studied her curiously, as if she were trespassing on their property.

A lone woman stepped toward her. She only spoke Spanish, but she gestured toward Julian's door with a frown. *"Esta buscando el senor?"*

"Is someone in there?" Anna asked, knowing the woman didn't understand her.

Still, she walked toward the large door and reached for the handle. It gave to her grasp, and she pushed it open, stepping into his enormous workspace.

The sight of him hit her hard, straight in the stomach. He was sitting at his desk, wearing a familiar navy suit and white shirt. His top button was open, but tonight there was no tie.

Almost seventeen years had passed since she'd seen him that last night, but very little had changed. A few hints of gray peeked out at his temples. A few lines had deepened at the corner of his eyes, but otherwise, he was exactly the same.

"I waited all day for you to come." He spoke without looking up.

She walked toward his desk carefully, bracing for the onslaught of those eyes. In a blink he captured her, but at the same time, she could see the surprise register briefly. *Perhaps she captured him as well?*

"I came here earlier, but you'd already gone." Her voice was softer, slightly higher in contrast to his. She'd never noticed it before.

He glanced down and nodded. "I left early. Needed to talk to Dad."

She couldn't tell what he was thinking, but she knew why she was here. "You weren't at the reception tonight. I thought we might talk there—"

"Is there something you need to tell me?" He was holding himself back, but she didn't know that.

He wanted, no *needed* to know what she would say.

Chewing her lip, she walked toward the window. He knew she couldn't see out in the darkness, but he studied her while her back was turned.

She was slimmer than before. Her legs seemed longer somehow—maybe it was the dress? Her hair was even different. He'd always loved her wild curls, but tonight they were soft. They hung down her back in gentle waves that invited him to bury his face in them, inhaling the little flower scent he loved.

When she finally turned to him again, he wondered how he'd ever missed those shoulders. They were smooth and gorgeous, and her eyes flashed above perfect cheekbones.

"I don't know how to start." She was more confident now as well. "I have so many things I need to tell you."

"Just say the first thing that comes to mind." He leaned back in his chair watching her think.

It reminded him of when he used to watch her in class. Tonight she was so grown up, but at the same time, he still saw that teenage girl who captivated his imagination.

"I guess for starters… How are you?" She smiled, and it caught him off guard.

"I'm doing well. How are you?"

"Okay, I guess." She looked down, and turned back to the window. "I kept up with you… some. Sometimes I would let months go by, but then I'd get too curious. You've done very well here."

He held back a smile. He'd followed every report of her brilliant career as well. She'd stayed behind the scenes in production—writing and putting stories together, guiding the reporters.

She'd risen through the ranks all the way to News Director, but she'd stayed off the social circuit. He'd only ever gotten a posed headshot, and the occasional almost-miss at some function. It must have driven her bosses crazy, as smart and beautiful as she was.

"I've thought about that night so many times, all the things we said." She faced him again. "You were right. There were parts, small parts, I didn't tell you."

"I believe that was why we ended up fighting. I think it was even part of the reason you left."

"It wasn't the reason I left." She rubbed her hand across her chin. A new gesture. "I was so preoccupied back then with school and JYA and London, but all I thought about was you. I was studying to be a professional communicator, and I sucked at communication."

"Can I fix you a drink?" He motioned toward the small table.

"No. Thanks." She was momentarily flustered, and he wished he hadn't interrupted.

"Please continue."

"I didn't come here to make a speech." Those green eyes flashed at him, and he caught his tongue between his teeth. *Hazel.*

"Why did you come here?"

She reached back to catch her hair. A familiar gesture. "I wanted to see you alone because… well, I do have one secret I've been keeping. But now I think you already know what it is."

They'd arrived at the truth at last. "Tell me what it is, and if I already know it, I'll pretend to be surprised."

Her lips twisted into a frown. "Are you making fun of me?"

The strength in her was intoxicating. He remembered the feel of those lips. Was it possible kissing her would be the same? Watching her now, he was pretty sure it would be better.

"I'm sorry. I was trying to lighten the mood." He stood then, taking a step toward her. She took a step backwards, so he changed courses, going to the table. "You just seem a little flustered. I was going to fix myself a scotch. You can have one."

"I don't like scotch. I never have since…"

He glanced up at her wide eyes. "Since when?"

"Since the night of your accident." Her voice grew quiet. "When we thought you might die."

"Wasn't that also the night you found out about my parents? It was a pretty significant date."

It was the night she'd first told him she loved him, she recalled, although he was unconscious at the time. He'd told her the same thing, but she'd run away. Again, silly girl.

She wasn't that person anymore, and she wouldn't feel that way in front of him now. "I came here to tell you something, but before I do… that last night you said something to me. You said 'The camera always loved me.' Why did you say that?"

His brow lined. "I don't remember. It was a long time ago."

"I know, it was, but you don't have any idea where you might have heard it? You'd never said anything like that to me before. It wasn't your style."

"I honestly don't know." He took a sip of his drink. "But isn't it obvious? You're beautiful."

She shook her head. "Thank you, but that isn't why I'm asking. I've admitted I didn't communicate well. I didn't tell you things as quickly as I should've, but I wasn't trying to hide it from you. Once I'd figured out how to say it, or once we were together again, I would tell you. The problem was you already knew. How did you know? Were you spying on me?"

He straightened, the look on his face incredulous. She knew the answer to this question, but she had to lead him there for him to see it, too.

"God, no. Why would I spy on you?"

"Then how did you already know? How did you know about everything when I hadn't told you?"

He exhaled and walked back to his chair to sit. This wasn't the walk down memory lane he'd wanted to take. That year had been gut-wrenching for him. "I would get texts from 'A Friend,' photos of you and him."

"You didn't know who sent them?"

"I didn't care to know. All I cared about was you, and you weren't telling me anything. Whoever it was had my number. I assumed it was Brad or Rachel." He put the scotch on his desk. "I was too angry to worry about who it was."

"I was so confused and hurt." Her fingers were laced, and she pulled her hand up to look at it. No rings were there. "I trusted you so much. It never occurred to me that you might not trust me."

"I trusted you." He studied his hand on the glass, and the little dragonfly he'd inked beside his thumb all those years ago. "You didn't have the best track record when it came to him."

"You're right. And I guess it was because of that track record, I was afraid of what you might think, of how you might misinterpret things… and we were so far apart. But I'd promised to tell you everything."

In his mind he was back in that isolated place in college. He was working so hard, and all he saw was their future crumbling away.

"We were the only thing I believed in back then. My family was a disaster, my mom had taken away my trust. You were the one thing I counted on, and then you were gone."

"I was never gone." She had moved closer. He hadn't noticed, but she was slowly walking in his direction. "I was angry at you for giving up on us, but looking back, I realize I gave up, too. I left us behind."

His eyes flashed to hers across the desk. "You didn't." The memory of that night had always been like a knife jab over and over to the chest. It was an open wound that would slowly kill him. "I had the bruises to prove it."

"But it wasn't the truth," she said quietly.

Silence filled the office for a moment. He'd always known there was a possibility she'd find out about his lie. He wasn't sure she'd want to talk about the reason they parted, but he should've known as different as she was now, she wouldn't leave any stone unturned.

He said the only thing left. "We have a daughter."

She looked down, placing her fingers on the glossy desktop.

"Were you alone when you had her?" His voice was steady.

He wasn't ready to let her know the pain that thought caused him. Thinking of her alone in a foreign country; him not there for the birth of his only child.

"My parents were there."

"I wish I'd known." He lifted the glass and took a sip. "I'd like to know her now."

"Of course." Again those hazel eyes flashed to his. "I wouldn't have kept her from you. It was just... You were so different. I thought you might..."

She didn't have to finish. He knew what she thought, and while he could be angry at so many people in this scenario, he could never be angry with her.

"Then I guess I'll see you tomorrow night."

Without a word, she turned and left his office. Just like that, she was gone, and all the lies that had kept them apart were on the table. Only where did that leave them now?

He wanted to go to her, but it had been so long. He didn't have the right to barge in on this woman who'd occupied his office like the force she had become.

At the same time, what had brought her here if not some desire to mend the past? Was it only to tell him the truth about their child?

Riding down in the elevator, her insides were a mixture of relief and misery. The secrets had been revealed, and now they both knew the truth. Everything that had come between them was now out in the open. Correction, all but one thing.

She couldn't go back to her parents' home yet. She remembered her daughter there upset, but she knew what she was doing here was just as important, possibly more.

She walked out to the beach and stood in the pavilion as the mist grew thicker in the air. Her heart beat pain through her chest with every pulse, and the stress of all the years of loneliness and longing sent tears spilling from her eyes.

Without thinking about it, she started walking. She knew the way from the summers they'd spent running down here. It wasn't far, and it was the only place she wanted to be.

The rain was growing steadier. Her dress was wet, and her hair was ruined. The short distance was covered, and she looked up at the cottage. Rain mixed with the tears on her cheeks. It was dark and quiet. The garage door was closed.

She wondered if the door opened, would she find his studio? Would the easel still be there? From their first night to prom night to the summer before she left for New Orleans, so much of their history was bound up in this place.

Still, it had been seventeen years. She didn't even know if he still owned the property. It was a foolish dream.

Turning back, she looked up and saw a figure in the dim glow of the streetlights. It was too far to make out if it was a male or female, or if the person was even moving in her direction.

She stood and watched, heaviness pushing down on her lungs. That old, familiar cramp in her stomach.

After a few moments, the person was closer, and she could tell it was a man. It was Julian. He didn't have his coat, and his white shirt and slacks were soaked. He was walking fast, without looking up. Why hadn't he driven?

When he saw her, he stopped. "What are you doing here?"

It was all she could do to speak. "I needed to walk. I wanted to walk, and I guess… I wanted to come here."

"You're soaking wet."

"So are you."

"Come inside, and you can dry off." He reached into his pocket and stepped past her, going up the porch steps to the door. "You can wear something of mine."

Looking up after him, she only hesitated a moment before following him up the stairs into the dark house.

He flipped the switch, thankful the cleaning service had come earlier in the week. Dashing to the bathroom, he grabbed a few towels off the rack. One was a small hand towel.

"Here. I brought you one of my tees and a pair of boxers."

She held up the smaller towel and glanced at him. "This brings back memories."

He could still see her eighteen year-old body not very well hidden behind a towel that size. The image sent a flood of heat to places she'd already inflamed in his office.

He cleared his throat. "There's also a larger one there, and you can use the bathroom if you'd like to..."

She stepped toward him, dropping the bundle on the floor. He waited as she reached out to touch his drenched shirt. It was warm rain, and his skin was hot beneath the thin fabric. His torso was plainly visible through the wet material, and with her palm flat against his chest, he didn't seem to breathe.

He was waiting, just like she was. Holding his breath, just like she was. His elbow bent, and his hand covered hers. Slowly her eyes closed and she leaned forward. His hand moved to her cheek, his thumb touching the velvet lips he remembered so well.

Rain dripped from the tips of his dark hair, and he covered her mouth with his. The tiniest whimper came from her throat, and she was in his arms.

Lips parted, tongues crashed together. She was up—*did he lift her?* Holding his cheeks, her body fused to his. Their kisses came faster, and it was hard to make out what exactly was happening.

The noise of a chair falling over, his hand reached out to find the doorjamb.

Her lips pressed to his cheek, his eye, back down to his mouth. These were the only things he felt, other than the burning need expanding low in his stomach.

Waves of heat unfurled through his limbs. They were finally

in his room, and she had managed to get every button undone on his shirt.

Her dress was defying him. Why did the neck have to be so high?

"It's a halter. Wait." She reached behind her neck to pull a string and it dropped to her waist. She was bare beneath it.

"I love this dress." He breathed, touching her before she crashed her body against his, arms around his neck, mouths reunited.

Pushing everything down, their clothes were left in a soggy puddle on his floor. He didn't care—he actually hoped for a watermark, something to commemorate this moment. It was monumental.

He ran his hands down the length of her torso to the curve of her lower back. Her body had changed since the last time they were together. She was more lines and angles, less curves. A new portrait was unfolding in his mind when he noticed her shiver.

"Are you cold?" he whispered, but she shook her head no, desire burning in her eyes.

Their mouths came together again, as they moved onto the bed. She was below him, then she was above him as their bodies entwined in a desperate need to be reunited.

He kissed her everywhere, remembering the taste of her skin, until at last they were one, and it was as if all the stars exploded in the sky.

He could hear the sounds coming from her throat, but his mind was a hazy blur of longing finally satisfied, desire fulfilled. She was everything, she was part of him, she was the air and the sea.

Their frantic pace calmed, and once again, she was beneath him.

Her hands moved to his cheeks, and she held him, eyes closed. Like their last reunion, she was overwhelmed by the way they fit together. He was hers, just like before, and his strong arms surrounded her, the softness of the sheets behind her, the prickly feel of his chest hair, the scent of the ocean clinging to him. The taste of rain was in her mouth, and her entire body vibrated with the most intense happiness.

"Jules said you were considering moving back." His low voice vibrated warmth against her heart. His elbows were bent, and he smoothed back her hair.

Her eyes drifted open, and his blue ones creased with a smile. "I'd like to come home. I miss everything here."

"Everything?"

She lifted her head and pecked his lips. "Some things more than others. Some things not at all." He actually laughed, and the sound made her laugh. "What's so funny?"

"What do you not miss at all?"

Her lips puckered into a frown, and he kissed them. She kissed him back, and for the next several minutes, his question hung in the air as they had another private reunion.

"I don't miss your brother Will at all." She was above him again, her head rested on her hand.

"Hmm... the ultimate buzz kill. What in the world would make you think of him right now?"

She exhaled and fell on her back in the bed. He was on his side above her just as fast.

With a finger he gently pulled her chin toward him. "Tell me."

She moved up to her side, facing him. It wasn't the greatest timing, but she might as well get it out there. "He was the one sending you those pictures. Of me with Jack at Loyola. He was the *Friend.*"

Julian's brow creased. "But why? I mean, what does he care? Other than I guess he'd be the type to get off on Jack and me fighting."

"It was because of me." Her eyes dropped. "Or more precisely, to get rid of me."

His lips curved into a grin, and he leaned forward to kiss her nose. "What did you ever do to Will?"

"That's just it! I have no idea!" She lay on her back again, and he caught her waist, pulling her close against his chest. She traced a finger through the light dusting of hair across the top. "Why don't I remember this?"

"I had it installed after you left. I got sick of Brad trying to buy me butterscotch Frappuccinos."

She snorted a laugh, and rolled her face against his skin. She took a deep breath before moving back to find his eyes. "You never changed, and then you did."

"Just a few little things. Now tell me why Will would want to get rid of you."

"I want to hear more about these little things."

"Anna…"

She pushed into a sitting position, holding the sheet under her arms. "I don't know, really. It started when I was dating Jack." Then she frowned. "Can I even say I dated Jack?"

"No. Continue."

"Well, whatever I was doing with Jack—he met me once, and decided I was not going to be a part of his family." She shook her head at the lunacy of the whole thing. "He was very annoyed by my presence in the office when I was interviewing your dad, and then he threatened me at Mardi Gras."

She examined her fingernails, hoping to let that last bit fly past. No such luck.

Julian sat up quickly. "He threatened you?"

"That's probably an exaggeration."

"Anna." He held both her hands in his. "What happened at Mardi Gras?"

"It's so stupid, really. He just danced with me—it was a masque, remember? So I didn't know it was him. Then he told me I would never be a part of his family…" Her voice broke off, and for some stupid reason, her eyes grew hot.

"You're crying." Julian's jaw clenched and he pulled her to him. "Did he scare you? I'm going to punch him in the face the next time I see him."

"Oh my god, don't you dare." She sniffed and wiped her eyes roughly, sitting straighter. "I'm not crying over stupid Will, it's just… He almost succeeded."

She blinked up at him, and his blue eyes creased with a warm smile. "Don't cry, Hazel. You *will* be a part of this family. Nothing's ever taking you away from me again."

"I thought you were Hazel."

"I'm butterscotch Frappuccino." He slid down in the bed, grabbing her waist and pulling her under him.

She laughed as his mouth started a sizzling trail from her jaw, down her neck, working its way lower until they were once again lost in a glowing haze of reunion.

Light streamed through the east-facing windows, and Anna opened her eyes to the olive walls and navy curtains of a room she remembered well.

Julian was on his stomach on the other side of the large bed, and she kissed his shoulder before slipping out, stopping to collect the damp denim dress, which was her only article of clothing in the house.

He'd given her two towels and dry clothes in a bundle the evening before. Creeping out of the room, she found them lying in the pile where she'd dropped them. His tee and boxers. Pulling them on and tying her hair back in a band, she quickly scribbled out a note for him to meet them at lunch today. Then she set out toward the beach, where she'd left her mom's old car.

It was still early when she crept into her parents' home in Fairview. She tried to be quiet, but Gabi and Jules were both in the kitchen having coffee.

"Shackin up!" Of course her best friend would start yelling.

Anna stood straight and went to the laundry room to hang her dress on the drying rack. When she re-entered, Jules was focused on the toaster oven and wouldn't look at her. Gabi, on the other hand was bouncing on her bar stool.

"He's as awesome as always, isn't he? You don't even have to answer that. I know the answer is yes."

"Gabi…" She made big eyes and tilted her head toward Jules.

"Hang on. Time out." Her best friend waved her hands. "You're the one who didn't come home last night, and now you're wanting me to pretend like you're not standing there in Julian's tee and boxers?"

Anna rolled her eyes and went to her room for a change of clothing. Once she was in her own underwear as well as her own clothes, she went back to the kitchen, where her daughter was eating a pop tart and drinking a large mug of coffee.

"I need some of that." She went to the coffee pot.

"I thought you didn't like pop tarts. Said they're fake food or something." At least Jules was speaking to her.

"I'm sorry for being out so late. I got caught in the rain, and then it sort of… one thing led to another." This was not going the way she'd hoped.

"How exactly did you get caught in the rain?" Her daughter's bright blue eyes were narrowed.

"I'd gone to talk to your dad. To be sure he knew about you, and well, it didn't go the way I'd hoped. I decided to walk it off, and this storm came up suddenly—"

"It was misting rain all day yesterday, Mum."

"I guess I didn't notice."

"She doesn't notice all *kinds* of things when your dad's around. Get used to it, Twerp."

"Gabi!" Anna grimaced at her friend. "Anyway, your dad took me to his place. I mean, his mother's… Well, they have a little cottage right down by the water."

She stopped at that point and changed directions. "How are you feeling today? Will you tell me why you were so upset last night?"

Her daughter had been slowly chewing her pop tart throughout the entire explanation, and now she was studying it like it was the early phases of the shuttle landing, as Gabi was quick to note.

"I don't think I will tell you now, since you're clearly biased in your position." Jules finished her breakfast and lifted her mug. "I will say I think you must've sustained a head injury in your youth the way you can take him back after what he did to you."

Her mother's brow pierced. "What he did to me? Sweetie, I don't know what you're talking about."

"Maybe it's early-onset Alzheimer's disease?"

"Juliet. I'm not pleased with this attitude. Either tell me what you're talking about or knock it off."

"She's acting like an eighth grader!" Gabi called from the living room, where she was on the couch eating popcorn. "Maybe she's getting messages from the mother ship."

"Gab, are you having popcorn for breakfast?" Anna's phone buzzed, and she picked it up.

JULIAN

Don't like waking up to a note.

Energy flooded her core, and she was unable to stop the grin spreading across her face.

ANNA

I'm sorry. You were so cozy, I had to go or I would've stayed.

JULIAN

What's wrong with staying?

ANNA

Nothing, except we have a daughter, you know.

JULIAN

When will I see her again?

Her eyes lifted to Juliet, who was watching her with an expression of disgust.

"You shouldn't make that face," Anna scolded. "You look exactly like your Uncle William, and he's a wank."

Jules's eyes flew wide. "Mum!" But as she expected, the girl started to laugh. "That is so wrong coming from you!"

"We're meeting your Aunt Lucy for lunch today. She's divine, she has four kids, and your father wants to join us."

Their daughter's shoulders dropped.

"I'll tell him you can't wait to see him again."

She punched a text in her phone.

ANNA

Jules is being a crank. She thinks she knows something and might be angry with you.

JULIAN

She found our sex tape?

Snorting, Anna rolled her eyes.

ANNA

Don't think we ever did that, love.

JULIAN

You just didn't know about it.

ANNA

Meeting Lucy for lunch, come with. Will send deets.

JULIAN

Love you.

She froze, staring at the words and trying to remember how

to breathe. In all the times they were together last night, they'd said so many things, but they hadn't said that.

Or maybe they had? There were so many ways to tell a person you loved them apart from using three little words.

ANNA

I love you. Xxx

JULIAN

Xoxo

* * *

LuLu's was crowded as always for a Saturday in April, but Lucy had managed to find a large table overlooking the playground. She stood and waved when the three of them entered the open-air restaurant on the canal.

"Oh my gawd!" She ran forward, grabbing Jules in a tight embrace. "You're gorgeous. The most amazing combination—just like I said. And you're an artist?"

Jules nodded. "And a writer."

Anna leaned forward and kissed her friend. "*You* are gorgeous as always. Where are these boys?"

"Out on the play maze. I'm fat as a cow after Meggie. I think I gained fifty pounds."

"I don't know where you're hiding it."

They went to the table, where Meggie was in a carrier on an upside-down booster chair.

Jules went straight to the white-haired infant and picked her up. "She's so cute!"

"You can walk out and chat with the boys if you'd like." I pointed over the railing where two skinny blond boys and one husky brunette were making their way around a rope maze.

She shrugged and headed to the entrance, Lucy's infant over her shoulder.

"I went on and ordered sweet tea for everybody, but get whatever you want. I just didn't want the kids to be thirsty. It's so hot."

"Julian's joining us." Anna took a seat across from her friend.

"I know! He told me. Are you about to *die?*"

Gabi fake-coughed too loudly, and Anna gave her an annoyed smirk. "I'm not sure what you mean, but I did see him yesterday."

"And spent the niiiight." Gabi pretended to murmur behind her hand before she took a pull from her straw.

"OH, YAY!" Lucy clapped. "So you're getting back together? That is so great. Can I help plan the wedding?"

"Hang on—slow down!" Anna held her hands up.

"What? You're thinking you won't get back together?" Lucy's light brows were clutched over her eyes.

Anna's eyes drifted over the railing out to the rope maze where Jules stood watching the boys, Meggie contentedly perched on her shoulder.

"We have a lot of bridges to cross before we start talking matrimony."

"Oh, please. She'll love Julian. *Everybody* loves Julian."

Anna laughed, looking down and remembering the first time she'd heard those words out of Lucy Kyser's mouth, only they were about her twin brother.

"Is Jack joining us?"

Lucy's eyes darted around the room. "Oh, well… I didn't know if that would be a good idea with Julian and you and all."

"Lucy! Text him right now and tell him to come!"

"Are you sure?" But she was already tapping on her phone.

Gabi took a packet of melba toast out of the narrow basket on the table. "Might as well smash them all together in one fell swoop."

A warm hand touched Anna's back, and she looked up into the eyes that sent her insides bursting into a shower of fizzy sparkles.

"I hope I'm not too late." Julian bent down to plant a light kiss on her lips. More fizzy sparkles.

Lucy let out a peal of laughter. "I'm so right! And I called it. Don't you dare go hiring anyone else to plan it."

"Oh my lord." Anna complained under her breath. Then she jumped to the side. "Ouch!"

Gabi's elbow was digging into her side.

"He *is* better," her best friend hissed into her ear.

"Gabi, hey!" Julian reached over the table to hug her, and it was possible her best friend, the very serious astrophysicist almost fainted.

Julian sat in the chair beside Anna and leaned forward toward his sister.

"Okay, I'm just going to be honest with all of you, since we're all friends here…" He rubbed his palms on the front of his black jeans. "I'm kind of nervous."

"Can you possibly get any cuter?" Lucy shook her head at him, but Anna kissed his cheek.

"Don't be nervous. She's out there holding Meggie if you want to spy."

"I haven't even seen Meggie." He sat up straighter, looking over the railing and frowned. "But I don't see anybody out there except the boys."

"Looking for me?" Jules's voice was terse, and the four grownups sat back quickly in their chairs.

Meggie was squirming and grunting.

"Oh, my little piggy's hungry!" Lucy laughed. "I swear she eats more than the boys ever did."

She rose, taking the infant from Jules and walked quickly towards the back of the restaurant. Anna stood, hoping against hope her daughter would reserve judgment.

"Jules, I know you kind of already bumped into each other. This is your dad. Julian."

Julian studied his daughter, and it seemed he could read what was happening behind her narrowed blue eyes, identical to his.

"Hullo, Dad." A definite tone of sarcasm soured their daughter's greeting.

Julian's lips puckered into a frown as he coolly watched her take a seat. "Jules."

"You're the old tosser I met at the beach. What's new in the world of wankdom?"

"Jules." Anna's voice had a tone of warning, but Gabi jumped up.

"Hey, I'm going to check on Lucy. It must be crap balls trying to have some privacy in a place like this."

Anna's best friend left, and the three of them were alone. For a moment, nobody spoke, then Julian took the lead.

"So hey, Jules. Trust me, I know. It sucks air not having a dad for sixteen years. I'm sorry about that."

"He didn't know." Anna hummed under her breath. "Jules, if you'd just say whatever's on your mind, we can at least try to address it."

"Yeah?" Her voice rose, and she put both hands on the table. "I read your sodding *private* tumblr, Mum. I know he was shagging some chav named Renee, and that's why you left. He's not just a wanker, he's a sodding git."

Julian leaned back in his chair and snorted a laugh. "Wow. First, that was freaking awesome. I don't think I've ever been insulted so well. Second, you kept a private tumblr?"

"Oh my God, Jules! You did *what*? Things were in there you should *not* have read!" Anna covered her burning cheeks with her hands. Then she lowered them fast. "What the hell were you doing reading my private tumblr? It was *private*."

"Mum. You are *such* a div. You put me in your bedroom for two days, then you leave a laptop open to 'Anna's private tumblr' on your desk? Like I'm not going to read it?"

"It's called *invasion of privacy*, young lady. I have never done anything like that to you."

"Can we all just take a breath?" Julian reached forward and lifted one of the drinks off the table. He took a long sip then winced. "Dang, *sweet* tea."

"I love it." Jules grabbed the one nearest her and took a long swig. "Sweet iced tea is the best part of America."

"Jules… part of what your father and I discussed last night was the *lie* he told me back then."

Her daughter cut disbelieving eyes at both of them. "Really. The lie. That sounds mighty convenient. Did you make that up on the spot, old chap?"

Julian laughed again. "We are seriously going to be tight. Eventually."

"He didn't tell me. Rachel told me. It wasn't possible for them to be together." She turned to Julian. "Renee had already gone." He looked down at his hands as she continued. "You said that… to make me take the job." Her eyes were hot. "And I slapped you so hard."

"Stop." He reached forward and slid a thumb under her eye. "You're forgetting I was still really mad about what I thought was going on with you and Jack."

"Wait." Jules's mouth fell open, and she wasn't even trying to close it. "You're saying it really *was* a lie? You weren't shagging bloody Renee?"

"Somebody knows I'm a sucker for a British accent." Jack's friendly voice made Anna jump two feet. "Hey!"

"Jack, my goodness." Anna stood, and he gave her a quick peck on the cheek. She motioned to a chair beside Jules. "Please sit. Lucy's feeding Meggie."

"Mother of flippin Christ!" Jules fell back in her chair, blinking rapidly as if stunned.

"He has that effect on all the females in our family." Julian took a pull from the straw in his drink and frowned again. "It just doesn't get better."

"Hey, man." Jack reached a hand across to his brother. "How's it hanging around the office? How's Dad?"

Julian returned his shake. "Good. Put that degree to work and see if you can figure out why he keeps having these spells."

Jack's expression fell slightly. "I'm a pediatric surgeon. But I know someone who specializes in geriatrics."

"He's not going to like the sound of that."

"Is something wrong with your dad?" Anna's brow creased, but Lucy interrupted all of it.

"We're all here! I hope you don't mind, I just went and ordered a little bit of everything for the table." Meggie was over her shoulder and an entourage of servers followed her, placing several Cheeseburgers in Paradise, seafood baskets, and two chicken wraps on the table.

"Those are for us," she whispered in Anna's ear.

"Looks great, Sis." Jack stood and kissed his sister's cheek then took baby Meggie from her again.

"Are you planning to steal her?" Anna laughed, watching the infant nuzzle into her uncle's neck.

"I might." He winked, and Julian's hand moved to Anna's thigh under the table.

She reached down and covered it with her own, then she leaned over and kissed his ear. "I love you," she whispered before straightening again.

He leaned back, looking over her shoulder. "I'm sensing a shortage."

"Jack, this is our daughter…" Anna paused to stifle a laugh. "Juliet."

"No way," Jack exclaimed. "I had no idea you had a kid."

"At least I wasn't the only one." Julian straightened in his chair, but Jules was watching her dad closely.

"It's really cool to meet you, Jules." Jack continued. "I'm your uncle, and trust me. Your parents have been in love since… well, hell. Before I came along and screwed it all up."

"You didn't—" Anna started, but Julian's hand on her thigh tightened. She started to laugh. "Welcome to your family. It's still evolving, but hopefully the worst is behind us now."

PART VI
DRAGONFLIES

Julian arrived at the house in Fairview an hour early to pick up Anna and Gabi for the final reunion event. It was a formal affair, so he wore a suit and tie, and while the women finished dressing, he sat on the couch with his daughter not watching television.

"Do you have a boyfriend back in England?"

Jules was dressed in black leggings and a tunic, and she leaned against the opposite arm of the couch with an enormous bowl of popcorn. "You're not really starting with that, are you?"

He laughed. "What should I start with?"

"I don't know, but I'm not about to discuss my love life with you."

"I only asked if you had a boyfriend."

Her eyes narrowed. "No."

"Why not? I never had any trouble getting dates."

"Of course you didn't!" Her foot shot out and kicked him. "Look at you, you old tosser."

"I looked up that word. I think we should find a new nickname." He leaned toward her and grabbed a handful of popcorn.

"Whoa! What the bloody hell happened to your hand?"

The knuckles were swollen, and he'd put tape over the backs of two. "I just smashed it… moving furniture."

"What were you doing moving furniture?"

He moved back to his spot and put popcorn in his mouth, not answering.

She studied him a moment, and then her eyes narrowed. "You're not some saint, you know. So you lied to her to make her chase her dream, but if she'd stayed, I'd have been born here. It would've been a different story, but it would've been just as good."

"I wasn't being noble," he said, finishing the handful of popcorn. "I was pissed, and I said it. I thought she wasn't being honest about Jack, and maybe… I wanted her to go away again. I didn't know she'd stay that long."

"Have you kicked that git's arse yet?"

Julian laughed. "You mean your uncle, my brother? Anna doesn't want me to."

"Screw that. He needs to be taught a lesson."

Her father's blue eyes twinkled just like hers, and he looked down at his hand. "People usually get what's coming to them, Jules. Just be cool." Then he lifted her feet into his lap. "I'm sorry I wasn't around for you."

She grabbed her wild dark curls in a ponytail at the nape of her neck, and he smiled at the familiar move. "It wasn't your fault, I guess."

"You know, I was thinking about asking her to marry me." His voice was as certain as the way he made the decision.

"What?" Jules sat straight up, almost dropping her popcorn.

"Would that be okay with you?" He glanced at her. "I know it's just been the two of you, and we don't know each other. But I want to know you. I want to be a part of your life."

Jules's stunned expression slowly melted into a smile as he spoke. "I'd like that. I'd like that very much."

"What would you like very much?" Anna stepped out in a knee-length black cocktail dress, her chestnut waves smoothed over one shoulder. Gabi struck a pose in a leopard print smoking jacket over a velvet, emerald green dress.

"You know I'm loving the drama here." Julian said, standing.

"I'm loving the two of you so cozy." Anna stepped forward and caught his lapels, kissing his lips softly.

"Hey dad?" Jules called out from the sofa. He glanced back, and she winked. "Keep her out late tonight."

Gabi went to the kitchen. "I'd better take the other car."

* * *

The Phoenician IV was decorated in the same white tulle and twinkle lights as the gymnasium had been the night before, but the only theme was "FHS: Twenty Years Later."

"We've gone from cliché to boring and unimaginative." Gabi complained.

Anna held Julian's arm as they entered. "Give Rachel a break. She gets no help with these things, and all she hears are complaints."

"Well you can't argue with that banner." Gabi grabbed a champagne flute off a passing tray shaking her head. "I leave and the whole place falls apart."

"Who am I going to see at this thing?" Julian's voice at Anna's ear sent a whisper of tingles down her back.

"You'll see me." She turned and kissed him, and he pulled her into his arms.

"I'd rather only see you."

"Okay, I'm out of here." Gabi sauntered off in the direction of her drama friends, waving from a table in the back.

A slow song was playing over the dance floor, and Anna and Julian started to sway in place. His arms were around her waist, and her hands rested on his chest. "Is this going to be like prom, where you want to ditch?"

"I see these people all the time."

"Because you never left!" She laughed, touching his chin. "I haven't seen these guys in years."

"You're coming back."

"Oh, am I?"

"Yes. You are."

Rachel and Brad were the next to arrive, and the swaying couple parted to greet their friends.

"I'm so happy my cutest couple has been reunited," Rachel said. "The awards presentation is going to be perfect now."

"You're not doing all that again, are you?" Anna cried.

"Of course! Every reunion has the revisiting of the class favorites." Rachel put her hand in the crook of Brad's arm. "If you two hadn't gotten together, you were up for 'Most Improved.'"

Anna's lips twisted into a frown. "Why does that feel like a back-handed compliment?"

Julian cut in. "You'd better hurry it up. We're not going to be here much longer." Anna elbowed him in the side, and he leaned into her ear. "This dress has driven the existing shortage to critical levels."

Rachel caught the whole exchange. "I'm not sure what that means, but I'm guessing it's something dirty."

"It's not dirty." Anna tried to cover. "It's just something we used to say. About being apart."

"Oh, it's dirty." Brad rejoined the group, slipping his phone into his pocket. "What are we talking about?"

The four started to laugh, and Julian pulled Anna to the dance floor. "I love being in your arms again," she sighed, resting her head on his shoulder. Julian didn't answer, and her head popped up. "What?" He smiled, but she could tell something was on his mind. "Tell me."

His smile turned more genuine then. "I have something

important to ask you, but first… I have to dredge up the past a little."

Anna groaned. "No more past dredging. I'm sick of it."

"Jules mentioned someone named Brandon?"

Anna's lips poked out, and her eyes dropped to his collar. "Jules and her big mouth," she breathed. "What did she tell you?"

His expression turned serious. "That you were married."

She didn't speak. For a moment her finger only traced a line along the lapel of his suit coat. "I was. For a little while."

"Did you love him?"

Her head tilted to the side as she considered the question. "I liked him very much."

"Ouch. Poor Brandon." Julian pulled her close and kissed her temple. "Five words no guy ever wants to hear from the woman he loves." They swayed a few moments in silence. "He probably hates me."

She exhaled a laugh. "He probably does. Sorry."

"You could've at least tried to sugar-coat it."

"Julian LaSalle, you know I've always been completely honest with you." She straightened up to find him grinning, and her heart melted a little. "I'm just not always incredibly punctual with the news. Why are you grinning like that?"

"I miss hearing you say my name that way. Everybody calls me *Kyser* now. It was important to Dad."

"You're very good to him."

"He's been very good to me, and he loves my mom. They're finally happy, I think."

"Will they ever marry?"

Julian shrugged. "You know how Mom is." Then he took her hand, leading her off the dance floor. "Come with me."

She followed him out of the ballroom to the back patio, down the short steps leading to the soft, white sand. Stopping her, Julian bent down to remove her heels then he slipped off his own shoes and cuffed his slacks.

"What happened to your hand?" She held it up when he stood.

"It's nothing. I just jammed it moving furniture. Come on."

Her thumb glided briefly over his dragonfly ink, and she straightened her ring now securely on her finger.

They walked hand in hand in the moonlight down to the shore, where they stopped right at the water's edge.

"It's so beautiful," she sighed, and he pulled her to him, holding her back against his chest.

His voice was low and right at her ear when he spoke. "Anna, I want you to marry me." He felt her jump, and he pressed his lips against the soft skin at the base of her neck before he continued. "I want you to be my wife. I want you and Jules to move back here and live with me. I want us to be a family."

Anna pushed against his arms, and he released her. She turned to face him, and he could see her eyes shining. "I can't think of anything in the world I want more than that."

Slipping his hand into his breast pocket, he pulled out a small, silver ring. "I made this a while back, when I was still in Savannah…"

A painful knot tightened in Anna's throat, causing her voice to crack. "You've had it that long?"

"I've loved you longer." He slipped the slim band onto the finger where her dragonfly ring sat, and it fit with the previous piece, adding a sparkling diamond upon which the tiny, glittering insect appeared to perch.

Anna gasped. "It's perfect! Did you know it would be like that?"

He smiled looking at the set a moment before he shook his head. "I didn't. I only guessed it might work."

She lunged forward, throwing her arms around his neck, pressing their mouths together. Lips parted, tongues met, she turned her cheek to hold her hand out in the moonlight as his kiss traveled to her jaw and up, into her hair.

"Lucy is going to be ecstatic," Anna laughed. "She was right."

"Let's get out of here." His voice was low against her hair, and his tone caused a little shiver to move through her.

"Okay," she whispered, and they started back for the ballroom, hand in hand.

They were almost there when Brad came rushing out the back doors. "Jules, dammit, there you are. You left your phone on the table."

"I didn't want to be disturbed just then." Then he noticed the strained expression on his friend's face. "What's happened?"

"It's your dad. He had a heart attack."

PART VII
END OF AN ERA

The halls of South County Hospital were filled with Kysers when Julian and Anna arrived. Lucy was sitting beside Lexy, and both women's faces were red and blotched from crying.

Julian's mother clutched a ball of tissues, and she pressed them to her eyes repeatedly. The soft noises of mourning filled the air.

Jack was at the nurses' station with Robert, discussing his father's status and plans for treatment. Anna caught sight of Will, alone in a row of chairs on the other side of the waiting area. She pulled Julian's hand, and he didn't fight her. But as they got closer, she saw Will's left cheek was bruised and swollen.

His cold gaze fell on them. "I'm still considering pressing charges," he growled.

"I'd love to see you try it," Julian snapped back.

Anna stopped and lifted her fiancé's hand. "I thought you did this moving furniture?" He didn't answer, but rather cut his eyes toward his eldest sibling.

She turned and pulled Julian to the side, speaking low. "What happened?"

"Let's just say he'll never threaten you again."

"You probably broke something." She turned his swollen knuckles over.

"I don't care. He's had that coming for twenty years." His voice trailed off as he scanned the faces of his family. "I need you to go and get Jules. Hurry."

Anna's eyes cut to his, and reading his expression, she nodded and took off back down the hall, fear twisting in her stomach.

She knew what Julian was thinking, and she feared he might be right. This could be his father's last night.

* * *

How many times had she made the panicked drive through Fairview to the hospital? At least she was only going to her parents' home, which was just a few short blocks away.

Jules was still on the couch in her black leggings and tunic when her mother arrived to get her. The two were out the door and in the car again without a moment to spare.

"Is he going to die?" Jules whispered from the passenger's side.

Anna reached over to hold her daughter's hand. "I don't know, sweetie. He didn't live a very healthy life for a long time."

The girl was quiet a few moments. "I'd hoped when I saw Nana again it would be a happy time, and I would beg her to adopt me."

Anna pulled her daughter against her shoulder in an awkward hug. "You'll have plenty of time to beg Lexy to adopt you, and I doubt it'll take much."

Back inside the waiting area, Anna knew they were too late. Julian held his mother tight against his chest, and Anna could see her body shaking violently as they ran up the hall toward the family.

Tears were in his blue eyes, and Anna's instantly flooded.

Jack was holding Lucy, and Robert was discussing a prescription for Ms. LaSalle to help her sleep. Naturally, she resisted.

Lexy shook her head, her smooth dark hair now shoulder length and streaked with gray.

"I'm not taking drugs," she whispered, her voice broken and shaking. "I'll get through this like I've gotten through everything else."

Her dark eyes lifted, and she saw Anna standing with Jules. Blinking back her tears, Lexy held out a hand to her granddaughter, and Jules rushed forward straight into her arms.

"I've been waiting to see you again." The girl's voice was broken, and they held each other. "I can look after you. Let me stay with you."

Robert handed the small prescription to Julian, and he glanced at his daughter before looking up at Anna.

"I don't mind if that's what Lexy wants," she said.

His mother walked over to Anna and pulled her into a hug. "You're calling me Lexy now? I've always wanted you to do that."

Anna looked down and smiled. "I guess I feel older these days."

His mother lifted her hand and studied the engagement ring with the little dragonfly perched on it. She nodded. "This is good. It's how it should be. I'll take Jules with me back to Port Hogan."

Lucy came up behind her, wiping tears from her eyes. "Are you sure? You can stay with us out on Hammond. We want you to be there. I want you there."

Lexy hugged her goddaughter and a fresh wave of tears filled all their eyes. "I never belonged in that house," she whispered. "I'd rather stay in my old place. With my lovely granddaughter."

Julian was discussing the medication with Jules, who nodded. Jack stepped forward, clearing his throat. Anna had only seen tears in his blue eyes once before, and it was when Lucy was lying in a hospital bed in this same building.

"I can drive you out there if you'd like. I don't mind."

Robert spoke up. "Or I can. If you want to stay with your family, Jack."

Lexy straightened her back. "I'm able to drive." Then her voice grew quiet. "I've driven myself through heartbreak before."

Anna couldn't stop the tears then, remembering the source of her words, her drive from the hospital following her friend's death when Julian was only a little boy.

"Do you want to see him again before you go?" Jack touched her back, but Lexy shook her head no.

"He's not here." A lone tear rolled down her cheek. "He's riding a horse down to Soldier Creek, or he's in his pickup, coming to find me. I'll be waiting."

Julian stepped forward again and kissed her, and Jules took her hand. "I'll check on you in the morning. Jules, call me if you need anything. I can be there in less than five minutes."

Jules nodded and the two of them walked slowly out to the parking lot. Their gait almost identical.

* * *

The funeral for Bill Kyser was as big an event as his wedding had been more than forty years earlier. Everyone in South County, it seemed was there, and the church and grounds were flooded with plants and flowers from all over the globe.

Only the family and the Brennans were inside at the service. Lexy wore a straight, black shift with a hat and veil to hide her tears. Anna had extended her stay, and she and Jules wore matching black knit dresses. Jules hadn't left her grandmother's side, and the two were quickly becoming inseparable.

Julian was beside Anna, mourning along with his brothers, but Lucy seemed to take it the hardest.

She had found her way to her father's heart, and the two had become closer as the years had passed. Jack held Meggie as she leaned into his chest and wept. Robert stood by with the boys, but Anna knew the twins had always been able to comfort each other better than anyone else.

Casey had cancelled several dates on her small tour to fly down and join them. Her light blonde hair was still cut in a pixie, and she wore a black tailored suit. She watched Jack and Lucy from where she stood beside Robert and the boys.

Brad's father and the rest of his family were across the aisle from the Kysers, and Will took a seat all the way in the back, alone. Anna wished there was a way to bring him into his family's fold, but it was a worry for another time.

Julian rose and went to the front to give the eulogy.

"As a young man, my dad grew up on a horse ranch, back when this area was nothing but farms. It was working in that punishing heat that drove him to dream big and to see what his hometown could become. He wanted to find a way so he would never have to work in the heat again."

He looked down and smiled, and Anna glanced across the aisle at Mr. Brennan, who was also smiling, his eyes shining with unshed tears.

"He had good friends to help him, and he was determined to succeed. I think he'd be the first to say his success came at a price, and he wasn't proud of the mistakes he made. But he was proud of his family, and he loved us all.

"I talked to Dad just a few days ago about love and loss, and in addition to quoting 'Mother's Little Helper' by The Rolling Stones, he told me something I think you will all appreciate."

The group chuckled, and Julian continued.

"I asked him how to find my way back to something I had lost. Something that was very dear to me, and that I was afraid was gone for good.

"He said, 'When you truly love someone, time, distance, nothing matters. You'll come together, and love will fill all the cracks and damaged spaces, and it will be whole again. It'll be stronger than it was before.'

"He also told me he was proud of me, and I was lucky enough to tell him I loved him one last time." His chin dropped, and Anna's eyes grew hot.

"So while our family might feel broken by this loss, he's still with us, and we still have each other. Our love will fill the space left by his passing, and we'll be stronger because we had him in our lives. We love you Dad, and you're always here with us in spirit."

He stepped away from the front and returned to his seat beside his future wife, and the service concluded.

The three Kyser sons, Brad and Bryant were designated pall-bearers, and Juliet walked with her grandmother out to the waiting limousines that took them to the cemetery.

It was a solemn event, but Anna was able to see how they had all come together, all except the one.

* * *

Anna and Jules stood in the airport with Julian, waiting to board their flight back to London. Anna had spent the majority of the last two weeks with her future husband while Jules hadn't left her grandmother's house on Port Hogan Road. Both were miserable at the prospect of leaving what had become their family.

"Kyser-Brennan can handle the entire relocation," Julian said, holding Anna in his arms. "You don't have to go back if you'd rather stay."

She shook her head. "I need to wrap up my desk, say goodbye to friends, pack up things I can't live without."

"I can take you back in a few weeks to do all that."

She smiled and kissed his nose. "I've already stayed longer than I'd originally said I would."

"Yes, but you're moving back here. It doesn't matter."

"It does matter. Let me do this, and you can finish wrapping up your dad's business without me here to distract you."

He breathed heavily, and they walked slowly toward airport security. His arm was around Anna's waist, and Jules caught his hand on the other side. He lifted it around her shoulders, and pulled her wild dark head in for a kiss. "You're not a distraction, you're a relief."

They stopped to embrace each other one last time, one last kiss. Jules went on ahead through the screening process. Anna held the front of his shirt, smiling up into his adoring face.

"We won't be long, and now that the date is set, it's actually kind of exciting. After so many years, we're starting our life together as a family."

He leaned forward to claim that mouth once more. "I can't wait."

They said goodbye, and two headed across the ocean, while one headed back to face the storm brewing along the Gulf.

Bill Kyser's will had been opened, and the lawyers were already discussing the contents when the family gathered at the house on Hammond Island to listen to the reading.

The house on Port Hogan Road went to Alexandra Marie LaSalle along with a generous annual allowance for maintenance and repairs for the rest of her life. The Hammond Island home was left to the Kyser children to dispose of as they wished.

As neither Jack nor Lucy expressed interest in Kyser-Brennan Equities, Bill named Julian chief executive officer of the corporation and gave him total control of his father's share. No mention was made of the eldest Kyser sibling.

Will was out of his chair in an instant. "When was this will revised?"

"Several months ago," his father's attorney replied. "I understand this is a shock to you, but your father's mental condition was never in question."

"Of course his mental condition was fine," Will continued

shouting. "However he was sexually manipulated by this gypsy squatter in her efforts to install her bastard son in the wealthiest development company in the area."

Lexy pressed her lips into a frown and stood to leave the room.

"You're the bastard, Will!" Lucy shouted, going after her. "Don't start this again or I'll do more than throw my supper at you."

Julian only sat quietly, watching his brother. "He was my father, too."

"Are we just going to accept that? Was a paternity test ever run?"

Jack leaned forward in his chair. "You're really grasping for anything now, aren't you, Will. It's because of this behavior that he cut you out. Dad only ever loved Lexy, and his entire life changed when she and Julian came into the picture."

The two younger Kyser men's eyes met, and in that moment, any past conflict between them dissipated for good. Julian stood and walked to the desk.

"It isn't right for my brother to be cut out of the business. He's worked hard, he's good at what he does, and he's an asset to our team." He turned to face Will. "We'll make this right. Your position is not in jeopardy."

His brother muttered a curse and stalked to the door, but before he left, he turned back. "Don't think this changes anything. You are not one of us."

The room was noticeably quiet when the door shut, with only the lawyers, Jack and Julian, Robert and Casey left to hear the remainder of Bill's dispensation. Once it was over they filed out into the kitchen, where Lexy was holding Meggie, and Lucy was pacing furiously.

"He's such a rat pig. I hope you punched him in the face again, Julian."

Her brother coughed a laugh, and the rest of the family turned to face him. Lexy's eyes were stern.

"He, ahh… He threatened Anna," Julian managed to say.

With that, they all collectively relaxed and the kids started digging in the refrigerator.

"I'll fix something for the boys!" Casey jumped forward. "Would the adults like me to order takeout?"

Lucy stopped pacing and smiled at her. "That sounds great."

Julian slipped to the outside patio, the last place he'd spoken to his dad. His phone buzzed, and he took it out of his pocket. Seeing the name he smiled, grateful for the relief.

ANNA

Made it home. Just a few things to collect, then
I'll take you up on that KB relocation offer.

JULIAN

Good. I want you back here now.

ANNA

Me too. Jules and I took one look at all this
furniture and screamed your name.

He exhaled a laugh.

JULIAN

I thought I heard something. I miss you. Can you
be here by Sunday?

ANNA

No. But we'll be there in two weeks. Then never
leaving your side again.

JULIAN

Deal. Bound for life.

ANNA

You holding up okay?

Slipping the phone back into his pocket, he walked toward the small table holding a decanter and two glasses. Then he turned and walked to the railing, with its eastern view.

It was a clear night, and his eyes rose to the stars. Mist clouded his vision, but he wasn't crying. He wasn't sure how to name the mixture of emotions he felt after this night, the funeral, that will.

"Thank you," was all he said, gazing at the thick bands of swirling twinkle-lights mixing in the sky above. "I'm glad I was able to know you."

For a moment, he felt peace. As if the broken shards and scattered bits had finally been found and brought back together.

He remembered his father's words about love filling the spaces. He was an artist. He knew from his craft that the finished piece would be stronger than the original.

Bill Kyser started this journey a long time ago with a dream, and it brought all of them to this point in time. Mistakes were made, a life was lost, and many pieces were broken as a result. But assembled in this house was the best of the broken.

They were cemented together with love, and they'd learned his father was right. Love changes everything. It will pull you under, but it's stronger than time or distance. It had seen them through the past, and it would hold them together in a beautiful work of art, strong enough to face their future, whatever it might hold.

EPILOGUE

Jules ran through the old house on Port Hogan Road carrying a heavy bunch of pink hydrangeas, white gardenias, and lavender flowers until she got to the base of the antique staircase, where her father stood in beige linen pants and a loose, blue oxford.

"Bloody hell," she cried, jumping back.

"I still haven't decided if that's swearing or not." Julian grinned at his daughter, all dressed up in a knee-length yellow chiffon gown. "You'd probably better get out of the habit before school starts in the fall."

"I'll be a senior, Dad. We get special privileges."

"Not in South County."

She pushed her father's chest. "We can discuss it later. You can't be here! You'll see her before the wedding, and that's hideous luck. Get out!"

He caught his daughter's slim wrists, dodging her bouquet. "I think we've managed to beat enough hideous luck to last a lifetime. I'm just stepping in to get the guys some drinks. It's hot out there."

"You're not getting pissed are you?"

"Juliet." Her father gave her The Look. "Have you ever seen me drunk?"

"No, but Christ! Send Uncle Jack in or something. You can't be here."

"I'm the only one who knows where anything is in this house."

"Then text me." She grabbed his arm and dragged him to the door. "I'll carry whatever you need out to you."

"It'd be much easier if you'd just let me get it. I'm already here!"

"Five minutes!"

The antique wooden door with its arched, stained-glass inlays slammed in his face. Jules was back to the staircase in a flash, dashing up to the bridal party on the second floor.

Female clothing was scattered across all the upstairs rooms in the large home, and natural light streamed in through open, oversized windows. Jules found her mother in Lexy's room, smiling and speaking quietly with her nana.

"There you are," Juliet cried, running to where they were.

"There *you* are," Lexy smiled, hugging her pet granddaughter. "Did you find them?"

"I don't know how you get them to grow right now. It's completely out of season."

"Your nan is a gardening wizard." Lucy swept into the room wearing an asymmetrical-cut knee-length chiffon dress in antique lavender and took the heavy blossoms from her niece's hands. "I'll add these to the bouquet, and we'll have all the colors represented."

Lexy put an arm around Jules. "The lady who owned this house, who adopted me when I was much younger than you, taught me all about flowers and how to trick them into growing, how to manipulate their colors..." She leaned closer and whispered, "She also taught me the benefits of a greenhouse. Your aunt told me which flowers she wanted months ago, and it was just a matter of cultivating them at the right time."

The two smiled at each other. "Miss Stella sounds divine. I'll let you adopt me like that, and we'll just spend all our time gardening. I can sit on the shore and paint and do everything you did at my age."

"I was actually kind of lonely as a child until I met Meg." Lexy's smile was wistful as she straightened the strap on her own dress, another chiffon ensemble in pale rose.

Her graying dark hair was pinned up in a French twist.

"Well, you won't be lonely with me here. We'll do everything together."

"You still have to go to school, Jules." Anna kissed the top of her daughter's head. "But you can spend every other minute here."

"Come with me, Nan, your son is demanding drinks for all his groomsmen, and we have to help Gran carry them out."

"She keeps me young," Lexy winked at Anna and allowed Jules to drag her out of the bedroom and down the stairs.

Lucy had just returned with the large bouquet finished and wrapped in a champagne silk bow. "You've got to get into your dress now. We're at the ten-minute warning."

For a moment, Anna paused in front of the oval mirror with her future sister-in-law looking over her shoulder, and she couldn't help remembering another set of girls she'd read about. Anna's hair wasn't as dark as Lexy's, but Lucy was the image of her mother, smiling from the past.

"Everything is gorgeous." Anna hugged her friend before following her across the hall. "You've really done an amazing job planning it all out."

"It was a cinch once you decided to have it here. This old place has the perfect landscape for a wedding."

It was true. With lush, oversized gardens leading out to an

arbor covered in wisteria and opening to a clear view of the Gulf, it was breathtaking.

Her remaining three bridesmaids were already downstairs hanging with the guys. Anna peeked out the window and saw Rachel dressed in antique lavender chiffon like Lucy, only without the asymmetrical skirt. Gabi was in a grass-green chiffon dress that was short in the front and long in the back. The two were laughing and chatting with Brad, Julian, and Jack, who had Casey, also in the grass green chiffon, holding his arm.

They'd only invited a small group to the ceremony, and Anna was cautiously pleased to see even the eldest Kyser sibling had chosen to attend, albeit alone.

Lexy and Jules marched out at that point, each carrying a glass pitcher filled with what appeared to be lemonade. Anna's mother was right behind them in her own rose chiffon dress carrying cups and ice.

Anna leaned further, and just then Will looked up.

She jumped back with a squeal. "I almost got busted!"

Lucy laughed and hopped over to the window then waved, then she let out a little growl. "Oh, goody."

"What?" Anna frowned as she took her floor-length champagne-colored gown off its hanger.

It had a sleeveless lace bodice that went over her shoulders in two panels, forming a deep V in the front. A single fabric rose clustered with seed pearls was in the center at the base of the V, and a beige underlay extended from her breasts down to her knees.

"I see old rat-monster Will's down there."

"I'm actually glad he came. He needs to be a part of this—of the family."

"You're seriously a saint for inviting him." Lucy gently lifted the floor-length, full chiffon overlay that made up the skirt and sighed. "When that breeze starts, this is going to billow out and be gorgeous. You've got really great legs. I don't know why you hide them all the time."

"I don't hide anything! I just wear the clothes I've got."

"Well, then we're going shopping. But first we'd better get down there and get you married. Hang on." Lucy caught her friend and dusted powder on her nose. Then she straightened a few of the pins holding her loose up-do in place and tugged on a few spiral tendrils. "You're perfect."

In the yard below, Julian waited as his daughter attached the boutonnière to his blue dress shirt. "I like the yellow," he said, watching her eyebrows clutch as she worked. "Do all these colors mean something?"

Finishing with a pat, Jules met his blue eyes—the same color as her own. "I think I'm in yellow because you always gave Mum those yellow flowers on her birthday."

He couldn't stop a smile at that memory. "Who told you about that?"

"Oh, please. Mum has all kinds of sappy details in that private tumblr of hers."

"And according to her, some not so G-rated details as well." He frowned as his daughter's face flushed.

"Trust me. I skipped over all of that business."

Lexy walked up and inspected them both. "Look at you two. My absolute favorite surprises, both of you."

Julian draped an arm around her waist. "I have to say, it made a big difference to me, knowing you'd only found out about her a year before I did." He kissed his mother's cheek. "Although knowing you could keep her from me a whole year is troubling."

"As many things as I asked Anna to sit on through the years, the least I could do was honor this one request of hers." Lexy shook her head. "She'd never asked me for anything before."

"You know what?" Jules interrupted. "We're all together now, and that's all that matters. Right?"

"Yes." Julian put an arm around his daughter and squeezed

them both. "And I think it's time for me to head to the front. I'll be glad when all these formalities are over."

"You look really handsome." Jules caught his hand as he left. "Good luck."

* * *

The minister finished speaking and turned to introduce the wedding vows written by Anna and Julian. The pair hadn't taken their eyes off each other the entire time, but now Julian blinked down to his hands.

"I'm sorry I don't trust my memory." He fumbled a sheet of paper out of his pocket as Anna giggled along with everyone else. "You've got more experience at public speaking than I do."

She had to fight the urge to lean forward and kiss him right then.

"Not true," she whispered. "I was always behind the camera."

Julian cleared his throat and glanced once at her hazel eyes before starting. "Anna Sanders, I told you once before I was in love with you in tenth grade. You quickly pointed out that I didn't do anything about it until we were seniors, and you were right. I think I said something like, just because I found you didn't mean I was ready to trust myself."

A soft ripple of laughter floated across the group.

"Trust was something we had from the start in our relationship. It was something we thought we lost for a little while, but we should've known we never did. I'm so thankful we found each other again. I'm so thankful you came back after saying you never would. I'm so thankful you flickered into my life and changed it.

"You are my Anna Sunshine. I hope we have many years to go on discovering all the amazing things about each other.

"I promise to love you always, to take care of you, to never leave you, and to never give you a reason to want to leave me again. Of all the things you are, you're my angel, and I can't live without you. Thank you for my beautiful daughter, and thank you for agreeing to be my wife. I loved you then, but I love you so much more now."

Sniffs punctuated the silence all around, and Anna giggled as she touched her eyes. "I don't know if I can say mine now. I've already started crying."

More laughs echoed from the group. She cleared her throat and began. "Julian LaSalle Kyser, you said you loved me first, but that was only because I was a terrible communicator when I was young. Even still, I'm pretty sure I said those three little words before you ever did, even if you weren't awake to hear them.

"We've been through so much together, but the only thing I remember is your smiling face always waiting for me, always coming for me. The one time it didn't, I realized I couldn't live without you, and I had to come back for you.

"I'm so thankful I'm better at math than you." His brow clutched and she exhaled a laugh. "So I was able to be your tutor. And I'm so thankful you're brilliant at art. You taught me to surf, you taught me to love, and you gave me two beautiful gifts, one being our gorgeous girl.

"You say I'm your angel, but I'm no supernatural being. I'm just a girl who fell in love with the most romantic boy she ever dreamed she could never have. And then she could.

"I promise to communicate very well and very quickly from this day forward. I promise never to give you a reason to doubt me again. This next one's easy. I promise to love you until I die, because I'm pretty sure I've now lived longer in love with you than I have out." Her brow creased. "If that makes sense."

He was grinning, and she caught him bite his lip. Their eyes met, and she knew he was dying to kiss her just as much as she was dying to kiss him.

"I think that's all I wrote. It's all I can remember." She laughed with the group. "Oh, except you dreamed of this day, when we'd never be separated again, and I'm so, so happy you shared your dream with me. You turned us into art, and now both our dreams have come true."

The minister moved quickly through the vows for the rings. Julian's was solid white gold, with a dragonfly engraved inside the band against his finger. Anna's was another of his handmade creations. A white-gold band, thicker than the other two, that fit perfectly under her dragonfly and engagement rings.

They had arrived at the part everyone was waiting for. "I now pronounce you man and wife. You may kiss the bride."

Anna was in Julian's arms in a sweep, and he only held her a moment, looking deep into her eyes before covering her soft lips with his. Her fingers threaded into his hair as that old swarm of fizzy butterflies took flight, swirling through her stomach and up to her arms as the audience broke into clapping and laughter punctuated by tears.

Their mouths parted as they hugged each other so tightly. Julian's lips pressed against the top of her shoulder, and for a moment she held him just a little longer while the applause continued. A few of the guys and Gabi whistled through their fingers, and more laughs broke out.

At last they released each other and were introduced as Mr. and Mrs. Julian LaSalle Kyser, and Anna reached out and pulled Jules to them as family and friends rushed together to hug and laugh and cry happy tears over the long-awaited union.

* * *

Pictures taken, a live band started playing. Friends were going through the buffet line, and the reception was set to last all day. Anna and Julian had promised to stay as long as they could take it, although Julian kept saying they should do a quick surfing break and come back.

"It only seems right, since that's how I finally got you to admit you love me." They were dancing to a slow song, and she kissed his nose.

"I admitted I loved you when you foolishly tried to kill yourself racing Brad's car. I don't think we should do that today either."

He laughed and squeezed her tight against his chest. "I've heard there are some good spots around here for skinny dipping. We should explore."

A thrill tingled in her stomach, and she leaned forward to whisper in his ear. "Later. We need to thank all our guests for coming to our special day."

"Silly guests." He kissed her neck, and she wrinkled her nose in a smile.

The two parted, and Julian went off in search of Brad and a beer. Anna headed into the house to change into a lighter sundress. She was headed toward the stairs when she noticed the door was ajar on the large downstairs room Lexy used as her art studio.

Taking a short detour, she walked over to see if someone was inside. "Hello?" Anna called as she entered the room.

It was filled with stretched blank canvases and a few easels that held paintings in varying stages of being finished. The actual finished works were stacked along the walls, and all were in Alexandra LaSalle's signature style.

"She's very good isn't she." Will's voice made her jump, but she managed to control her skittering nerves.

She'd hoped to have a moment to thank her brother-in-law for putting in an appearance, and now it seemed she was getting that wish.

"Yes, she is," Anna said. "She always has been, but she put the brush down for a long time."

"After my mother died." His tone was different than it normally was.

The cold cruelty was gone, and Anna almost detected a note

of vulnerability, however slight.

"That's right." Anna nodded as Will came from behind one of the easels out into the center of the studio to face her.

His eyes narrowed at her like always, but the usual sneer was absent. "I guess you think you've won. You showed me or something."

Anna's eyes flickered over his face. "I don't think anything of the sort. I'm glad you're here."

"I wanted to see it for myself." He pressed his lips into a line. "You changed your dress and lost some weight, but you're still the same girl you always were."

Only six months had passed since the reunion, since he lost his father. Anna mentally reminded herself of these facts, and while Julian had gone out of his way to secure his oldest brother in the family business, he had no power over her.

She stuck out her chin. "That's right, I am. I hoped your being here meant you might've changed a little."

"I'll never change." His voice wasn't angry or sinister. It was resigned.

"Anyone is capable of change. If they choose to be."

He let out an impatient breath, and she knew he wasn't ready for that. Instead she changed directions. "You know, Will. I'm glad I have this chance to thank you."

She glanced to her right, and as she expected, his brow was creased.

"You scared me once," she continued. "You threatened me once. But I'm not afraid of you now. Your scheming drove me away, but it only made me grow up and become the person I needed to be. Without you, I might never have realized the strength of Julian's and my connection. So I want to thank you."

His expression grew more irritated as she spoke, and Anna had to fight not to burst out laughing as she said the words she now realized were too true. It was so crazy how life could turn everything around.

She was silent, waiting, until finally Will cleared his throat and started for the door.

He paused before exiting to mutter "You're welcome," then he left.

Anna's shoulders dropped with her exhale, and she took one last look around the room before following him out the door and heading back up to her room to change.

Whether she would ever see the day when Will Kyser gave up hating everyone, she didn't know. For all of them it had been a matter of finding the right person to help start the healing process. She looked forward to the day when that might happen for her new brother-in-law.

Later that night, back at the beach cottage wrapped tightly in Julian's arms, she remembered the day she'd dreamed of living in this little house with him and having his children.

All of their dreams had come true. Her life was complete, and with so much pain behind them, they looked forward to a better future together.

She was where she belonged, and their love had filled all the cracks and missing pieces. Now they were not only stronger, they were a beautiful new work of art. She had everything she had ever wanted, and as time passed, she was confident they would only have more.

* * *

Thank you for reading Mosaic!
I hope you loved the Dragonfly series as much as I do. Be sure to download your *Free Deleted Scene HERE*, or scan the QR code below.
More books are coming, so be sure you're signed up for my newsletter, and you'll never miss a thing!

Mosaic Bonus/Deleted Scene

ACKNOWLEDGMENTS

Finishing a series four years in the making, I know there are a bazillion people I need to thank. I've tried to thank specific folks along the way in each book, so hopefully this round won't be ten pages long…

First and foremost, I have to thank my husband, Richard, my best editor, who never once allowed me to give up on this series. He's always believed in me, and he's helped me in so many ways —most especially by letting me be a little crazy at times and a lot (mentally) absent at others. I love you so much.

Second, I have to thank my little girls Cat and Laura, who were just babies when I started *Dragonfly*. Thanks for understanding when Mommy says "just one more minute," it really means an hour. Thanks for being so incredibly patient with me when you were too little to understand why I was always on the computer. Thanks for being excited and asking if I'd written any more on *Mosaic* when you got older and understood. Thanks for praying for me (Aww!). I'm so blessed and lucky to have you both. I love you so much.

Special thanks to my family—my mom, who said, "I know when I haven't heard from you in two weeks, you must be writing." My sweet dad, who's always ready to "take the children off your hands." My extended family and my "Moore family," who read and share my books with friends and book clubs. All of you touch my heart so much. I love you guys!

Some amazing people have emerged during this last installment to encourage me and offer support and expertise. Huge thanks to Ilona Townsel, whose cards and notes of encouragement made me look forward to checking the mail, and whose beta reads and brainstorming are tons of fun. Love you!

Mandie Jones, my right arm, my best personal assistant *evah!*, my Master Teaser Maker, the most organized person on this team of two… You are the greatest, most intuitive helper. You are never allowed to leave me—haha!

Christi Allen Curtis, who approached me about doing the cover and then knocked my socks off with the most gorgeous photography. You are the best. Thank you so much for loving these stories.

My beta readers and friends Kim Barnes, Sharon Hattenstein, Tracy Womack, and Melissa Ott. You guys mean the world to me. I know I can put a book out if you all give me the thumbs up. Love you guys!

To my writer-friends, who are some of my best friends, to the Indelibles and Indies Ignite and the Listies and my blog buddies and YA Confidential, *Thanks* for understanding my absenteeism, but most of all, *Thank you* for always supporting and encouraging me. Love you all~

To all the amazing readers who've contacted me on Facebook, who've sent me emails and tweets. To Tina and Chad, whose personal dragonfly love story touched my heart—even if I only just found out about it! To my readers on Wattpad and the administrators there, who fell in love with the story and couldn't wait for more.

To Giselle at Xpresso Tours and Natalie and Jennifer at Love Between the Sheets for doing such a fantastic job with cover reveals and release day blitzes. And to all the bloggers and readers who helped me spread the word. I feel like I know so many of you personally, and I appreciate you all so much.

Being independent takes a village, and I love love *love* all my fellow villagers. You all have a very special place in my heart. Thank you for buying and reading and sharing my books.

I hope you loved this final installment as much as I do.
<3 Leigh

BOOKS BY LEIGH T MOORE

THE DRAGONFLY SERIES

Dragonfly (#1)

Undertow (#2)

Watercolor (#3)

Mosaic (#4)

All available in Kindle Unlimited. More to come—be sure to sign up for my newsletter HERE or use the code below, and never miss a thing!

Dragonfly was the very first book I ever wrote all the way back in 2009. At the time I was a newspaper journalist living in Baldwin County, Ala., and I was a massive fan of the Twilight series.

One night, I decided to try my hand at writing a novel, and what resulted was four books about a billionaire who developed the coast but never found happiness.

I felt like Anna venturing into this world, learning the old secrets, falling in love with the next generation.

The series was very popular when it first came out in 2012, then with time, it fell off the radar, and I eventually unpublished it.

This year, with the rise of social media and the renewed interest in romance novels, I thought it might be time to pull these books off the shelf, polish them up, and see if a new generation of readers might love this story as well as the previous one did.

The "Kyser editions" have gone through extensive revisions, edits, scenes have been changed and updated based on new technology, and the bonus content has been enhanced.

Still, the story remains the same. It's one that is close to my heart, and I love it so much. I hope you do, too.

Happy reading,

Leigh

ABOUT THE AUTHOR

Leigh T. Moore is a wife and mom by day, a writer by day, a reader by day, a former journalist, a former editor, a chocoholic, a caffeine addict, a lover of great love stories, a beach bum, and occasionally she sleeps.

A south Louisiana native, she currently lives on the Alabama Gulf Coast with her best friend turned husband and one clumsy grand-cat.

Connect with Leigh

•Sign up for my newsletter using the QR code below and never miss a new release or sale, also you'll always know what's coming next.

•**Get Exclusive Text Alerts** and never miss a Sale or New Release: Text LEIGHTMOORE to 855-902-6387 (U.S. only)

•You can order **Signed copies** of the Dragonfly series in my online store at https://geni.us/LTMstore

Scan to sign up for my newsletter.